A PLEASANT AFTERNOON ON TITAN

Daniel Kitajima got off his space sled and stood on the nitrogen-methane ice, surveying the unfamiliar scene.

The sky glowed a dull orange-yellow on the horizon. Toward the setting sun—Saturn—the jagged icebergs glowed. The sea surrounding the ice floe looked completely black except for the caps on the wavelets. Large, soft flakes of yellowish methane-nitrogen sleet fell on Daniel's upturned face.

It was a pleasant afternoon on Titan. And unless his mission succeeded, one of Titan's last . . .

SUN'S END

RICHARD
A.
LUPOFF

BERKLEY BOOKS, NEW YORK

SUN'S END

A Berkley Book/published by arrangement with
the author

PRINTING HISTORY
Berkley edition/September 1984

ISBN: 0-425-07022-0

KBL

1

DANIEL PULLED his arm back so his fingertips brushed over the keyboard inside his spacesuit sleeve. He thought for a few seconds, his eyes taking in both the metal plate covering the processor and the visible portion of the earth some 167,000 kilometers beyond.

"How're you coming, Dan?" He looked up as Avram Novon's voice crackled through his helmet radio.

"Okay. Be a lot happier once this glitch is cooled." He could see Novon, his flat-white suit marked with distinctive incandescent green recognition panels, riding a medium-duty materials hefter. Dan could make out the howitzer-like barrel of a 150-centimeter-diameter telescope clutched in the hefter's waldoes.

"You 'stronomy kids never cease to," Dan dug at Novon. "All the radiation-sensing work of the past fifty years, and probes to go look at the local dumps, and here you are playing with optical gear again. What's next, horoscopes?"

"Never mind, bucko," Novon snapped back. "You get that coffin full of tubes and wires working and then we can talk about something real." Novon turned back to his work, gingerly fitting the massive barrel to the brackets where it would remain while it was sighted in.

Forgetfully, Dan started to wipe his forehead with the back of his hand. He remembered his spacesuit and instead moved his head against the helmet pad. The suit's air-recycling system and monitoring circuits carefully adjusted the level of moisture

1

at all times, just as the temperature control maintained a steady comfortable level for him. Dan shouldn't be sweating. Certainly the sweat shouldn't roll down his forehead into his eyes and make them sting fiercely. Not here in free-fall balanced carefully at the leading point of a static earth-moon triangle.

But it did.

He returned his concentration to his work. He spoke a log entry into the suit's recorder pickup and tapped out a set of instructions on the keyboard inside the suit's elephantine wrist.

Servos hummed softly and the suit retracted the electro-stethoscope Dan had been using; in its place, the suit extended a hex-collared Phillips-head blade.

Dan nodded, blinked, pressed the blade against the plate-retainer nut nearest him and twisted a gnarled cylinder.

The blade responded, locking against the retainer nut, and began smoothly to revolve.

When the last retainer nut was undogged, Dan swung the plate back from the processor service panel. He looked away again, his attention caught by the planet below. He could see his native California, the Sierras looming rugged and slatelike, sloping away through autumn-brown farmlands to the low coastal region and the offshore fogbanks and cloud systems that covered the eastern portion of the Pacific.

He didn't check the time on any chronograph other than the steady progress of the terminator across the North American continent. Robert and Elizabeth would have finished their afternoon naps by now, and their mother, Marie-Elaine, would be getting them up, changing them, putting them in their playpen.

Probably Daniel's mother Janice was with Marie-Elaine, chattering, offering advice, providing companionship while Dan carried out his duties halfway to the moon. He knew that his mother enjoyed being with Marie-Elaine and the twins; she was performing no selfless service staying with them in his absence. Still, he was relieved that Marie-Elaine had the older woman to provide help and company.

Over Dan's shoulder the sun was a perfect white disc.

He pressed the display command override on the processor module and grunted at the numbers that glowed back at him the color of a polished emerald. He tapped out a message on his wrist-keyboard, watched the Phillips-head blade retract and a skeletal full-hand waldo hum into position in its place. He laid his hand over the waldo master-plate and ran a series of exercises, smiling at the performance of the hand. He had designed most of its control circuits.

"You busy, Avram?" he radioed.

"What, bucko?"

"Hey, just for fun, give me something easy for this box to translate."

"Any particular languages? Hebrew to Oglala Sioux?"

"Hey, make it easy for starters."

"Okay." A pause while Novon gathered his thoughts. "Okay," he repeated, "English to Esperanto. 'How many kilometers to Venus, Jack?' That do it, Dan?"

"Fine."

"Let me know."

Daniel glanced at Novon again, centering on the other man's green square panels. Past Novon a huge crane, holding itself stable with little vernier puffs of compressed air, fitted giant plates into position for welding crews.

A touch to a pressure plate brought the processor keyboard to life. The letters on the keys glowed red; the numbers, yellow. Dan turned on readout display, checked the printer to see that it was turned off. He entered Novon's message into the processor's in-buffer, read the sentence back from red lettering, then hit the controls for *translate*, *from*, tapped in the code for English, hit *to*, coded Esperanto, hit *read*, then *execute*.

The machine didn't make any sound. Dan provided that in his imagination, summoning up the clicks and chuckles of a spaceborne computer center from fifteen or twenty years before, from some television show seen in the living room of his parents' house on Steiner Street in San Francisco, or a big-screen spectacle at the Northpoint.

The readout display flashed a meaningless jumble of red letters and yellow numbers.

Dan wiped the entire procedure from the machine and started over, carefully double-checking each step, muttering log entries via his suit-mike.

Again he hit *execute* and again the readout flashed a senseless garble of yellows and reds. He tried to wipe the sweat from his eyes, batted his waldo-hand against his helmet, cursed vehemently and leaned against the absorption pad inside the helmet. At least that worked the way it was supposed to. It was almost as good as wiping your forehead with a big old bandana.

"How did it work?" Novon's voice crackled inside Daniel's helmet.

Dan flashed a glance at the Israeli worker. "Terrible. I'm going to pull this damned processor and work on it in the shuttle. If I can't fix it there, I'll have to take it back to Palo Alto and fix it. Or more likely, just throw the damned thing away and have 'em send up another."

"Must be sunspots."

Daniel looked at the sun, his helmet polarizing and darkening to shut out the blinding glare and actinic rays that would otherwise damage his retinas. "You kidding?"

Novon paused before answering. Daniel waited, holding himself steady with one hand on the processor cover plate. "I don't know," Novon finally said. "I thought I was kidding, but if solar flares can knock out video transmissions—"

"Oh, they can glitch up computers all right! That's not even a question, Avram. I didn't know there'd been any unusual solar activity, is all."

"Oh, yeah. That's part of the rush on this scope. We want to study the corona—the visual astronomy gang does, that is. Nothing naked-eye visible, but there's been a little extra activity lately and they're pretty excited."

"Swell. Is anything going on now?"

Beyond Novon, the sun glowed unchangingly.

"Now?" Daniel could see Novon shift his position to cast a brief look at the sun, then turn back. "Well, at 150,000,000 kilometers—"

"You know what I mean. Anything happen up there eight minutes ago, that would be glitching my circuits now?"

"Can't tell. But it's been going like this for a while."

Daniel cursed again. "I don't know why they never tell me anything. Maybe nobody knows how to put things together. That's probably the cause of all this mess, and I'm up here, they're spending a fortune on me, using up shuttle space; all they need to do is wait for the flares to die down. Or just shield these processors better, the way we're always begging them to do."

"What are you griping about, Dan? Don't like the bucks?"

"I like 'em fine. And my family can really use a little extra money. Kids are expensive."

"Hunh."

"But it's still a waste." He glared angrily at the processor, tapped a message into the keyboard and waited for the display that would contain the machine's response. "Look, Avram, I'm going to run some more diagnostics anyhow, just to make sure. I wouldn't want to go home and start bitching about inadequate shielding and solar flares causing all the trouble we've had up here, and then find out that some assembler slipped in a module backwards to start with and that's been the trouble all the while."

"Yeah. I'd better get back to this tube anyhow. Don't want Cris chewing on me for dogging on the job."

Dan squinted at the sun as if he could have seen the causes of his problems crawling across its face, then turned back to the keyboard. "How many kilometers to Venus, Jack?" he whispered to himself. "Nov shmoz ka pop. Ask a silly question."

He reached into his service kit and extracted a read-only memory chip containing a diagnostic program. He slipped it into place on the processor, hit *read*, waited for the machine to blink its completion signal back to him—it took the readout lights longer to glow into legibility than it took the machine to absorb and store the program from the ROM chip—and hit *execute*.

Garbled yellow and red.

Dan took a hard copy of the message, muttered a log entry, pulled the diagnostic and began demounting the processor. "The gostok distims the doshes," he grumbled to himself. "I had one grunch but the eggplant over there. Glitches, glitches, glitches."

The perspiration spreading from his forehead stung his eyes and he remembered to move his head against the helmet pad instead of trying to wipe his forehead with his hand.

HOURS later he sat at dinner, inside the shuttle, with Avram Novon and Novon's boss, Crista Balbo. They used a combination of Esperanto and half a dozen natural languages for conversation, but English predominated.

"It's too bad your problem couldn't hold off a little longer," Cris said. "Once we turn on the spin and get some gravity in the Island, things should be a lot pleasanter." Her blue Piedmontese eyes flashed.

"I don't mind working without it," Dan said.

"You've been up before?"

"Couple of times. You know, things got so specialized in my field, for a while there, nobody could do anything outside his little bailiwick." He gave a short, barklike laugh. "I remember for a while, a circuit designer, a materials engineer, a machine operator, and half a dozen kinds of programmers would have to have a meeting and a building full of support people to do anything. Anything!

"Got so cumbersome, we couldn't slice a leaf of lettuce in half without a ten-megabuck conference. Now, at least, we're giving people a few skills again. Maybe we'll catch up with our Russian pals yet."

Avram Novon grunted, "We'd better."

"Eh?"

"You'll be uncomfortable if you don't," the Israeli said. "But *we'll* be wiped out."

"Yes."

There was an uncomfortable silence as the three of them concentrated on their food.

Crista broke the tension. "How about something a little more amusing? Vidi, anyone?"

Novon reached and turned on a wall unit. "We're in line with the satellite; we ought to get a good projo."

The framed area on the shuttle's wall glowed into life. In the illusion of a window, pseudo-three-dimensional figures took form. Novon studied the figures for a moment, then adjusted the controls, sharpening and brightening them.

"You a sports fan, Daniel? That's your team. It's World Series time, isn't it? I could never understand the fascination of American baseball. Could you, Cris?"

She shook her head, *no*.

"Well, I'm not a big fan," Daniel said. "But it is my hometown team there. My dad used to take me down to Seals Stadium to watch 'em now and then. I always had a good time. Besides, the park was in the warmest part of the city."

In the holo window an Asian-featured pitcher in a green baseball cap was throwing warmup pitches.

"That's Skeeter Nakamura," Dan said. "Twenty-three and nine this year. Lives over in San Leandro, I think."

Novon turned to the other man. "Is he on the—what do you call them—the Seals? You pull for them, he's your hero?"

Crista Balbo said, "I think he looks a little like you, Daniel."

He shook his head. "We're not related. And he's not on the Seals. He's pitching against us tonight."

"Well, if you are not really fanatical about it, I'd like to pass up this game and see what's in the general news."

"Go ahead, Crista. I'm not an athlete. I'd just like to live like one. Do you know what Nakamura makes a year? More than the President of the United States does!"

"Huh! He's probably better at his job, too."

. She switched the vidi to a news broadcast, adjusted controls until the focus and gain were in balance and slid back on magnetized boots to her seat.

"Look at that. More stuff on the Russian stations. How many people do they have up now?"

"Three hundred, the last I knew," Novon supplied.

"Huh! They'll be beaming power down in another year if nothing goes wrong." Crista Balbo turned a mildly accusing glance on Daniel. "Why didn't you push on with your work when you were ahead? You could have been as far along as the Russians are now, ten or twelve years ago. More interested in baseball, I suppose."

"Hey," Daniel said. "Don't point the finger at me, Cris. I didn't make those decisions. I was a little kid playing with yo-yos twenty years ago. I didn't make those decisions." He didn't feel as blameless as he claimed to be, and wiped his hand across his face, embarrassed at his own heat and growing hotter at the embarrassment.

"Besides, we were busy carrying half the world with us. Where would Europe be now if the U.S. hadn't spent a hundred billion bucks to build it up and hold the Russians back for forty years?"

"*Hmph.* I suppose," Novon raised a finger tentatively, "somewhere between the Ural Mountains and the Atlantic Ocean.

Pretty well where it is now. Don't you think?"

There was a brief silence while Balbo and Novon waited to see whether Daniel was going to explode or not. When he indicated that he was not going to explode, they relaxed.

"Well, if we succeed," Cris said, "we'll be ahead of them again. I've always felt that earth-orbit technology was self-limiting."

"LaGrange Islands aren't the ultimate answer either," Dan asserted.

"No, I didn't mean to imply that they were. But it's the next logical development. I think the Russians are just staying in earth orbit because they're inherently cautious. It's part of their culture. They always have wanted to expand, but they've also wanted to keep their lines of supply and communication as short and as direct as possible. Any time they tried to go too far, to jumptoad—?"

"To leapfrog."

"Thank you. To leapfrog they have suffered for it. Look at what happened to them in Cuba!"

"I remember it well," Dan said through clenched teeth.

"Well, but we of the West—I include Israel in the West, Avram, even though it is technically an Asian state."

"You are too kind."

"We have always made the breathtaking leaps. Da Vinci, Columbus, Fermi, Marconi."

"Do I notice a pattern?" Novon shot at Daniel.

Dan grinned.

"The facts are the facts," Crista Balbo shoved away a lock of soft platinum hair that had swung before her eyes in the gravityless environment of the shuttle. "Oh, what a pleasure it will be once we get gravity going in the Island!"

"Hah! That won't be for months." Novon took a bite of hamspread sandwich and chewed it seriously. "You'll be long gone by then, Daniel. Home happily in California, eh? While we intrepid space pioneers suffer the deprivations and perils of homesteading humanity's newest frontier here in the heavens. Pass me a can of Piper-Heidsieck, will you? Thanks."

He popped the seal on the can and slid his thumb over its plastic drinking nozzle. "Anybody care for a drop? Well, here's to the sabras of tomorrow, the first generation of kids born up here in the LaGrange Islands!"

"That won't be for a while," Cris said. "Daniel, are you going to have to ferry that processor down with you, or do you think you can get it running right up here?"

Daniel blinked a couple of times. "I'm not certain yet. It would really be something if it's just sunspots causing the glitch."

"Then you won't need to repair it at all?"

"Not immediately. But that will be the worst case, actually. If this processor is really faulty, we'll get 'er running again or just replace the damned thing if we have to. And that's no big problem."

"No? At the kilogram charge on the shuttle?"

"I didn't mean it wouldn't be expensive. But even so . . . But if there's nothing wrong with the processor, and we have to reshield all our electronic gear up here, what a blow! Do you know what a complete retrofit would—"

"The vidi seems to be working fine."

"By God, Crista, you're right! Why didn't I think of that? Now, why would something as trivial as an entertainment holo run like a jewel, and something as important as a major control-system data processor glitch up? We must have a Jonah up here with us."

"I doubt that. Or if we do, Daniel, I suppose it's you."

"Oh no. You're not going to pin that on me. The problem turned up first, then you sent for me, at straight passenger-kilo rates, too, if you remember."

"Your company will take a charge-back, Dan. The machine is their responsibility. They have to make it work."

"Well, the lawyers and accountants will take care of that."

"How soon do you think you're going back down? The next shuttle down should be in a day and a half."

"I'm going to try for it. In the meanwhile, what about taking another look at that ball game. Anyone object?"

LATER he was back in his flat-white and rust-red spacesuit, reinstalling the processor in the shell of the Island. Inside the shuttle, laid out on a test-bench, the machine had performed perfectly. He'd even surprised Avram Novon with a perfect Esperanto version of "How many kilometers to Venus, Jack?"

A brief conference with the astronomy gang had got him a

new reading on the sunspot and solar flare situation. Cycles upon cycles, it was like the old Ptolemaic model of the universe with the earth surrounded by concentric shells of blackness and specks of light.

Here the shells were not physical constructs but temporal ones. Short cycles and longer epicycles and still longer, what could you call them, hypercycles? Sometimes they ran in opposite directions, a high point on a lower level cycle coinciding with a dip in a higher level cycle, the two phenomena damping each other's effect, or canceling it totally for the moment.

And sometimes they ran parallel, a minor and a major cycle peaking or dipping simultaneously and reinforcing rather than damping each other. And when all the cycles moved in the same direction, piling their effects one upon another . . .

He had the processor reinstalled, carefully placed a diagnostic ROM chip in position and hit *read*, then *execute*. The pattern of red and yellow lights in the display matched the result that his service kit predicted. He exercised the circuits a few times, ran some more diagnostics and decided that the processor was running flawlessly.

The glitches had all been transient, and Daniel was more worried than ever. When he got his report in to his company, the shuttle and the Island would swarm with instrumentation gangs lashing additional shielding onto every bit of electronic gear they could find. Meanwhile, downstairs on earth they'd be cranking new specs into the next generation of processors so the shielding would be implicit in the hardware design and not have to be lashed onto the outside like—Daniel smiled to himself—like so many old tires lashed onto the gunwales of a tugboat.

He bolted the cover plate back onto the processor and checked his chronograph. Time to kill before the next shuttle flight back downstairs. He looked around at the shuttles that were tethered to the half-finished Island. They were used as temporary housing for the onboard construction crews, makeshift warehouses, workshops, mess halls and rec centers. Once the Island was airtight and spinning most of the shuttles would be freed up and returned to their proper use, as passenger and cargo transports.

Dan spotted his friend Avram Novon emerging from the

same small port above the cargo bay of the shuttle he had himself left a while before. He called to Novon and the Israeli waved back.

"I am just about finished with the scope, Daniel. How is your work coming along?"

Dan said that he was finished and just about to head back into the shuttle.

"How would you like to peep through my toy?" the Israeli asked.

Dan decided that would be good fun. Something to tell his wife and friends about when he got home in another day or so. Otherwise it would be the old story. What did you do up in space, Danny? Nothing very interesting. Was it exciting? Spectacular? Frightening? No, none of the above, just a job. But what about the vistas of the universe? Well, I was busy running diagnostics on a data processor and the ROM chips kept jiggling around in null-grav, so I was too busy with that problem to look at the Milky Way.

Daniel left his safety tether hooked to a locking ring near the processor cover plate and shoved himself in the direction of Novon and the howitzer-like telescope barrel. He felt a sensation of movement only for a second, then floated effortlessly, Novon's green-on-white figure growing larger as Daniel glided toward him. Beyond Avram, Daniel could see the heavy construction crew still at work, their huge cranes jockeying plates into position over the already completed skeleton of the Island.

Workers with vacuum electro-welders swarmed over the girders and the plates, making the permanent attachments that would turn the vast numbers of separate components into a single entity. Later Islands would draw their resources from the raw materials of the moon and the asteroid belt, processing materials and fabricating parts here in space. The Island civilization, if plans were met, would quickly become a self-sustaining economy, returning much of its surplus wealth to earth in the form of tightbeamed energy and absorbing emigrants from the swarming planet as the number of Islands grew exponentially. It would be generations before Avram's *sabras* were born in sufficient numbers to obviate the need for emigrant citizens for the Islands.

But this was still the start-up phase. The half-completed first Island had to be built with components fabricated on earth and ferried up painstakingly and at the cost of constant shuttle flights between the downstairs spaceports and the LaGrange points.

Novon caught Daniel by the shoulders, steadying him with his thickly gloved hands.

"What would you like to see?" Novon asked.

Daniel said, "Can you point that thing downstairs? It would be fun to tell Marie-Elaine what she was wearing today if I could spot her in front of the house!"

Avram laughed. "Wrong time of day. I could show you what they're wearing in Australia, except there would be no resolving the image from up here."

"I thought you stargazers were so hot for putting telescopes up here because the seeing was so good. What was that line I heard, 'We can see better from a pair of opera glasses in space than we can from Palomar?' What about that?"

Novon's chuckle crackled inside Daniel's helmet.

"That's an exaggeration, I'm afraid. But it is not really much of one. The biggest problem with seeing, downstairs, is the few miles of earth's atmosphere. Light that travels for millions of parsecs with perfect clarity gets fuzzed up and fogged out— if not completely lost—coming through the smoke and atmospheric moisture and miscellaneous gunk that covers the earth.

"That's why we've been so eager to get our scopes upstairs. So we don't have to watch everything through a smokescreen.

"But you see, if we look down through the atmosphere and try and see something, it's just as bad as looking up through it. The way to see is *away* from here!"

He pointed dramatically.

Daniel nodded. "All right. What about a look at—" He paused and considered. Beyond the telescope and the tethered shuttles, a crane was swinging a gigantic cylindrical section of stressed metal toward waiting men. Daniel watched the operation. The mass of the plate would crush the workers like ants if it were not slowed almost to stasis before it reached them.

"How about Cerberus?" Avram suggested.

"Hey?"

"You know, the little sub-satellite of Pluto. That'll be something to tell about back home. They only found Pluto's own

moon, Charon, twenty years ago. Nobody downstairs has *ever*
seen the little chunk of rock that orbits Charon. Too small.
Too remote. We had to come upstairs to get a peep at the
thing."

Daniel grunted.

"Here, hang on a minute," Novon said. He pressed the
transparent bubble of his suit against the eyepiece of the big
scope's little sighting scope.

"Damned inefficient way to work," Daniel said. "You sky-
boys going to suit up and exit the Island every time you want
to do any observing?"

"Don't be silly," Novon grumbled. "Feeds and controls from
inside. We're going to have a luxury box in there that would
put a World Cup soccer stadium to shame. This is temporary,
till the Island is sealed. After the box is working, we will leave
the controls and eyepieces out here as auxiliaries, but I think
we'll seldom use them. If ever."

He shushed Daniel's next question, concentrating on the
eyepiece and the sighting controls of the telescope. Daniel
watched huge cranes swinging their loads through the vacuum
as he waited.

"All right," Novon's voice crackled.

"You keep an ephemeris in your head, Avram?"

"Most of one. Doesn't everybody?" He guided Daniel to
the sighting scope. "All right, I am going to give you a peep
through the sighter, just to get a glimpse of the region we're
interested in. You should have no trouble seeing Pluto, and
the dim speck at two o'clock, that will be Charon. Go ahead,
look. Here, use this for fine focus. It is very tough to get a
good focus when you have to wear a bubble over your head."

Daniel pressed the front of his bubble helmet against the
flexible eyepiece of the sighting scope. "Where—" He felt
Avram guiding his hand to the focusing control of the scope.
Daniel had tapped out the messages on his wrist keyboard that
retracted all of the spacesuit's waldo-hands and extended flexible gloves from both sleeves.

All he could see through the eyepiece was a pale, rounded
blur against a dark background. The blurry object exhibited no
clear-cut features but had a number of dark blotches scattered
across its face.

"Looks like the moon," he said to Novon. "The way it would

look from the bottom of a full swimming pool on a smoggy night."

"Hah! Not a bad approximation. All right, try the focus. You just have to play with it."

Daniel tried. The pale, fuzzy disc in the middle of the sighting scope grew slightly brighter and considerably sharper. "Looks a *lot* like the moon!" he said.

"All right. Do you see a pale blob off the edge of the disc, upper right quadrant?"

Daniel grunted. "I *think* I do. Is that Cerberus? That little blob?"

"No, sir! That is Charon! That's a couple hundred kilometers in diameter, Dan. Cerberus is about the size of a soccer field, maybe a hundred, hundred-twenty meters long. There is no way you could see Cerberus through that little sighter.

"Now, you have got to switch to the big scope."

Daniel let Avram guide him from the little sighting telescope to the main barrel. "This one has electronic enhancement, doesn't it?" he asked the astronomer.

"Yes, but you should be able to see Cerberus with just the optics. Here." He guided Dan to a position at the eyepiece of the big telescope. "Now, you should have just about the same field of vision that you got through the sighter."

"Yeah. Oh, but a *lot* brighter and sharper! Say, this is really something! I wish Marie-Elaine could see this!"

After a minute Avram said, "Now, you want to see Cerberus. Look, I am going to change the field of vision." Daniel kept his bubble pressed against the big scope while Novon adjusted controls, using the sighting telescope for himself.

The disc of Pluto swelled until it spilled over the edges of his sight. The features of the remote planet slid past his eyes until the upper right edge of the disc reappeared. The telescope continued to swing until Pluto's arc cut only a lower corner. The moon Charon now occupied the center of Daniel's field of vision, a slightly oblate spheroid marked, like Pluto itself, with craters and rays.

"Okay, Avram, there it is. But where's Cerberus?"

"You need sharp eyes to spot it, Dan. It has a very high orbital velocity, is close to Charon, and has an unequaled rate of libration."

"So?"

"So it pops from behind the edge of Charon at a different point each orbit. And you'll only be able to see it for a very short time before it passes over the face of Charon, and then it's almost impossible to see it. But it has a high libido. Probably the highest in the solar system, unless you count an object like Jupiter that generates radiation of its own."

"Huh! What do I look for?"

"A very small object, possibly just a point source. Very bright, almost a beacon. Amber-colored. Popping from behind the edge of the moon, it will appear to hover for a moment, then dip back either over the face of Charon or behind its rim. You will lose it in either case."

Dan waited, felt an itch on his scalp, overcame the need to scratch. "There it is! I can see the bugger. Wow! Gone already! Where did you say it would appear next? And how soon?"

"About fifteen minutes, and—where did it appear *from*, Daniel?"

"Six o'clock."

"You'll have to keep watch for it between eleven and one. Could you tell whether it passed over the face of Charon or behind its rim?"

"I think, over the face. I'm not sure. I think I can still pick up an occasional glint of the thing. Like polished bronze. What *is* it?"

"Metallic rock."

"Are you sure?"

"Do you mean, have we sampled the rock? Of course not. Have we done spectroanalysis? Not as much as we'd like. It is so damned hard to get a good image with pure lines. But we are pretty sure."

"How do you know it isn't a spaceship? Some old orbiting station, maybe still working, maybe dead."

"Come on, Daniel. Whose? The Russians? They are not that far ahead of us. And it is surely not ours. Maybe Sri Lanka has a secret space colonization program, do you think?"

"No, I was thinking more—" He pulled his bubble away from the eyepiece and watched the cranes at work behind Novon. The nearest, swinging a heavy metallic wall section, seemed to be having trouble. Jets of compressed air became visible.

The crane itself seemed to have suffered a structural failure and the metal was jack-knifing halfway up its main arm.

"I was thinking more of, ah, some of those older theories."

The crane had partially buckled and its cabin rose at the base of its arm.

"You know, ancient astronauts, chariots of the gods, that kind of stuff. It was a fad in my parents' day. My dad kept some old paperbacks around. Intriguing stuff."

"Hooey, Daniel, all hooey, believe me. Hey!"

Other voices were crackling in their helmets as emergency override signals came into play. The crane operator was calling Mayday. Other workers were shouting advice or crying out in panic. The crane itself had begun to spin like a pinwheel. No, Daniel thought. It was more like a hammer being swung by an athlete. At one end of the crane was the control cabin; at the other, the massive plate that the crane had been fitting into the skin of the Island.

Majestically the crane swung toward Daniel and Avram.

In an access of panic the two men released their grips on the telescope. Like drowning swimmers they clung to each other for support.

Daniel could see Avram's dark, desperate eyes through the front of his bubble. Reflected from the rear surface behind Avram's head he could see the curved plate swinging silently toward them.

There was a crackling sound at the moment of impact, then Daniel felt as if he had been struck from behind by a fist the size of a semi-truck. The stars leaped toward him, the darkness was filled with exploding lights.

2

THE VOICE came to him from some remote locale, like the voice of a ghost calling back to the land of the living. So faint, so remote, that he was unsure whether it was perceived or imagined.

At first he ignored it. At some level of consciousness he decided that he was sleeping, that the voice might fade away and leave him to his warm and infinitely comfortable sleep, if he did not rise to the bait of its call.

But it persisted.

"Mister Kitajima."

Daniel tried to burrow deeper into the warm blackness.

"Mister Kitajima."

Let me be!

"Mister Kitajima. Daniel. Mister Kitajima. Daniel."

It was hopeless. The contest of wills was unwinnable. The voice would not let him be. Daniel heard a second voice. Its response to the first was an inarticulation, a single syllable that amounted to little more than a grunt.

"Mister Kitajima. Can you open your eyes? Can you speak?"

He grunted some semblance of an affirmative.

The voice was agreeable, encouraging, supportive. "Wonderful! You can hear me. You can speak. Now, can you open your eyes? Come, the room is dark, it won't hurt. Come on, give it a try."

Daniel wanted to please the voice. It had characteristics of his mother (or the idealized recollection of his mother), his wife, a friend, a sister . . .

He tried again to speak an affirmative, heard a slightly less inchoate sound, and opened his eyes. Didn't open them. He tried—he made the effort of thought and will that had set off the synapses and muscular responses to open his eyes, the effort that had worked unquestioningly for as long as he could remember.

This time it didn't work.

"You're trying," the voice said.

Daniel wondered if it was the voice of God. (Was God a woman? The voice was warm, strong-timbred, deep for a woman's voice, but he was almost certain that it was nonetheless the voice of a woman.)

"We can monitor your channels, some of them. That was a good try. Won't you give me another, please?"

("That was wonderful! Won't you try it again? Take another step for Mommy. Dada will be so pleased when he gets home!")

"Try again, please."

He strained to open his eyes. It was an incredible effort, a daunting task. Strain! Pull! He wanted to reach up and literally try to pry his eyelids open, like a drunk in a cartoon propping his eyes open with twigs.

"Come on, Mister Kitajima!"

A burst of dazzling light struck him, sent his mind reeling, disappeared, leaving burning afterimages that swung from red to green and back again, gradually damping, fading, disappearing into a neutral darkness.

"How was that, Mister Kitajima?"

"Eh. Hurt." He heard himself speak, realized that he had managed an articulate word.

"That's wonderful," his mother—no, the voice—the voice —said. "That's enough for now. I'll let you rest. But that was very, very good progress. Speech and some sight. Sleep."

The voice ceased and he slipped back into the warmth. Some time later he probably dreamed, or perhaps he actually regained a small degree of consciousness and merely ran ancient memories through his mind. Pictures and sounds and feelings. Hot dogs and frozen malts at Seals Stadium with his father, watching the Seals in action against the L.A. Dodgers, the Houston Astros, the Denver Giants, and hearing stories from fans his father's age of the time when the Giants had been a San Francisco team and played their games before sparse crowds at a terrible ballpark down at Candlestick Point.

Sneaking off to X-rated movies on Market Street with his friends from Balboa High, lying to the cashier about their age to get into the theater and then lying to each other about having done the things they saw being done on the screen.

Bringing home school assignments and running programs on his family's little keyboard link to the Ma Bell computer, hearing the praise of his parents when his programs ran uncorrected on the first attempt. But it was all so easy for Dan, all so easy, he couldn't understand people who failed to grasp the concepts involved, or who—even more incomprehensibly—claimed to understand the concepts but couldn't keep the details of a simple search-and-sort or an elementary Sysgen routine.

His terror when he walked to the house on Post Street to pick up his girl for his first date. Taking her to a fast-food joint for hamburgers. Wondering how she would react if he . . .

It all faded again.

Some internal clock told him that a long time had passed before he returned to consciousness. He heard the woman's voice calling his name once more, the woman's voice that he had mistaken for the voice of his mother.

He said, "Yes."

He opened his eyes.

Once more the room was dark, but the darkness was relieved by a gentle grayish light that seemed to pervade all of space. Daniel smiled inwardly at the thought. Cosmic, cosmic. Silly.

He was, for the moment, unable to distinguish any particular color or shape in his surroundings, but he was aware that there were shapes around him. One of them moved.

"Mister Kitajima," the shape said.

Ah, so that was his mother; no, the woman whose voice reminded him of his mother's. "Mister Kitajima, can you see me?"

He said, Yes.

"Wonderful. We're going to keep you up for a while today. It's been a long struggle, but this will be all right. Can you make out my face?"

Somehow the dim light in the room seemed to grow slightly

less dim. Before him Daniel could see a suggestion of a face. He blinked, held his eyes shut for a moment, then opened them a mere slit. He could still see her, and the pain to his eyes grew less.

She seemed to be a small woman. Not that he could gauge her height or body configuration. Just her face, but that was the face of a small, slim, fair person. Light-colored hair; he could not tell if the hair was white with age or blonde with youth. Pale skin. He could not tell the color of her eyes. Possibly they were blue.

He tried to say, "I can see your face." Somehow the words tumbled over one another as he spoke them, but the face nodded as if she understood.

"Good," she said. "Very good. I am Doctor Royce. I've been with you the past two years, getting you ready for this. I'm very happy with your progress, Mister Kitajima."

There was a brief silence. Then Daniel said, "Two years?"

The room grew dim and he fell asleep.

Doctor Royce was back. Daniel had trouble at first in deciding whether this was another dream or reverie of some sort, like his journeys back to Seals Stadium with his father. His father was no longer living.

"How are you feeling, Mister Kitajima?"

She was probably real. He would assume that she was, act as if she was. If it turned out to be a dream, there was nothing lost. Consider it a rehearsal for reality. If she really was before him, all the better.

"Don't feel very much," he said. "What happened? Where am I?"

"Med Island," Doctor Royce said. "Don't worry about that now. You're making good progress. We have lots to do. Today I'm going to turn the light up higher, and we'll talk for a bit longer than we have. Here."

She must have moved her hand, Daniel thought, unless someone else is here, picking up cues from her. The light grew brighter than it had been and he could see her face more clearly, surrounded by some sort of shapeless, neutral-gray garment. She was blonde, not very young, he decided, more thirtyish. Her features were on the edge between graceful slimness and sharpness. Her eyes were definitely gray.

"What island is this?"

"Med Island."

"As in Club Med?"

"No." She smiled, almost laughed. It was the first time he'd seen her do that. "Med as in Medical. I'm Doctor Royce. Do you remember me? We've worked together."

He grunted, Yes.

"I'm going to turn the light up again, Mister Kitajima. I'll try to make it very gradual. Tell me if I go too fast. There's no big hurry. I don't want to cause you pain."

The room grew slowly brighter.

Medical? Was he in a hospital?

He tried to see if he was in a hospital room. Where were the white sheets, the omnipresent tables and stands. Was there an IV rack overhead? How had they fed him?

"What happened?"

"It's been a lot of work. A long time. You're doing very well, Mister Kitajima. Very, very well."

"Are you my doctor?"

She said, "I'm the head of the team. Your team. There are others, of course. There have been a lot of us over the years."

Oh yes. She'd said something about two years. Two years? What had happened to him? Had he been in the hospital for two *years?* He hadn't even been sick!

"What happened?" His voice sounded very strange.

"There was an accident." Doctor Royce turned away from him, moved away from him. She must be walking. In the increased light of the room he could see her moving away from him. He'd been right about her. She was a slight woman, slim.

She turned back and asked him, "Can you remember it? The accident?"

The room didn't seem to be a hospital room. There were no medical appurtenances there at all, that he could see. Wait. There were electronic monitoring panels, indicator lights and displays. It looked like the monitoring room of a process-controlled factory, not a hospital room.

He'd been unconscious for two years? Had medicine changed that much in two years?

"I was working with . . ." He struggled to remember. "I'd been sitting with Avram Novon and Crista, ah, Crista Balbo. In the shuttle. We were working on the first big Island."

He struggled to remember.

"We went outside. Novon and I. He was an astronomer. Optical astronomer. I was looking at Pluto and Charon, looking for Cerberus. I thought it was artificial and Avram said that was a load of—of—"

He paused.

"The crane. There was a heavy crane nearby fitting main skin panels of the Island onto the skeleton. The crane buckled and one of the panels . . ."

For the first time his vision had cleared sufficiently to permit him to look beyond his room. Amidst the panels and indicators there was a—yes, it must be a door. Daniel was amused at detecting this sign of the commonplace in the presence of so much exotic. And there were, yes, windows! Through them he detected greenery, rolling hills and pathways and trees. The hospital must lie in the center of a park.

"You said this was an Island, Doctor Royce?"

"We're at a LaGrange point. Yes."

"How many Islands are there?"

He tried to read the expression on her face. At first it had been merely a blob, then her features had become clear, and now he was looking for the signs that would betray her thoughts.

She seemed to be worried.

"I don't really know. Mister Kitajima, you've been here a long time. Your progress is really remarkable. I think I'd better—"

"Wait a minute," he broke in. "I was working on the first full-scale Island. You mean to say that it's all finished, and there are others now, so many others that there's a special Island devoted entirely to medical use? Are there others, then? Resorts, factories, ah, ah, religious communities? How many Islands have been built? How fast could they go in two years?"

"I don't know how many. I—yes, everything you say, and more. War Islands, too, like gigantic battleships in space. It's been—it hasn't been just two years."

He would have sat bolt upright in his bed but the reflex seemed to be disconnected. He felt the shock of startlement and would have spread his hands on the coverlet, palms down, automatically pushing himself forward and up, but nothing happened.

"Not two years? But you said— Hold on, Doctor. Isn't this 2011?"

"I'm going to get help." She started toward the door. "I'm

going to get Doctor Kimura. He'll talk to you. You'll be more comfortable with him, I think. I'll be here too unless you want me to leave."

Daniel closed his eyes. "Please. Before you go, Doctor. Just tell me how long I've been here. What year is it?"

She said, "It's 2089." She pressed a panel beside the door and it slid into the doorway. The door slid back into place behind her.

Daniel sat watching the door, letting his gaze slip away from its plain gray surface to the blinking lights and dials that covered most of the room, to the windows and the greenery outside. If this was an Island, then the park might stretch away to an upward-curving horizon. The world was shaped like a hollow cylinder with all life, all homes, all structures on the inside.

At least, that had been the plan in 2009.

It was eighty years later. Eighty years! Dan Kitajima's head spun—or seemed to.

The sunlight that illuminated the parklike area would be reflected from great mirrors mounted outside the Island, geared and calibrated to provide twelve hours of day and twelve of night to the zones inside the Island—unless the engineers and psychologists had decided that some other arrangement would work better.

The door slid aside and Doctor Royce walked back into Daniel's room, accompanied by a middle-aged man. They were both dressed in some kind of medical whites.

"Mister Kitajima," Royce said, "this is Doctor Kimura."

Kimura stepped close to Dan, then halted. He didn't offer his hand, but instead made a sort of friendly-polite gesture, half a casual nod of the head, half a self-conscious bow. He had jet-black hair, worn short. Jet-black eyes. Skin the same color as Dan's, and features that suggested the same Japanese ancestry as Dan's.

"It gives me pleasure to meet you at last," Kimura said. "That is, to be able to converse with you. I've seen you many times, worked with you, along with Doctor Royce. And others. Many, many others."

"Doctor Kimura. I want to know. Are you going to level with me?"

Kimura looked concerned. "Of course. Anything you want

to ask me. Where shall we start?"

"I—" Dan hesitated.

"Mister Kitajima was telling me about the accident," Royce said. "His recollection of it. Shall I play it back, or—"

Kimura turned toward a wall panel and punched a series of instructions. A readout screen glowed with color. Rows of characters sprang to life.

"You're familiar with these, of course." Kimura flicked his glance to Dan, then back to the screen. "This is an extract of your medical history, Mister Kitajima. Of course there was great interest in your case at the time. But so much has happened since, so many years have passed."

"Eighty years," Dan gritted.

"Yes. Eighty years."

A stray thought came to Dan, almost an irrelevancy. Yet he felt that he had to know. "Doctor Kimura. Doctor Royce. Look at all the hardware here. And eighty years of care. This Island didn't even exist when I was—when, when the accident happened."

"That is correct."

"Who the hell is paying my bills?"

Kimura smiled. In fact, Daniel almost thought he detected a faint laugh.

"Don't worry about that," Kimura said. "That's all taken care of. And you have plenty of money, if it comes to that."

"After eighty years? Eighty years of hospitalization?"

Kimura smiled more broadly. "You can have as many details as you wish, but the essence of it is this. When that crane buckled and smashed into the tethered shuttle, there was a huge outcry to save the survivors. The U.S. Congress passed a special act, the United Nations got involved, there were insurance claims, and one of the networks started a special fund for the survivors. The survivors, and their families, and the families of the, ah, nonsurvivors."

"I see."

"I don't think you see it all, Mister Kitajima. For one thing, 'survivors' was only a temporary category. Most of the people up there were killed outright. Of the remainder, all of them perished before we could stabilize their conditions."

"All but me?"

Kimura nodded.

"Ave Novon? Crista Balbo? All the construction crew? Everybody?"

"Everybody. I'm very sorry. But consider, if they had survived and recovered, they would almost certainly be dead by now anyway. Eighty years, Mister Kitajima."

"Huh. I suppose so." He looked past Royce and Kimura, and watched a family strolling past in the parklike area outside. Well, surely, even at a medical Island there would be marriage and homes and children. The group passing looked like the vision of some former utopian predicting the paradise of the future. The parents were both tall, slim, youthful-looking. Their children circled around them, tossing some sort of flying toys to each other, running off to retrieve them when one of them failed to make a catch.

"You seem a little doubtful."

Daniel looked back at the doctors. Kimura had spoken. Daniel said, "Eh?"

"How old were your friends at the time of the accident?" Kimura asked.

"I'm not sure. I think Avram would have been . . . huh, I never asked him, but by his appearance . . ." Daniel shut his eyes, conjured up an image of Avram Novon as he appeared across a lightweight eating-counter top inside the shuttle. "Probably forty or so. Fortyish."

Kimura nodded. "Longevity research has accomplished a few things, but we haven't brought the normal lifespan anywhere near one hundred and twenty, Mister Kitajima."

"I see."

"Well, this has been a good session. I think it would be best for you to rest, now. You've a lot of catching up to do. Eighty years worth of news. And, of course, now that you're back with us, we've a job ahead getting you up and around again. You'll never have to work for a living again, but I suspect you'd prefer to get back in the swim."

Dan agreed.

"Well, then . . ."

"Oh."

Kimura and Royce stopped just at the door of the room and turned to face Dan again. Royce asked if there was something else he wanted before his rest.

"When that crane smashed into me..."

He saw Kimura and Royce nod simultaneously, similar grim expressions on their faces.

"What did it do?"

"Well, it, ah..." Doctor Royce took a step back toward Daniel. "Its impact was severely traumatic. You are aware, certainly, that even in a weightless condition, objects retain their mass. Being struck by a hundred-kilogram mass traveling at twenty kilometers per second will be as much of a wallop in free-fall as it will in plus-G conditions."

"I understand that," Dan said impatiently. "I know the crane gave me one hell of a wallop. I'm surprised to be alive. And grateful."

Royce and Kimura exchanged glances.

"Uh. I think I'm grateful," Dan amended. "What I want to know is, 'severely traumatic' *what?* If the impact didn't kill me, I'm surprised I didn't die of vacuum-decompression. Bends, explosion, asphyxiation, cold. There must be a whole catalog of ways to die in that kind of accident, and it's just roulette, which way should have got me."

Royce's face showed relief. "Yes, it seems a miracle, I'm sure. Your suit held its vacuum. The damage was caused by crushing. There's a complete history of your case in the files. Under law we are required to show you the contents of your file, so nothing will be held back from you."

"Hey, I'm no medic. I wouldn't know a scapula from a skateboard."

"What is a skateboard?"

"Never mind. What I want is, just give me the straight input. What happened to me? How badly was I smashed up? It must have been pretty badly. And how did you get me fixed? I think I feel pretty okay."

He gestured—or tried to gesture. Nothing happened.

He looked at his hand to see what was wrong with it, and found he could see nothing but Royce and Kimura, her blonde Caucasian features and his darker Asian ones; nothing but the two doctors, the hospital room that more closely resembled an electronic laboratory than a sickroom, the park outside with its grass and trees and brook and strolling families.

He could see nothing of himself, nor could he move.

"Oh, Jesus," he moaned. "Oh, holy bloody bleeding Jesus Christ."

His vision blurred with tears. Through the blur he saw the doctors exchange another glance, saw Kimura gesture. Royce turned toward a control panel and punched a series of instructions into a keyboard.

"Don't do it," Daniel pleaded. "Please don't. Don't turn me off like a fucking TV set. Please—"

"Now try to calm yourself," Kimura said. He stepped toward Dan, toward Dan's visual locus at any rate. "We just want you to—"

"What am I? What am I, damn you, tell me! Am I just a goddamned brain hooked into a voder? What did you take away from me? What do I have left?"

"Please, please," Kimura gestured placatingly.

"Why can't I feel? I can't move! I—"

"Please, Mister Kitajima."

"Did it kill me? Am I just a computer program? Tell me that at least!"

"No," Kimura shook his head. "Really, nothing like..." His voice was fading.

"Don't turn me off!"

"Please, Mister Kitajima." Kimura's figure bent and wavered like an image in a funhouse. "We're just wann yoor-resss..."

"Wha?" Dan tried to hold his eyes open, to ask Kimura...

"Eelaxann ress laretawgain..."

The room was dark, or Daniel's eyes were shut, he couldn't tell which. He was floating in a sea of black in the temperature of blood.

He remembered sensory deprivation experiments he'd heard of where subjects' eyes were taped shut and their mouths taped shut and pure oxygen was fed them through nasal tubes and they were floated in tanks of body-temperature fluid and they developed bizarre hallucinations and...

He was hallucinating, he realized, this whole experience, everything since the construction crane had buckled and the curved wall plate had swung toward himself and Novon and the gimballed telescope. He had been injured by the impact.

Unconscious, he had been carried by a rescue team to some medical facility and placed in a flotation chamber and for some unknown medical reason subjected to sensory deprivation techniques and thereafter had hallucinated the interview with Doctor Royce and Doctor Kimura, the room full of flashing electronic gear, the story of his eighty years of unconsciousness, the completion of the medical Island with its parklike region outside his hospital room.

Unless—

A horrifying thought struck.

Unless he had not been subjected to deprivation by the medical team. Unless in the course of his injury he had suffered neural damage. Unless the seat of his consciousness, whatever that was, wherever it was located in his brain, had been severed from all sensory inputs.

For all he knew his eyes were functioning normally, his ears were responding. But somehow the messages flowing from the nerve endings throughout his body were failing to reach his mind. His mind, his consciousness, his psyche had access to all recollection up to the moment of the accident, but was cut off from all inputs that it should have received since that moment.

His body might be anywhere, in a medical facility, lying on a hospital bed, suspended in a flotation chamber, even— for all he could know—still floating between the shuttle and the half-completed Island. He might be slowly dying of injuries received in that moment of impact, and not know it, never know it, simply fade out, softly fade out as the flow of blood to his brain tapered off and the cells of his brain went into temporary dormancy and then into permanent death.

He tried to conjure up an image of his wife Marie-Elaine, of her face, her dark, sympathetic eyes, her black, glossy hair, her soft skin, her slim body. He could feel her with him in their bed, responding to his lovemaking, her dark-aureoled breasts soft beneath his hands as brown nipples rose to hardness, her mouth whispering warm and moistly against his face as he slid away, his cheek moving against the smooth gold of her body toward blackness...

He blinked.

He rose from the blackness, dizzied by the bright sunlight

pouring through small rectangular windows and the bright artificial light filling the room from unseen sources and the bright image of Doctor Royce in her white tunic, her pale Caucasian face, her pale eyes, her platinum hair. She looked at him. She looked concerned.

Daniel Kitajima could see her and could see beyond her that he was again—or still—in the hospital room that more nearly resembled an electronics laboratory. Beyond Doctor Royce he could perceive Doctor Kimura. Kimura was devoting his attention to a screen, presumably monitoring Daniel's medical readouts rather than watching Daniel himself.

Tentatively, Royce called his name.

He chose not to reply, but Kimura said something to Royce, turning his head to transmit the words over his shoulder. Royce nodded.

"I think you can hear me, Mister Kitajima. Please reply."

Daniel waited.

"Mister Kitajima, we know you're there. Doctor Kimura is monitoring a neuroscanner-encephalograph. The trace indicates that you are conscious and aware of us. Please reply."

Dan said, "Are you real?"

Royce's face showed surprise. "Real? Of course we're real. Why—"

"How do I know you're not hallucinations? Why can't I move? Why can't I feel anything?"

"I assure you, Mister Kitajima, I am a totally real woman. Doctor Kimura is a totally real man. You are definitely here."

Kimura left the screen and stood beside Royce. He nodded at Daniel.

"Mister Kitajima, Doctor Royce and I are physicians, not philosophers. Please understand that. But I did take a few electives in philosophy, epistemology. Eh?" Kimura smiled tentatively. "There is no way that any of us can be certain that the exterior universe is real. Even if we go all the way back to Descartes and his famous 'I think, therefore...'"

Daniel waited silently.

"So," Kimura resumed, "what can we do? Any evidence of external reality may itself be merely part of the illusion. The old 'Pinch me, I'm dreaming' syndrome, you see? It's no problem for a cow or an unsophisticated mind. They equally accept reality at face value. The question never occurs to them.

"The sophisticated mind must perform an act of faith. Assume that the universe is real. Even if it isn't, treat it as if it were. The alternative is catatonia, Mister Kitajima. Please don't go catatonic on us."

Daniel looked out the window. A group of youngsters were passing his room, riding on some sort of futuristic bicycles.

"We're all real, eh?"

Royce and Kimura both nodded.

"Can we shake hands on that?"

Kimura looked at Royce. "Not yet. We will, Mister Kitajima. I'm afraid that you aren't able to shake hands yet, but you will be able. If you work with us, you will be able."

"Do I have any hands?"

Royce said, "You will."

"But I don't."

A hesitation, then, "No."

"Do I have—huh, why go through a catalog! Do I have *anything? Am* I anything? What am I? A self-aware computer program? All right, Doctor, I'll grant that the universe is real, at least probably real. But am I? Am I real?"

"I assure you, you are real. You are still a protoplasmic being, a human being. You suffered some losses. We'll get around to the details. But you are still—you are still *you*. We've already constructed an elaborate prosthesis, and we're going to have you functioning again, Mister Kitajima. All we need is your help."

Daniel closed his eyes and waited for a while. Then he said, "Why should I help? Why don't you just let me go, let me die, let me fade back into that blackness where I spent the last 80 years? Is it just that you're protecting your jobs?"

Doctor Kimura let out a short angry laugh that was almost a bark. "We could do very well in another practice, sir! Be certain of that!

"No, Mister Kitajima. We're not just keeping a sinecure."

Daniel looked at the park outside the window. More bicyclists were passing, dressed in brightly patterned clothes of an unfamiliar cut. Well, the outfits of 1999 would have looked strange to someone from 1919. At least the people were recognizable. No bizarre mutations had occurred in the human form. Sunday-paper speculations about five-meter-tall human mantises bred in weightless Islands didn't show up here.

"Look, Doctor Kimura. Doctor Royce. I guess I should be grateful for everything you're trying to do for me. But I'm really not sure I want to come back."

Kimura reached into a pocket of his medical whites and pulled out a plastic rectangle. He faced Dan and cleared his throat. "Under the Uniform Personal Dignity Act of 2063 it is your right to refuse any treatment designed to prolong your life against your wishes, or to require the termination of present courses of medical treatment. You may also request a prompt and painless termination of your life through accepted means of euthanasia, subject to a reasonable period of delay for consideration. This period is normally of seventy-two hours' duration but may be shortened or waived in cases of severe and unmeliorable suffering."

"You mean you'll just shut me off if I demand it?"

"I think we would insist on the seventy-two-hour delay-for-consideration, Mister Kitajima. But if you really want to throw in the towel, it's your life.

"We'd have a tough time explaining things to your family, but we'd just—"

"Wait a minute! What family! Is my wife still . . ." Dan let the question trail away.

Behind Kimura, the blonde Doctor Royce had already punched up a series of entries on a display keyboard and read back the information to Daniel. "Your wife, Marie-Elaine Tanaka Kitajima, was lost in the San Francisco earthquake of 2031. Your son, Robert Albert Kitajima, died of Ulyanov's Syndrome in 2055. Your daughter, Elizabeth Kitajima Hasegawa, is still living. Her permanent residence is in San Francisco but she is presently domiciled with her son and daughter-in-law and their family on Hokkaido Island."

"Hokkaido! You mean—they emigrated back to Japan?"

"Oh, no!" Royce shook her head. "I keep forgetting that you've been unaware of events for eighty years. Hokkaido Island is a space island like this one. It's located—let me check on that . . ."

She tapped more keys beneath the display screen.

Daniel Kitajima looked at Doctor Kimura. Neither spoke.

Lights flashed on the screen where Doctor Royce was working. She read the information, then punched the screen back to quiescence. She walked toward Daniel.

"Hokkaido Island is located at the edge of the solar northern hemisphere of the asteroid belt. It is listed here as a cultural experimental colony, dedicated to recovery of former terrestrial social institutions and values. Economy is intensive agriculture. Major export is foodstuffs. Import is metals."

"Oh boy, oh boy. I've got a lot of catching up to do." Daniel focused his vision on Doctor Kimura. "You say you'd have trouble squaring it with my family if I chose euthanasia."

"Yes."

"Then why aren't they here?"

"I'm afraid that Missus Hasegawa—your daughter—is quite elderly and not in the best of health. I don't think she would take the trip very well. And I frankly doubt that she has sufficient command of her faculties to make very much of it if she could.

"Your grandson—as I recall, he was born Edward Albert Hasegawa but has reverted to the name Ieyasu Hasegawa— Mister Hasegawa has been in communication with us. He feels that it would be improper of him to visit until such time as you are prepared to receive visitors. And until you choose to extend an invitation.

"I haven't been to Hokkaido Island, Mister Kitajima, but—"

"You *are* Japanese, Doctor Kimura!"

"About as much as you are, sir!" Kimura drew a hissing breath and bowed slightly. Daniel couldn't tell whether the gesture was made seriously or in mockery.

"What's that mean?"

"It means, Mister Kitajima, that my family came to America about the same time, I think, as yours. We've been Americans for generations. We've been citizens for a hundred years or more. How long does it take to stop being Japanese, or Japanese-Americans, and just be Americans whose ancestors happened to come from Japan? Do you speak Japanese?"

Daniel grunted a negative.

"Neither do I."

Daniel was silent.

"Do you—did you have a hobby?" Kimura asked.

Daniel shrugged, or tried to shrug. Nothing happened. "I was a baseball fan, if you call that a hobby. Followed the Seals for years. Used to play hooky from school and take a cable car down to the stadium to watch them play."

"Not sumo wrestling? Not paper folding?"

There was a silence. "I get your point," Daniel finally conceded. "Well, do you think I ought to invite Edward Albert . . . Ieyasu Hasegawa . . . over for a visit?"

"That's up to you. I'd suggest that you push on with some rehabilitation work before you invite him in."

"What does Doctor Royce suggest?"

"I'm inclined to agree," she said. "I think you'd feel better if you could move around when your grandson arrived. And I think he'd be a lot more comfortable, too. I've spoken with him—by screen of course. I think he'd have a little trouble dealing with you just now."

Daniel tried to breath a sigh. "All right. Let's get with it. But you have to tell me straight. Why can't I move? What's left of me—the original, organic me—and what kind of prostheses have you rigged up?"

Royce nodded. "That's a good attitude, Mister Kitajima. That's the kind of thing Doctor Kimura and I have hoped to hear from you. All right, we'll give you the full information. You just tell us if you're getting tired or if you want to take a break and assimilate some of this data before we give you the rest. There's a lot to tell."

She brought a tall stool from a corner of the room out of Daniel's field of vision, set it in place in front of him, and hoisted her slim form onto it. She began his briefing.

3

TOSHIRO MIFUNE on a bicycle!

This is absurd, Daniel thought. He flashed a look at Doctor Kimura, got one back that showed the medico had caught his meaning and counseled him to stay cool, play things by ear, see to it that nothing too drastic took place.

The rehabilitation period had been less painful than Dan Kitajima had feared—physically. In fact, there had been almost no real pain. A good deal of discomfort, half-physical and half-psychological. Vertigo, confusion in the interpretation of sensory inputs and physical orientation.

Maddening frustration in learning to operate prostheses as if they were his own body.

There was nothing really new in his restoration to a semblance of human normality. The first clever individual to fashion a peg leg or a hook to replace a lost hand was the ancestor of the most sophisticated prosthetician of the present century. But where that long-ago pioneer had attached a simple piece of wood or metal to a liquor-numbed stump (at least Daniel surmised that some primitive anesthetic must have been involved), Kimura and Royce and a crew of their associates had used the most complex technology in existence to get him back together.

They hadn't started with an almost-whole man lacking a hand or a leg. They had started with the cryonically preserved central nervous system of a man whose body had been crushed and mangled and frozen to virtually total destruction. Even the

34

brain and spinal column were incomplete. What had Royce said, carefully monitoring the flow of benzodiazepines to Daniel's minimal remaining organic component?

"You lost about half of your brain, Mister Kitajima. Most of the medula, almost all of the hypothalamus, about a third of the cerebrum, the entire pineal body. When we first tried bringing you around, our chiefest question was not so much concerned with the functions of control or even intelligence, but whether there would be any awareness left.

"Some of our cyberneticians were interested in keeping your brain going even if there was no self-awareness. In fact, especially if there was no self-awareness. They wanted to work with it—you—as an experimental computer. See what kind of input and output channels they could establish with your brain. What its storage capacity and computational abilities were."

Daniel exploded a loud "Huh! Well, I can hardly blame 'em. That's the kind of experiment I would have loved to get involved with myself, back in those days. I'll tell you, though, it certainly looks different when it's your brain they're planning to play with. Well, but that didn't happen, hey?"

"As soon as we determined that you had some degree of self-awareness, that established that you were still a legal person. No experimentation without permission. And we had no way of obtaining the permission, until we had restored communication with you."

"Catch-22," Daniel said.

Royce looked puzzled. "I don't understand . . ."

"Just an old expression. Some kind of literary reference, I don't remember the details myself. Makes no matter. Listen, I'm taking this all pretty damned calmly. Isn't that a little bit strange?"

"It's the benzodiazepines in your bloodstream." She flicked her glance at a readout, nodded almost imperceptibly, turned back toward Daniel.

"At least I still have a bloodstream for you to pump that stuff into."

"Just barely."

"And here I am." He raised a hand before his eyes. "Looks like the real thing to me." He laced his fingers together and flexed his back muscles, feeling his shoulders creak with the effort. "Feels real, too."

Royce smiled. "And yet there isn't a bone or a muscle in your body. We did manage to grow your optic nerves back into the optic sensors. But they're not organic eyes either."

"Hah! I don't *feel* like a robot!"

"We didn't want you to. You can't imagine the meetings we went through. I said, 'We.' Those meetings started long before Doctor Kimura or I were born. In a sense, you're the most expensive medical experiment that's ever been carried out. If you feel like looking through the files, old news bubbles, whatever . . ."

"Maybe sometime," Dan said.

"No need if you don't wish to. But there was a terrible uproar over your appropriations. Politicians kept yelling that it was an elitist plot, that the money should be spent providing food for the poor, housing for refugees. They just wouldn't believe that what we learned from putting you back together would be the biggest fund of medical information ever to come from a single source! People at the other end wanted to cut you out and use the money for weapons."

Daniel looked out the window. There wasn't very much activity in the park outside the hospital. A few picnickers sat beside the brook, sharing a meal. They had an infant with them, creeping around on a blanket. The path on which they had approached wound into invisibility in both directions. Dan thought he could see someone approaching from the right, a distant figure little bigger than a speck.

"How did I win out? How did you keep them from shutting me off? Once that initial save-the-space-hero thing died down?"

Royce smiled and put a hand to her light-colored hair. "You're probably here because you're Japanese. Part of the complaint of the anti-elitists was that the money spent on you was a racist plot. Part of white-inspired genocidal tactics aimed at the Third World. Did you use that expression in your time? Third World?"

Daniel nodded.

"I could never understand what it meant, originally."

"No matter. Like Catch-22."

"Well. When your identity came out, it became genocidal white racism to *oppose* spending money to save you! And the weapons people came around to the idea that you could become the prototype of a new army of mostly mechanical super-soldiers. They'd spend money to make up divisions of killers."

"But they wouldn't be robots. Where were they going to get the—ah—" He paused and gathered his determination. "If it takes one human being to make each robot-soldier, what's the advantage?"

"Believe me, Mister Kitajima, if you went up against any ordinary man, he wouldn't have a chance. Your rehabilitation has come along fine, as far as learning to use your prosthetics goes. You're back to what we'd call normal functioning. But you haven't begun—we haven't begun to switch on the abilities you're going to have."

She turned away nervously and stood looking out the window.

"What abilities?"

She turned back. "I've discussed this with Doctor Kimura. He agrees that we can start now. Just sit down for a minute." She punched a series of commands into the now-familiar keyboard. "Do you notice any change?"

Daniel shook his head.

"Let me know."

As she continued to operate the panel the windows of the room darkened, then became opaque. The lighting in the room dimmed until total darkness was reached.

"Can you see anything?"

"No." A moment passed. "Yes! What did you do?"

He could see her clearly in an eerie, dark-red radiance.

"I didn't do anything. Just turned off the lights. But first I enabled your infrared vision."

"You—how?"

"The enable control came from my keyboard. But now it's your own. You can use the infrared or cut away from it any time you want to. How is it? Do you want to move around a little? I can't see you at all, Mister Kitajima. The room is in complete darkness."

He stood up and walked to the window. He could see it clearly—see the window as a panel set into the wall of the room. But he could see little of what lay outside. He asked Royce the reason.

"That's a surprise," she admitted. "We just didn't think of that. I suppose that the window material is opaque to infrared."

"I can see everything fine in here." Daniel looked at his hands. "I'm pretty dim myself. You're much brighter, Doctor."

"Infrared is associated with heat. I suppose you're seeing me by body heat. The rest of the room is illuminated by—whatever ambient heat is present."

Daniel laughed, a single barklike exclamation. "What other mystical powers do I have now? I feel like some kind of television super-hero. Am I going to find that I can fly? Shoot death rays from my eyes? Can I shrink and travel over fiber-optic lines?"

She shook her head, looking distressed.

"Oh. What's my magic word? Or am I the kind of hero who changes clothes in a vidi booth?"

"Would you do me a favor, Mister Kitajima? Please come over here and run up the top-left dial on this panel. I'd have to do it by feel, now. You can see it, I think."

He complied.

The room returned to normal lighting. Royce hit another command and the window cleared. Daniel looked from it and saw a man on a bicycle slowly making his way toward the hospital locale.

"How do I turn my infrared vision on and off, Doctor?"

"It's hooked into your brain."

"Huh!"

"Now that we hit the master enable, you can cut the infrared in and out at will."

"That's a nice little touch. And do I have other surprises in store for me?"

She nodded.

"How do I get hold of a copy of the operator's manual?"

"Doctor Kimura and I. And other members of the staff here. We'll work with you."

"All right, damn it. But how about a briefing? What do I have? Radar?"

"Yes."

"How do I turn it on?"

"We haven't—enabled that yet. But it's built into your prosthetics. Once it's enabled, you can control it mentally."

"How much brain did you say I have left?"

"About forty percent. Of your organic brain, that is. While you were in cryonics we tried to clone it, but there were technical problems. And—legal obstacles."

"Don't grow us a Frankenstein in the man-vats of the Islands, hey? Who was the mastermind of this project, Doctor Moreau?"

"I don't think I know the name."

"Never mind. Just more of my regressive acculturation."

"So we used electronics instead. Some of your own work, in fact. That helped get the appropriations through, and your company made some very large contributions."

"Oh, boy. What can I do, Doctor Royce? I thought I was kidding when I asked you if I could fly. But—can I?"

She shook her head. "No, nothing like that. Your physical powers are not so extraordinary. You'll find that you are very strong. Your body runs by servo-motors, mostly very small fractional-horsepower motors. Doctor Kimura is more conversant with the details than I am.

"But the major muscles are—I should say, the servo-systems that perform the functions of the major muscles—are quite powerful. Your hands and your legs are very strong. And of course you have no fatigue to contend with."

"Just need to get my batteries charged up now and then?"

"Yes."

"Oh, Jesus. Oh, Jesus. I was joking, Doctor."

"I'm sorry."

He took a deep breath—or tried. Nothing happened. "No lungs? No digestive system?"

"Mister Kitajima, do you think it possible to hold two contrary ideas at the same time? To use each for its pragmatic value, even though you realize that they're logically inconsistent?"

"Hmm. Such as?"

"Oh—in your former time, did you regard radiant light beams as particles or as wave phenomena?"

"Okay. Sure, we dealt with that dilemma. Some clever folks decided to call light wavicles, and not deal with doublethink. But I didn't see the need for it."

"Yes. What did you call that technique?"

"Doublethink. From another old book."

"A wonderful concept! Hugely useful. Who devised it?"

Daniel waved his hand dismissingly. "Somebody named Blore or Blair, I don't know. It doesn't matter. It was just what you described."

"Well. Part of the work we've been doing, Mister Kitajima, is designed to integrate you—*you*, you understand—with the prosthetic system we've built for you. Eighty years of effort, Mister Kitajima. And what we need desperately is for you to become a whole man once again.

"Your hands." She took them in hers, held them up between them. "These are *your* hands. This is your body. This is *you!* The old you, the old body that was destroyed years ago in the accident—that's gone. This is really *you!*"

He could feel her gripping his hands with all her strength.

"At the same time, you have to use your body as an—object." She dropped his hands and turned her back. He could hear her voice clearly. He suspected that his hearing, like his vision, had been augmented.

"I'm a cyborg," he said.

"You are a man!" She spun and faced him. "But—yes, you're a cyborg. You can deal with that. I know you can. Doctor Kimura is sure of it also. But you have to—to doublethink. You have to integrate your psyche with your new body and become a single being. And you have to realize that your psyche, your self, is an entity in *itself*, and that this body—this *machine*—is a possession, too."

"Huh."

"Mister Kitajima. You're going to have a visitor today."

"I've been waiting for that. Who is it?"

She nodded toward the window. The bicycle rider had placed his bike in a rack beside the path and was walking toward the building.

"He can't see us," Doctor Royce said. "This is a one-way panel right now. We can control it from inside, but usually it's set on transparent-out, opaque-in."

"Ah-*hah*. That's my visitor? That—character? He looks like an actor out of some kind of old-time slice-'em-up movie."

Royce shook her head.

"You know, this is really something. I was conked out for

eighty years, you say. And you don't understand half the things I'm talking about."

"I'm sorry. Times change. If they didn't, you wouldn't be here."

"Thanks." He made a sour face. He knew the expression had appeared. He'd practiced before mirrors, getting his new features to form expressions that had come automatically with his old ones. The new Daniel Kitajima face was like the old one: dark eyes, thick brows, black hair, broad cheekbones. But when first he had tried to smile, or frown, or weep, nothing had happened.

After a while the features had begun to respond, but he'd had to learn to match expression to feeling. A sneer when he intended a look of joy was worse than a dead pan. By now, his control was fairly reliable.

"We've done our best," Royce said. There was a trace of bitterness in her voice.

Daniel said, "Thanks," again, this time without the sneer. "I know you've done a terrific job. You and Kimura and the rest. It's just that—you know, I didn't only lose my hands and feet and half my brain. I lost my world, too. My wife and..."

"Not everything, Mister Kitajima."

A signal flashed on the control panel Royce habitually used. She pressed an accept code and a voice murmured. "Hold a second," Royce answered. To Kitajima she said, "Your visitor is waiting. Shall I have them send him in?"

"Why not?" Kitajima said dispiritedly. "Another medic?"

"He's your grandson, Mister Kitajima."

Dan covered his eyes. He said nothing.

"Ieyasu Hasegawa. He's your daughter's son. He skittered here from Hokkaido to see you. We've been expecting his arrival. But I can have him wait, if you want. Or send him away. I think you ought to see him. You're going to have to get out of here sooner or later, Mister Kitajima. Not that your money is running out or anything like that. But there's no point in spending the rest of your life in rehab. We want you to find your place in human society again."

Daniel smiled. "Human, eh? I can enter hold-your-breath contests. Never lose a one! Say, do you think I could try out for the Seals? I wonder if the commissioner would rule that I was a robot and inelligible to play in the big leagues. If he did, I might be able to get a job as a pitching machine for spring training."

Royce frowned.

"Please. It isn't fair to keep Mister Hasegawa waiting at the desk. Shall I have them send him away, ask him to come back? Or should they send him in?"

Dan hesitated. "Send him in, send him in."

HASEGAWA took one step through the doorway, bowed deeply to his grandfather. *"Konnichi wa, ojiisan."* He faced Doctor Royce and bowed. *"Konnichi wa, isha."*

Daniel looked at Hasegawa. "I'm sorry," he said, "I don't understand you. That's Japanese you're speaking, isn't it?"

"Ojiisan," Hasegawa repeated. He bowed again to Daniel.

Embarrassed, Kitajima returned the gesture. From a corner of his eye—at any rate, from the edge of his field of vision— he could see Doctor Royce inconspicuously withdrawing to a corner of the room. It seemed the wisest course, to hold herself out of the dialogue between Daniel and Ieyasu while remaining present in case of need.

"Ha," Ieyasu barked. *"Watakushi iu Nippongo, ojiisan."* With the first syllable he had snapped his head forward in a quick gesture of assent.

"Well, I'm sorry," Daniel said. "I don't speak Japanese. Look, Mister Hasegawa, do you know English? It's the only language I'm comfortable with, except for things like Cobol and Sysgen. And a little Esperanto. *Mi parolas Esperanto. Mi parolas multa Britia. Mi ne parolas Japania."*

Hasegawa drew a hissing breath. "My grandfather is from a different time. Of course, you struggled bravely to survive and permit your descendants the opportunity . . . the opportunity to regain the heritage which had been taken from you." He bowed again. He wore kimono, breeches and gloves. A ceremonial scabbard poked out from beneath his kimono.

Daniel hoped that the scabbard was purely ornamental and that the fancy handle that protruded from its upper end wasn't attached to a real sword.

"This is a very strange situation, sir."

"Please," Hasegawa half-bowed still again. "I am the younger. You are entitled to be called sir, Grandfather."

"Now wait a minute. You look older than I do. I'm only thirty—" He stopped. "Wait a minute. If I was out of action for eighty years, then I'm a hundred and, ah, fourteen. I was thirty-four when I got squashed."

"And I am your grandson."

Daniel narrowed his eyes. "How old did you say you were, Mister Hasegawa?"

Hasegawa half-bowed. "I am fifty-five years of age, Grandfather. By earth reckoning, of course. At Hokkaido, years are more or less under our control. We usually prefer to remain in a solar-stationary orbit, permitting the asteroid belt to revolve beneath us. We have access to all resources, in that fashion."

"Ah, uh." Daniel put his hand to his brow, expecting to find that he'd broken into a sweat. He had not. "Look, ah, Mister Hasegawa, there's an awful lot coming at me awfully fast these past, ah, these past couple of months. Since I woke up and found that I was essentially a pair of optical scanners in the middle of a wall of data processors."

"Of course."

The damned guy bows every other sentence, Daniel thought.

"Uh, what I'm saying is, this is a very strange relationship. I understand that I am your grandfather. Doctor Royce has told me about the death of your grandmother and your uncle Robert. Believe me, those two pieces of information were hard blows for me. And knowing that your mother and you were still alive were the best bits of news I've had."

Hasegawa bowed. "My grandfather honors me."

I will *not* get into this crazy business of bowing every few seconds! "But still—look. I'm a man in my thirties. Where it counts. Here, in my head. Even this body—I know it's half robot." Daniel held his hands between himself and his grandson.

"Even this body. They were right to make it *look* like a man my age. And you—I believe that you're my grandson biologically, Ieyasu. But you're older than I am. For all practical purposes. You're old enough to be my father, not my grandson. Don't you have a family of your own?"

"*Ee,*" Ieyasu moved his head. The gesture could be read

as a vigorous nod or a small bow. Daniel chose to interpret it as the former.

"I have a wife and two concubines and many sons and daughters."

"Jesus!"

"That is the way, in Hokkaido."

"Don't you know—" Daniel felt the frustrated reflex of drawing a deep breath and exploding it through his lips. Somewhere inside his torso he could hear the steady humming of a wankel rotary pump that kept the blood steadily circulating to the small amount of organic material that remained of himself.

He saw Ieyasu Hasegawa politely waiting for him to speak.

"Look here, Ieyasu. I'm sorry, I've got to get used to this." He put a hand to his brow.

Ieyasu stood listening respectfully.

"Doesn't your wife object? I mean, if you're less than a plaster saint, that's understandable. But to openly . . ." He shook his head. At least he could shake his head.

Ieyasu lowered his head. *"Ojiisan.* Honored grandfather. Perhaps it would be pleasant to walk in the parkland. If your condition permits such exertion." He looked inquiringly toward Doctor Royce.

"You should be all right, Mister Kitajima. I can still monitor your condition from here. It's time for you to get outside anyway. Mister Hasegawa, your grandfather is probably stronger and more capable than you are. But please be careful with him."

She checked the time.

"It's almost nightfall."

Daniel looked through the window. The grounds outside his room seemed still to be bathed in sunlight. He had paid little attention to the outside area and did not know what to expect at dusk.

"If you'd rather wait another day," Doctor Royce suggested, "maybe that would be . . ."

"Will my infrared vision work out there?"

"It should."

"Then let's go. I think I'm suffering from a sudden attack of claustrophobia."

He headed for the doorway. His comment to Royce had

been made mostly as a mild wisecrack. But now he realized that he was itching to get out of his room, to get out of this building with its dials and screens, its monitors and its keyboards, its glowing oscilloscopes and flashing readouts. He had not set foot on a grassy lawn for months—or for decades, depending on how you counted his eighty years of virtual death—and he felt a yearning for the experience.

Outside the hospital building he crossed a paved plaza and walkway, almost running with the sudden eagerness that overcame him. He jumped the last fifty centimeters to the lawn, landing off-balance. He reached for the ground with one hand, his instincts dictating a stable three-point contact so he wouldn't tumble to his knees.

He was astonished at the quickness of his reflexes. His hand reached the grass and touched; he stopped his tumble with the heel of his hand, pushed up onto his fingertips, shoved himself back toward the upright and was standing, grinning, feet a meter apart in the lush grass, before his grandson could reach his side.

A thought flashed through Daniel's mind: Thank God it isn't astroturf. I couldn't have dealt with that!

"*Ojiisan,*" Hasegawa said.

Daniel looked around. There were oak, maple, and towering eucalyptus trees scattered through the area. The massive, fast-growing eucalyptus drew his eye upward, up along their strong, graceful trunks to the limbs that spread scores of meters above the ground.

Through the branches he could see vague mist accumulating in the high atmosphere, and through that a bright sun pouring its warmth on him. He held his face and hands toward the sun. The prosthetics were fitted with a variety of pseudo nerve endings: photovoltaic cells, optical sensors, pressure-sensitive miniplates.

He held his eyes shut, prosthetic lids drawn across the optical sensors so the glow of sunlight penetrated them and produced the warming glow of natural sight. He felt the warmth of the sun on his prosthetic skin.

Daniel heard Ieyasu Hasegawa's voice. "Is my honored grandfather well? Shall I summon *Isha* Royce?"

Daniel lowered his face and opened his eyes. "I'm fine,

Ieyasu, I'm just fine. This is the best thing I've felt. It's like being on earth!"

"But we are not on earth."

"I understand. It looks as if the Island concept worked out just as planned. If we dug down through this soil . . ." He poked a finger into the earth, working its carefully fabricated fingernail between the blades of grass and into the rich, almost black humus beneath. He pinched a bit of the soil, spread it on one palm and studied it closely.

"If we dug down through this, what would we find? Not the searing magma of earth, eh?"

"No, grandfather. We would find the metallic plates of this Island."

"Come on, I feel like a stroll." Daniel set off at a comfortable pace, or what he considered a comfortable pace. Almost at once he became aware that Ieyasu Hasegawa was trotting and panting, yet was slowly losing ground.

"I'm sorry," Dan said. "Didn't mean to set such a pace."

Hasegawa stood panting for breath.

"Would you rather just sit here and talk? Or I could try and set a slower pace."

In a few minutes they had worked out a solution, Hasegawa pedalling his bicycle along a smooth pathway while Daniel set an effortless pace striding in the grass beside him. "I hope you're comfortable, Ieyasu. A man your age shouldn't strain himself."

"Thank you," Hasegawa nodded. "My grandfather is most considerate."

Daniel chewed that for irony.

"What happens at dusk?" Daniel asked. "I never paid close attention to the plans for these Islands. I was too busy at home, downstairs. The Islands were other people's problems."

Ieyasu stopped his bicycle. "I think it's just about time." He checked his chronometer. "It is a fine sight. In Hokkaido we have revived the art of *tsukumi*, grandfather."

"Hey?"

"You would call it, moon-viewing."

High overhead the sun shifted its position. It seemed to go into eclipse, a perfect chord slicing across its face as if a screen were sliding into place. In moments the sun was gone and a strange hush fell across the parkland.

There was a call from overhead, then another.

The daylight and its warmth were replaced by a silvery glow and a tangible drop in temperature.

Through the latticework of eucalyptus limbs Daniel could see the moon, larger than he had ever seen it from earth.

"That sight, *ojiisan*, we cannot enjoy upon Hokkaido. But we have our own *tsukumi* as we view the asteroid belt beneath us. Still . . ."

He sank gracefully to the earth, sitting cross-legged with his hands in his lap.

Daniel positioned himself similarly. He could see tiny specks high above, grains of blackness silhouetted against the moon. Then, closer, he saw a shape rise from the top of a eucalyptus and disappear into the darkness.

For half an hour the two men watched the dark silhouettes move gracefully above them.

"They are nocturnal birds, grandfather," Ieyasu said. "They nest in the tops of the trees, and hunt in the night."

"And the more distant ones?" Daniel asked.

"Some species have adapted to weightlessness. Some falcons. In Hokkaido we have made an art of observing them. Here they are less attended."

"Where are their nests?"

Daniel turned his face toward Ieyasu. The older man, his grandson, was graying at the temples. He still sat, watching raptly. "Some of them nest in the center of the Island. They learned quickly that they could remain in free-fall, in the center where there is no gravity at all. There is even vegetation there. Crews must visit the region and sweep it clear from time to time, but the birds return and build there, and vegetation that draws nourishment from the atmosphere, grows.

"A few individuals from the free-fall zone visit the treetops occasionally. And venturesome individuals hatched in these parks fly higher and higher until they join the other community. There are those who see a metaphor in the lives of the birds, grandfather."

The two men locked eyes, then simultaneously turned back toward the sight overhead.

I wonder. Daniel concentrated on the distant specks silhouetted against the moon. I wonder. Royce has been a little bit tightlipped about the full range of these prosthetics. Law or no law, the info comes slowly.

He tried to focus his eyes on those specks, calculating the distance from the inside surface of the Island to its center. He couldn't tell whether he heard servo-motors hum and gears slide into position. Probably not; that much of it was almost certainly his imagination at work.

But the birds leaped into focus. He could see them, graceful long-winged creatures with dark feathers and bright eyes, sweeping through the mist at the center of the cylinder. He wished he'd studied species of birds and been able to identify these. He was certain that they were some sort of predators, probably falcons.

Who had brought falcons to the medical Island? Who had planted eucalyptus trees here?

When the lungfish moved from sea to land it had carried its ancient home with it, the salt-sea of blood that circulated through its body. And when *homo sap*. left earth, that move, too, was accompanied by a movement of the environment into its new locale.

Falcons and eucalyptus trees in a metal Island hundreds of thousands of kilometers from the earth! The new humanity was astonishingly like the old humanity—or was that a temporary carry-over only, the immigrant generation in American speaking the language of the old country, and their children growing up speaking the old language to their parents at home but English to one another, and their children assimilated into the new culture, alien to the language and the country of their grandparents.

A shard of mist or a clot of free-fall vegetation momentarily obscured the moon. A gust of cool air swept across Daniel and Ieyasu. The murmur of the nearby brook combined with the call of nocturnal birds and the sounds of insects concealed in the grass and bushes.

"I wonder how the fishing is in that stream," Daniel said. He rose to his feet. He looked overhead while Ieyasu followed suit.

The moon, momentarily obscured, became visible again. Daniel focused on it. The craters and rilles were sharp and brilliant. He could see the mounds of industrial installations that were buried in tons of lunar soil to insulate them against solar radiation.

All of it was astonishingly faithful to the predictions in the glossy magazines and television shows of Daniel's boyhood.

I have lived to see this, he thought.

A great light flared unexpectedly at the edge of a lunar crater. Daniel blinked. Another reflex in working order. Could there be an explosion there? A volcanic eruption? A meteor strike?

"Ieyasu, do you see that?" Daniel pointed.

His grandson bowed his head. "The moon has become active again, grandfather. The deity Atago has awakened from long slumber. *Amaterasu no Ohokami* will again rule supreme, *oji-isan*."

You bet. "Let's go. This *tsukumi* is very pleasant but I think I'd rather do something a little more active. I've been cooped up for too long."

"As my grandfather wishes."

They found a cafe. No one took notice of Daniel, or possibly everyone had been alerted and briefed, instructed to take no notice. Daniel ordered nothing. Ieyasu asked the server for tea.

"My grandfather lacks an appetite?"

Daniel shook his head. "I don't think I'd better eat. I don't think I could, anyhow. But if I tried, I'd probably gum up the machinery and have to go in for an overhaul. Do you think you could get me back to the hospital, Ieyasu?"

"I would call for assistance."

"That's smart. I don't think you could lift me. Do you know what I weigh?" He held his hand above the tabletop and let it fall from a height of ten centimeters. The table shuddered with the impact.

"A little over three hundred kilograms. What do you weigh, about seventy kilos?"

Ieyasu nodded. He had gone pale.

"How much did they tell you about me before they let you in to visit me, grandson? Do you know how much of me is still a man, how much is chips and servos and waldoes?"

"I understand that you were nearly killed, grandfather. Long before I was born. When my mother was a small child."

"Yes. And they rebuilt me. But how much of *me* is left? Did Doctor Royce tell you? Did Doctor Kimura?"

"Not in great detail, *ojiisan.*"

"Well, I'm mainly a robot." Daniel fixed his grandson with a steady eye. "I want you to be candid with me, Ieyasu. Why did you come here? Why did you want to see me? I can't believe this is just a social call. Was it morbid curiosity? If so, you can probably pick up a spare part or two for souvenirs."

Ieyasu sucked breath inward. *"Ojiisan.* It hurts and shames me to see you robbed of your heritage. If you had been raised in traditional fashion, you would know that I came to you out of love and duty. I am your descendant. I am your grandchild, your *mago.*"

"Fine. What do you suggest I do now, grandson? What's your thought? Am I going to travel around like a Barnum show, a medical miracle, a scientific prodigy? Where do I go from here?"

"Grandfather. I came here to bring you back to your people and your family. I beg you to return with me to Hokkaido Island. You are the most senior member of our family. And we are an important family in Hokkaido. We are known to the royal personages.

"The Prince Shotoku himself has visited my home. Should you return to Hokkaido, you would become a great person. Honor would reflect upon our house."

Daniel closed his eyes, resisting the impulse to shake his head in disbelief.

"You are referring to an Island, Ieyasu? An Island like this, a construct in space. You are not referring to the island of Hokkaido on earth?"

"Grandfather, that is correct."

"But it sounds to me like time travel! Aren't you talking about ancient Japan? Prince Shotoku!"

"Yes, grandfather. The original Prince Shotoku made his house, the Soga, supreme in their day, a millennium and a half ago. And the new Prince Shotoku has made his house supreme by creating the new Island of Hokkaido. We are now ruled by Shotoku IV of the new Soga dynasty. The Hasegawa Clan is a great clan, but with you as its leader it would become the Kitajima Clan and would become the greatest house beneath the Soga."

Oh, Jesus! This is all I need. "Look, grandson, this all takes some getting used to. I'm still a man of my own times, you see? Eighty years ago, but I feel as if I'd fallen asleep and traveled a thousand years into the future, or the past, or some loony never-never land."

"If my grandfather would agree to travel to Hokkaido Island with his grandson, he could leave at any time, with honor. Perhaps *ojiisan* would like to visit the earth once again, also."

"I think I would." Daniel leaned his head on his hand, pressing his forehead against his palm, his elbow on the edge of the table. His new body seemed to know no fatigue, but his mind was growing weary.

"Look, Ieyasu, what about my hospital bill here? Royce and Kimura say everything's taken care of, that I have a bunch of money that was set aside when the accident happened. But I can't believe they'd just let me out of here without paying anything. Look—I don't have a susie to my name."

He tried to pull out his pants pockets and show his grandson that they were empty, but he had no pockets.

"You owe nothing, grandfather."

"How do you know that? What do they charge patients here? Who picks up the bills, the government?"

"Grandfather, there are no patients here. None but yourself. This Island was built to create you. Everyone, here, is here for your assistance, directly or indirectly."

"What?"

"Grandfather, *ojiisan,* you own this Island. Everyone here is your employee. You may leave and return whenever you wish. Did they fail to tell you, grandfather, that you are a wealthy man?"

4

"Ee, ICHIBAN KIREI, ojiisan."

"Eh?"

"Forgive me, grandfather. I was merely agreeing with you. The sight is indeed beautiful."

Daniel grunted. As Ieyasu returned to the controls of the skitter, Daniel turned back to watching the sights from the window of the little ship. The skitter was a far cry from the crudely thumping shuttles of Daniel's former time. Those old shuttles with their roaring, inefficient chemical rocket engines had permitted the development of the Island civilization, or had at least got enough persons and technology into space to permit the civilization to self-start.

But today's skitters with their scoops and mass-driver engines were clean, quiet, elegant.

The trip from the medical Island had had a dreamlike beauty to it. At Daniel's request they had followed a course closer to the moon than Ieyasu would have chosen, but of course Ieyasu had deferred to his grandfather's wishes. There was something to this business of being an ancestor.

Moving out past the orbit of Mars they had plunged into increasing darkness and emptiness, for all that Ieyasu had assured Daniel that there was plenty of microdebris present for the skitter's scoops to pick up and feed into the mass-drivers.

"Once past the orbit of Mars we will leave the plane of elliptic," Ieyasu had said. "Then microdebris will become scarce. Prior to that we will build a reserve for the mass-drivers. Else

52

we would have to call to Hokkaido for aid, or send a broadbeam distress signal."

Daniel sat with his chin in his hand, an old habit that his new machine-body followed as a matter of course. Even without the enhancement offered by his new eyes, the sight of space from the skitter would be breathtaking. There was none of the blurring and dimming of earth's atmosphere to peer through. It was the kind of sight that Daniel wished his friend Avram Novon could have shared with him. The stars were still merely points of light, but they shone with a steady brightness unlike the twinkling and dancing of their images on earth.

They were well out of the plane of elliptic now, above it or below it a matter of arbitrary judgment. Daniel turned, peering in different directions, trying to orient himself as he would gazing at the night sky from earth. He found the Milky Way, here a band of glorious light like a bank of incandescent fog, its hundred billion stars blending into a single mighty glory.

Directly overhead the scatterings of lights were more sparse. Some of them were the stars here in Sol's arm of the galaxy; others were great, remote objects: other galaxies and clusters of galaxies, distant bits of the cosmic firecracker still tumbling away from the point of the first great detonation.

Daniel wondered if his new eyes could resolve the distant objects into two-dimensional images rather than the multiple point sources they appeared. He shut his eyes and tried to feel out the controls, the pseudoneural connections that would shift his new eyes to an appropriate mode.

His grandson interrupted his concentration. *"Ojiisan.* If you will watch directly overhead. We have reached our approach point. I will turn the skitter."

Daniel abandoned his project. There would be plenty of time to shake down his optical system and the rest of his new body. He followed his grandson's suggestion.

The universe tilted and slowly swung around the skitter. The Milky Way was directly ahead of the little ship now, the sun was behind it. Overhead, Daniel could see the beginnings of the asteroid belt. From this distance it resembled one of the rings of the giant planets, a disc of solid matter, thinly spread, that caught the rays of the sun.

Before long the illusion faded. The disc resolved itself into uncounted specks of irregularly shaped rock, eternally dancing and tumbling about one another, each a point or small disk of light.

"Are you going to try and navigate that, Ieyasu?"

"No, *Ojiisan*. Hokkaido is well out of the belt. We visit the belt when we need materials from it, but the Island itself is kept in its position safely away from the asteroids."

Daniel nodded. "We're looking for the Island?"

Ieyasu pointed to a glowing panel. "Hokkaido sends us a homing beacon." The panel was circular, a bright ultramarine color. In its center a point of brilliant magenta pulsed twice a second. "If we deviate from our course, the beacon moves from the center of the screen."

He turned the skitter; the pulsating magenta point slid toward one edge of the plate. He turned the ship back; the point returned to center.

Daniel looked forward. The Island appeared, at first a shining point of silver indistinguishable from a star. It grew and assumed a definite shape.

"This is remarkable. They really followed the designs that O'Neill projected a hundred years ago."

"There are Islands in many forms, *ojiisan.*"

"Still, it looks pretty much like the classic cylinder with alternating regions for day and night, and external mirrors to direct the sunshine."

"That form has been successful."

The skitter came in above the cylindrical Island. Beneath the ship, Daniel could see the flattened end of the cylinder, and beneath it the great belt of asteroids, flowing like a river in an endless circle around the sun.

The Island rotated around its long axis but a gimballed disc held stationary at its end.

"We're going to land there?" Daniel pointed.

Ieyasu nodded. "There is a small amount of true gravity, but our skitter will be held by grapples. Magnetic grapples. We can remain in the skitter until it is hauled belowdecks, or exit in spacesuits, as my honored grandfather prefers."

Daniel rubbed his chin. "Tell you what. I want to try something. You go ahead and climb into a spacesuit, Ieyasu. Let's get out on that landing disc."

Hasegawa's eyes widened. "I fear for *ojiisan's* well-being."

"Look, I don't need air for breathing, Ieyasu. I don't breathe any more. I don't think there'll be any pressure problem. What can happen? Radiation? I doubt it. Will I fly off from lack of gravity? I think 300 kilos will hold me down. Or else I can hang on to the magnetic grapples you talked about. I have to test out this new body of mine. I didn't go through all that rebuilding to live like an invalid!"

Ieyasu bowed his head.

The skitter came in over the disc, banked and made a second approach in the manner of an airplane approaching an aircraft carrier. In classic fashion it dropped a hook, was caught by arrester cables, slid to a halt on runner-like skids.

Ieyasu opened a locker. "If *ojiisan* is certain? There is a second suit here."

"Thanks." Daniel shook his head.

Ieyasu climbed into vacuum gear. He walked to the ship's port, turned a final time toward his grandfather. They exchanged no words this time. Through the ship's windows Daniel could see crew working on the landing disc. The arrester cable had been disconnected from the skitter and the grappling hook retracted.

He looks like a samurai, Daniel thought. The spacesuit that Ieyasu had donned was cut to stylized Japanese style. The helmet was a functional vacuum helmet but its shape was that of—Daniel didn't know the name, but he remembered seeing them in slice-'em-ups in San Francisco. The whole suit suggested samurai armor, and its exterior was covered with designs of traditional Japanese motifs.

Ieyasu reached toward a vacuum control. Daniel nodded.

Ieyasu hit the control. Pumps throbbed and the air hissed out of the cabin, back to recycling tanks. A dial swung down indicating that the cabin had been emptied.

Through the faceplate of Ieyasu's helmet, Daniel could see his grandson's lips moving. He heard nothing. Of course not —vacuum wouldn't conduct sound, and if Hasegawa was transmitting over a suit radio, Daniel wouldn't pick it up. Unless— there might be another capability built into his new body to permit him to communicate by radio.

What could he—or couldn't he—do? One way or another,

he'd have to return to the medical Island and get Royce and Kimura to check him out more fully on his new equipment. What he needed, he thought—not for the first time—was a thoroughgoing user's manual for his hardware.

He gestured to Ieyasu.

Hasegawa spun a wheel and the door of the skitter swung open. Hasegawa stepped from the ship. At least there would be no Alphonse-and-Gaston act over who should leave the ship first.

Daniel paused for a moment in the doorway, then stepped onto the landing disc. He kept one hand momentarily on the metallic body of the skitter, gazing around. It was the first time since the accident with Avram that he had seen this sight, the sight of space, from space, and not from the cabin of a ship.

The stars blazed and the Milky Way swung its brilliance across the sky. He couldn't see the asteroid belt from here; it lay beneath the cylinder and he stood in the center of the wrong end of the Island to see it.

But he could see the sun, a clear, small, brilliant disc. He felt a momentary urge to fall to his knees in an attitude of adoration, so beautiful was the sight, and so overwhelming the majesty of the sun.

He was startled to see that his grandson had actually done what Daniel had felt impelled to do: he was kneeling there on the disc, the decklike plane where the skitter stood. He held his arms outspread and his face directed toward the solar disc. The faceplate of his helmet had darkened in response to the brilliance of the sun.

Of course—if the cult of Amaterasu no Ohokami had been revived here at Hokkaido, Hasegawa would appropriately pause to worship before entering the Island.

Feeling a strange mixture of diffidence and joy, Daniel Kitajima sank to his knees, spread his arms in imitation of his grandson's gesture of worship, and gazed into the sun. His optical sensors compensated for the sun's direct, if distant, rays. He felt the brilliance and the warmth of the distant sun filling his entire being. An exhilarating warmth spread through his body, centering in his chest where the rotary pump served in place of his heart.

He saw Ieyasu rise and did the same. He was not certain

whether he had undergone an authentic religious experience, or had simply hyped himself into an illusion of one. Too much had happened to him since his return from the long freeze for him to make any judgment.

Deck workers rushed to greet Hasegawa, bowing before him. Hasegawa returned the bow to each. Daniel saw Hasegawa pointing toward him, gesturing as if he were speaking over his suit radio to the crew. Like Hasegawa, they wore spacesuits cut to distinctive Japanese style, with external markings that had to reflect their rank and functions. Clearly, all were of inferior station, compared to Hasegawa.

When Ieyasu finished speaking, the crew approached Daniel. Simultaneously they prostrated themselves on the deck.

Daniel flashed an inquiring look at his grandson. In reply he received a gesture. He bowed to the prostrate crew, then gestured them to their feet.

Ieyasu moved again, apparently speaking. The crew members bowed toward Daniel, then returned to their regular work.

Ieyasu took Daniel by the elbow and guided him respectfully toward an airlock.

As Hasegawa operated the lock, Daniel thought, Oh, boy! I'm not just a tourist here. I'm some kind of big shot. This is too much, too mucking fuch! He shook his head.

Hasegawa checked a meter, operated a second sealed portal, led Daniel through and began to remove his spacesuit. A uniformed worker scurried up, bowed, took the space gear from Hasegawa. Daniel could see that he had somehow managed to keep his sword with him inside the spacesuit, and that he kept it still when the crew member scurried off with the suit.

"*Ojiisan,*" Ieyasu said.

Oh, lord, that bowing business again! Daniel returned the bow, waited.

"Truly my grandfather is a miraculous being! But you still wear the clothing of the medical Island. You would honor all of your house and all of Hokkaido by changing to the garb of a *Nihonjin.*"

THEY approached Hasegawa's village on horseback.

The journey from the landing disc had been easy enough,

pedalling through the null-g zone that ran along the Island's axis. When they reached a position opposite the village, Ieyasu had signalled a halt. Here, as in the medical Island, life had found its way to the null-g zone and made its own peculiar adaptation, but there had been no difficulty in skirting the air-ferns, and the flying creatures that nested among them had given Hasegawa and Kitajima a wide berth.

They descended through a transverse brace and emerged at a maintenance station some twenty kilometers from their destination. Here they picked up their horses—Hasegawa had messaged ahead and they were ready when they arrived.

"I'm sorry, Ieyasu. I don't know how to ride." Daniel felt himself blushing with embarrassment, then berated himself for being embarrassed. Horseback riding was simply not a useful skill in his world. If it was here in Hokkaido, he would learn.

"I will summon a palanquin and bearers, *ojiisan*." Ieyasu looked flustered.

"Don't forget. I weigh three hundred kilograms. How are you going to account for that? I'll go right through the bottom of the thing!"

Ieyasu sucked air.

"For that matter," Dan resumed, "how could a horse hold me anyhow? I'd probably break the poor beast's back."

"Ah, grandfather, that is no cause to worry. The beasts are bred to carry *samurai* with full armor and accoutrement. Your weight alone would be little more than that of a *samurai* and his gear."

"Huh! In that case, maybe I'll give it a try. Shouldn't be too hard. I was always good on a bike. Is there anything I need to know about?"

Ieyasu gestured. "My grandfather's courage and spirit of adventure are an inspiration."

And so, dressed in kimono and breeches, head-cloth and doeskin gloves (doeskin?—where did they get doeskin, Daniel wondered), he climbed into the ornate saddle. The horse was docile. It wasn't so bad after all, Daniel thought.

They crossed agricultural lands where laborers prostrated themselves at the sight of the horsemen. Daniel was acutely uncomfortable at the self-effacement of the workers. This was nothing like the California farmlands he had known eighty years ago. But then, he was an alien here.

The village itself was composed of a half-hundred wooden huts. It was surrounded by rice paddies, and in the distance Daniel thought he could hear the lapping of water against a rocky shore.

He asked Ieyasu if there was a body of water nearby, and was told that there was a small sea where fishermen went for bream, scup and similar food fishes.

Hasegawa's house stood atop a hill, surrounded by a high wooden wall. At the gate Hasegawa and Kitajima were met by lackeys who prostrated themselves, then rose, helped the men to dismount, and led the horses away.

There was a formal garden with rake house, and a koi pond with has not seen you in many years. stopped old woman, much overcome by feebleness."

to "I understand, Ieyasu. This will be very strange for me. I haven't seen her since she was a little child. She was four years old when I last saw her. My children, Robert and Elizabeth, my twins. Now she will be—eighty-four! And I'm still young."

There was a bitter taste in his mouth. Probably a minor flow of lubricating oil. He'd been using the voice synthesizer quite a lot, and his body's self-maintenance devices would be called into action.

"My uncle is known in family annals now as Tatsuya. There is a memorial post to him in the rear garden."

"His name was Robert."

"We have reclaimed the old ways, *ojiisan*. It is my hope that you will honor your heritage by adopting a suitable name very soon."

Dan grimaced.

"My mother awaits within, *ojiisan*."

"I suppose you don't call her Elizabeth, either."

"Her name is Yakami, *ojiisan.*"

"Let's go in. I want to see my daughter."

Ieyasu held out his hand. "A moment more, grandfather. Please. My mother is—*very* aged. Very feeble. Much of the time she does not know where she is. She stayed in Beikoku—"

"Where?"

"Beikoku. The United States."

"Yes. Weren't you born there, Ieyasu?"

"Such is my regret, grandfather. But all of my children have been born here in Hokkaido."

"I ?"

Hasegawa su to Yakami who you are. She knows grandfather wishes. Please co She chose to remain ath. I have she

THE old woman was propped on cushions, surrounded by fresh straw mats. A number of younger women hovered around her, performing no identifiable task. Daniel saw Ieyasu approach the old woman and humble himself. *"Kannichi wa, okāsan."*

The old woman did not look up.

Ieyasu touched her, took her wrist and shook it gently.

"Okāsan. Okāsan."

The old woman looked up, looked at Ieyasu. Standing behind his grandson, Dan studied the old woman's face. It was wizened, her skin stretched tight over fragile bones. She appeared to have no teeth. Her eyes were clouded and vague. Her hair hung in thin wisps of gray about her face. She was dressed in a rich kimono that hung loosely from her withered body.

She mumbled something to Ieyasu. Daniel could not understand what she said.

Ieyasu spoke to the old woman in Japanese, gesturing toward Daniel. The old woman followed her son's gesture. A new light came into her milky eyes. She tried to get up.

Instantly the younger women took her by wrist and elbow and helped her to her feet. She attempted a few steps forward, reaching for Daniel. He stepped toward her instead.

"Elizabeth?" Daniel managed.

Her mouth trembled. The old woman muttered a few words that Daniel could not understand, in a mixture of English and Japanese. She put her hands onto his chest. He looked down at the thin, almost-transparent hands. They had almost no weight at all.

She said, "Father?"

He said her name again.

She stared into his face, her eyes becoming watery. "Father. Mother." She paused. "Mother says you were hurt. She says you were injured. You are getting better. Mother says you will be home, but not for dinner. Not for goodnight. We waited. Robert and I waited. Robert said, 'Elizabeth, father will come home.'"

"Father is home."

She drew her face away from his chest and looked into his eyes. A sweet, childish smile played around the corners of her toothless mouth.

"Father is home," she said again. "Home, home. Now Mother will make dinner. Robert, Father is home."

Daniel looked over his daughter's head, at his grandson, Ieyasu Hasegawa.

Hasegawa gestured to the old woman's serving companions and they guided her gently back to her cushions. She sat on them, smiling happily up at Daniel, crooning the word *father* over and over. A small line of spittle appeared at one corner of her mouth. She gave no sign of having noticed it, but one of her serving women gently wiped it away.

The old woman rocked softly, adoring her father.

Ieyasu spoke to her servants in Japanese. They nodded understandingly and bowed their heads. Ieyasu spoke a few words to his mother, using English, touched her hand, then ushered Daniel out of the room.

In Ieyasu's study the two men seated themselves on clean *tatami* mats. A woman brought a jug of saki and set it on a miniature charcoal brazier. She set two cups beside the brazier.

"Will my grandfather take saki?" Ieyasu asked.

Daniel shook his head and made a rueful expression. "I'm afraid I don't eat or drink anything any more. This rig has a great little power pack in it."

He tapped himself on the torso with his thumb.

"Kimura told me they cooked up a slow-fission alloy-pellet that self-breeds. Some short half-life elements and some much longer-lived elements. The whole thing just keeps cooking away. Won't wear out until long after I'm gone."

He laughed.

Hasegawa looked at him questioningly. "May you live for many years to come, *ojiisan.*"

Dan nodded.

"But if your grandson may inquire," Hasegawa resumed, "does my grandfather have any idea how long his life is to be? With the body of a living *haniwa* ..."

"A *what?*"

"A figurine."

"Um."

"Grandfather, your heart is a rotary pump. Your stomach is a fission pile. Your limbs are wondrous mechanisms, and like any mechanisms, should they wear down or break down or even be destroyed by mishap, they can be replaced. Is that not correct?"

Dan rubbed his chin. "I never went into that much, with Royce and Kimura. But—yes. At least, I'd think so."

"Then how long may you live, grandfather? A century? A millennium?"

Ieyasu filled one of the saki cups and raised it before his face. "If I may, *ojiisan?*" Daniel nodded abstractedly. With irony in his eyes, Ieyasu said, "To your very long life and very good health, honored ancestor." He sipped at the hot saki, then placed the cup again near the hot jug.

Daniel tried to exhale a long breath. He was able to purse his lips and synthesize the sound, a softened half-hiss. "That's another thing I'll have to check out with the medics. There's some medical principle about brain cells wearing out, dying off and not regenerating."

Hasegawa refilled his cup and looked attentively at Daniel.

"We have so many billions and trillions of the damned things." Daniel tapped his cranium just above one ear, using the tip of his middle finger.

"So damned many of the things, even at the rate they die off, unless there's some kind of big problem like a stroke, you don't have to worry about using them up and turning to a vegetable. Not in a lifetime of a hundred years, not in five hundred! I think."

He shook his head.

"But I don't know how long I'm going to live. It might be a real problem. Maybe they can just keep chopping out my brain and slopping the hogs with it," he laughed bitterly. "Keep on shoving more microcircuits into my genuine artificial imitation skull here, till I'm all machine. Then there's nothing to worry about."

Hasegawa grunted. "At what point, *ojiisan*, does one cease to be a person, and become a machine? A—forgive me, *ojiisan*—a *thing*?"

Dan shook his head again. He made a gesture of puzzlement.

"Am I a man now? Or a thing?"

Ieyasu bowed his head and waited for Daniel to continue.

"I think I'm still a man because I still feel like one. I'm conscious. I'm aware of myself. I have a viewpoint. I don't know." He shrugged.

"'*Cogito, ergo sum.*'"

"Is that an old Japanese proverb, grandson?"

Ieyasu blushed. "I did not mean to offend, grandfather."

"No, no. I'm just being touchy. I just—just never gave any thought to that possibility. To . . ." He looked at Ieyasu, locked eye to eye with him. "How long has she been like that, Ieyasu?"

"You mean my mother."

"Of course."

"She wishes to return to earth. To Beikoku. She wishes to live in San Francisco, grandfather."

"She does, eh? How do you know? When she's like . . ." He let the words trail away.

"Sometimes she is more aware of her surroundings. When I brought her to Hokkaido, she was more aware than she is now. There was a time—this is my shame, *ojiisan*." He bowed his head.

Daniel waited.

"She spoke of *seppuku*. This is why the subject of—your own aging, is difficult for me, grandfather. She spoke of *seppuku*. To die by her own hand, while still she possessed enough of her faculties to perform the deed."

There was a long silence in the room. As Daniel watched, Ieyasu filled his saki cup again, lifted it and gazed into the clear, shimmering contents. He poured the hot saki back into the jug and set his cup aside.

"Grandfather, it was my weakness. I convinced her to live on. Of course, I wished to keep my mother with me. And the presence of the Lady Hasegawa here brought luster to our house.

"But I was wrong. I permitted my selfishness to keep her until she could no longer make her own decision, could no longer perform the act. And so, the shame is mine. For what you saw."

"How do you keep time here?" Daniel asked.

Ieyasu looked at him in surprise.

"How long till nightfall?"

Ieyasu said, "It is very near."

Daniel rose. "If you don't mind, Ieyasu, I'd like to be excused. To go to my room."

"Of course, grandfather." Hasegawa scrambled to his feet and bowed. "I did not mean to tire—"

"No, it's all right," Dan said. "In fact, I was kind of surprised, myself." He looked at his arms, flexing them before himself. "I didn't think I'd have to worry about fatigue in this new body."

"Of course, grandfather."

"No, it's not 'of course.' I *don't* get tired. Not physically. This machine can just run and run. It self-lubricates, it seems to be so damned tough and strong. I guess I just have to take it into the shop for a tuneup like an old-time truck. *Hah!*

"But up here—" He tapped his forehead.

"Ah, fatigue products, yes."

"No," Daniel shook his head.

"Then—"

"Something I never heard of. Royce brought in some kind of sleep therapists. Dream therapy theorists."

"Ahhh." Ieyasu nodded as he made the drawn-out sound.

"Was funny, they kept insisting there was a close analogy to computer programming, that programs get cluttered up with junk when you run 'em, and you have to debug to get the junk out. *Uh*-uh!" He shook his head. "Doesn't work that way. You debug a new program. Well . . ."

Ieyasu nodded.

"Of course, if there are still bugs and you get into a production run, they can gum up the coding, especially if you aren't using transparent routines." Daniel could see Ieyasu's eyes beginning to glaze. It was precisely the expression he'd seen eighty years before whenever programmers tried explaining their work to outsiders.

He managed to synthesize a sigh and excused himself.

Minutes later he stretched in his Japanese-style bed, between layers of soft quilting laid on fresh *tatami* mats. His room was comfortable, attractive, yet simply furnished.

He laid his head on the carved pillow and closed his eyes.

He could turn off his sensors, he knew, and drift voluntarily back into that void where all sensation had ceased to exist, and pure mind held awareness of itself. But he knew, by now, that that way lay not peace or any knittings up. That way lay hallucination and terror.

Before leaving the medical Island he had got Kimura to devise and install an interval-timer in his circuitry, an electronic counter that served no more function than a ticking clock: it gave his nervous system, what remained of it that was organic, a kind of temporal yardstick. A substitute for the body's usual rhythms of heartbeat and respiration cycle. Something that would let him know that he was part of the physical universe, that its throbbing pulsations marked the beats of his life now even as they had before the collapsing crane had crushed his body in its spacesuit.

He listened to his internal clock now. He was able to manipulate his senses to hear that clock not as a metallic ticking but as a deeply reassuring throb, like the beating of a mother's heart that is felt and heard by an unborn fetus.

His quilt lay lightly and warm upon his body. Over the heartbeat of his body-clock he heard a soft sound, the sound of a screen sliding on its track. He heard breathing, the pad of soft slippers on *tatami* mats, the closing of the screen.

He turned his head slightly, opened his eyes. In the dimness he could see a figure advancing toward his bed. The figure was slim and richly dressed. It knelt beside him.

"Kitajima-san."

He sat up. "What is it?"

"Lord Hasegawa sent me because I speak English. Few in Hokkaido know other languages than Japanese."

Daniel grunted.

"My name is Kodai-no-kimi."

"And why did Lord Hasegawa send you to me?"

She turned her face away; Daniel could not tell whether the reaction was one of embarrassment or coquettishness.

"Lord Hasegawa thought Lord Kitajima might enjoy companionship. A suitable welcome to the new land of his ancestors."

Daniel blinked. Kodai-no-kimi was slim, dark-haired, graceful. There the resemblance to Marie-Elaine ended but— his mind whirled. By normal measure he was a widower, had been one for decades. By his own subjective experience, he had seen his wife just a few months ago.

He had to return to San Francisco, walk the streets where he had walked those few months or those eighty years ago. He had to see his home. He had to visit the graves of his wife and his son, to come to terms with the events of eight decades.

He knew almost nothing of conditions on earth, he realized. Since his return to consciousness at the medical Island he had been totally involved in his personal, immediate reality. But the world had not stood still for eighty years while he was kept in frozen storage.

What were conditions on earth? Did his former home still exist, or would he return to San Francisco and find a totally changed setting? He was a new Rip van Winkle, except that he had been gone four times as long as his prototype!

He looked down. Kodai-no-kimi had reached to touch him, her slim hands moving with the shy grace and beauty of two doves.

He turned back the upper quilt of his bed and invited her to lie beside him. "You are very beautiful," he told her. "I only hope—"

She turned her face toward his, inquiring.

"I only hope that you don't feel—lowered—by this."

She smiled. "In old Nihon, we are taught, the art of the courtesan was regarded as a true art, and achievement in it, as true artistry. If my master Lord Hasegawa did not hold me in high esteem, he would not have insulted his grandfather by sending me here."

He put aside his worries, at least for the moment, and stroked her hair. Unlike the other ladies of his grandson's household, whose hair had been worked into elaborate patterns, Kodai-no-kimi's was let down. It framed her face and hung over her shoulders, glossy, black, reflecting the dim ambient light that found its way into the room.

Beneath Daniel's hand, her hair felt soft and alive.

With her slim hands, Kodai-no-kimi slid open the front of Daniel's sleeping kimono. She laid her cheek against his chest. He wondered if his artificial body felt natural to her, if she felt his false flesh and the machinery that lay beneath it as the body of a living man or as a perverse simulacrum.

At the same time he could feel her breath, warm and moist, against his skin. His doctors had fitted him with a perfect exterior replica of a human body. There was even a thin sprinkling of black hair on his chest, as sparse as it had been on his original body. There were sensors near the surface of his false skin that gave him the same sensation—or something close to the same sensation—that he would have felt from Kodai-no-kimi's breath as it stirred the hairs on his chest.

He slipped one of his hands inside her kimono. She did not prevent him. In fact, she seemed to turn slightly, to make it easier for him to reach inside the silken garment.

The flesh of her back was surprising to him. It was warm, smooth as satin, soft. Why was he surprised? The feel of her was no different from the woman-feel he had always known. He had no reason to think that women would feel any different now than they had eighty years ago. There was as much difference between the sensation of Kodai-no-kimi's skin against the palm of his hand, and his recollection of Marie-Elaine's skin, as there was between the feel of any two women, both of them warm and young and slim.

That much difference, but no more.

He laid his other hand against Kodai-no-kimi's face. He brushed his fingers lightly across her forehead, the softness of her closed eye and her nose. He brushed a fingertip across her lips, felt their moist warmth. He felt her nibble playfully at his fingertip, then flirt her tongue along his finger, into the vee where his fingers met.

He pressed her body against his own, felt himself rising sexually for the first time in this new life. She dropped her hands to undo the sash of his kimono. He held her by the shoulders.

If the sexual encounter were completed, he wondered suddenly, what would the outcome be? He felt suddenly the cold gagging sensation that was his new body's simulation of nausea.

Would he and she, Daniel and Kodai-no-kimi, bring each other to climax? Would his orgasm pour machine oil into her body instead of semen?

His hands began to shake violently. He felt his erection collapse, suddenly and totally.

"Kitajima-san?" Kodai-no-kimi whispered. "Lie back, my lord. You have traveled far, it has been a long day. Permit me to please you. It will be my pleasure to please you."

What could he tell her? What would she think? Could he tell her what he was? That she would only be soiled by his love? That he was a robot, a mechanized *haniwa*, an elaborate dildo?

He was suddenly as cold as ice.

"Go, Kodai-no-kimi. Please! This is not your fault—I—but I mustn't—"

"Lord!" She was out of his bed, kneeling beside it, holding her hands toward him.

"Go away. You don't know what you're doing. If you see Lord Hawegawa, tell him I must speak with him in the morning. I have to leave Hokkaido at once!"

He watched her in misery as she drew her kimono about her, pulled soft slippers over her feet and stood up.

"I am sorry, Kitajima-san." She started toward the door.

"You didn't—" He tried to explain. It was all too much. There was nothing he could say, he realized. He turned his head so that he watched the opposite wall until he heard the sliding screen close behind her.

He rearranged his sleeping kimono, drew the upper quilt over his body once again, placed his head carefully on the pillow block.

He put his consciousness into the controls of his new body, carefully checking out its parts, turning off as much of it, as much of his sensation, as he could. Finally, maintaining only as much contact with his body and with the external world as was needed to avoid sensory deprivation and its accompanying disorientation and hallucination, he drifted off into sleep.

It was the first sleep he had had, away from the medical Island with its monitors and chemical infusions into his bloodstream. In the last fragmentary play of consciousness before lapsing into full sleep, he wondered if he would dream. If his sleeping mind would work to sort out the recent events. If he could possibly debug his mental programs, or if they would degenerate inevitably into chaos.

He saw the image of his daughter, a senile, toothless hag, a narrow line of spittle unnoticed as it dribbled from her toothless mouth.

5

THE SKITTER PILOT was polite to the point of obsequiousness, but he spoke almost no English and Daniel clenched his fists in frustration at his lack of Japanese. The skitter headed away from Hokkaido, its scoops gobbling up the microdebris above the asteroid belt, its mass-driver engines using the microdebris as reaction mass, shoving it behind the little ship and leaving it for other passes to use again.

The note from Ieyasu had been polite, also, although not nearly as elaborate as the conduct of the pilot. Hasegawa had been summoned away to the court of Shotoku. Surely his revered grandfather would understand that there was neither refusing nor delaying one's response to such an invitation.

Nor would Hasegawa think of delaying his grandfather in the latter's wishes to return to Beikoku. It was regrettable that Ieyasu's mother, the Lady Yakami, was unable to travel with her father as she had wished, but her extreme age and its obvious ravages clearly precluded such a course.

Lord Hasegawa sent his humblest respects and warmest filial best wishes to his grandfather Lord Kitajima, and expressed his hope that his grandfather would return, once he had finished his visit to Beikoku, to Hokkaido.

From the distance of lunar orbit—but opposite the position of the moon at the time—Daniel's pilot made radio contact with an earth outpost. Daniel was astonished to hear his pilot conversing with a control post in Japanese. It seemed to mean that Japanese had supplanted English as the international language for aerospace commerce. Or perhaps that each nation of earth had established its own commo net, in competition with the others.

The skitter headed toward an immense, shimmering shaft that pointed like the haft of a spear from space, thousands of kilometers, toward the earth. The shaft disappeared into the cloud banks and general obscuring haze of the planet's envelope.

The landing atop the shaft was astonishingly like that of an airplane on a naval carrier. The pilot approached the shaft from the west. The shaft was moving toward the east; if its base was fixed in some manner to the surface of the planet, at this altitude its outer end was whizzing through the near vacuum of cislunar space at something like 1500 kilometers per hour. Even so, that speed was nothing compared to the approach speed of old-style spacecraft that Daniel could remember from films and videotapes, that had returned to earth from their missions at ballistic speeds. It wasn't even as fast as the approach speed of the shuttle that he had ridden eighty years before.

The skitter moved up on the vertical shaft, seemed to hover over the shaft's terminal pad, then dropped softly into place. It was an even softer landing than the one Ieyasu Hasegawa had made at Hokkaido Island.

Inside the disc whose upper surface was the landing pad, Daniel met controllers and crew members. To his surprise they spoke a number of languages including Esperanto and Japanese, but English was the language in widest use. Daniel asked a spacecraft controller if Japanese was used for communication with landing spacecraft. The controller laughed and told him that the radio had language translator circuits built into its electronics.

"Son of a bitch," Daniel muttered.

"Sir?"

"Sorry. I didn't know about such things—not that they should have surprised me."

"No sir." The controller looked puzzled.

"I think I'll have some built into my own gear."

The controller continued to look puzzled. "There's no need to build the circuitry into every ship, sir. Not when it's automatically included in landing locations."

Daniel didn't explain that he meant to have it built into the circuitry that was replacing half of his brain.

The controller turned him over to a bureaucrat who ushered Daniel into a posh office. Yes, he knew who Daniel was, he had expected his arrival. He had identification papers waiting for Mister Kitajima, had cleared his downstairs bank accounts, and would Mister Kitajima oblige, please, by placing a radio-phone call to Doctor Royce and the medical Island.

If Mister Kitajima didn't mind, his temporary host would be honored to order up a meal or a round of beverages for them both. He didn't get a chance to play host to such a distinguished guest very often. The President of Westuria had passed through this office once, as had the Tierra del Fuego Gigantes—what a team, what a team, the bureaucrat had got them to autograph a pole for him to send home as a memento for his niece.

Daniel wondered where Westuria was and what kind of team from Tierra del Fuego traveled to outer space and autographed poles for their fans. He didn't bother his host with those questions. They could be filed under a low priority. He wouldn't mind phoning the medical Island but he'd have to turn down the offer of refreshments, with thanks.

"I don't eat or drink," he explained.

"How about a small glass of wine?" the bureaucrat offered.

Daniel made a face. "I never drink wine."

"I'm sorry. I didn't realize that you had a moral commitment to—"

"No, no." Dan shook his head. "I guess they missed that in the briefing. I carry around a power pack." He tapped himself with the tip of one thumb. "If that ran down, I might ask you for a nice little radio-isotope cocktail. But otherwise, I'd just gum up the works."

The bureaucrat said, "I see." His expression suggested that he did not, but if he was willing to let it slide, so was Dan. He was not eager to get involved with lengthy explanations.

A technician put through his call to Doctor Royce.

She appeared on a small screen, looking worried. "How are you holding up?"

Dan smiled. "Physically, just fine, thanks. I'm afraid there's a certain amount of culture shock. And maybe a few other matters we ought to discuss one of these days. But for the moment, I think I'm all right."

"And your plans? I'd like to check you out soon."

"I'll be back. Not yet, though. I want to take a look around Beikoku and—"

"Around *where?*"

"Sorry. I want to get back to earth. I want to see my old stamping grounds in San Francisco. How will this body hold up downstairs? It seems to work fine in earth-normal gravity."

"How did you do at Hokkaido?"

"That's part of the culture shock I mentioned, Doctor Royce. Those people..." He let it trail off.

"I understand. After a long period of growing homogenization on earth, the development of the Islands has encouraged renewed cultural diversity. It was like going back to old Japan, wasn't it?"

"How the hell should I know? I'm American."

"Of course. And Doctor Kimura and I were somewhat concerned about letting your grandson carry you off that way."

"It was strange. By appearance, my daughter ought to have been my grandmother, and my grandson should have been my father. We didn't really get along too well."

"I'm sorry to hear that."

"Yeah." He didn't go into the problem of Elizabeth's wishing to return to earth with him. In her physical condition, he doubted that she could have handled the trip anyway. It was a marvel that Ieyasu had got her from earth to Hokkaido Island without killing the old woman.

And she was his daughter!

He looked up, startled. "What?"

"I said, are you all right? You looked—upset, Mister Kitajima."

"Just that culture shock again." He made a wry face. "Look, what about earth? Everything should be all right for me there, shouldn't it? I had no physical problems on your Island—"

"*Your* Island, Mister Kitajima."

"Whatever. Or on Hokkaido Island. I even rode a horse there! The poor creature got quite a surprise!"

"Well, I'd like to check you out again as soon as possible. But if you're determined to spend some time on earth first, it should really be all right. Just be careful. Don't take any risks, all right? Let's save mountain climbing or bull fighting for some other time. After we're a little more... certain that everything is as reliable as it seems."

Daniel grinned. "If that horse at Hokkaido had a surprise, what do you think a bull would think of trying to gore a three-hundred-kilogram iron man! What about swimming, Doctor?"

"Better not try it. You might crack the diving board."

"I didn't have that in mind."

"Better not. Not even a shower yet, please. You can clean your skin, and it *should* be safe, but if there's a leak anywhere, you could get some nasty electrical effects."

The conversation was dribbling away. Daniel had wanted to ask Doctor Royce if anything could be done for his—he almost thought *mother,* then corrected himself—if anything could be done for his daughter. Weakened tissues, failing functions, but worst of all the mental deterioration of age and disorientation. Could the team that had brought him back from the deep freeze, little more than a mass of pulped protein, do anything to help Elizabeth?

Somehow, he hadn't been able even to broach the subject. Another time, another time.

He heaved a sigh and smiled inwardly at his ability to do so. The old reflexes were finding new channels of communication through his electronic network. What next, yawns?

He promised Doctor Royce that he would avoid risks, that he would return to the medical Island for a thorough check-out. Almost as an afterthought, he asked her another question.

"Listen here, I understand that I'm something of a rich man now. I'd have to be, to own that Island! But how much is it costing me? Even if I'm as rich as an Arab or an athlete, there have to be limits somewhere!"

The doctor shook her head. "I have no information on your private finances, Mister Kitajima. Nothing beyond common knowledge. You *are* a fairly famous person, you know. But as for the Island, why, we run at a profit. Everything we learned from working on you, sir, went into commercial products. Half the people alive use one product or another that pays royalties to the Island.

"Did you have the expression in your day, Mister Kitajima—the rich get richer?"

"Uh-*huh.* And the poor have children. Ain't we got fun?" He terminated the hookup.

The chief bureaucrat insisted on riding downstairs with Daniel. "You've been in Elevators before?" the bureaucrat asked. Daniel could hear the capital "E" in his voice.

"How far down does this go?"

"All the way to Rejkjaviko."

"Rejkjaviko?"

"I'm sorry. Is the city new to you? The capital of Islando."

"Oh, sure. But—how far do we ride down?"

The bureaucrat scratched his head. "Let's see, I think this shaft is fifteen hundred kilometers in length. The ride down will take seven hours."

"They finally did it. They finally got one right, hey?"

"I don't understand, sir. Who got one what right?"

Daniel leaned back in the plush-cushioned couch and lifted his feet to a hassock. Even with no physical fatigue to deal with, his mind was so accustomed to his old body that he felt more comfortable with his feet up. His host sat opposite him in an overstuffed wing chair that seemed to be covered in real leather and studded in brass.

There was a low table between them and a thick carpet on the floor. Although the room was really an elevator car, it seemed more like the nineteenth-century private railroad cars that Daniel had seen pictured in his boyhood. All they needed was a staff serving brandies and fat cigars and roasted squab—for all the good any of those would be to Daniel!

The bureaucrat was still waiting for Daniel to speak.

"I mean—building this. This space elevator. Is that what you call it? The Elevator?"

The other man nodded. "There are half a dozen of them. Most are close to the equator—gets them maximum catapult effects in launching heavy loads. But we have this one at Rejkjaviko, and there's one down at Apio in Okcidenta Samoo, so the northern and southern regions have some service, too.

"All run by the International Aerospace Commission. When were you last on earth, sir?"

Daniel found himself rubbing the back of his neck in thought. "Let's see—the last I remember, being on earth, was in 2009. Actually, I was up at the first Island construction site then, but I'd just come up from earth. Things were in pretty bad shape downstairs then. They had me back after that, in the freezer, but I don't suppose that really counts. I certainly wasn't aware of anything going on. They woke me up in the medical Island after they'd got me rebuilt."

The bureaucrat rose and walked to a control panel. He punched in a sequence of commands. "I think you'll find this interesting, Mister Kitajima."

The far wall of the room was decorated as a nineteenth-century salon—plush, flocked wall-covering, draperies, gas-lamps, a huge vulgar romantic mural in a gilt frame. All of these faded out. The wall itself flickered briefly, then disappeared.

The room was open to space, to the thin atmosphere more than a thousand kilometers above the surface of Islando.

Daniel took a few steps, put out his fingers and felt the invisible wall.

"That's very good."

The bureaucrat smiled smugly.

Outside the Elevator car, the night sky was still black, dotted with distant stars.

"We're facing east, sir. The moon is behind us just now. It makes quite a sight as we come down through the stratosphere."

Below them the upper surface of a cloud layer was visible, glowing in bright moonlight. "How fast are we falling?" Daniel asked.

"Hmm, well, I'd prefer not to use that terminology. We're approaching the earth at two hundred kilometers per hour. Nothing to the speeds you're accustomed to, I know, sir. But respectable."

"And this car is just for us?"

The bureaucrat flushed. "A perquisite. And a courtesy, of course, for such distinguished travelers as yourself, Mister Kitajima."

"Incredible. I've never seen this sight before. I wouldn't have thought the moon could be that bright."

"Huh. I suppose it is a trifle brighter than it was back in the last century." He checked the time. "Watch this, now!"

Dan stood beside the bureaucrat, looking out the seemingly vacant end of the car. The farthest edge of the earth's cloud cover glowed purple and orange. Brilliant rays of color shot into the sky. The distant blackness lightened toward gray and the stars near the eastern horizon faded.

The sun's brilliant edge emerged from behind the earth's cloud cover and the clouds were transformed into a rolling sea of orange and purple and blue. The car continued to descend as the sun rose; the perspective changed constantly until the Elevator car plunged into the uppermost surface of the cloud layer. Wisps of gray shrouded the end of the car.

"Amazing. I keep expecting the clouds to come in here."

"It's a good thing they can't. Without the wall, we'd either be swept from the car or smother for lack of oxygen. We might even get the bends!"

Daniel smiled. "I don't think I'd have any problem with lack of oxygen. But bends—that's an intriguing notion. One more question to take up with the medics next time."

By the time they plunged through the bottom of the cloud layers it was full daylight in Rejkjaviko. The clouds themselves had spread into thin, broken formations that let almost all the sunlight through. Daniel could see vast fields of grain stretching for kilometers in all directions from the city. He shook his head at that development. The Elevator car disengaged from the descending cable and shunted into an unloading area. Daniel and the bureaucrat debarked.

Dan fought his way through more bureaucracy and immigration, getting deferential treatment throughout. He finally found himself seated aboard a suborbital transport headed for the new landing port in Sacramento-Stockton Bay. He took a suite in Unruh House and placed a radiophone call back to the medical Island. This time he got Doctor Kimura onscreen.

From Kimura he got the name and location of the management group for his financial interests on earth. He called his office and set up a drawing account at a bank in San Francisco.

Then he put his feet up, laced his fingers behind his neck, and wished he could still drink liquor. A good belt or two of scotch would relax him enough to work out some of his problems before he headed for San Francisco. He'd have to get Kimura or Royce to fix up his innards so he could dump a little alcohol into his bloodstream now and then, either by drinking it (he'd have to get a chemical processor built into his new body) or by some sort of infusion.

Jesus! How many things did he need to have them do up at the Island, next time he went there? And how many things did he still need to find out about his body?

When his host had faded that wall out of the Elevator car, he'd really thought the wall was gone, for a moment. He'd felt it with his hand to make sure it was still there.

But his new eyes had more capabilities than he'd fully explored. If they could act like telescopes, maybe they could work as microscopes, too. Or sense a lot more of the radiation spectrum than he'd tried. He could use his eyes to sense in the infrared. Could he detect ultraviolet? X-radiation? Could he *see* radio waves?

He was abnormally strong. He didn't know exactly *how* strong, but with his machined musculature, he could probably perform marvels of strength. He could hardly be hurt, either. He didn't have to breathe, so he couldn't be suffocated or gassed or drowned. (But some caustic gasses might muck up his circuitry or eat away at his artificial skin. And while he couldn't drown, Royce had warned him that immersion might cause short circuit. What a laugh!)

He wasn't abnormally intelligent—certainly no more intelligent than he'd been in his older life, and back then, he'd always known, he was no more than a run-of-the-mill computer technician. Now, even his modest expertise in computers was eighty years out-of-date. About on a par with a fabric-biplane-era aviator, suddenly transported to the space-shuttle era and told to pilot a ship up to orbit and back!

Still, he had a lot of computer circuits inside him, and between getting some more installed, to his own specifications, and learning to make the best use of what he had, he might yet turn into some sort of mental prodigy, with incredible ability to learn and store and call back information.

Altogether, he was pretty close to being an old-style television-type superhero.

What good did it do him?

He hadn't been able to do much with his new powers. He hadn't even been able to screw a woman when his grandson had thrown one at him!

He turned on a vidi wall and tried to stop thinking about himself. He was lucky. He tuned in on a Tierra del Fuego Gigantes game and saw the team in action. At least that small mystery was resolved! It was a good game, and the Gigantes won it handily. No wonder his acquaintance's niece was a fan of the Gigantes.

When the game ended he twiddled dials on the vidi wall, found a dance performance that seemed, at least, soothing and coherent, and put himself to sleep.

Again his dreams were chaotic and disquieting. He awoke feeling unsettled and confused. He checked out of Unruh House, traveled by rail to San Francisco, and walked through the city. There was something to be said for having a body that knew no fatigue.

He tried to find the house where he had lived with Marie-Elaine, Robert and Elizabeth. A hotel stood on the spot. He visited the manager's office and discovered that he was the owner of the hotel.

"We've preserved a suite, Mister Kitajima." The manager was respectful, almost trembling. Daniel wondered just how important a man, how wealthy and powerful, he had become in his eighty years refrigeration.

He told the hotel manager that he'd like to move in for a while. He thought the manager's choice of words was odd—if they'd *reserved* a suite for the absentee owner, that would make sense. But *preserved?* As in strawberry jam?

He stepped through the door and stepped eighty years backward through time. The room he entered was furnished entirely with replicas of the furnishings of his old Steiner Street house. He waved the manager away, closed the door behind her, sat gingerly in the wooden-framed easy chair that he'd last occupied before his ill-fated trip to the Island construction site, drank in this return to his home.

His chair still faced the old-style vidi box. The table beside his chair still had a vidi program card lying on it. He picked up the card and punched it on. It still held the program information for the week of his departure eighty years before. He held it closer, obeying the command of habit rather than refocusing his optical sensors.

The card was in perfect condition, bearing no trace of dust or age. But it still was marked with a brown circle with the diameter of a small man's palm: the ring left by his coffee cup eight decades ago.

He crossed the carpeted room and pulled back the old-style

fabric curtains. The windows were fitted with wooden frames and a good approximation of glass, but the scene outside could never be mistaken for the San Francisco he had last known. Still . . . still . . . dusk had fallen, lights were starting to glow in buildings around his hotel. In the northwest he could see a glow that suggested that the Golden Gate Bridge was still standing. He wondered if the city had simply spread to Marin County across the Gate; probably it had.

The day had been abnormally warm, Dan thought. He realized, with a start, that he didn't know the date. He lifted the old-style telephone handset but before he could punch any buttons an in-house operator responded. Yes, could the desk be of any service to Mister Kitajima?

He asked the date, received the information and hung up. The beginning of December. Huh! Really abnormal for San Francisco. In the street below his window he could see a thin fog. He'd never lived in the city's heavy fog belt, but occasionally Steiner Street got its share. The day had been warm, but the night was no less damp for that.

Stranger had been the wheatfields of Islando. How had the Icelanders been able to grow grain on their rocky land, to start with? There had been no evidence of hydroponic techniques; that kind of farming should have been discernable even from the Elevator car. And even if they had been able to manufacture soil, or import the incredible masses of it needed to turn the island into the vast farming tract it had become, how was it that they had a great harvest waving beneath brilliant, warm sunlight—in December?

He punched the vidi into life, tuned it to a news channel— and found himself watching the news for the first week in December, 2009.

Eighty years ago.

He smiled. They'd really gone to a lot of trouble, ginning up an array of tapes just on the chance that he'd feel like watching. He drank in the old war news and disaster reports, switched to a sports channel and watched a college hockey game till he tired of it, then killed the set and wandered to the kitchen, yearning desperately for a can of beer.

He slammed the refrigerator shut, sighing. It was stocked with Kirin and Dos Equis. There was even the soft burbling sound that used to fill his house. He walked to the bedroom. Yes, they'd put in the fifty-liter tank that Marie-Elaine had kept on her dresser. It was stocked with the right tropical fish and the supposedly soundless air pump that had never performed soundlessly. A tiny African frog swam to the surface, gulped a breath and dived back to the safety of the bottom.

Daniel stood over the bed silently for a while, rubbed his hand across his face, then returned to his easy chair, put up his feet and closed his eyes. He slid into total darkness for a while.

Later he opened his eyes again. The room was dark. The lights from outside barely penetrated the curtains of the old-fashioned room. He got up, looked into the street. There was almost no traffic, there were no pedestrians. He saw one dark figure dart from a shadowed alleyway to a gutter and disappear. It might have been a cat or large rat.

He followed the sound of the bubbling air filter toward the bedroom. He'd forgot to turn off the low-wattage bulb on the aquarium, and its orange light filled the room with a dim, warm coloration.

The quilt was folded back on the bed and Marie-Elaine sat in the bed, propped against a pile of pillows. She was busy and did not look up as Daniel stood in the doorway. He was glad that she hadn't noticed him. He stood and watched.

Her black hair framed her face. The skin of her forehead and cheeks looked soft and smooth. She was wearing an ivory-colored nightgown, pulled away from both her breasts.

She held their twins, each wrapped in a soft blanket, each nursing at one of her breasts. Her face was turned down to watch the infants; her expression was one of quiet, of total beatitude.

He was filled with joy, was awed by her beauty and the beauty of the two infants nursing at her bosom. He felt an inexplicable impulse to fall to his knees in worship. He felt a heated illumination and understood, at least for a breathtaking, overwhelming moment, the meaning of the adoration of the Madonna.

Almost in the same moment he felt a mighty, overpowering surge of lust, a throbbing, almost painful erection that rose before him. A need to plunge himself into Marie-Elaine, to penetrate her to her center, to unite with her with the complete unconcern of the rutting lion mounting his mate.

He pulled his robe open, threw it to the carpet, put one knee on the edge of the bed and leaned forward on his palms.

Marie-Elaine looked up at him and smiled. Her expression was one of welcome, and of understanding, and of agreement. She smiled down at the two infants who lay against her breast now, sated and drowsy.

Daniel reached and took one of the infants from her. He put the child across his shoulder and walked back and forth, patting the infant's back rhythmically. He heard Marie-Elaine's laugh, warm and with no trace of mockery. He looked at her, saw that she was patting the other twin but looking at him. He looked down at himself and saw that he was naked, his penis huge and erect, while he paraded back and forth with the baby on his shoulder, patting its back. He laughed also.

They laid the infants down and covered them for sleep.

Marie-Elaine climbed back into the bed, her ivory gown now lying across its foot. She sat as she had, propped against the pillows, her black hair falling across her shoulders. Daniel could see a tiny drop of leftover milk on one of her nipples.

He came to the bed and knelt on the quilt, facing her, his penis still erect before him.

He leaned forward, placed his hands against the stacked pillows, and closed his eyes. He felt a shudder of coldness shake his body. He opened his eyes and looked down. He was alone in the bed. The only light came from the aquarium on the dresser. The only sound in the room was that of the imperfectly functioning air pump. He couldn't hear any sound of himself breathing; he pressed his hand to his chest trying to feel the soft thudding of his heart, but detected only the steady, barely perceptible whir of a wankel rotary pump.

The optical sensing devices he was fitted with performed their marvelous functions of switching through radiation bands, radiation intensities, variations of focus, by electronic networks of splendid versatility. There were no moving parts; there was no need for lubrication; there were no fluids in the system; there was no purpose, his designers had determined, to furnish him with tear ducts.

With a moan he pulled his clothing back on. He called the

desk and found that the hotel operated all its services, around the clock.

He left the hotel and set out walking through the fog. A night manager had tried to dissuade him from leaving the hotel at this hour but Daniel responded curtly and pushed into Steiner Street. He headed eastward, in the direction of the Bay.

The night was warmer than he'd expected, but the fog had grown surprisingly thick. It was an unusual combination of warmth and atmospheric moisture, something that he'd never experienced in San Francisco before. It made the air seem full of dancing prisms that caught and diffracted the light of street-lamps into tiny floating rainbows. But mixed with the beauty of the unfamiliar fog was a feeling of cloying, almost debili-tating heaviness to the air.

Sounds were dampened, smothered. He felt his hard-bottomed shoes striking old cement sidewalks, but the sharp sounds of his steps were softened, almost obliterated by the heavy air.

Somewhere music was playing.

Daniel realized that he missed the cocktail of odors that should permeate the night air. His new body seemed to have no sense of smell. Since he did not breathe, he realized, it was only for show that he had a nose at all. He chuckled to himself, made a mental note to ask Royce or Kimura about installing a set of olfactory nerves.

The music was not very complex, and not skillfully played. Some local resident must be holding a late-night party complete with band. Daniel heard mainly a powerful if clumsy rhythm section throbbing away. Against the almost tangible thuds a chorus of voices were singing, *Something-something-fucker-in-the-ass-baa-baa-baa/Something-something-in-the-ear-laa-laa-laa.*

A rat scurried from under a discarded carton and disappeared behind a rotting fence.

The neighborhood was a mix of high rises, older well-kept commercial buildings and houses, and deteriorating derelicts. Another neighborhood in transition brought to you by your friendly twenty-first century society.

A sleek-looking vehicle with police markings on its sides purled by. Daniel could detect a rotating infrared spotlight on its roof. Its occupants either failed to notice him or saw fit to pay no attention. The vehicle disappeared into the fog just beyond California Street, apparently heading north on California, toward the Richmond district.

The sound-smothering fog was shredded by a shout and the sound of a scuffle coming from Perrine Place.

Daniel sprinted into the little street, headed from Steiner toward Pierce. There was no light here, and the fog had gathered in the stillness.

The sounds were louder. He could hear grunts, the dull sounds of fists striking flesh, a tearing sound as of ripping cloth. A grunt of pain was accompanied by a woman's shriek somewhere between a scream of fear and a shout of anger. He heard another voice of indeterminate sex shouting, a man uttering a string of obscenities, a woman yelling angrily.

There was no one in Perrine Place.

Daniel stopped in the center of the block, searching for the source of the voices. They were coming from a still smaller alleyway that opened between two old brick buildings. He sprinted toward the alleyway. He could see nothing from within, by normal light. He strained to make his optical devices shift spectra, to pick up images by infrared.

He saw three distorted figures, all of them on the ground, struggling and rolling together.

He ran into the alleyway, his three hundred kilograms of weight thudding against the old tar surface with every stride.

He saw the three figures on the ground, a woman lying face down on the ground, a second, heavier woman crouching on her, her knees on the other woman's shoulders, her hands around her throat, grunting and throttling her. Behind her a man leaned against her, his body at an angle, his hands pummeling the ribs of the woman on the ground. His knees were on the ground, between the woman's legs. His pelvis was thrusting against her in rhythm with the blows his fists delivered to her ribs.

The woman being raped was still struggling feebly to raise her hands and resist her attackers, but her movements were nearly as weak as the choking sounds that she made. The woman sitting on her back was talking steadily to the victim, commanding her again and again to shut up and lie still. The man was uttering an unbroken stream of almost incoherent foulness.

Daniel grabbed the man by the belted trousers that had slid halfway down his thighs. With his other hand he grabbed a fistful of the man's unkempt hair. As he pulled him off the victim, the man gave a convulsive thrust and grunt. Daniel tugged him away, lifted him a meter off the ground. There was a liquid squelching sound as his penis slipped from the victim's anus.

Daniel raised the man over his head. He balanced on one foot and kicked with the other, as hard as he could, striking the heavyset woman low on the spine.

There was a sick, snapping sound and she skidded forward, over the head of the victim, tumbled once end-for-end and lay moaning on the ground.

Even before the heavy woman had finished her tumble, Daniel threw the man away from himself, threw him as hard as his machine muscles could act.

The man struck the brick wall of the old building two meters off the ground. There was a loud sound, a wet smack. The man bounced off the wall and fell to the ground a meter from the wall, landing with a softer repetition of the sound. He shuddered once and lay unmoving.

The heavyset woman was continuing to moan. Her inarticulate complaint reached a peak, held on for a moment, then toppled back to a low repetitious wailing.

The attacked woman had managed to get her hands beneath her shoulders and had shoved her body a few centimeters off the tar. She was making a loud, repetitious gagging sound. *Aak-aak-aak-aak*.

The sound stopped and was replaced by a mushy gurgling. The woman had vomited copiously. Her arms lost their strength and she fell, her face landing in the puddle of vomit.

She moaned loudly, managed to shove herself sideways, pushed from the ground with one arm and sat up, peering toward the mouth of the alleyway.

Daniel realized that she might barely see him silhouetted there, against the only slightly less black opening to Perrine Place.

He made a gesture with one hand, trying to reassure the

woman. He said, "You need help. I'll call a cop."

The woman stared at him dully.

"Can you stay—you'll be all right for a minute. Should I go for a cop—a police car—"

The woman shuddered, her body thrusting forward, a loud gagging sound that seemed almost a shout coming from her. She spasmed violently, puking out one more blob of unidentifiable matter. It splattered on her shin and dribbled onto the ground.

She held up one hand, leaning, reaching toward Daniel, swaying her head from side to side negatively. "Don't—" she managed to get out. "Don't. No. Don't."

Daniel moved toward her again, knelt beside her.

She grabbed him with both hands, with astonishing strength. She put her head against his chest, pulling him toward her and rubbing her face, almost scraping it, against his garment.

"They—they—"

"Wait. It's all right now."

"They—" She shuddered and gestured vaguely toward the two bodies on the ground. The woman was still moaning softly. She was making feeble attempts to do something with her hands but only managed to scrabble them on the tar surface.

"Are you injured?" Daniel asked.

The woman shook her head; he could feel that, against his chest. "I don't think—they—they—" She gagged, tightened her gasp on his arm, gasped for air. "Don't go," she said again. "Don't leave me."

Daniel blinked. Of all situations to fall into! His own bizarre circumstances with all their puzzling prospects retreated. They were things he could worry about in the morning, and morning seemed incredibly remote. He had to deal with the situation he was in.

"Look," he said, "Miss. Uh, do you think, uh, if I help you, if you lean on me, do you think you could . . ." He tried to encourage her to stand, putting gentle pressure beneath her elbow.

She said yes, pushed herself upward, leaning on his shoulders. He stood up with her, doing most of the work for both of them. She stood a half meter away from him, steadied herself with one hand against him. She dropped her hand, straightened her clothes the best she could. Her garments were torn and soiled but she managed a slight semblance of order.

"Uh—could you . . ." She covered her face with her hands. By using infrared vision Daniel could see that her hands were torn and bleeding from her struggle and from futile scratching against the pavement.

"The police?" Daniel asked. "Or a hospital? You should get to a hospital."

She shook her head. "I don't know. I don't know. It was my own fault. I think they doctored my drink."

"Never mind that now." Was this how a hero acted when dealing with a victim he's just rescued from brutes? Daniel searched his memory for some kind of rules to follow. Make sure drowning victim has not swallowed his or her own tongue. Grasp person who is choking on food from behind and squeeze. Do not attempt to move victim as broken bones may cause internal injuries.

"What should—"

"Come on, lean on me. We'll get help."

He half carried her out of the alley. Superman would fly over the city with Lois Lane in his arms. He got her as far as Perrine Place, looked left and right. It was a shorter walk to continue up to Pierce than back to Steiner. In Perrine he could hear faint, distant music. There was a vocal. *Something-some-thing-fucker-in-the-eye-baa-baa-baa.*

He turned her left on Pierce, heading vaguely back toward his hotel. The fog was thicker and warmer than ever. Moving was like struggling through loosely wadded cotton.

He heard a soft purling sound from the deserted street behind him. He looked back. His infrared vision penetrated the fog. It was another police vehicle—or perhaps the same one that had passed him earlier.

He waved a hand trying to hail the police car.

"What are—" the woman started to ask.

"It's the cops. You'll be all right now."

"Oh, no! You—let's—"

The police vehicle pulled to within a meter of them and screeched to a halt. A bank of glaring blue-white lights blazed into life. A voice amplified to a deafening roar poured from the vehicle.

"Don't move! Stay perfectly still! Weapons are trained on you and any movement will be interpreted as an attack with deadly weapons! Don't move! Stay perfectly still! Weapons are . . ." The tape loop or whatever it was continued to repeat.

The woman with Daniel was standing with her hands at her sides, trembling.

Daniel could hear the doors of the police vehicle slide open. Booted feet hit the ground.

"There, we'll be all right now," Daniel said.

"You moron!" the woman sobbed.

"It's all right," Daniel repeated.

Silhouetted against the blue-white glare, Daniel could see a pair of figures advancing cautiously toward himself and the woman. They were bulky, almost inhuman. Each was helmeted, he realized, with a thick transparent face covering and breather, flak jacket, heavy gloves, padded trousers and thick footgear.

"Turn around," a police officer commanded. "Hands behind your back. Obey or die."

Daniel complied, shrugging at what seemed extremes of caution on the part of the police.

"No more warnings!" the officer barked.

The woman had been slow to obey. Now she stood with her back to the officers, as did Daniel.

Daniel felt his hands covered with something softly thick and gooey. He gave the stuff a quick, slight test. It was strong, so strong that no muscles could have broken it or squirmed out of it. He was confident that his new body could cope with the stuff, but obviously no organic human could. Old-style handcuffs must be strictly for museums now.

Beside Daniel his companion uttered a muffled sob as the stuff enveloped her hands.

"Listen here, this woman was attacked! You needn't—" Something hard and heavy thudded against the back of Daniel's skull. The blow did no damage to him but its sheer force sent him reeling forward and toppling to the ground. With his hands gummed together behind him, he landed on his shoulder and lay flat.

The officer kicked him once, hard. "Up! One more word and you're dead!"

They were prodded into the police vehicle, placed in a windowless, metal-lined compartment flooded with the same blue-white glare of the vehicle's outside floodlights. Daniel looked at his companion. Her answering look warned him against making any further protest.

At the police station they were thrown into a similar room that was a little larger than the compartment in the vehicle.

They were seated back-to-back on the metal floor.

A loudspeaker in the ceiling of the room gave out a metallic voice.

6

THE DOCTOR drew Daniel aside in the doorway of his suite. "I'm surprised but very pleased, Mister Kitajima. I don't think she's going to have any problems except for being terribly sore for a few days. But please call me at once if there's anything. There may be some bleeding in urine or stool. Don't worry at a little, but if it's extensive, call me at once."

Daniel nodded. "Thank you. I still don't see why she refused hospitalization, but . . ." He shrugged.

"I understand her feelings. It's just too bad that this happened outside the zone of her policy coverage. But she'd have been in hock for years if she'd had to pay the bills."

"But I would have taken care of that. I can afford it."

"She wouldn't take that. You heard her. So did I."

"But she let me hire you."

"Mister Kitajima, what can I say? Let it be. The young lady is very fortunate. From the double encounter she had in that alleyway and with the police, I think she's a very lucky person. She just didn't want to risk getting enmeshed with another institution. I really can't say that I blame her.

"And now, if you have no other questions—" He paused. "Very well. Thank you for the payment. You can reach me if you need me." The doctor left.

Daniel looked over his shoulder once more at the woman sleeping, sedated, on the living room couch. She had adamantly refused to be taken into Daniel's bedroom, for all her gratitude at winding up in his suite instead of remaining in City Jail.

After some discussion, Daniel and the medico had agreed that it was more sensible to leave her on the sofa rather than agitate her further.

She slept in a set of Marie-Elaine's pajamas (or a facsimile of them—Daniel couldn't be certain). A heavy, soft comforter was thrown over her. Her dark hair and rich skin color made for a resemblance, at a quick glance, to Marie-Elaine. But her facial features were different, her bone structure heavier, far less delicate than Marie-Elaine's. And before she had fallen asleep, her piercingly brilliant blue eyes had established themselves as the strongest feature of her appearance—far different from Marie-Elaine's soft, nearly black eyes.

Daniel breathed a sigh almost as if he still had lungs and a diaphragm. He turned away from the living-room scene and threw back the fabric drapes.

It was full daylight outside. The fog had totally burned off the city—or this neighborhood, at any rate—and the sun beat brilliantly on Pacific Heights toward the Bay. People moved along Steiner Street and up and down Post, astonishing numbers of people. As deserted as the thoroughfares had been in the night, that full had they become by day. Pedestrians overflowed the sidewalks and filled the streets themselves, moving angrily out of the way of huge vans that barely passed in opposite directions, even on the wide thoroughfares.

There were almost no private motor cars.

Behind Daniel, the woman on the couch moaned. Daniel turned and saw her sitting up. Her hair was tangled and matted, her face badly abraded and marked with the red of antiseptics and white patches of bandage. One eye was slightly blackened; the other, swollen wholly shut and colored a livid purple. Her nose was not broken, but was swollen and bandaged.

"Oh, my God," the woman said. She put one hand to her face and the other to her side, feeling the bandages and tape there.

"A couple of cracked ribs," Daniel said.

The woman nodded. She asked for a glass of water and Daniel fetched it for her from the facsimile of his old kitchen. "What time is it?" she asked. "My God, what *day* is it?"

Daniel told her.

"Oh, my God, I'd better call my office. I can't afford to lose my job."

Daniel was surprised. "Lose your job? After you were assaulted, beaten half to death, dragged away by the police and treated like a criminal instead of the victim? Don't worry about your job."

The woman turned grimly toward him. "Mister, I don't know what you've been melting under your tongue, but you don't know anything about jobs. They're too hard to get and too easy to lose. They don't want excuses, they want you there when it's starting time, preferably a half hour or so before. I've got to get to work!"

She tried to stand up and fell back onto the sofa, unable to balance on her feet.

"Oh, no," she muttered, "I can't do it." She tried again to rise but got only halfway up this time.

"Listen," Daniel said, "I'll bring the phone over. It's voice-only, will that do? Or I can get you a screen."

She sat on the sofa, the quilt pulled around her, staring at him dumbly.

"If you can't handle it, I'll call for you," Dan offered. "I'll tell them what happened. You shouldn't go back to work for at least a week."

She attempted a bitter smile, at that. Daniel could see that she had lost several teeth. Her lips were badly swollen.

He pulled up a chair near the sofa, brought the old-style telephone.

"I feel like I've fallen into the past," the woman said.

Daniel nodded. "In a way, you have." He paused. "Look, you have to tell me where you work. Do you know the number? Who's your boss?"

She shook her head slowly and with care. She gave him a lengthy number and the name of her supervisor. Daniel felt a fleeting flash of pleasure as he realized that he retained all the digits in the number the first time she said them. He punched the digits into the telephone, heard a voice respond with the name of an electronics firm he'd never heard of. Well, it had always been a volatile field with major competitors springing from the ground like soldiers from dragons' teeth.

"I'm sorry, I'm not receiving any image," the voice said.

"That's okay. I don't have a screen set, just voice."

Daniel could almost see the other's eyebrows rise. "Is this a jape?"

"No, really. I'm using an old phone. No screen."

"Have it your way. What do you want?"

Daniel asked for the woman's supervisor. There was a delay, another round of explaining why there was no picture. Finally the person on the phone said, "Well, what is it anyway?"

Daniel started to explain the situation, realized that he didn't even know the name of the woman in his wife's pajamas, but before he got that far the woman's supervisor said, "Oh, yes. That would be Lydia Haddad." She pronounced the first name with Hispanic values, the second with Semitic. It came out as *Leed*-ya Kha-*tod*.

"She used to work here, yes."

"Used to?" Daniel exploded. "What do you mean?"

"She's not here, she's out of work. Plenty more eager to get employment and off the dole."

"But—it isn't her fault. She was attacked and beaten. She's covered with bandages now. She can hardly move."

The supervisor said, "Hold on." There was a pause during which Daniel could hear the tapping of a keyboard and the clatter of a printout unit. "Not in the company hospital. She's not our employee now. And I'm really very busy, so—"

Daniel blurted, "Wait a minute! What kind of—never mind. Listen here, I want to talk with someone higher up. This is an outrage!"

The other person laughed.

"Listen," Daniel tried again. "If there's any trouble concerning Miss Haddad's salary for missed time, I can take care of that. My name—you can verify my credit standing—my name is Daniel Kitajima and I—"

"Come off it, bozo!" the other interrupted. "This is a good gag but I've had enough."

"What do you mean! I'm not joking. I can make up Miss Haddad's salary for the days she'll be out. I don't see why she should be penalized for—"

"You're Daniel Kitajima?" the voice said. "No screen on your phone, and you're Daniel Kitajima and you're going to make up Lydia Haddad's back salary when she returns to work. And we're not to penalize her in any way, even though she left the Company zone and got in trouble with the police. Any more instructions, Mister Kitajima? Shall we promote your protégé? What about a two-day holiday for all employees? Do you want us to send up fireworks to celebrate your return?"

"Forget it, forget it." Daniel hung up the phone. He leaned back. His chair creaked threateningly under his kilograms of weight.

Lydia Haddad turned sideways on the couch and looked at him through one eye. "Are you really Daniel Kitajima?"

Daniel nodded. Haddad's voice was deeper and pleasanter than he would have expected under the circumstances.

"You *really* are? No jape?"

Daniel spread his hands in amazement. "Yes, yes, I'm really Dan Kitajima. So what?"

Haddad laughed. There was a rough sound to her laughter. "Then why did you bother with my boss, Mister Kitajima?"

"Oh, please. What could I do? And don't *mister*, will you? I thought you knew who I was at the police station. That got us out of there, don't you remember?"

She rubbed her forehead. "I guess I do. Last night—last night is such a jumble. I—" She started to cry, blotted her eyes with the sleeve of Marie-Elaine's pajamas. "Oh, shit, Daniel. You're sure you want me to call you Daniel?"

"Or Dan. I prefer Dan. May I call you Lydia?"

Her smile of agreement was a grotesque mask.

"Lydia, I could get the doc back here. Or at least bring in a nurse for you. Are you sure you don't want to go to a hospital?"

"I'll be all right. *Oofh!*" She winced as she shifted position on the sofa.

"Are you sure you want to talk?" Daniel asked.

"A little. A little. Then if I could just rest . . ."

"Look, then. About last night. Unless you don't want to talk about it. I mean, it must have been a terrible experience for you. It would have been for anyone. I mean—"

She shook her head. "My own fault, Dan. There was a certain risk in leaving the company zone, but everybody does that. But—"

"Slow down. People keep talking about these zones. I don't know what they are. *What* zone?"

Lydia's one open eye opened wider in surprise. "Oh, yes, you've really been away. Well, look." She struggled to sit up straighter on the sofa. "The company provides security on its own property. Employees are expected to live on the reservation. They don't *have* to, you see, but everybody does. And the company sees to it that things are pretty peaceful and safe on the reservation, the zone. You see? We have full benefits, medical coverage, there are stores in the zone, schools and so on. You could live there all your life and never leave. Or if you have business with another company, there's reciprocal coverage."

She looked at him, waiting for some response.

Now Daniel shook his head. "But the government. Aren't there public schools any more? I know there are municipal services. The streets, the police . . . we know about the police now!" He grimaced.

"Yes, we know about the police now," she agreed.

"Well, but what you describe—it sounds like anarchy. Or feudalism! I don't understand."

"How long were you away?"

"Eighty years." He waited for her expression of surprise and for the inevitable questions that statement must provoke, but they did not come.

"Oh, yes," Lydia nodded. "I'd forgot how long you were gone."

Instead of creating surprise, Daniel experienced it. "Look, I didn't realize I was that much of a celebrity. Does everybody know about me?"

"You *were* a pretty famous figure," Lydia said. "But no, not much more. You're not exactly a headliner on the vidi news, Dan. But you're a legend at the company."

"Why? Why?"

"You haven't been briefed."

"No."

She laughed. "That's good! You *own* the company!"

"Nonsense. I had a few shares in the old computer outfit I worked for, up to 2009. But everybody had a few shares. All the employees. Management encouraged it. Supposed to be a motivater, if we had a piece of the action. Keep us loyal and productive, you know. Less likely to listen to headhunters from the competition. But I never even *heard* of this outfit you work for."

"Yep. Your, ah, estate—I guess it wasn't really an estate

with you alive. But anyway, there were a lot of contributions
to you while you were frosted. And your trustees kept socking
bucks into the company. They went through some mergers and
takeovers, that's where the company of today comes from. And
you own fifty-one percent of the stock."

Daniel sank into an easy chair. He put his head into his
hands. "Oh, boy. Oh, boy." He pulled at his hair, then looked
up at Lydia. "Okay. For one thing, you have your job back,
as of now."

She smiled tiredly. "Thanks." She shifted her weight. "Oh,
Christ, do I ever hurt! Look, would you help me to the bath-
room, Dan, I have to piss something fierce. And then I guess
I'll use that bed after all, if you don't mind."

"Sure, I'll watch the news for a few hours while you rest.
I need more catching up than I'd realized."

"Fine. But you don't have to stay here on my account. I'm
not going anywhere."

"No, it's not—"

"And I'll phone for help if I need it."

"Okay."

"You look better. Feel any better?"

She nodded. "I never had eggs and beer for breakfast before.
But I don't suppose I could handle much else till I get my
mouth fixed up."

Daniel nodded.

"Listen." She put her hand on his wrist and he could see
that the swelling had grown less although most of her discoloration remained on her hands. Her face, too, was beginning
to look a bit better. Her lips were less puffy than they had
been, and her empurpled eye was no longer completely shut.
"Listen," she repeated, "I really want to thank you for getting
me back my job. You don't know what it would mean, to lose
it."

"I guess not."

"I want to get back to work. I want to get back to my job
and my partner. You've been very kind, Dan, taking care of
me in so many different ways. Putting me up here, taking care
of my med costs, getting my job back for me. But I'm getting
itchy."

Dan nodded his head. "I've been down to the police station a few times. They don't kid around."

"No jape."

"That couple who attacked you—they'll need a statement from you. The police will." He saw Lydia grow pale. "It's all right," Dan reassured her. "You were the victim, for heaven's sake. Why are you so worried? You're not in trouble over something else, are you?"

"No. No." She shook her head. "Haven't you seen what the police are like?"

"Even so. Even so." He stood up, looked at her for a moment, then walked across the old carpet. "They can't be *that* bad, Lydia. I'll stand up with you. You were the one attacked. The cops can't be *that* bad," he repeated.

"Yes, they can." She looked away, then back at him. "What happened to Jed and Millie?"

"Eh?"

"The people who were," she squeezed her eyes shut for a second, "raping me."

"Oh. He's dead. She's paralyzed."

"Uh-*huh*. How badly?"

"Badly. It's ironic, I met a police medic who says she'll probably get most of her function back if they install some bypass circuits and neuroprosthetics that were developed for me. If she can afford it."

"I doubt that."

"Or if I'll pay for it."

"Will you?"

He shrugged. "What was it all about? I mean—it was pretty clear, what was happening when I got there. To Perrine Place. But did they just jump out at you? Were you just walking by and they grabbed you? The streets seemed awfully deserted to me, that night. Every night."

"Well, it was my own fault. I just got so bored in the company zone. And my partner didn't want to do anything much. So I came up to the city. It's not that uncommon. It's a little risky but everybody does it. Everybody does it."

She stood up and walked to the window. Daniel watched. It had been a few days since the attack, and she was walking steadily. She could go back to work tomorrow, he supposed. If she wanted to. It had been pleasant, in a way, having someone to care for and to talk with. But he couldn't keep her here. He wasn't sure, for that matter, that *he* wanted to stay here much longer. Certainly not indefinitely.

Living in this replica of his old home was too much like retreating into a nostalgic fantasy. All he'd have to do would be to hire an actress to pretend she was Marie-Elaine, keep the vidi stocked with eighty-year-old tapes and order up a facsimile newscard subscription and live in the past of eight decades ago. It was too tempting, too easy. Before he slipped more deeply into that fantasy, he'd better leave it and begin making his peace with the world of December, 2009—and the years that would follow.

He realized that Lydia was still speaking, and he'd paid no attention to her. "I'm sorry. What was that?"

She frowned. "I said, I'd met them in a dive. One of those, no-last-names, don't-do-anything-grossly-illegal-till-you're-off-the-premises places. You know? Did you have them in your day?"

"More or less. I didn't go there."

"I do."

He shrugged.

"But maybe I won't any more. You always hear of terrible things happening, but they always happen to the other person. Then one time—"

She shook her shoulders as if to shake away a clammy touch, then continued. "Then one time it does happen to you. I met them, Millie and Jed, in this dive. They seemed like nice folks, especially Millie. We melted a few tabs under our tongues, had a few drinks, danced. Then they invited me to run the curfew with them, back to their digs."

Daniel interjected, "Hah! Your place or mine?"

"Eh?"

"Just a cliché."

She thought about that briefly. "Oh, yes. I get the drift. Yes, it was exactly that, although the expression is a little odd. Well, they were city folk, didn't live in any company zone. That made the whole thing seem kind of daring and glamorous.

"Look at me," she said, holding her arms in the air. "I'm a big girl, Daniel. I ought to've known better. But I'd led a charmed life until then. Bad things always happened to somebody else.

"I still don't know if they had anything in mind other than getting their keekees."

"Their *whats?*"

"Keekees. You know. Um, thrills, enjoyment. Especially sexual enjoyment."

"Oh."

"Yeh. I thought we'd go to their place, hear some music, maybe melt another tab and climb under a quilt. All friendly and wholesome. I'd be up and gone in the morning, head for Palo Alto, the safe zone, and be at work with time to spare. And I'd have a nice little adventure to tell my partner about under the quilt, later."

"Well . . ." She looked down at her bruises.

"Yeah." Dan looked out the window at the sun-drenched street. "Yeah. I guess they were getting plenty of keekees when I arrived."

"I really want to thank you for that. I don't know where they would have stopped, Dan. Maybe the big climax for Millie comes from somebody dying."

"I've heard of that kind of person."

"Well." She stood up, looked at the old-fashioned clock across the room. "I think I should get back to the zone, Daniel. If the city police haven't put an official hold on me, they can get to me through the company."

"All right." He started toward the door with her.

"Oh, listen, you don't have to escort me back. I said, I'm a big girl. Thanks again but—"

"If you don't mind. I *am* the owner of the company. You told me so yourself. I'd like to travel down there and look over my possessions, meet some of my employees. I do have people managing my holdings for me, but I think I'd like to get back into the game myself. Learn something about the new technology. I'm not cut out for a life of idleness."

THE smooth road to the company zone at Palo Alto was lined with intensively worked agricultural projects alternating with high-rise architecture.

Daniel shook his head sadly. "This used to be gorgeous countryside. Lakes and wooded hills. The developers kept trying to get their hands on it and the do-gooders kept trying to keep the land away from them. I guess the almighty buck won. As usual."

Lydia looked at him. "You're one to talk."

Daniel grinned a wry grin. "Touché."

"But this wasn't just bucks in action." Lydia waved at the passing scene. "We had to have somewhere to put all the people. More and more countries have been getting too hot to live in. The people had to go somewhere. Of course, the north is opening up, too. But this was just about inevitable."

"What do you mean, too hot to live in?"

"Didn't I hear you remark that San Francisco was awfully warm for December?"

"Well, yes. But we always had a freakish climate. Cold spells and hot spells and midwinter thaws. I just thought . . ."

"The whole world is getting warmer. Some kind of solar radiation cycle. It'll reverse itself soon and get back to normal. But for a while now it's been getting a little warmer each year. It all balances out. Not to worry."

"You're kidding, Lydia."

"No." She seemed unconcerned.

"But that's like—oh, some funny old disaster tape. You know. The volcanoes all go off and cover the world with lava, or all the octopusses come marching out of the ocean muttering, 'Kill, kill,' or there's a fire in a skyscraper and people are trapped on the umpteenth floor screaming at each other. The sun goes out and oceans freeze or the sun flares up and the ice caps melt. That kind of stuff."

"Yes."

"Wait a minute. If what you said is right—how come the ice caps haven't melted? They always used to have the ice caps melt, the oceans rise, cities flooded. Where's the flood?"

"Christ on a crutch, Dan, how the hell do I know? I'm just a circuit planner, not a meteorologist. Wouldn't the water evaporate? There'd be more water in the atmosphere and the oceans would lose as much that way as they'd gain by melting. Hey, and doesn't water expand when it freezes? If it melted it would take up less room. How do I know anyhow? Ask me about PNP dipole IC monofilm networks, you know. Ask me about something I know about."

"Huh. I guess that's why Islando is covered with wheatfields now."

Lydia looked at him. "I wouldn't know. But here we are at the zone gate."

They were expected at the gate and passing the X-ray scanners was a mere formality. Lydia passed without a hitch. Daniel sent the alarms into hysterics of flashing lights, ringing bells and screaming sirens.

A squad of security troops in full combat gear surrounded them with weapons drawn.

Lydia said, "Oh, no, not again!"

The Director of Zone Security was a tough individual with short hair and an androgynous appearance but her assistant was an old-timer who was tuned into company history. She got the Director to call the Resident Manager instead of the police. The Resident Manager knew who Daniel was, apologized for the inconvenience and led him toward her office.

"Look," Dan said, "could Miss Haddad join this session? She knows me and I have a high regard for her knowledge."

The Resident Manager and Director of Zone Security exchanged looks. "You're the boss, Mister Kitajima."

"Fine. I wonder if I could get a little work area, maybe sit in on some classes. I used to be a fair systems engineer but I'll have a lot of catching up to do."

The Resident Manager put her hands on her hips. She was a gray-haired woman, sixtyish to Daniel's estimation, with eyes the color of her hair. "You can have anything you want, sir. You own this company."

Daniel laughed. "I keep forgetting that. I'd still like to sit in on those classes, and I'd like a cubbyhole for myself if I can get it."

IN the Resident Manager's office they sat on comfortable furniture while Daniel got his briefing on eighty years worth of changes in the company's role and in the technology it had developed. Network processors and data storage facilities were everywhere. Their manufacture had become so cheap that they were ground out for every conceivable use.

The company was immensely profitable and provided its employees total security and lifetime employment. Most companies did the same. But there was not enough work to go around, and much of the populace lived precariously on a massive dole of the necessities of life. Land utilization was kept in a state of delicate balance as the tropical zone became increasingly uninhabitable while the farther reaches of northern Kanado, Gronlando, Spicbergeno, and Eurazio were developed.

"Listen here," Daniel interrupted. "Are you certain that these changes are just temporary? That they're going to reverse before things go too far?"

The gray-haired Resident Manager locked glances with Daniel, her bright-textured gray eyes connecting with his artificial scanners.

"Of course," she said. "Can I offer you a drink, sir?"

"No, thanks. And that was too simple a response. I don't like what I'm seeing and hearing lately. Those space Islands seem to have worked out pretty well. You know, we were just getting started on them when I . . . had my accident. Now, well, the medical Island is a going concern. I visited Hokkaido with my grandson and that seems to be a big success. Although I can't say I found their social system very congenial. Still, it works. And the technology works."

"I'm not an authority on Islands, Mister Kitajima. But I have the same impression, yes." The Resident Manager nodded.

"Look, then." Daniel leaned forward earnestly, laying his arm on the Resident Manager's desk top and pointing at her. "Why don't we start packing people off in mass numbers, to Islands. If the sun really keeps heating up, then, it's not hard to move the Islands. Scoot off to a spot a couple of AU's farther out; if the sun heats up any more, scoot out a little farther. When the sun goes back to normal, bring the Islands back."

"That's wonderful, Mister Kitajima. That makes it all sound simple."

"Uh-*huh*. I suppose you're going to tell me I've omitted this factor and that, I don't understand the complex considerations, et cetera, et cetera. Right?"

"I'm afraid so."

"Okay." Daniel leaned back and laced his fingers together. "Let me have it."

She flushed. "We've done a lot of work for the responsible agencies. U.S. agencies, international groups. So I'm a bit better informed about this than the ordinary citizen. I don't mean that this will be classified information or anything like that. But some of it is a trifle...delicate."

"I understand. Oh, Miss Haddad. I'll take responsibility for Miss Hadded. All right, Lydia? Word to the wise."

She nodded.

The Resident Manager looked doubtful. "I don't know, sir. Well, every informed person understands this anyway. What was world population when you experienced your mishap? Do you recall, roughly? Or I could check it by the almanac." She reached to punch a control sensor built into the top of her desk.

"On the order of eleven billion," Dan said.

The manager punched at the panel. A number glowed. "Yes. What was the date?"

"May 24, 2009."

"Eleven billion, two hundred sixteen million, five hundred eighty seven thousand, three hundred fifty-four."

"Yes. And in these eighty years—well eighty years and seven months—what has it become? We were still working toward ZPG in 2009."

"Eh?"

"Zero Population Growth. We'd made considerable progress. If that continued, plus emigration to the Islands..." He spread his hands and tried to look and feel hopeful while a cold sinking feeling grew in his iron belly.

"I'm afraid it didn't work. Your, ah, ZPG."

Daniel waited for her to say more.

"And as for emigration to the Islands—well, let's gen up a couple more numbers." Her hands sped over the control sensors, bringing glowing answers onto the desk's display screen. "On a total of fifty-three functional Islands and twenty-seven more under construction as of today, there's a total off-earth population of 885,922. Of those, 463,105 are emigrants. The remaining 422,817 were born in space.

"You see, sir, what the sociohistorians have told us all along, is that emigration has never been a solution to large-scale or widespread population pressure. It can offer an escape valve for temporary, local overpop situations. But over large regions of territory and over long periods of time, people persist in breeding faster than they leave. The only historical answers to overpop have been massive plagues and massive famines. Even wars and natural disasters aren't enough to stop popgrow. I'm sorry."

Daniel looked sadly at the floor. "So the whole ZPG effort failed, also?"

"Right now," the Resident Manager began her reply. She paused and tapped a few more instructions into her desk. "Right now, total worldpop is—damn, I see we just passed another meterstone, twenty-six billion."

"Twenty six billion?"

"Actually, it comes to 26,001,396,428. Of course these figures have some fudge in them. We try for a world census and we know we miss a lot of people, double-count some, the census people deliberately introduce some fudge to try and adjust for their known errors, and then we try to keep births and deaths and emigration figures running through the mix. But I'd say that's pretty accurate. Twenty-six bill."

"Oh, my God."

There was a lengthy silence, broken at last by the Resident Manager. "May I ask, sir, what you'd like to do now? A tour of the zone? I'd be pleased to show you around myself. Or maybe you would prefer the company of Miss Haddad?"

Daniel caught a glimpse of Lydia's expression at that. "If you don't mind, I think I'd like to get back to my job," she said. "I've already missed several days of work."

"There will be no penalties assessed against Miss Haddad," Daniel said firmly.

The Resident Manager nodded, her face expressionless.

"And I'd like to have Miss Haddad assigned as my personal aide. If you don't mind, Lydia."

She hesitated, then shook her head.

"Fine."

Daniel stood up and walked around the office, his hands laced together behind his back. "I don't know. I don't know about this whole thing. Maybe I need a general briefing on the state of the world. A brushup course in modern history. Or just a session in the library looking at news vidis for the past eighty years."

"Easily done."

"All right. Let's make that the first order of business. I'll spend a day here, catching up on the company. Lydia, please, will you be my guide? Thank you. Then, I'll head back to San Francisco and do my homework. I don't suppose I could just go back to my old high school and pass for a transfer student." He grinned at the thought.

"I hope you won't need me up in the city," Lydia said. "I want to get back to my regular work."

"And your partner, eh?"

She nodded.

"Of course. I can understand that. But look, is your partner as intelligent and reliable a person as you are, Lydia? What a foolish question," he stopped himself. "What answer could I expect!"

The Resident Manager said, "I know Miss Haddad's partner, Mister Kitajima, and the answer to your question is definitely yes."

"All right, then." Dan folded his arms across his chest. "I'm going to have to build myself a staff. Suppose you both come up to the city. There's plenty of room in my suite, the two of you can have a room. Would that be all right?"

He directed the question at Lydia rather than at the Resident Manager. He saw Lydia flash a questioning glance at the Manager, get back a barely perceptible nod. She said, "Of course, Dan. We can move up tomorrow."

And that night Daniel Kitajima lay in bed watching abstract patterns move soothingly across the ceiling above his pillow. They were ordinary convection currents of warm air set up by the room's small heater, invisible to the human eye and certainly not part of anyone's plan. But to his infrared-sensitive vision they suggested the slow, steady beat of foam-crested waves against a still, rocky beach. The deliberate rhythm was as pleasant and soporific as that of waves would have been.

And Daniel lay, thinking calmly about his future. Once he had caught up on the missed decades of knowledge, once he had renewed his modest expertise in electronics and data systems—what would he do? He could return fully to business, devote himself to piling up additional wealth. But to what end? He could travel back to Islando or another of the planet's Elevator locations, and skitter back to the medical Island, or back to Hokkaido and live like a feudal Japanese lord. He could tour the—how many were there?—fifty-three functioning Islands that had been built, the twenty-seven more under construction. Or he could visit whatever planets had been colonized—if any had! He'd not even thought to ask that. With the development of space Islands, there seemed little if any reason to struggle for survival against the furnace of the Venusian environment or the arid frigidity of the Martian. Still— if there were even research stations, his money could almost surely gain him *entrée*. If he wanted to use his money for that.

But did he?

He was an ordinary man with ordinary talents and ambitions. To earn a decent living at work that was not too oppressive, to have a comfortable home, a hobby, a family. He knew that he was not a man of exceptional brilliance or talent or drive. And he did not *want* to be one!

That was the irony of all that had happened to him.

He *liked* being ordinary—or *had* liked it for the first thirty-odd years of his life. He would have been well contented to spend the rest of his years being equally ordinary, watching his children grow, his world change only at a reasonable and comprehensible pace, and his grandchildren come into the world, in the normal progression of generations—not encountering the horror of seeing his own daughter a senile crone and his grandson a gray-haired, middle-aged man while he himself was still young and strong.

But that unordinariness had been thrust upon him. He was both a superman and a freak, a misfit. He had exceptional physical powers and he knew that he would achieve exceptional mental ones as he learned to make use of his electronic implants. And he was vastly wealthy, and knew that his wealth would make him vastly influential in the world.

And he did not like that thought, either.

He fell asleep and dreamed of himself at the scene of the rape of Lydia Haddad, but this time he was not the rescuer but the rapist, and he felt himself dragged from his victim's body and thrown across the alleyway to smash headfirst into a brick wall and not die but awaken, shaking.

7

OSVALDO MGOUABE reached over his desk and delicately lifted a single rose from the arrangement of the flowers that gave the entire room its focus. The roses were arranged concentrically by shade, ranging from an almost-perfect black through deepest crimson and on to pink, yellow, and pure white.

The rose he removed carefully from the arrangement was a white one.

Daniel Kitajima watched from his chair—of astonishingly strong woven straw. The rose stood in brilliant contrast to Mgouabe's jet-black hands. Framed in a beam of brilliant African sunlight, the hands and the flower moved like three performers in an unaccompanied *pas de trois*.

Mgouabe turned the white rose, examined it carefully, trimmed away a single petal that had begun to turn yellow-brown. He discarded the petal, returned the rose to its position in the arrangement.

He smiled at Daniel and said, "I have you to thank for this, Mister Kitajima. Not all your wealth nor all your power could have got you in here to see me. I am far too busy and far too committed to my work to see anyone not directly connected with that work. But you, sir, are more than welcome, and will be at any time.

"You see, these are your doing."

He held his hands above the flower arrangement, palms toward himself, fingers extended upward, like a surgeon about to don sterile gloves.

"This arm," Mgouabe continued, "was utterly destroyed. It has been surgically replaced, up to here." He tipped his head, gesturing to his own right shoulder. "The other," he continued, "wasn't nearly as badly damaged. The flesh was ruined but they managed to save my bones and a little tendon. All the rest is restored with prosthetics. Prosthetics developed for you, Mister Kitajima, and furnished by your medics.

"So you see." He reached and touched a dark red rose near one edge of the arrangement. His touch was so delicate that just one petal was moved. "I was most pleased to honor your request for a meeting. I hope that my staff has been good to you, that the quarters we furnished are comfortable?"

Daniel nodded.

"And I understand, sir, that you traveled here with two companions. Your personal aides?"

"Yes."

"They were satisfactorily provided for?"

"They were indeed. Most pleased."

"Well, then, Mister Kitajima. I wonder just what it is that I can do for you."

"What you can do for me, Mister Mgouabe, is give me some information."

Mgouabe grinned broadly. "Of course. I don't know why you had to come to me for information. We're a public international body, sir, and our findings are freely available everywhere. I'd have thought you could just tap into any data-link to learn whatever you need. But as chief administrator of the International Geophysical Organization, I'll be very happy to answer your questions. Just what do you wish to know?"

Mgouabe reached behind him to an informal spray of roses and abstracted a black rose from it. He turned back, holding the flower carefully by its stem. "Do you know, if I prick myself on a thorn, I bleed? Such remarkable technology, and all of it to your credit, Mister Kitajima. Think of it! My own lifeblood, flowing through prosthetic vessels, my own skin— or is that a proper designation?—artificial skin, so sensitive that I can distinguish textures more finely than I did before my accident."

He held the rose delicately in one hand. With the other he carefully touched one fingertip to a thorn. He pressed the pad of his finger until the thorn pierced it, then pulled back. A drop of blood appeared.

"Yes, Mister Kitajima? What questions have you?"

"I'm not sure," Daniel said. "Since I got back to earth, I've had to deal with a lot of changes. Things that have accumulated over nearly a century. Things that you probably take for granted, that may have happened decades ago. Even before you were born."

"Such as?"

"California splitting in half, and the southern segment seceding from the United States and becoming part of Mexico."

"I didn't know about that."

"When were you born?"

Mgouabe smiled. "In 2054. Why?"

"Happened before your time. I suppose the world we're born into is the world we all take for granted. Anything that happened before that was part of the act of creation, whether it was two weeks before birth or back during the Big Bang."

Mgouabe delicately transferred the drop of blood from his fingertip to a petal of the rose he still held. The dark red drop was visible against the black petal, more by virtue of its higher reflectivity than by the difference in shade.

"Local politics don't interest me very much anyway," Mgouabe volunteered. "But I ask again, Mister Kitajima, and certainly with no intended implication that I'm trying to hurry you along, just what was it that you wished to ask me?"

"It's this change-of-climate business," Daniel said. "Everybody is so soothing about it, so calm and certain that it's a temporary thing. So reassuring. Nothing to worry about. Just keep cool—I'm sorry, I didn't intend that as a play on words—and things will get back to normal in a little while..."

Mgouabe nodded. "Quite so, quite so."

"I thought I'd do a little checking myself," Daniel said. "Back when I was a youngster, toward the end of the last century, there were still quite a few hard-copy reference facilities around. Libraries with microfilm newspaper files. Even a few that kept bound copies of the papers themselves. Real *paper* papers."

"Remarkable. But as you say, that was all before my time." Mgouabe lowered his face to inhale the fragrance of the black rose. Over it he studied Daniel.

"You can't do that any more," Daniel continued. "It's all stored electronically and accessed from data-links."

"Far more efficient. You see, there is true progress in the state of humanity. Is it not inspiring, Mister Kitajima?"

"I couldn't get the info I was after."

"My, my, what a surprise! What could you have been after? Certainly published information could hardly be anyone's secret."

"That's what I thought. That's why I checked carefully back at the company. Had my assistants check it out for me. I'd put in my call-sequence and it would get shunted aside. The wrong stuff would come back. World Series box scores for the year 2026. Music reviews of symphonies premiering in 2080. Election returns from the Chinese Peoples' Congress race of 2053. By some fluke I even got a readout of a news story on the accident that got me in 2009."

"Remarkable."

"Remarkable cow-pies, Mister Mgouabe!"

"Please call me Osvaldo."

"There's something rotten in the state of Denmark!"

Mgouabe sat up straight. "Denmark? What do I have to do with Denmark? Isn't that some little country up around the Greater Finnish Empire? Here!" He leaped to his feet, tossed the black rose onto the flower arrangement on his desk, where it lay against a white flower, smearing it with the still tacky drop of Mgouabe's blood; Mgouabe crossed the room to a huge terrestrial globe.

"Denmark? Isn't this Denmark?" He pointed.

"I've had enough of this game playing," Daniel shouted. He grasped the arms of his chair and pushed himself to his feet. The woven straw creaked beneath him, then gave way with a screeching, tearing sound.

"The info I was after was just weather reports for the past century. I wanted to graph them, compare them with past eras. See if I could figure out the curve on this temperature thing. See if I could project the cycle, see how hot it's going to get before it peaks, and when that's going to happen!"

"I see. I see." Mgouabe took several roses from the informal arrangement behind his desk. He arranged them carefully in his hands. One white, one yellow, one champagne. "And what did you learn, Daniel? I may use your Christian name?"

"I didn't learn a goddamned thing!"

"Oh. Perhaps your access codes were incorrect. Or you used an incorrect command structure. I understand that you were one of the leading computer systems designers of your time—"

"An exaggeration."

"In any case—" Mgouabe spread his hands, holding the yellow and champagne roses in one, the white in the other. "In any case, the systems are quite different today, I'm sure you'll agree."

"I used correct coding. Any child could use this command structure."

"Well. I certainly did not wish to upset you. I don't wish to quarrel with my benefactor." Mgouabe brought his hands back together, making an equilateral triangle of the flowers. "Does it really matter, anyway? Who cares whether they had a mild winter or a severe one some forty or fifty years ago? What difference does it make? Are you contemplating a new career as an historical vidiist?"

"I'll tell you what I think is going on," Daniel said. His voice was low. Mgouabe flashed a brief glance out the window of his office, then looked back at Daniel. "I think this whole line about temporary climatic changes and transient increases in solar activity is a lot of bullshit.

"It was abnormal solar activity that got me *this*." He smacked his torso with the open palm of his hand. The impact made a loud sound, distinctly nonorganic in quality.

"I think maybe the changes are permanent, and the people on this planet are going to have to get used to things as they are now. And you politicians and bureaucrats and technocrats and the rest of the gang running the show don't want to own up to it. You're afraid there would be an uproar, and you don't know how to deal with that, so you're pretending things will go back the way they belong. But they won't. And you're blocking access to the weather records that might give people a clue that the nice reassuring word from the vidi isn't quite the truth!"

Mgouabe laughed. He sat down behind his desk again, tapped a few codes into its receptor-top, and tossed the three roses he still held into a corner of the room. "This is very funny, Daniel. Oh, please don't try to leave. The door won't open, now."

Dan looked behind him at the door. He couldn't tell anything.

"And while I certainly admire your strength," Mgouabe continued, "I must ask you this. Please don't tear up any more of my furniture. That chair cost me a lot out of my very limited budget. But please be comfortable. Here . . ." He swung another chair from its place against the wall, slid it toward Daniel.

"I'm just as comfortable standing, thanks!"

"Of course. I forgot. This too, too weak flesh. Daniel, did you by any chance try to access the science columns of the past several score years, in your little research project? You could have got most of them, but there were a few you would have missed."

"That didn't happen."

"Ah, I suppose you just made no lucky hits, then. Or unlucky. But I can call up the ones you would not have reached. In fact, I would really like you to see these."

"I don't think I'm interested."

"I think you will be."

"What if I just walk out of here, Mgouabe?"

"Osvaldo. Please, Daniel. Osvaldo."

Daniel synthesized the sound of hawking phlegm and spitting it, making the appropriate gesture in the direction of Mgouabe's immaculate desktop flower arrangement.

"You can't 'just walk out' unless I unlock the door. On the other hand—forgive me if I anticipate—you could do to me what you did to my poor wicker chair, there. So I don't suppose I could really keep you here against your will, Daniel Kitajima.

"But let me put it this way. If you'll stay, voluntarily, and let me show you these old vidi clips, you'll learn a lot more than you would have from those weather reports you couldn't get. I promise it. For that matter, you can have the weather data, too. But it wouldn't prove that things are as bad as you'd suspected. Oh, no."

He lifted a bright yellow rose from the arrangement and held it to his face, brushing the soft petals delicately against the black, finely pockmarked flesh of his cheek.

"Oh, no," he said again. "Things are far worse than you

had suspected, Daniel. This world isn't going to stay as it is. Unless we can do something to alter nature's course, this planet is going to die, along with every living creature on it."

He held the yellow rose to his lips, inhaled its delicate fragrance, and closed his eyes with pleasure as an ecstatic expression crossed his face. "Do you know, Daniel," he murmured, "I think that the scent of the rose is the most lovely thing in all of creation. Do you agree? Can you think of a lovelier?"

THE vidipic filled one wall of Osvaldo Mgouabe's office. Mgouabe swung his chair around to face the pic wall; at the tap of a command sequence the desk sank into the floor of the room, leaving an open field of vision. Mgouabe asked Daniel Kitajima to sit down while they screened the vidis. "I'll feel more relaxed—I know you don't experience fatigue, Daniel, but it makes my bones tired to watch you standing so long."

Daniel sat, gingerly. The chair held him.

The first clip showed a vidi announcer in clothing that Daniel found familiar. Even the announcer's face was vaguely familiar in appearance. The announcer's expression was grim as she read the script from an offscreen cue-feed.

"An unusual burst of solar flares today knocked out communications and caused electrical upsets the world over. At the construction site of the LaGrange space Island, a crane used in moving huge wall plates malfunctioned, smashing a multi-ton plate into a crew of engineers programming a computer-guided telescope."

The visual cut from the announcer's face to a reasonably accurate animation of the Island construction site.

"That's—" Daniel said.

"Yes," Osvaldo completed.

"Huh! I don't know how you program a telescope."

The visual changed to an apparently live scene of a tarmac where ground crews rushed frantically to prepare an old-style space shuttle for lift-off.

"As many as thirty deaths may have resulted," the announcer went on. "Space agency authorities in contact with the crippled construction site say that one electrician working on computer wiring may have survived a direct impact by the heavy plate. A freak accident vacuum-froze the worker and his body is being held pending return to earth and slow-thaw therapy."

The newscaster's face filled the screen again as she continued to deliver her lines.

Mgouabe leaned over and tapped a code into the desktop panel. The wall monitor turned back to its previous appearance—that of rustic bamboo strips native to the region.

"Electrician!" Daniel laughed.

"Well, they had the general idea."

"So, that was the day I got squashed, eh? Frankly, I was a little scared to try and call that up. I finally did but the readouts I got didn't have anything on the accident. So I decided that it just wasn't regarded as news."

Mgouabe shook his head. "It is not that at all, Daniel. The event was a major story. We had to block access because of the solar flare aspect, you see."

"Not fully. What else do I get to see?"

Mgouabe ran a series of quick news items past. One in November, 2009 reported continued high levels of solar flare activity. It was played for humor—high numbers of complaints when a flare storm wiped out a vidi transmission at the climactic moment of a soap-opera episode, a sequence on a model aviation meet with radio-controlled miniatures buzzing their frantic owners. The weather segment of the same broadcast dealt with the long summer and mild autumn that the northern hemisphere had been experiencing, and the mild winter and early spring of the southern.

In April of 2027 there was dramatic footage of the forced evacuation of Cairo. The vidi went inside the city's largest synagogue for poignant closeups of aged bearded Jews weeping at the deconsecration of the Ark. Exterior shots showed crowds trudging through the city's narrow streets carrying their poor possessions in packs on their heads. Only the relatively wealthy could afford even hand-drawn wooden carts.

The newscaster contrasted the event with similar evacuations of Bagdad, Singapore, Jakarta, and Caracas. The emptying of Cairo had produced the greatest hardship because there was no viable land route away from the city. Only desert stretched west, south, or east. Aircraft carried the powerful and wealthy to cities in northern Europe. Tramp steamers carried the rest down the old Suez Canal, into the Red Sea, to refugee centers in southeastern Africa. Reluctant host nations set up armed perimeters around the camps with stern warnings of death without mercy for refugees trying to leave their encampments.

Daniel Kitajima cast an acidulous look at Mgouabe. "I see why you don't like people reviewing these vidis, Osvaldo. Where does it lead, though? You're not just showing me these to depress my spirit, I'm sure. But they're having that effect."

Mgouabe heaved a heavy sigh. He stood over the informal flower arrangement near the wall. "It isn't caprice, I assure you." He squatted and held his face just above the roses. With both hands he pressed the arrangement inward, concentrating the flowers beneath his nose, and inhaled gratefully.

"No, not just caprice. You wanted to know where the solar changes and climactic warming were headed, Daniel. Surely you're able to draw those curves you spoke of, now. Where do you think we're headed?"

"I don't think it's going to get any better." He stood up and walked to a window, looking out over the northern tip of Lake Njasa. The gleaming white buildings of Lilongwe curved around the shores of the lake. It was a beautiful sight. The refugee encampments beyond the city proper had long since lost their air of temporary existence. They had hardened into hill slums reminiscent of the *favelas* above Rio de Janeiro.

"At least they get a pretty view," Daniel said.

"Eh?"

"The poor souls up there." Daniel pointed.

Mgouabe dismissed the slums and their occupants with a subdued grunt. "You're right, Daniel, I regret to say. And the petty problems of this or that residential group here on earth pale in comparison with the cataclysm that is coming."

"How bad?" Daniel asked. He suspected that he knew, but a forlorn hope that he might be wrong impelled him to seek confirmation.

"That bad," Mgouabe smiled bitterly. He held a rose before his eyes and studied it. "Essentially, we're expecting the end of life on this planet. Your own meteorologists in the United States were the first to project the trends and predict the outcome. The findings were discounted as sensationalistic ravings.

Fortunately, by the time the scientific community was ready to accept the truth, we had co-opted its most influential members.

"Even so . . ." He shook his head.

"What about emigration? What about colonizing the more remote planets? Or building more Islands and moving there? If necessary, moving the Islands way, *way* out?"

"Is that question intended seriously?"

"No." Daniel turned back from the window. "I know better. What's the population now, twenty-six billion?"

"Close enough."

"There's no way, then."

"No. No way to evacuate twenty-six billion people, or even any sizable portion of them. We might try to get away an elite group, but that would have to be done in secret. It would have to be a perfect conspiracy. Otherwise—can you imagine the riots?"

"I think I saw an old tape of a story about that."

"It must have been a long time ago. That tape has been withdrawn. Nobody sees it any more. Too close for comfort, as I believe you say in your country."

Daniel sat down heavily, planting his iron arse and feet on Mgouabe's carpeted floor and drawing his knees up, clasping his arms around them, leaning one cheek against his knee.

"Ah, bitter despair, eh, Daniel? Well, but things are not hopeless."

Daniel looked up.

"I didn't drag you—lure you—all the way to Zambio just to cause you distress. There are a number of things in the works, that may offer some hope for humanity. Cheer up, friend! Look at this vidipic." He sat near Daniel, reached to his control panel and punched a code sequence.

The news item was a drab bureaucratic handout of bigwigs making speeches and throwing ceremonial switches but the event was more interesting than the coverage. It was July, 2030, and the space island Tereshkova was the site. Tereshkova was the first full-scale astronomical observatory built entirely in space. It was positioned in the plane of the elliptic in the orbit of Jupiter, trailing the Jovian family by ninety degrees and moving at the same rate as Jupiter. It circled the sun once in just under twelve years.

Almost at once, Tereshkova made news. Even as the Island's instruments were being tuned, radio signals were detected from a source forty degrees out of the plane of the elliptic. The question of deciphering a message was treated as co-equal in importance with that of identifying the source. A source identified as the star Menkar in Cetus was the first suspected source. It was not even known whether it was a natural body or a machine placed in its strange orbit by parties unknown.

Finally a Czech astronomer working in Tereshkova suggested a source orbiting Sol, but doing so out of the plane of the elliptic.

She proved to be correct.

The radio source was an object in orbit around the sun at a distance of roughly ten billion kilometers, double that of Neptune. The object's orbit was tilted a full ninety degrees from the elliptic, and it was moving far too fast. It would circle the sun once in six hundred years, cutting the plane of the elliptic every three hundred years.

By August of 2030 radio astronomers on earth and in other Islands confirmed the work that had been done at Tereshkova. There was as yet no physical description of the transmission source. It was not even known whether it was a natural body or a machine placed in its strange orbit by parties unknown.

The latter theory led to the growth of cults who attributed the transmission to Atlanteans, to ancient alien astronauts, to Jesus. None of the cults got very far.

"Who was it?" Dan asked.

"Eh?"

"Was it people from Atlantis? Aliens? Jesus?"

"Oh, oh, of course." Mgouabe tapped controls again. Once more the room resumed its bright appearance. "What do you say, I'd like to get a little grub now. You don't eat, do you? Would you mind, though? I could order up a snack, but it would be more pleasant, I think, in the executive dining room."

"First I want my answer."

"Oh, all right, as you wish." He tapped a control and his desk rose to its normal position. "Someone will come in and replace that chair you dispatched, Daniel. We can walk to the dining room.

"No, I have no idea who sent the messages from Zimarzla. I think I would have put my money on Atlantis if I'd been around at the time. Of course, I wasn't. But I suppose I'm a romantic at heart."

He put his arm around Daniel's shoulders and guided him through plush corridors. The executive dining room was fitted like an exclusive club of a century before. The air was chilled— that alone had to cost a fortune, Dan thought—and a fire blazed beneath an ornate mantel. The floor was thickly carpeted, the walls were darkly paneled and hung with gilt-framed canvasses, the tablecloths were immaculate linen.

"I would hope that you could enjoy the atmosphere, at least," Mgouabe said. "The feel of fine things, the scent of woodsmoke and old wine. But I am a romantic, as I said."

"I have no sense of smell," Daniel said.

Mgouabe showed surprise. He changed the subject. "The astronomer who found the radio source—I did mention that she was a Czech, did I not? Wonderful people, the Czechs. Such a subtle and sophisticated people, perhaps a trifle decadent, even, but then, that adds a touch of the attractive *petit péché*, the little sin."

He signaled a waiter in traditional livery plus Arab tarboosh. The waiter salaamed. Mgouabe ordered goose-liver *pâté*, a fresh *szekely* goulash, and *gewurztraminer*. The waiter scurried away.

"Now," Mgouabe resumed. "A pity you don't have any sense of smell or taste. It was gauche of me to mention the scent of roses. Still, we have an excellent chef here, and the cellar is quite adequate, within its limitations."

"We were talking about those radio transmissions," Daniel reminded him.

"Of course. Well, the precise nature of the source was not identified at the time, but the astronomer who had made the discovery thought it most likely a planet. That notion set off all sorts of controversies. What was a planet doing in that strange orbit? Was it an extraterrestrial wanderer that had been captured at some remote past time? The odds against that were— pardon my play on words—astronomical."

He paused to spread a dab of *pâté* on a bit of hard-crusted bread and to eat it slowly.

"But for the planet to be a natural part of our own family of worlds seemed even more absurd. The whole notion of stellar and planetary formation, of course, depends so heavily on the idea of rotational motion. Fantastic! But then—how could a planet get into that orbit? Perhaps the Atlanteans did it. What do you think?"

"I'm no astronomer." Daniel frowned.

"Well, the lady who had found the planet or whatever-it-was decided to name it as a planet. Conditionally, don't you see, like a priest baptizing a miscarried fetus. Of course that involves all sorts of doctrinal oddities, does it not? Why should the soul of a miscarried fetus need absolution for its sins, eh? What kind of sinning can an unborn child do?"

He took some more *pâté,* placed it in a makeshift cup formed from a bit of lettuce and popped it into his mouth. The waiter arrived with the *gewurtztraminer* and Mgouabe sampled the wine and approved it. To Kitajima he said, "We're very informal here at IGO. I hope the absence of the sommelier does not offend you. We try to dispense with his direct participation except at the dinner hour. Budget, you know. Always budget, budget, budget! Well." He toasted Daniel.

"I'm afraid you wandered a little," Daniel said.

"Eh?" Mgouabe halted with his hand halfway to his mouth.

"Somewhere between theories of Atlantis and the doctrine of original sin. I think you were talking about a Czechoslovakian astronomer."

"Oh, yes. Of course." Mgouabe popped the morsel of *pâté* into his mouth and gulped it down with a swallow of wine. "Of course. Well, she decided to name the radio source conditionally as a planet. I have always loved the selection of the name." He grinned.

"It was?"

"Zimarzla."

Daniel waited for an explanation.

"A Slavic deity. Her epithet is 'the frozen goddess.' She used to have full charge of winter weather in Russia. Her attributes included, as I recall, breath of ice, clothes of hoarfrost, a mantle of snow and a crown of hailstones." He laughed loudly.

Daniel waited for Mgouabe's laughter to subside. "Yes. I see. And did we ever find out what this Zimarzla was? Is it a planet? Were the transmissions ever decoded? Did you figure out how it got into that remarkable orbit?"

"Well, we've had almost sixty years to work on the problem. I think we've made a certain amount of progress."

"In secret."

"Yes, in secret."

"You don't trust the ordinary folk very much, do you, Osvaldo?"

Mgouabe adopted a serious mien. "Please don't forget, Daniel, that you are in effect a time traveler from a simpler and a happier age. Certainly from a less crowded one. What do you think would happen if we announced to twenty-six billion people, most of them living in conditions of almost unbearable crowding, enforced idleness, and on the most minimal of diets—ah, but just a moment."

"Ah, here's my *szekely.*" The waiter placed the steaming dish before him. "To all the Czechs," Mgouabe toasted, "and to all their inventions and discoveries, of which Zimarzla and *szekely* compete for the honor of being the greatest!" He mouthed a forkload of steaming pork stew and followed it with a sip of *gewurztztraminer*. "Thank the fates for air conditioning," he added. "Without it, such a meal would be unpalatable here in Zambio."

Daniel pursed his lips in impatience.

"I digress," Mgouabe said. "My apologies. Well, if we told the populace—already existing under conditions of rather severe privation, don't you agree?—that the world was going to end in another century or so, that between now and then conditions will be slowly but steadily worsening—"

He speared a dumpling with his fork and popped it into his mouth, smiling appreciatively and murmuring, "Superb, superb."

"Well, you must see that the result would be catastrophic. We have to keep things going, as best we can, for as long as we can."

Daniel said, "Why?"

"Why? Why? My dear friend and benefactor, simply because—you'll pardon my switch on the classic response—because we're here!"

"Hmph. Not with a bang, eh?"

Mgouabe lifted a forkload of hot red cabbage to his mouth,

then blotted delicately at his lips with a linen napkin. It came away marked with a small red stain of cabbage juice. "I think that would really suffice for a reason. If we are to die, we might as well do so in as civilized a manner as possible. Why rob the last generations of *homo sap. sap.* of their turn on the carousel, eh? Why smash it all up before we have to?"

"Will the Islands survive?"

"Probably. The increase in solar emissions seems to be very gradual. One Island, in fact, set out for Centauri some years ago. More are considering trying for other suns. But this star," he jerked a thumb vaguely toward the ceiling of the dining room, "should provide a good living for humanity in Islands. And there are a few planetary bases, really just outposts, of course. But they are so set up to survive terrible conditions anyway, they may well survive the increase in solar activity. It isn't getting very much hotter, you see. Not really, on the cosmic scale."

He smiled and sipped wine.

"Just enough to make earth unlivable."

FROM the dining room they left the building instead of returning to Mgouabe's office. The afternoon sun was huge and Mgouabe and Kitajima both donned broad-brimmed white panamas and linen ponchos. They strolled on gleaming white sand, flanked by gleaming white buildings and the blue of Lake Njasa.

"I don't really need these," Dan said. "This body of mine has a damned good homeostatic temperature control."

"Yes, but we don't want to look strange."

Daniel scuffed the sand with one shoe. "I find it hard to accept, Osvaldo. That things are as bad as you say. Just look around." He stopped and gestured. "I'd say this is closer to utopia than to purgatory."

"Yes, yes. Ecclesiastical imagery. Isn't it strange how God and all the old Bible-walloping habits keep coming to the surface, even among us enlightened men, even in the days of the approaching apocalypse.

"Well, I assure you, things are as bad as I painted them, and maybe a little worse. The IGO is kept going at almost any cost, and with almost any privilege. We're the last hope, you see. Emigration just won't do it, we've been over that till our ears rang and our eyes went blurry, but the numbers won't go away. Mass evacuation is simply impossible. But maybe IGO can find a way out. That's what the world politicos hope. So we get to work in our happy little utopia here."

"All right." Dan halted at the water's edge. Out on the lake huge sea-farming platforms stood like metal giants rising to stalk the earth. "What *are* you doing? Is this Zimarzla an answer? Have you done anything about—" He shrugged; for the moment, words failed him.

"I know what you mean," Mgouabe supplied. "The first time it hits you, really hits you, it's overwhelming, isn't it?"

Daniel grunted.

"First," Mgouabe said, "let me tell you that Zimarzla is indeed a planet. Some planet! It's larger than Jupiter by a sizable amount. If it were any larger, the astrophysics people tell me, it would have ignited. By a sort of cosmic spontaneous combustion. It would have become a second sun and we would have found ourselves living in a binary system."

"Huh!" Daniel turned his face to the afternoon sky, as if he expected to perceive that remote second sun blossom into life there in the brilliant African December. "And the planet was the mysterious radio source, Osvaldo? Were the signals natural phenomena? Or were there Zimarzlans with tentacles and claws waiting to invite juicy earthlings up for long pig fricassee?"

"That we don't know yet. Even after all these years. Do you know anything of the history of astronomy, astrophysics, radio astronomy, Daniel? No? Did you know that when cosmic radiation was first detected—before your birth, even, no less mine—it was believed that cosmic rays were the work of alien intelligence? People sat down seriously and worked for years trying to decode the messages, before they realized the radiation was a natural phenomenon.

"No." He shook his head and the shadow of his broad-brimmed hat swung back and forth across his linen poncho. "No, we don't know even now whether the Zimarzlan transmissions are messages from aliens, or just Mother Nature teasing us once again. As she did with the so-called cosmic rays. Isn't that a marvelous term, though? Sounds like something out of Man Ray."

"But surely you were able to find out what Zimarzla was. The source itself. Was it really another planet?"

"Oh, yes indeed! Once Tereshkova had got some other observatories to triangulate on Zimarzla, they just pointed their scopes and there it was! In fact, it became an object of such curiosity that your country and several others sent probes to investigate it. That was before IGO had come into its own, of course."

"And they found a planet."

Mgouabe laughed. "They found a lot more than a planet! Look here, Daniel. Black man take stick and make picture for strange visitor!"

He squatted on the beach, pulled a stylus from his garment and sketched a diagram in the sand. It was the familiar stylized representation of the solar system, its scale squashed down to make it manageable. But circling the sun at twice the distance of any other planet, and at right angles to the plane of the elliptic, Mgouabe placed a huge body, larger even than Jupiter and nearly as large as the sun itself. It was ringed like the gas-giant planets of traditional astronomy; it had an even larger and more complex family of satellites—moons?—possessed rings and satellites of their own.

"That's only an approximation," Mgouabe said.

"Holy moley," Daniel muttered. "You weren't kidding, it's more than just another planet! That looks as if—hold on! What are you doing?"

Mgouabe was scraping his diagram away with the toe of one shoe. To Daniel he said, "Security. Even here in Lilongwe we have to observe the rules. After all, what if there's a nasty spy hiding behind a palm tree, mini-camera in hand, ready to scurry out here and copy this sensitive document the moment we stroll away?"

He finished his scraping, then took Daniel by the elbow and guided him back toward the IGO office building.

Daniel let Mgouabe direct his steps. His head buzzed with new ideas and unanswered questions. Why had Zimarzla gone undetected for so long? Even at its remote distance, it made Sol into, effectively, a light-dark double star system. Zimarzla's gravity alone should have given Sol a wobble that astronomers could have detected centuries ago. Why hadn't it?

He guessed at one answer to his own question: the tug of Jupiter and other masses circling in the plane of the elliptic had had a gyroscopic effect, stabilizing Sol's movement against the tug of Zimarzla.

Why was Zimarzla a dark body? And even though it was dark, was it entirely inert? Certainly Jupiter wasn't, Jupiter which was the closest analog of Zimarzla known to classical astronomers. Had Zimarzla ever been more active than it presently was? Had it ever given enough heat and light to support life on its satellites? Its—planets seemed a more apt term for them than moons.

Were there Zimarzlans? In all the history of space exploration, whether by optical telescope, radiation telescopy, crewed travel or automated probes, there had never been a shred of the illusive aliens that popular storytellers loved so dearly. No tentacled Martians nor satanic Overlords nor bubble-gum pink Chickladorians nor any of the other endlessly varied creatures sprung from fertile human brains.

But maybe there were Zimarzlans! Were—or once had been.

8

DANIEL KITAJIMA stood before his own front door, ignoring both the old-style annunciator and the new electronic sensor grid. He knocked.

There was a pause during which he thought there might be no response, but before he was ready to let himself in the door swung open. Lydia Haddad stood in the replica of his long-ago foyer and grinned at him. "Dan! We thought you'd never show up! We've been having a great time here, but we figured you'd got involved with IGO and forgot all about us."

"No chance of that." He smiled back at her, stepped into the replica foyer and shut the door behind him. For a moment it was as if he had succeeded in stepping back those eighty years, that he was returning to his home from a routine day of work down in Palo Alto rather than having skittered in from Lake Njasa.

An old reflex snapped into place and he reached to give the woman a brief embrace. Even as he raised his hands and lowered his face toward hers he realized the *faux pas* he had committed and tried to draw away, but she stepped within the reach of his arms and turned her own face toward his.

"It's all right," Lydia whispered. "Really, it's all right."

He held her against him, squeezing his eyes shut and doing all he could to hold his consciousness away from intellectualization. He struggled for pure sensation and pure emotion: the feelings, the tactile and what passed in his mostly-machine body for endocrine realizations of the moment, with no analysis, no interpretation, and, God help him, no anticipation.

Lydia said, "That's fine, Dan. Really it is. I like it."

He opened his eyes, returning to the present, losing that timeless moment and reentering the stream of ever-moving time and ever-changing reality. His surroundings were those of 2009 but the world had not stood still, it was the world of 2089; no, he realized with a tiny shock, it wasn't even 2089 any longer, the new year had come and it was now January of the year 2090. In another decade the calendars would click over to the new century, the twenty-second century, in all likelihood the final century in the history of life on earth.

If the Islanders survived, and it seemed entirely reasonable to believe that they would, at least most of them, they might in later eras return to earth, visit the now sterilized cradle of life. They might erect, somewhere, a great, final memorial obelisk with some message on it, some suitable epitaph for a world:

On this planet there arose life in uncounted species, and one of those species, homo sapiens sapiente, *escaped the death of the world, bringing for companionship a few other lucky survivors to find eternal life among the stars. Earth, RIP. Amen.*

"Is Tovah—" Daniel started to ask.

"Oh, she won't mind," Lydia interrupted. "What kind of narrow-minded people do you think we are?"

Daniel blinked and shook his head. That wasn't what he had had in mind. He wasn't worried about Tovah Decertes's jealousy at her partner's embracing him. He was hammered emotionally by his recurring problem: that his flesh was not flesh, it was metal and plastic, his blood was oil, his nerves superconducting electronic circuits, his memory encoded bubbles, his heart a wankel rotary pump and his sexual equipment an ultra-advanced erector set.

Lydia knew that now, not in detail but in its broad reality. Her partner Tovah knew it, too. And when one of these women said to him, said to his embrace, "It's all right, really, it's all right," she was throwing the problem back to him. It was no favor. A quick and passionless rejection would have laid the question once and for all: it would have meant we will be friends, but not family, surely never lovers.

But what did "It's all right, really, it's all right" mean in the end?

Daniel walked through the recreated house. Decertes was in the kitchen. It was her turn to prepare food, and the atmosphere of the kitchen lent coloring to her normally pallid, neutral appearance. Her hair was a rust color; she wore it cropped close to her skull and curled in tiny ringlets. Her eyes were a transparent shade, nearly as neutral as her skin; a faint suggestion of green was the closest they came to pigmentation. Her figure was generous to the borderline of excess.

She looked up from her work as Daniel stepped into the kitchen. "Well, it's the lord of the manor. Come to sample the kitchen's wares? Soufflé, salad, beer? We never lived like this in the zone!"

Daniel said, "I'd love a beer. I wish I could drink one."

"Well, here's to ya!" Tovah opened a Kirin and downed a swig. "I've been working on those conversion circuits your specs call for," she said.

"What do you think?"

"Looks easy." Tovah lifted a heavy knife and a head of iceberg lettuce. She laid out the lettuce on a cutting board and began slicing. "You have any idea what most people would pay for a single leaf of this stuff?"

Daniel shook his head.

"Or what you could get from an antique dealer for a knife like this, or for this cutting board? A family could live for ten years on what this cutting board would bring. And the fridge—" She pointed. "You could live like a sports headliner on what that would bring!"

"We don't need the money."

"No. That I understand, Dan. If by *we* you're speaking in the royal plural."

"I'm not."

"Well, you'd better take another look around, then. Lydia and I are still wage-slaves, you know. It's a labor-surplus economy, in case you hadn't been brought up to date, and anybody who steps out of line can get chopped off before she had a chance to dodge back into place."

Daniel started to reply, but before he had a chance, Tovah added, "By the way, there was a lady here today from the police. I've never seen anything like it. She actually apologized for intruding and asked if you'd call her when you had a chance."

"She must have been investigating that assault on Lydia."

Tovah faced Dan, her hands balled on her hips, the heavy knife still clutched in one fist. "Of course she was investigating the assault on Lydia. If you weren't who you are, they'd just have sent a squad around to drag you in. The cops don't operate the way this broad did."

She turned back to the cutting board and resumed work on the salad.

"Did she—say why they were checking again?"

"Yeah. That bitch finally cashed it in. Good riddance! How do you feel about paying her hospital bills?"

"You mean there's no court procedure? No criminal case?"

"Are you kidding? Who's going to bring the charge? And what charge, anyhow? Oh—you and Lydia might both have to pay a fine for curfew violation, that's all. Listen, this is about ready." She stowed the salad in the refrigerator. "Let's relax a little before we eat. Lydia's in the living room already with a beer."

Tovah draped her apron over the refrigerator handle and preceded Daniel into the living room. She sat heavily on the couch beside Lydia, putting her beer on the low table that stood before the couch. She laid one arm across Lydia's shoulders and nodded to Daniel. It was as if the gesture signaled the opening of a new conversation, unrelated to the one they had just held.

"Okay, we're sure as hell earning our salaries. The hardware they shipped up from the zone is all set up and running now. A good console with general channel links and a wireless couple to the company's central tech comp center.

"What you're going to need, I'm pretty sure, can be accomplished best with a single all-purpose conversion rig. There's always a temptation to try and build special-purpose circuits for this kind of work, but you wind up with more bells and whistles and patches than Robbie the Robot."

"So?"

"I think I can design it. I know Lydia can build it—at least a breadboard model. We got enough hardware shipped up from the zone for that. We can gen up the coding, build in the micros or put 'em in on read-only stores, and furnish you with a set of macros to activate the little buggers and send 'em scurrying down the right pathways. I think it will be a terrific sys, no jape."

"No, huh? Well, I'm glad to hear that. What do you think, Lydia? Can you build it?"

"Just a breadboard."

"That's enough."

"Then there's nothing to worry about. We can do it for sure." She snuggled into Tovah's side.

"Well, I'm not quite as sanguine about this as you two," Dan said. He stood up and paced to the window, drew back the drapery in his familiar fashion and looked down into Steiner Street. "This isn't supposed to go into some comp center somewhere. I want it built into me." He patted his torso and grinned self-consciously. "There isn't that much spare room in here. We'll have to flit up to med Island and see how good a job they can do of miniaturizing and toughening the hardware."

"I wouldn't worry about that. They're—oh, damn!" The timer sounded from the kitchen. "You two go ahead and sit down, I'll bring in the soufflé."

Daniel sat with Tovah and Lydia during dinner, trying to act as he would have in the old days, had he dropped in on friends who were about to eat an informal meal when he had himself already had his dinner.

After the salad was eaten, Tovah left the table to bring the soufflé from the kitchen. Lydia put her hand on Dan's arm and spoke in a low voice. "I don't really understand, even yet. What did this Osvaldo Mgouabe *want* from you?"

"He's planning a big expedition and he wants me along. Gave me a big recruiting type pep talk. Implied that I'd be running the whole show but I found a lot of loopholes and calculated vagueness in his plan. What I really think is that he wants an iron man along to handle dangerous chores that might fall beyond the limits of mortal flesh."

"Such as what?"

"You remember the old Adam Link vidipic?"

She shook her head. Daniel heard Tovah clattering in the kitchen, saw Lydia turn her face to see if Tovah was returning yet. "I don't," she said.

"Huh. Before your time. Link was a—" He was cut off by the pressure of her hand on his wrist. Lydia jerked her face almost imperceptibly toward the kitchen. Tovah was advancing, her bulk nearly filling the doorway, the steaming soufflé in a hot tureen to which she held the handles in padded holders.

Tovah put the hot food on the table, seated herself and began to divide it between her own dinner plate and Lydia's. "They'll never believe this in the zone," she remarked. "Real vegetables and actual animal cheese, and eaten off actual crockery dishes with metal implements! I doubt that the Resident Manager herself can eat like this!"

Daniel shook his head.

Tovah laughed. "You know what you are, Dan? You're a time-traveler. You're an alien. But instead of being from another planet you're from another time."

"I think you're right," he agreed sadly. "Look, how long do you think this work will take? This converter that you're both working on for me?"

"You asking officially or unofficially?"

"What difference does it make?"

"Hah! You aren't *that* much of an alien, are you? Look here, Dan. Lydia and I get to live in this old-style house. We sleep in a double bed with real cloth sheets and an actual animal-wool blanket. We get to eat food that nobody but an athlete or a top-grade bureaucrat can afford. I don't think you really understand life in the zones, nowadays. And the people in the zones are the lucky ones. Places like *this"*—her gesture took in the replica house and the hotel it surmounted— "are the equivalent of old-style imperial palaces."

She swung her chair in a semicircle so she could gesture comfortably toward the window. "The people out there are struggling to survive in crowding you wouldn't believe, on food doles that you wouldn't *want* to believe. And even they are lucky to be here. If they were in some countries, they'd probably survive just long enough to produce a flock of scabrous babies they couldn't feed or support, and then they'd die."

She turned back to the table and took a forkful of hot food.

Daniel looked from Tovah to Lydia. Lydia had grown pale and sat with her hands in her lap.

"I don't see what this all has to do with my question," Dan said. "Or with whether it's official or unofficial."

"All right," Tovah inflated her cheeks, looking exasperated. "I'll show it to you in takes of one frame, Daniel. We are living better—Lydia and I—than we ever have in our lives. We were born to this world, not to your golden age of animal protein every week and life expectancy of half a century or even more for everybody.

"We were born to *this* world, and we clawed or cringed our way into a zone where we know we'll have two square meals a day and medics when we need 'em, and if we keep out of trouble and do our work six days a week we'll keep our jobs and our cubicle. As citizens of this glorious era go, we were well above the median and happy to stay that way.

"Then along you come and save Lydia here from a couple of sadistic loonies—that's all I could ever figure out, they didn't seem to have anything else in mind, from what Lyd told me about 'em. And then you took a shine to her and plucked *her* out of the zone and set her up in a style of living beyond her wildest dreams."

Dan looked at Lydia. She was listening to Tovah's speech, her expression absolutely neutral.

"And as a kind of fringe benefit," Tovah continued, "because we're partners and because Lyd asked you to, you saw to it that I got subbed into the deal also. For which, kindly master, please do not for one instant doubt my unmeasured gratitude."

Her bow added to the bitterness of her speech.

"So you ask me how soon we're going to finish this job you've got us doing. What happens when we finish? Do you skitter back to your private med Island and play around with the prosthetics gang for a while? Or do you opt for Hokkaido Island, your high and glorious lordship? And play samurai-and-portugees with your toy swords and your geisha girls waiting to put you to bed when you come home all tired out and sleepy."

She jabbed her fork at her dish so hard that the dish skidded off the table and fell to the floor. It landed on its edge and cracked. Tovah dropped the fork on the tablecloth and put her hands to her mouth. She drew a sudden breath and sat staring at the two pieces of her plate on the floor.

Daniel started to pick up the fragments, scraping the spilled soufflé with the edge of one onto the flat surface of the other. Two dark-complexioned hands joined his, helping him with the job. He looked into Lydia's eyes, then turned his attention back to cleaning up the spilled food.

"I'll go start packing," he heard Tovah's voice. "That wasn't Lyd's fault at all. It was my fault." She slid her chair from the table and stood up.

"Wait a minute!" Dan stood, drew Lydia to her feet also. He carried the broken dish to the kitchen and dropped it into a waste receptacle, then returned to the dining room.

"Look, you're upset, Tovah. You broke a dish. So what?"

"So what?" Her always pale complexion was now deathly white. "Do you have any idea what that plate was worth? Wait, let me get the pieces back out of the waste. They can be bonded together. The plate won't be worth as much, but it still—"

"Now stop!" Daniel shouted. "God damn it, Tovah, it's a stupid piece of chinaware. You're acting crazy, making all of this fuss about it. I'm sorry you're so upset. But we can talk—"

"Even repaired," she cut back in, "it's worth more than I earn in a year! Didn't you understand what I told you? You're an alien in this world, as alien as a Martian or a Neanderthal. You don't understand this world. You don't know what anything's worth."

"And *you* don't understand where this world is headed! I'm sorry. This is supposed to be super-hushed material but you'll just have to use your judgment. This so-called temporary change in the climate isn't temporary. It isn't going to get any better and it isn't even going to stabilize until this planet is rendered uninhabitable. The people in the Islands can survive, probably will survive, because the heating-up seems to be gradual, and they can just slowly pull back until they're at a safe distance from the sun. But the earth is going to cook, and anybody left on it alive is going to cook. But there will probably be nobody left alive by then."

There was a lengthy silence in which Daniel walked to the window and looked out into the street. In the window he could see Lydia still seated at the table, her head bowed and her hands in her lap. Tovah stood behind her chair, one hand resting on Lydia's shoulder as if to comfort her. Her other hand was raised to her brow.

Tovah turned toward Daniel. In the window he could see the movement of her lips as she spoke a single word. "When?"

Daniel turned to face her. "Not right away. It will be very gradual. If this planet had a small population and a great industrial plant, we might conceivably build enough ships and Islands to get a sizable proportion of the people away in time. As it is . . ." He shook his head slowly.

"When?" Tovah asked again. "You can do better than 'not right away,' Daniel. When?"

He rubbed his face, four fingers on one cheek and his thumb on the other, rubbing his artificial flesh against the prosthetic materials of his artificial teeth and jaw. He even had a new, flexible tongue in his mouth—for all the good it did him. Between his ability to synthesize sounds, and his regained skill in using his mouth, teeth and tongue as an infinitely variable sound chamber, he had a far greater vocal range now than he had had in his original body.

Maybe, he thought, I should give away all my unearned fortune. Become a traveling troubador. The one-man band *par excellence*. He could gen up drums, organs, whole choruses of singers, banks of fiddles and ranks of horns, all the while performing amazing feats of strength and endurance courtesy Doctors Royce and Kimura and the entire staff of his personal medical Island.

If there are still any tourists at Fisherman's Wharf—if there's still any Fisherman's Wharf—I could head over there bright and early in the morning and pick up enough change to pay for my lunch, Daniel thought. Especially since I don't eat lunch any more.

That would show Osvaldo Mgouabe and his scurrying servants.

Tovah Decertes made a loud throat-clearing sound, an almost vocalized "Ahem." She shot her question at Daniel with her eyes.

Jerked back to reality, he put one hand on the table edge. "I'm sorry. Just wool-gathering for a moment. Does anybody say that any more? No? Well, my attention wandered, let's leave it at that."

"For God's sake, Dan, you've just told us that the world is going to end." Tovah pounded her fist once, striking the wooden table near Daniel's extended fingers. "When is it going to happen?"

"I don't know, exactly." He shook his head. "Just by running out the curves, things shouldn't get really sticky until about the last quarter of the next century. I mean, not that it's so great now, what with the Sahara growing at the rate that it is and the tropic regions getting the roasting they have been. But new regions are opening up, too. Greenland, Siberia, Baffin, Victoria, Sakhalin, Kamchatka. And we've hardly touched the Antarctic! Once that opens—"

"Stop!"

"Eh?"

"For Christ's sake, Dan, I didn't ask for a lecture."

"But you asked—"

"When is the shit *really* going to hit the fan?"

"Oh. Well, as I said—we're actually gaining usable land a little faster than we're losing it, according to Osvaldo Mgouabe. But that won't go on much longer. He anticipates equilibrium in about sixty years, then twenty or thirty years of approximately stable conditions. And then—and then, all downhill from there."

"All right."

"What—but I don't understand—" Daniel showed his puzzlement at the whole line of conversation.

"You wanted to know how long it would take Lyd and me to get these conversion circuits designed and a breadboard built, and the programming done."

"Yes."

"Then you listen to me." She struck the table top with the blunt tip of her forefinger, emphasizing each word with a thud. "We don't give a flying fuck, mister."

"What?" Daniel stared from Tovah to Lydia, then back at the heavyset, pale-complexioned Tovah. "Are you serious?"

"You bet I'm serious. I care about my partner and me. The world is going to end in a hundred years, give or take a few decades? We'll both be dead and gone long before that. What's going to happen in an hour, is what I care about. Will I get laid tonight? Will there be anything in the fridge for my breakfast tomorrow? How long can I stay in this palace, or do I have to move back to the zone? What's going to happen to me and Lydia in twenty or thirty years, when we're getting too old to work and the company flings us away? Can we stay in the zone, or do we wind up out there"—she jerked a thumb toward the window—"with the rest of the dregs and the losers?"

She reached across the table and took one of Lydia's hands in her own, holding it with a combination of desperation and protectiveness.

A tear rolled from Tovah's eye. She scrubbed it away angrily with her free hand, pushed herself up from the table and started to clear the meal. "I've got work to do," she growled.

Lydia followed her from the table, carrying a glass in one hand and a dish in the other. Daniel rose, resisted an impulse to follow them both into the kitchen and try to continue the conversation. But he decided that it was hopeless at the moment. He could only worsen the harm that had already been done. He strode to the console that had been installed at his direction and sat down before the control panel.

He called up an elementary tutorial on data-processing systems architecture and worked on bringing his ancient and hopelessly obsolete expertise—never really that sharp to begin with—up to somewhere near the level of the year 2090. The biggest problem was not that the newer technology was much more complex than that he had been used to. If anything, it was simpler, marvelously elegant, but its simple elegance embodied all of the advances of eight decades of progress, and even the most elementary tutorials seemed to assume familiarity with concepts that Daniel found alternately exciting, shocking, or simply baffling.

After an hour of heavily concentrated effort, Daniel wiped the tutorial and called up deep-stored tape of the San Francisco Seals playing in the World Series of 2006. He stopped the vidi on a camera pan of a foul ball off the bat of Mongo Murakama as a fan in the second deck pulled it in. He hit the zoom and brought the fan up to fill the screen, along with his companion.

He sat staring at the screen for a while, then rose and walked to the deep, musty-smelling hall closet. He rummaged through the clothing there, reached the rear of the closet and located a large wooden box, his onetime footlocker used at summer camp near Yosemite and later as his combination hope chest and repository of personal treasures.

He squeezed his eyes shut, concentrated on shifting spectra, opened the box and pored over it, using infrared to see. The ball was still there, in pristine condition save for a smudge on one side where Mongo Murakama's bat had slammed into it and a faded wavery line on the other side, where Murakama had scrawled his initials after Dan had waited an hour outside Seals Stadium to plead for his autograph.

He carried the ball back to the console screen and sat down. He held the ball as tightly as he could without crushing its still-white covering into its dried cork center, and stared into the screen. There he was, excitement in his features, the old battered mitt he always carried to Seals games on his hand, and the white blur of the baseball a meter away from his outstretched hand. He advanced the pic frame by frame, watching the white blur falling past the rows of faces, falling, falling, then landing with a sound and an impact Dan could still hear and feel.

He looked away from the screen, into his hands, startled for an instant at not seeing the mitt on his hand, but still holding the ball that Murakama had fouled off.

He put the ball away in his old footlocker, pulling some ancient garments together in front of it and closing the closet door behind him. He returned to the console, sat before the screen and studied Marie-Elaine's face as she jumped from her seat beside him. She held a hot dog in one hand and a paper cup of beer in the other.

He ran the brief footage over and over, watching the play of muscles in Marie-Elaine's face, the excitement, the glow in her eyes. 2006. October, 2006. She had been pregnant then. They had been hoping for a child and they were to have two, but she had not yet informed Dan when this pic was shot. But she knew. He could see, as the foul ball approached his outstretched hands, while his concentration was riveted on the falling white blur, that Marie-Elaine reached forward and down, crossing her arms across her lower torso, protecting her belly, protecting the new life that she alone knew had taken root within her.

He reached forward with one finger and touched the screen. He touched the tiny image of Marie-Elaine's belly, laying the tip of his finger across her own crossed forearms. He ran his finger up her body, remembering the feel of the garment she was wearing that October day. But now he felt only the cool, smooth surface of the screen, not the rough woolen texture of the garment nor the protected softness beneath which lay two new beings struggling to grow and live.

Still, he drew back his hand, did all he could to remember the sensations of that moment. The pounding excitement of his heart—what a contrast to the eternal low whirr of the wankel rotary pump in his present torso! The *thwack!* of Murakama's foul as it landed in his battered mitt. The happy embarrassment he had felt at the crowd's good-natured cheer when he made the catch. The smell of ball-park beer and the sharp taste of mustard on a hot dog...

The smell of beer. The sharp taste of mustard.

But he had no sense of smell, no sense of taste. He closed his eyes and concentrated. Damn it, he *could* smell the beer and taste the mustard, even across the decades. That meant that whatever part of his brain remained, or whatever function had been taken over by implanted circuitry, could still give him those sensations. He had no external organs for sensing odor or taste, no channels for conveying signals from the exterior world to those regions of his brain or pseudo-brain. But he himself was still capable of experiencing those sensations. He need only devise a way of getting signals in.

He opened his eyes, set the vidi to running again, and watched the rest of the ball game, partly paying attention to the screen and letting the rest of his attention wander off into abstractions and dreams.

Wool gathering again.

He felt a hand on his shoulder. He flicked off the console and turned to see Lydia Haddad standing behind his chair.

"It's getting very late," she said.

Daniel smiled. "I know it. I thought you and Tovah had gone to bed long ago."

She nodded. He looked into her face, searching for telltale symptoms. Her speech had a slightly abnormal tempo that he knew was associated with the tabs she occasionally melted beneath her tongue. Yes, her eyes were dilated also.

"We thought—Tovah and I thought you might like to come to bed, Dan."

"Oh." There was a pause. "That's, ah—I don't need nearly

as much sleep as most people. And I can catch what I need anywhere. I can stretch out on the couch or the floor, or use the other bedroom. For that matter, I can grab forty winks right here, sitting up."

She sat on the rug, cross-legged, wearing a set of pajamas that had been in the replica household when Daniel had first moved in. She reached up with both hands and took his, gently, in her own.

"Dan, Tovah was very upset before. She said some things that—well, I won't say that she didn't mean them. She's a very honest person, sometimes too honest and she gets in trouble for it. But I know she didn't mean them as anything hostile toward you. Do you believe that?"

He nodded.

"I—we talked it over, Dan. We'd like you to come into our bed."

He felt his hands tense and start to jerk away from hers at the suggestion, but he held them still. "It's nothing new," Lydia said. "You know I like threes. I talked it over with Tovah. She doesn't mind. She, well, she thinks it will help."

Daniel shook his head. "I don't—I really don't think I . . ." He shut his eyes, held her hands in his.

"Dan, ever since you brought me here . . ."

"I didn't want you to think . . ."

"That it was just some weird kind of pickup?" At her words he opened his eyes again and saw her smile at him. "I thought it might be something like that," she said. "Then when you left me alone, I thought you were just the most wonderful, considerate being. Then when you kept leaving me alone I decided you were a homosexual. Then when you told me about yourself—about your family—I decided that you hadn't always been homosexual, even if you are now."

Dan nodded. "And once you learned about my body—about my prosthetics—you must have understood why—why—" He halted, unable to formulate exactly what he wanted to say to her.

"Why you think sex isn't for you any more?" she supplied. He nodded.

"But a person with a false eye or a kidney implant would have no such problem."

"That isn't my problem."

"I know. Your body is all prosthetics, right?"

For all that his body had no such reflexes, no such functions, Dan felt that he had to swallow, to draw a deep breath before he could get out his single-word answer. "Yes."

"It's all right. Come ahead."

She stood up, her slim body in the loose pajamas; as she stood before his chair her feet were on the carpet, bare, between his feet. Her slim legs were between his own massive prosthetic limbs with their hollow metal bones and their powerful artificial muscles.

He managed an almost inaudible "All right."

She took him by one hand and led him through the replica house, to the bedroom. The aquarium light had been turned off for the night and the pump burbled familiarly, comfortingly.

Tovah waited, already in the large bed. Its rumpled furnishings indicated that the two women had been active there earlier, while Daniel had been scanning the vidipic of the old World Series game. Tovah sat upright in the bed; he could see that she was naked, but had drawn the sheet up, covering her breasts. She smiled tentatively as Daniel and Lydia entered the room.

Lydia released Daniel's hand and closed the door behind them, then drew him gently toward the bed. He felt his knees trembling and thought, This is absurd. An experienced man of my age, with my background—and besides, this body can't feel nervousness and shouldn't even be able to tremble. But still he did tremble, and he felt his hands grow icy.

He managed to sit down on the bed, sit on the foot of the bed, his feet still on the floor. The only light in the room came from a small lamp built into the headboard. It illuminated Tovah from above, the bedding, Lydia. Lydia stood before Daniel and slowly peeled off first the pajama top, then the bottoms. It was the first time Daniel had seen her body since he had carried her, violated, beaten, half killed by her attackers and then terrorized and further abused by the police, into this room, and placed her in this bed.

There were still a few shadows of bruises on her body, slow-fading souvenirs of her encounter with the couple in Perrine Place. But the fading bruises did not ruin the beauty of her body. Her breasts were small, delicate, perfectly formed. The graceful curves of her torso led inevitably to her slim, dark-skinned belly. The food they had been eating in San Francisco—that she and Tovah prepared daily in Dan's kitchen for each other—had added the faintest suggestion of a soft rounding to her abdomen. Beneath that slight roundness, her mons was covered with a luxuriant patch of darkness.

Daniel felt an impluse to run one hand across that soft, comforting belly; it was like the abdomen of a woman blossoming in the early months of pregnancy. Daniel felt a red-hot stinging and an aching vacancy where his tear ducts should have been. He wanted to stretch his arm around Lydia's waist, to slide it to her hips as he laid his face against her belly, then slide it downward to rest his cheek upon her mons.

He made two fists and held them on his knees.

Behind him he heard Tovah move, heard her switch off the light and saw the room plunged into nearly complete darkness. He could see by infrared, he knew, or simply by amplifying the visible-range inputs his eyes were receiving, but he chose not to do so. Let there be darkness.

He felt two hands on his shoulders, felt himself being drawn backward so that he lay on his back, his head on the bedding, his feet still over the edge of the bed.

Tovah, leaning over him, laid her cheek against his, her arms on his torso. Her heavy warmth complemented Lydia's slim gracefulness. He felt Tovah's hands begin opening his clothing.

He started to speak to her. "Tovah, about—before . . . About the things we were—"

"Stop," she said softly. "Never mind that. Never mind that now."

He could feel Lydia kneeling on the bed beside him and Tovah. He could see her and could see Tovah, vaguely, in the gloom. He could see that Tovah had taken one of her hands from his chest and was touching Lydia with it, resting her hand softly on Lydia's thigh.

Daniel wanted to move. Somehow, he realized, with a start, his clothing had disappeared and he was lying fully on the bed now. He felt in a dreamlike, almost hallucinatory state, and wondered if the effect of the tabs that Lydia—and he was sure

Tovah also—had melted, could be influencing him also.

He lifted one hand, then dropped it to the bedding again. He saw Tovah and Lydia move, Tovah bringing her hand from Lydia's thigh, Lydia placing her own hand, with Tovah's, on either side of his, one against the back of his hand, the other against the palm. Their hands gently teased his, running lightly over it like small creatures at their own love-play. He felt the three hands, like a strange organism, rise and move back to Lydia's thigh. Using their fingers like the legs of a single being they slid softly into the blackness of her pubic hair, caressing the delicate flesh beneath, savoring the heat and the softness and the moisture of that flesh.

He heard and felt Lydia draw a deep breath. She leaned forward, put her arms around him and Tovah. He felt her squeeze with surprising strength.

He felt Tovah sliding her body down along his own. For a moment she rubbed her face against his, then laid it gently on his chest while her breasts pressed warmly against his face. He opened his mouth and ran his tongue gently against her nipple, felt her shudder, hold him for an instant, then continue her slide down his body.

She reached and took his penis and scrotum in one hand. The hand was warm and strong; her grasp produced in him a mixture of tantalizing pleasure and delicious pain. He felt her snake her other arm under his body. He shifted and held himself up to let her reach under him. She slid her hand down the base of his spine, reached toward his anus.

At the same time he felt the light brush of something warm and moist—he identified it as a tongue, on the tip of his penis. He could feel Tovah's head on his abdomen; the new touch must be Lydia's. He felt the added weight as Lydia lay on him, with Tovah. He felt the heaviness of Tovah's lower abdomen against his face, then the roughness of her hair, then the marvel of her thighs and the flesh between them. At the same time he felt the full warmth and moisture of Lydia's mouth and the strength of Tovah's hand.

He closed his arms around them, and closed his eyes as well.

9

OSVALDO MGOUABE arranged for them to skitter directly from the Space Elevator at El Triunfo in Baja California. Mgouabe didn't come to San Francisco, or to El Triunfo to see them off. He was too busy, he explained apologetically, with urgent IGO business at Lilongwe.

In the hours rising from Baja in the Elevator, they reviewed the work that had been accomplished in San Francisco and in the zone at Palo Alto, the work that remained to be done at the medical Island, and their intentions for later on.

Basically, they had no plans beyond their work at Med Island. Or they had too many, with too many questions still studding them, to make a coherent picture.

They were pleased to be getting off the earth. They knew that its approaching demise would not arrive within their lifetimes. And, as Lydia and Tovah had repeatedly reminded Daniel, the two women had no children and intended to have none. Even so, the prospect of remaining on the overcrowded and socially unstable planet any longer was increasingly appalling.

They kept their secrets. Mgouabe would have no complaint against them for leaking repressed information.

But they were pleased to be away from the terminal ward, the planetary deathhouse that earth had become for them.

Daniel, Lydia and Tovah were the only passengers on the skitter as it fled through the blackness from El Triunfo Elevator toward the medical Island. In the informal atmosphere of the skitter, they were invited to share the control bridge by the pilot, an efficient young woman in trim IGO lieutenant's uniform.

Daniel was vaguely disquieted by the increasing number of uniforms he had seen on earth, and now on the skitter. A society in crisis, struggling to maintain order, he supposed, would lean toward an organization where order was built into the very structure of being. Any kind of hierarchical structure would meet that requirement: a priesthood, an academic system, a bureaucratized corporation—but best of all, the military.

The lieutenant turned from the controls of the skitter and introduced herself to the three passengers, shaking hands with each of them in turn. She was cordial with all, but to Daniel it seemed that she lingered momentarily longer with Lydia's hand in hers while the two women locked eyes.

She didn't know anything about Daniel, or at any rate she gave no indication of knowing his background and identity. She knew only that the IGO skitter had been placed at Daniel's disposal, under instructions from the director, Mr. Mgouabe himself.

Daniel walked to the front of the bridge and stood studying the locked controls as the lieutenant chatted briefly with Lydia and—he assumed—Tovah. To his surprise, he felt Tovah's heavy touch on his elbow. He turned and found her standing at his side, studying the controls as he was.

"I wonder if I could get the pilot to teach me a little about this rig," Dan said.

Tovah did not reply at once. She stood, rubbing her chin with one broad hand.

Dan watched a constant series of changing numbers appearing on readout displays. This skitter had different instrumentation from the one Daniel's grandson had used to transport him from the medical Island to Hokkaido, but they were no different, Dan thought, than the instruments and controls on different manufacturers' automobiles, back in the days when automobiles were common.

"Looks to me as if they're pretty thoroughly automated," Tovah said at last.

Daniel jerked his thumb toward the lieutenant. "Think she'd give me a quick lesson?"

"I was wondering." Tovah sat in the pilot's chair. For a

brief moment Daniel saw her raise her eyes from the instruments to the transparent screen that looked out directly on the lightstudded blackness. She turned back to the controls again.

Dan squatted beside her. There was no chair for him to sit on, but his new artificial muscles did not suffer from fatigue; he could hold the posture indefinitely.

"With that universal converter we're cooking up for you," Tovah said, "hmm— and maybe with a couple of new read-only memory modules—we might be able to get together some kind of instant tutor. Be easy enough for anything involving straight facts. You want to translate . . . hmm . . . just think the English word into the converter circuitry, execute a macro we could give you easily enough that would code in the language you wanted, uh . . ."

"And . . ." Daniel prompted.

"And back it comes, in French or Tibetan or Quichua."

"Just think, 'Doggie, Russian,' or 'How many kilometers to Venus, Jack, Esperanto,' and you get what you want?"

"'Doggie, Russian' would be a breeze. The other would be a tougher job, though. Once you get into syntax instead of single-word translation, it becomes very complicated. Very." She looked squarely at Daniel, apparently sitting on thin air beside her. Lydia and the skitter pilot had disappeared into a rear cabin. Tovah swung her fist and hit Daniel, backhand, a solid shot to the belly. Caught off guard he tumbled to the cabin floor and began to scramble to his feet.

"What did you do that for?" he demanded.

"You give me the creeps, sitting like that. On nothing. I kept waiting for you to fall on your ass!" She laughed heartily. After a few seconds Daniel joined in. It was the first time since his awakening at the medical Island that he'd had a good laugh.

It felt spendid.

"Okay," he said. "If that's what it is, just slide over a little and I'll share that chair with you."

Tovah shoved her substantial hips to the side. "Think this toy chair'll hold us both? She'll be pissed off if she comes back and finds that we've broken the furniture."

"I tell you what. I won't put any weight on the seat. I'll just pretend, and I'll hold all my weight off it. We don't want any pee-oh'd lieutenants running around here."

"Pee-oh'd!' That's wonderful! You are so very refined, sir," Tovah said acidly.

The hatchway behind them opened, and the lieutenant and Lydia Haddad reentered the bridge. They held hands; in her free hand the lieutenant carried a small package.

Tovah reached forward and pointed through the transparent screen. Their course had been programmed to carry them past the moon, to swing behind it and slingshot toward the medical Island. They had now reached their closest point to the moon itself, and were passing over its day-night terminator.

"I've never been in space before," Tovah said.

Daniel watched her face. The sight below was spectacular, he knew: the brilliant whiteness of the lunar day marked with the astonishingly sharp and black shadows of crater rims as the skitter neared the terminator, and beyond the terminator itself, the utter, blackness, punctuated only by the dazzling brightness of a few peaks near enough the terminator to poke up into the sunlight and catch its last brilliance, and by the even more startling lights of the scattered industrial installations that dotted the moon.

But Daniel had seen the sight often enough to become jaded to it, except for the mild surprise of the industrial lights. He was far more captured by the expression on Tovah's face. The cabin's lights were dim—or momentarily dimmed, anyway—and her plain, almost coarse features were transformed by the light reflecting from the moon. Her own pale complexion, in the brilliant but even more pallid light, became a scrap of an Italian fresco. Or, Daniel thought, if his grandson could see Tovah, a vision from an ancient Noh drama.

To Daniel's astonishment, a tear rolled from Tovah's eye; she ignored it. It fell to the instrument panel and beaded on a ruby-glowing readout. The single drop quivered there, resembling uncannily the drop of blood that Osvaldo Mgouabe had carefully placed on the red rose petal in his office in Lilongwe.

Tovah shuddered and emitted an embarrassed laugh. She turned her face back toward the cabin. "Say, Loot," she addressed the pilot, "how much do you have to know to jockey one of these sleds around the stars?"

"The stars?" the pilot laughed. "Forget about that. Nobody's ever gone to the stars."

"What about Galileo Island?"

"Oh, yes, I forgot that. That's ancient history, Miss Decertes."

"You think they'll make it?"

The pilot shrugged. "Who knows? They were doing all right till they got out of commo range. I suppose they'll make it, and their great-great grandchildren will send back a mini-Island to tell *our* great-greats all about the wonders of Beta Orionis or wherever it was they went."

"I wouldn't bet on it," Tovah said.

Daniel flashed her a warning glance.

"Well." Tovah stood up, staying near the controls. "What I wanted to know . . ."

"Uh-huh. Right. Actually, you don't have a hell of a lot to learn to do this job. Learning facts, I mean. But you pilot simulators till you're green in the face, then you pilot simulators till you're blue in the face. Then they tell you you have to start piloting simulators. Holy Mother, I thought I'd *never* get to run a real ship. Then when they let you go up in one the first time, with a senior pilot running the show and you just pushing an occasional switch. 'Here, kid, think we ought to boost a little? Got a little yaw problem there, what do we do about it? Hey, and watch out you don't get kidnapped by any UFO'S, *haw, haw, haw!*' And you give your response, which is almost certain to be wrong, and she says, 'Naw, that'd get us both killed, I'm afraid. How's about we try a little attitude correction with the magnetoverniers, and don't crumple the scoop or you'll have to go out and fix it with a crowbar and a pair of spaceshears, *haw, haw, haw!*' "

"All right." Tovah nodded. "But it seems to me that this skitter's been flying itself on automatic most of the time. In fact, you locked the controls yourself. What's so tough about setting controls and then just going along for the ride? Seems to me that you need a programmer more than a pilot."

"Good point." The lieutenant went on. As she and Tovah bored deeper into the programming aspects of space navigation, Daniel found himself thinking of his graying grandson Ieyasu Hasegawa. He'd made no fuss over piloting a skitter from Hokkaido to the medical Island alone, or of guiding the craft back to Hokkaido with Daniel as passenger. Daniel's emotions were strangely confused, as usual, he ruminated wryly.

He felt pride in Ieyasu. My grandson—space pilot, expert bicyclist, samurai lord, koi fancier.

Hokkaido Island had beauty and order, and if he returned there he would be welcomed, honored, installed in a position of high respect. He could even expect an invitation to court. Of course he would have to learn the language, he couldn't get along speaking English and having everybody translate for him indefinitely. And he'd need to take a crash course in the convoluted etiquette and propriety of neo-classical Japanese society.

As for the language, that might not be too hard after all. Learning a grammar was little different from learning the logic and architecture of a computer system. Not that he'd ever been a super-whiz programmer; he'd learned enough software to go with his job as a systems tech. But the principles were grasp-able; he could always achieve competence if not brilliance on any new system he'd worked with.

Using Tovah's software skills—he had by now developed immense admiration for her abilities in that realm—and Lydia's talents as a circuit designer... He gazed out the transparent screen. A distant glimmer of reflected sunlight caught his eye. They were drawing near the medical Island, would reach its landing disc within a few hours.

Hokkaido probably lacked the high-tech shops he'd need to get a full language-translation rig built and miniaturized to any convenient size, and installed in his internal circuitry, but if they could do the work at the med Island and then move on to Hokkaido Island. . . .

What about Lydia and Tovah? They could go back to the zone, of course. Not that they'd want to. But they could almost certainly find employment at one of the Islands, or at one of the planetary research stations Mgouabe had mentioned briefly to him. He found himself reluctant to contemplate that future, though. He'd formed no emotional attachments since his return from the freezer, until the sequence of events initiated by the encounter in Perrine Place near his replicated home on Steiner Street.

Since then—could he say that he loved Tovah and Lydia? He wasn't sure. Probably not. Their sexual contacts were hugely important to him. They had made him a man again, in his own consciousness. The alienation of mind from body had been setting his whole life-style, he realized. As he had seen his new body as something alien to himself, something to be dealt with at a remote and tentative level, so he had perceived this whole new world of the future—no, of the present!—as something similarly alien to him. He was a tourist, a guest, a pampered revenant of an earlier age. He moved, had moved, through the world of 2090 as some sort of ghost, provoking shudders in those around him, shunned by all.

No, that was not true, he realized. The alienation had been on his part. He had been strange to those around him, but they had been willing to accept him as part of the world. It had been his own sense of insurmountable separation that had kept him at a frozen reach from the world and its residents, and that had been only a larger version of his frozen separation from himself, his mind's separation from his body.

By drawing his ego fully into his body, Tovah and Lydia had made it possible for him to be drawn fully into the present, into the world as it existed, periled and precarious though it was.

No, he decided. Hokkaido Island was not for him. Not even if Tovah and Lydia were willing to travel there with him and remain permanently as his wives, his concubines, or simply as free ladies. It was too much to ask of them; more, it was too little to offer them and himself. He would not shut himself into a corner, retreat into a miniature enclave in this new world. He must find his way into the mainstream of humankind however he could.

". . . sighted on the so-called fixed stars in the early days. Now we use beacons from the various Islands. It's not one of the problems we have to keep us on our toes."

Daniel blinked and rubbed one hand across his eyes and his forehead. Both reflexes, of course, with little relevance to his new body. Well, but they *felt* right. Let it be, let it be at that. The lieutenant was in her pilot's seat once again. He could see that she had unlocked the controls and was setting an approach course for the med Island.

"Oh, listen," she said. She relocked the controls, swung around toward Daniel with a small package in her hand. "This was waiting at El Triunfo Elevator. It's for you."

Daniel reached for it. "Took you a while, didn't it?"

"Just following orders, Mister Kitajima."

He looked at her questioningly, holding the package against his ribcage.

"When Mister Mgouabe handed it to me, he said to give it to you an hour out of med Island. And here we are, and here it is."

Daniel sat down with the package in his lap. Why had Mgouabe traveled to El Triunfo to deliver the package, but not seen him off on the skitter? Even gone to the extent of sending a message explaining that he was too busy to come to El Triunfo?

"Maybe it's a box of bonbons," Tovah suggested. She laughed at her own barb.

Daniel unsealed the package and lifted its top; it came away neatly. He set it carefully to one side.

The box itself seemed to be made of some sort of super-lightweight metal, as smooth and white as aluminum but far lighter. It was filled with crinkled green tissue paper. Lying bedded in the green paper was a slim, elegant vase containing a single flower, a perfect moss-rose half-opened so its tough, green calyx had split and partially separated from the petals. These seemed to be of pure white, but at the center of the flower Daniel could see a heart of deep blood-red.

The entire flower was little larger than his thumbnail. Stem, vase, and flower stood in the palm of his hand, barely six centimeters tall.

When he removed the vase from the box he could see beneath it a vidipic bead. "Would you like me to project that?" the lieutenant asked him.

Daniel shrugged. "I suppose he'd have attached some notice if he wanted this to be super private."

She held out one hand. "There will be a security notice at the beginning of the projection, if there's any problem of that sort."

Daniel dropped the bead into her hand; she set it up and hit a control. The rear of the bridge lit up with an outdoor scene. What seemed like an entire garden of roses blossomed. Osvaldo Mgouabe stepped into the garden, looked at Daniel and smiled.

"I hope you enjoy my small token of friendship," Mgouabe said. "You see, I have it with me still, here in Lilongwe." Mgouabe produced the glittering bud vase and the miniature rose that Daniel held in his hand. Daniel felt the strangest sense of dislocation, holding the vase with its single tiny rose, seeing Mgouabe hold the same vase, the same rose, in a garden beside the IGO building in Zambio.

"I had hoped to join you," Mgouabe said, "but events here prevent my doing so. Thus..." He looked fondly at the rose in his hands. "I wonder, friend Daniel, if you ever have been inclined to look into the field of rose culture. It is very old, and very rich in beauty and tradition. Some genetic lines of roses stretch back to the time of the Caesars, and of the T'ang Dynasty in China.

"This little beauty"—he held the bud vase toward Daniel— "I developed myself. It's a miniature moss-rose. Do you know how roses are developed? We hybridize them. Here, let me show you."

Mgouabe walked toward a row of low-climbing roses. He knelt beside them, in soft, black soil. He set the bud vase aside and lifted a small pair of hand shears. He clipped a mature rose and a few centimeters of stem from their understock. The petals were already opened, but he pulled them away from the flower and let them drop to the ground where he knelt.

"You see," he said. The partially ruined flower swelled until it half-filled the bridge of the skitter. "The rose is hermaphroditic. Here, these little wavery stems with the swollen tops are stamens. The male organs of the rose. They carry a fine, powdery pollen. And these little shafts with the open tips—can you see the openings, so tiny and delicate? They're called stigma, and they carry the pollen to the seeds, here a centimeter—oh, actually a fraction of a centimeter—below."

Mgouabe looked up and smiled. His face was as tall as Daniel. He reached away, his hand seeming to penetrate the bulkhead of the skitter and reach into empty vacuum beyond. It reappeared, sliding through the bulkhead again, holding a tiny pair of tweezers between two careful black fingers.

"If we leave the flower to itself, the stamens will drop their pollen onto the stigmas—or would you say stigmata?" Mgouabe chuckled. "Well, and the result, naturally, will be another generation of roses genetically identical to their parent. But—"

He rose to his feet, shrinking as he did so, to the size of a man.

"If we remove the stamens"—he carefully plucked the tiny projections from the heart of the rose—"we have created a still-fertile, but emasculated rose. Very sad. A frustrated blossom, eh?

"So we simply keep the flower covered, to protect it from stray pollen floating by in the breeze, until the poor little stigmas grow moist and glutinous in their need. Then we introduce a rose of a different strain, its big male stamens quivering with eagerness and pollen."

He clipped a rose from a different bush and stripped away its petals, exposing a full array of stamens. He brushed the engorged stamens lightly over the stigmas of the emasculated rose, leaving behind a clearly visible dusting of pollen. He tossed away the unemasculated rose.

"Voilá!"

Mgouabe bowed. "Now," he discarded the clipped rose, laid down his gardening tools and retrieved the bud vase. "Out of two lovely strains of miniatures, the rosmarin and the beauty secret—the developer of a strain has the privilege of naming it, friend Daniel—I have created this lovely miniature moss-rose."

He held the vase forward. Mgouabe and the vase he held appeared fully as real as Daniel and the identical vase in his hand.

"Anticipating your kind permission, my friend, I have given this new hybrid a name with our brief acquaintanceship in mind. And because it is a miniature, you see, I have named this flower Daniel's Tiny Passion. White and chaste is the face that it shows the world"—Mgouabe raised the miniature rose to his face, peering into it and carefully drawing back its petal—"but at its heart, the color of flame."

He smiled and reached forward. The vase and Mgouabe's hand faded as they approached Daniel. He looked down at his own hand to see the vase still in it. Mgouabe stepped back. "And the scent," he said, "the scent, dear friend, is delightful. As you have no doubt learned by now."

Mgouabe and the rose garden in which he stood shrank down

to a tiny globe, to a glittering disc, then winked out of existence.

The skitter pilot handed the vidipic bead back to Daniel. He slipped it into his garment, still holding the vase. He peered into the heart of the rose, at its heart of flame. He raised it to his nostrils and tried to inhale, then frowned and set it aside.

"How many kilometers to go, lieutenant?" he asked.

"We're just about there," she told him.

Daniel strolled through the parklike preserve outside the hospital; Lydia and Tovah were with him. Barely in view of the hospital they stopped and sat beside a stream. Until now, no comment had been passed concerning the gift or the message from Osvaldo Mgouabe. Now Tovah raised the subject.

"I thought your dealings with IGO were strictly business, Dan. That was a very strange scene. Mgouabe planned that so we'd all see it. What was that all about? Why does he think you're such a bug on flower breeding?"

"It wasn't about flower breeding. Not just about that, anyhow. You don't think that was *double entendre?*"

Lydia snorted. "Of course. But still—why did he do it? Why come all the way to El Triunfo to drop off a package? Why not just send it?"

Daniel shook his head.

Lydia said, "Were you lovers?"

"No."

"Did he want you? Did Mgouabe make a pass at you? He seemed pretty annoyed. Well, not exactly annoyed. But—he was digging pretty hard, wasn't he?"

"Yes."

"And—?"

There was a long silence. Finally Daniel yielded. "And what, Lydia?"

"Listen to me, Daniel." She put her hand on his chest. "We're playing some kind of murky game here. I don't know what happened between you and Mgouabe in Lilongwe. And I don't care—"

He broke in. "Nothing happened. Nothing like that."

"I really do not care. But you don't understand what you're dealing with here. Osvaldo Mgouabe—"

"Runs the IGO," Daniel supplied. "He's a bureaucrat. A

highly placed one, sure. And I don't like a lot of what he does. Using his position to wallow like an old-fashioned colonial bwana. The whole business with roses and brandies while people starve. But he's still just a bureaucrat."

"You're wrong on that score. It's the bureaucrats who run this world, Dan. I keep forgetting you're from another era. Maybe the elected politicians or the generals ran things then. It's the bureaucrats now, and Osvaldo Mgouabe is the ultimate bureaucrat.

"He can snap his fingers and factories fire up in Tasmanio or gear down in Svedio, crops are planted in Islando, whole tribes are plucked out of Nepalo and plunked down in Asamo. He controls more budget, more industry—" She shook her head. "It's too bad you weren't lovers. If you were—"

"What do you think appealed to him, in me?" Daniel asked. "You think there's some special thrill in making it with the mechanical man? Everyone his own fetish?"

Lydia blanched.

"I'm sorry," Daniel said. "I—I didn't mean—you and Tovah—and I—" He stopped. There was nothing more.

"Is that it, Daniel? You think you're queer-bait, and you despise anybody who goes for the bait?"

"I'm sorry," he repeated. "I didn't mean..."

"Don't let it bother you." Lydia put her palms to her face and rubbed her cheeks, breathing deeply. Her color returned to normal. It was an odd gesture, one that Daniel had seen her use a few times before.

"Lydia, it's been very hard. You and Tovah have helped me more than I could ask. But you don't have to go on. You can go back to the zone, I'll see to it that you have any job you want there. I still own the company, you know. Or you can stay out here in the Islands. There's plenty of work. You'll be all right."

Tovah flashed a quick look to Lydia, then back to Daniel. "No. We'll stick with you. There's something going on. Your friend Osvaldo Mgouabe is up to some monkeyshines and it should be fun to find out what they are."

Daniel stood up. "Thank you." He looked away, looked into the park, into the woods beyond the stream. He felt a momentary impulse to opt for Hokkaido after all, or to find some other Island habitat where he could live a normal life, or as close to a normal life as his body permitted. But he knew he couldn't settle down again. Not in that fashion. His feet were planted on a new road, had been planted on that road since he first recovered under the watchful care of Royce and Kimura. He didn't know where that road would lead, but there was no point in trying to turn off it and settle down at some thatch-roofed cottage. The thatch-roofed cottages of the year 2009 were now overrun by 26 billion people who, if they weren't lucky enough to starve first, would in time be roasted to death.

"Royce and Kimura are waiting for us," he said. "They've rung in another colleague of theirs, a bioelectronics wizard of some sort. He'll need to work with you both, and with Royce and Kimura, to get these new gizmos running right and to get them installed properly."

Lydia said, "Look, I don't mean to sound negative about all this."

"But?" Dan and Tovah asked in chorus.

"But what's it all for? You've told us a little, Dan, but to be quite honest, I don't think you've played fair."

"In what way?"

"I don't think you've told us everything you could, about why we're doing this work. You're already a kind of cyborged superman. We're going to turn you into a kind of super-superman with these new circuits."

"I wouldn't call a language translator that extravagant, Lydia."

"No." She shook her head, her hair swinging softly against the screen of conifers between them and the stream. The stream made a rushing sound as it tumbled and broke over rocks in its bed. The cataract at Lodore, Daniel thought. He wondered for a fraction of a second why he couldn't smell the odor of pine forest, then remembered.

"No," Lydia repeated, "the language translator isn't that extravagant. But why do you want to keep adding to your powers? Is it simple ambition? Like a muscle-builder, just building for the sake of building?"

"I guess you're right," Dan conceded. "I haven't showed all my cards. But then, neither has Mgouabe. He's been keeping something away from me, I know it. And so, I suppose, I've been holding back on you."

He knelt to pick up a pine cone, turned it over in his hand and peered at it carefully. He looked up at Lydia and Tovah. "We're getting up an expedition to Zimarzla."

"To *what?*"

Daniel laughed harshly. "Zimarzla. The tenth planet."

"Oh, come on," Lydia pressed. "What is this, a rocket fantasy? That kind of stuff went out of fashion eons ago. The big thing nowadays is Viking adventures. And who cares, anyhow?"

"Right," Daniel conceded bitterly. "Who cares, anyhow?" He tossed the pine cone away. It clattered once against the trunk of a tall pine, then fell onto a bed of needles. "I don't suppose anybody knows or cares about Zimarzla any more. You're all too busy worrying about today. About here-and-now problems. Not concerned with remote places or future times."

He looked into the sky, hoping to see some of the creatures that had adapted to the null-gravity zone, but none were in sight.

"Okay. When they found that there was a tenth planet and that it was a radio source, the first question was whether the transmissions were a natural phenomenon, or whether somebody was actually sending messages. If there's somebody there, maybe we can talk to them. Get information from them."

"So what?" Tovah said.

"This isn't just pride of intellect, damn it! Maybe we can do something about this sun problem! Do you have any idea what it would mean, if we could stop that heating process? Or maybe put some kind of protective shield over the earth? Maybe there's a way to . . . I don't know. Look. Maybe we could manufacture a billion little mirrors and orbit them in a globe around the planet. Reflect away just enough of the sun's extra radiation to get things back to normal on the earth. Or—any of a hundred things."

"Why do we need this Zimarzla place to do that? Why don't you just talk it over with your friend Osvaldo Mgouabe? He has the power if he wants to do it."

"No. Look. I have no idea whether that notion of orbiting

a globe of mirrors would do any good at all. What I'm saying is that we want to get to Zimarzla as fast as we can, to see if we can find anything, learn anything there that—you just don't believe that the situation is as desperate as it is, do you?"

"Yes, we do." Tovah squatted, facing him, scattering a handful of pine needles with one hand. "We've come to terms with it, that's all, Dan, and you haven't. You're struggling and we're riding with the reality. Lyd and I will be all right. You're battering your head against a stone wall."

"Huh. Maybe so." He pushed himself to his feet. "But if nothing really matters, then just stick with me, will you? Will you both? I need your help. And in the meanwhile, you're at least as well off here as you would be back in the zone. At least as well off."

"Okay." Tovah rose beside Lydia. Each woman held one arm around the other. "But what's this business about Mgouabe not playing fair with you? You somehow managed to leave that part out, Dan."

He nodded. "I don't know what he's hiding. He gave me the code-keys to get anything I wanted out of the vidi files or any other stored data I chose. *I think!* But he left out something very important. He didn't tell me what questions to ask!

"If I'd happened to hit on the right question—or the wrong question, I suppose—I might have come up against another retrieval block in the system. So I infer that I didn't ask that crucial question. Or maybe there's some kind of bland answer laid into the system, that anybody gets who asks, unless you know the right way to ask. And then you bypass the decoy and get the correct answer. Meanwhile, you don't even know you're being led down the primrose path."

"Or the moss-rose path?" Tovah jabbed.

"Let's go see Royce and Kimura," Dan said. "If we miss our appointment, they're likely to cancel us and it'll take us six months to get onto their calendar again. You know how these medics are"

Somehow the joke had lost its meaning in eighty years.

THEY didn't meet in a hospital room or a medical lab this time, but a conference chamber with a chandelier, wood-paneled walls, a thick carpet and panoramic window showing the wooded area outside the medical building. The centerpiece of the room was a polished mahogany conference table, inset with data pads, screens, keyboards and styli.

It all reminded Daniel uncomfortably of Osvaldo Mgouabe's executive dining room in the IGO headquarters building. At least the chairs were simple and functional, not the elaborate antiques that Mgouabe favored. And instead of roses, the meeting was outfitted with hot coffee.

Daniel didn't know whether the presence of a cup at his own place was an oversight, a courtesy, or a subtle jab. He did not comment on it.

Kimura and Royce had dispensed with their medical whites and wore comfortable street clothing, as did Daniel, Lydia and Tovah.

Daniel introduced Lydia and Tovah.

Royce nodded to the sixth person in the room. "I've asked Mr. Monroe here to help us out. S.S. Monroe, Daniel Kitajima."

Monroe nodded. He sported a huge red-brown moustache. Daniel said, "S.S . . . ?"

"The kids called me Spaceship. Dopey name. So I took the Viking craze for a clue and poked around in an old encyclopedia. Found a minor norse god I liked called Mimir. If you don't mind."

Daniel shrugged. "As you wish."

"I designed a good many of the circuits that Drs. Royce and Kimura built into you, Mr. Kitajima. I've been monitoring the results. Well, as much as possible, from reports. And of course I was present during most of the testing and refinement process."

"I don't remember you."

"You wouldn't. We hadn't wakened you yet."

"All right. You did a good job. But I've been making plans and I may need some additional capabilities. And I'm here this time, awake, and I'll be monitoring you instead of the other way around. You'll not be working for a piece of tattered medulla in a deep-freeze. Now let me tell you what I need."

10

"SPLENDID!" Monroe pulled at the tips of his bushy mustache. He grinned and turned a smile at the others. "Let's give it a try!"

He's not such a bad fellow, Daniel thought, once you get past the goofy Viking nonsense. But at least Monroe had cut down on his antics once the preliminary sessions were over and they had begun seriously to work together.

And he had worked well with Daniel, with Lydia and Tovah, always keeping touch with Royce and Kimura for the medical aspects of what they were doing.

"All right," Daniel acceded, "Let's go."

Monroe hit the power switch, initialized the program, cleared his throat self-consciously and faced the audio input pickup.

"Cue macro test. Source Italian. Text, *Le particelle battevano all' esterno, producendo ognuna un suono talmente tenue che nessun orecchio unano avrebbe potuto percipirlo.* Source Esperanto. Text, *Estis glora mateno en la majmonat'.* Source French. Text, *Ils vinrent le chercher dans la cellule òu l'on enfermait les fous furieux.* Source Japanese. Text, *Ki iro no sugata. Sono ashi no shita ni: ankoku.* Source German. Text, *Eines der drei Decks war den Speisesälen, der Bar, einem Gesellschafts und einem Unterhaltungsraum vorbelhalten.* Source Portugese. Text, *Filetês de fumo cinza-claro grudavamse nos espessos cahos e nas longas barbas dando a impressão de que procediam dalguma fonte interior da roupa carmesim do mago e nao das fôlhas e gravetos agora em cinzas diante delê.*"

Monroe tugged at an earlobe instead of his moustache. "Input complete. Compile and translate, object language English."

He held his hand over the sensor plate. "Everybody ready?"

The others nodded. No one spoke.

Monroe said, "Here we go then. Skoal!" He lifted his hand from the plate. "Execute macro!"

After a momentary pause the room was filled with a perfectly ordinary voice, its timbre and modulation similar to Monroe's, even to the occasional mild nervous quaver.

"Outside the particles struck, each making a noise so tiny that the human ear, unaided, would have been unable to detect it. 'Twas a glorious morning in the month of May. They came for him in the violent ward. The figure in yellow; beneath those feet: blackness. One of the three decks was devoted to dining salons, a bar, a lounge and an entertainment area. Wisps of gray-white gas clung to his thick locks and lengthy beard, giving the appearance that they arose from some source within his crimson mage's garb rather than in the leaves and stalks that lay now in ashes before him."

There was a pause, then from the same miniature speaker a different voice, impersonal and uninflected. "Execution complete, macro canceled."

Along the table lights winked out.

Daniel asked, "What was that text?"

Mimir Monroe rubbed his nose. "Just random passages out of an old multilingual storybook. They don't mean anything."

"Okay." Daniel looked at the others. "I'm satisfied. What do you think?" Tovah Decertes smiled. Lydia Haddad nodded. Royce and Kimura, usually members of the team, had not been concerned with this aspect of the testing. They would learn of the success and move on to the next stage.

"The only trouble," Monroe said, "is that this gizmo is a meter on each side. You could have it shipped around with you, but I don't imagine you want to use it that way. Or you could get a tightcast link with it, but that'd be messy if you traveled too far. Start playing with delay times and you're in trouble, hey? Some carl starts to challenge you and hefts his broadsword, you don't want to take half an hour to translate 'Hold up, I'm your pal,' while you're getting smitten hip and thigh!"

"Don't worry about that," Lydia said. "This can be squeezed down to the size of your last joint on your little toe."

"Fine! Then let's get to work. Meanwhile, Mister Kitajima, we can fit you with a temporary linkup with the working model, if you want to do some more testing or just practice with the gizmo."

DANIEL sat in the armchair, letting his eyes trace the heavy cable that ran from his shoulder to the working model of the translation module. Like some kind of senile billionaire hooked into a life-support system, he thought. Old man betabucks planning his next corporate coup while greedy heirs plot to pull the plug on him and distribute the family fortune among themselves. Hah!

He'd worked with the circuitry until he'd become comfortable with it. There was no problem with its translation routines, and with Tovah's help he'd been working up its learning-circuit capabilities to do other forms of conversion: mathematical equivalents, spectrum conversions that would let him see by sound, hear by weight... if he ever needed to.

Their latest effort had been remote perspective viewing. The equivalent of reverse-shot camera work in a vidipic drama.

"I'm going to try it again," Dan told Tovah. "See if you can monitor this, okay?"

She nodded.

He slumped lower in the chair, looked out the window at the park outside the medical building. A few people strolled between the building and wooded region farther from the pathways. Dan caught sight of a small figure beneath one of the trees; it was an oak, he decided. He was turning into a small-time botanist.

The figure beneath the tree was that of a rodent, a chipmunk or squirrel. Dan adjusted the focus and magnification of his optical receptors, not using the conversion module yet.

The animal was a squirrel. It was standing on all fours, a few meters from the tree trunk. As if alerted to being watched, the squirrel sat up on its hind legs, balancing with its thick tail. It turned large, shining eyes toward the medical building. For an instant Daniel felt that he and the squirrel locked eyes, established a tacit mutual linkage.

He dropped back to all fours and turned away from the odd sight, scampering toward the tree trunk. A few hops from the trunk he felt something hard and round beneath a browning oak leaf and stopped to investigate. With the nails of one paw he turned the leaf over, knocked it aside. Beneath it lay a marvelous acorn, its cap gone, its shell already browned and cracked down one side.

He picked it up in both forepaws and peered at it, trying to tell whether the meat had been attacked as yet by insects. It apparently had not and he put it to his nose, sniffing the wonderful woody odor of acorn-meat. It was superb! The kernel would make a delicious meal later on, when he was hungry. For now, he didn't feel hungry and didn't want to waste a meal that he might need desperately another day for the momentary pleasure of tasting the kernel.

He popped it into his mouth, chattering happily around the hard shell, and dropped back to all fours. A scamper and one easy hop and he was a meter up the tree trunk, his claws getting a quick and easy purchase on the rough bark of the oak. It was only a matter of a few skips up the trunk to his favorite spot. There was a hole in the side of the tree where a limb had once grown. Now it was his home, his nest, and his best-stocked food larder.

He leaped into the nest, dropped the acorn from his mouth into his forepaws and placed it carefully with the rest of the food he had set aside for future use. He had not yet mated, but he'd seen several young females scampering through and under the trees in this region, and he had felt pleasant urgings in his loins. It would not be much longer, and once he had mated and there were young in the nest, this stored food would be all the more important.

He looked around his nest, found everything in order, and jumped back onto the edge of the hole. He scampered a few meters up the rough bark of the oak, then out along a limb. There had been an attractive flash of gray somewhere out there, and there was an intriguing tang in the air.

Nostrils twitching, he made his way farther out on the limb. The tang seemed to lead him, and he felt stirrings in his belly and his loins that distracted him from the wariness that had kept him safe and well all his life. There was no sight, anywhere along this limb, of the gray flash he'd seen.

Liquid eyes shining, he scanned the limbs above and beneath the one he stood on. Still no sign of anything. He stood up on his hind legs, balancing with his tail. He was easily fifteen meters above the ground, but his balance was sure and his claws sharp, his reflexes honed as sharp as his claws. If by any unlikely chance he should fall from this limb, he could twist in the air and catch safely at the next one below, and scamper back to the tree trunk none the worse for the experience.

But—no sign of any flash of gray. And yet, that deliciously overpowering tang persisted in the air.

He looked at the next tree. Something had moved there, and his shining eyes caught sight of a leaf shaking that should not have been moving. Yes, the limb quivered slightly at its tip and he saw a flash of gray along it, moving toward the trunk of the next oak.

The squirrel equivalent of a smile flashed along his synapses and he dropped back to all fours, scampered toward the end of his own limb, felt it begin to bend under his weight as he neared its thin, flexible tip. He launched himself toward the next tree, his nostrils filled with that marvelous tang. The odor was sharp, warm, earthy, dizzying: He'd detected it before now, but only in remote, attenuated form. What he'd felt previously had been only the merest suggestion of what now took over his body and his mind.

It was easily five meters to the next tree, and he would reach that tree two or three meters lower than he had left his own. He saw a flash of gorgeous gray pelt scamper from a limb onto the trunk of the tree and disappear around its edge. The air whistled past his ears, bent his whiskers back against his cheeks, filled his lungs with a delicious flavor and his whole body with an irresistable sense of urgency.

There was a moment of warning, a blackness as a shadow flashed across the squirrel, but he had barely time to twist his head, to raise his eyes, before the diving falcon struck.

Daniel looked down at the gray form, grown from a barely visible moving speck to an appetizing animal, as the falcon pumped once more with her powerful wings, adding their own force to that of gravity. She pulled in her wings, drew her head down between her shoulders, extended her taloned feet and struck.

There was a delightfully satisfying thump and a delicious feeling of impact as she hit her prey. The consciousness of the falcon was small but diamond-bright. She knew instinctively that the squirrel was dead. There had been no struggle from it, neither a desperate attempt to wriggle loose and escape nor an even more frantic fight. Once or twice these little creatures had turned on her, struck back with their chisel-edged teeth and talonlike claws. It was a pointless effort: the prey of the falcon never escaped once caught in her grip, but she bore a star-shaped scar on one leg and a tender spot on her body where a terror-crazed rodent had struck before dying.

Not this time.

She emitted a triumphant scree, spread her wings to brake her dive five meters above the ground, then pumped her powerful wings to begin the long climb back toward her lair. She knew from repeated forays into the heavy regions that the first minutes of her climb for home would be the hardest. Here her body weighed her down, her every movement was strained, and she knew that if she stopped her efforts to rest there would be no peaceful floating as there was at home, but a sudden and dangerous plummet back toward the ground, a perilous fall which would require her, at the very least, to start her climb again.

Other falcons had fallen prey to their own unwariness in this fashion, usually young birds lacking the wisdom and wariness of experience. Once they reached the ground their return to the high regions was unlikely.

She pumped her wings, thrust her body upward, pumped again. The lightening of her task was so gradual that she could not detect it from moment to moment, but she had flown often enough into these dangerous heavy regions of her world to know of a certainty that, as she rose, meter by meter, wing beat by wing beat, toward the high and weightless region that was her home, she would become gradually lighter until, home, she could float weightless and at rest.

She glanced upward. From her position, the sun was near the edge of a darkener. She enjoyed its warmth on her wings and her body. She feared what creatures might lurk in the darkness where sunlight was blotted out. She swooped around, circling away from the shadow. She passed through a small blob of floating mist, then rose above it.

The prey in her claws had not moved since the single convulsive twitch with which it had met her attack. Her flight now was a matter of a slow, rhythmic, methodical pumping of her wings against the warm air. It required little concentration. She had far, far to go to reach the high region where her home lay. Her young were awaiting, she knew, in the spongy nest she and her mate had built of the ferns and twigs that grew in the high region.

When she reached the high region and returned to her spongy nest she would tear the prey to bits, chewing and softening each morsel until it was suitable for her young to consume. There were two of them, hardly more than chicks as yet. There were still bits of shell caught in ferns near her nest. Her young had not left the nest, nor would they until their egg-down had all dissipated and been replaced by young feathers.

She was light enough now to divert part of her effort from her wing strokes. She continued the slow, unceasing rhythm, but she raised her prey slightly in her talons and tucked her head partway toward it, catching the scent of the still-hot meat in her sensitive nostrils. It was a delicious scent. She had dined earlier, satisfying her own hunger before her mother-instinct had taken control of her and caused her to seek more food, food to bring back to the nest.

The young were safe, she knew, guarded by her mate. The social organization of her kind was such that parents shared duties, one hunting for herself, then for the chicks, while the other mounted guard over the globular nest, keeping the young inside and keeping all intruders from entering the single round opening to the nest. When the hunting parent returned with food for the chicks, the guardian parent would depart to find nourishment for itself, then pursue the hunt until it had obtained more food to bring home.

Successful incursions into nests were rare. Loss of chicks to marauders—hunting birds of still larger species, or the dangerous creeping things that had no feathers at all but frightening rough skins like the outside of twigs, and that lived all their lives in the ferns and bushes of the high zone—occurred at long intervals. When chicks were lost the entire community of falcons would rage through the high region, screaming their anguish and their fury, searching for the marauder who had taken the young.

When such a melee took place the region was scattered with lost feathers, blobs of reeking blood and gobbets of ripped flesh for long afterward.

The falcon plunged her beak into the soft belly of her prey. The squirrel's fur and its thin abdomen-wall offered little resistance to her razor-sharp, powerful beak. A fresh rush of squirrel's blood and its rich, strong odor hit her nostrils. The taste of the blood on her tongue was even more intoxicating than had been the odor.

It was her posture, the downward-bent position of her head and neck, that prevented her instant death.

She was struck by a murderous impact, a weight several times her own, propelled downward in a dive almost identical to the one with which she had killed the squirrel. Had she been holding her head in its usual position during flight, her neck would have been snapped by the harsh impact of the diving eagle from above her.

Instead, she was sent tumbling, reeling through the air. She spun, using her tail feathers and her wings to adjust her position, to face upward toward the direction of impact.

The eagle had swooped past her, wings half-spread, talons dropping feathers and dropping blood that had been drawn in the moment of brief contact between the two birds.

The dead squirrel had been jolted from the falcon's claws by the shock of impact, and was tumbling away, shrinking to a speck as it accelerated into the heavy zone. It disappeared completely long before it reached the ground.

The falcon caught sight of her attacker and instantly assessed her circumstances. The prospect was grim.

The eagle was a larger bird than she, its beak and talons equally as sharp as her own. Its wings were far more powerful than hers. If she tried to fight it, she would almost certainly be killed, ripped literally to shreds by those razor-edged weapons. If she tried to flee, whether in headlong flight, in a dive toward the heavy region, or in a desperate climb toward the high region, she would be overtaken.

Her best chance, it seemed, was still to make for home. Her body was lighter than the eagle's; the climb might tire the heavier bird more severely than it would herself. She might distance the heavier bird, reach the sanctuary of her nest before—

No!

Her young were there. Her mate, too: possibly two falcons could overcome the eagle; if not kill it, then at any rate send it fleeing in defeat to seek easier prey. But the risk was too great. If they failed, if the two falcons were unable to stand off the eagle, their helpless young were doomed. They could neither flee nor defend themselves. They would be a meal for the eagle.

The eagle had turned and was accelerating toward her now. The falcon must draw him away from her nest. She dived, her keen hearing tuned for the telltale sound of the eagle charging after her. She managed three strokes of her wings against the air, four, then she heard the heavier, terrible beating of the eagle's wings.

Tail feathers spread, twisting in the air, she dodged to one side.

The eagle rushed past her.

It swiped at her with an outstretched talon.

For all her frantic dodging, the eagle's claws caught in her wingtip, ripped away a fluttering storm of feathers. The wing failed to respond properly now. She could use it still, but without the speed, the power, the precision she had been accustomed to all her adult life.

Even so...

She sprinted horizontally for half a dozen strokes of her wings. Out of the corner of her eye she spotted her enemy. He had located her and was climbing on an angle, aiming at her. She knew that it would be fatal to let the eagle get above her again, yet she knew that her weakened wing would give out before she could reach the high region, should she try to climb away.

She waited until the eagle's climb had brought him almost level with her. He was beating the air heavily, strongly.

She tucked her head against her breastbone and dived.

The maneuver bought her a few meters of separation before the eagle could adjust and renew his pursuit. That was her one chance in this uneven contest. The very mass that went with the eagle's greater speed and strength could be used against him. It translated to momentum, and that momentum made the eagle slower and clumsier in changes of direction than was the falcon.

As she plunged downward she could feel herself growing heavier. The ground beneath was clearly visible, with only wisps of mist occasionally screening meadows, stands of trees and lakes. She could see the strange hard-edged buildings where the humans stayed.

She could also see a terminator, separating a day-zone from a night-zone on the ground.

This time she cut horizontally before the eagle's flight had brought him even with her. She knew that he would adjust in middive and follow her, but she couldn't risk another frantic dodge like her last.

She crossed the invisible line from sunlight into darkness as the brilliant sun disappeared behind an opaque section of the world. She took a moment to look upward toward her home in the high region where eternal twilight obtained. Across her shoulder she saw her pursuer flash from brilliant illumination into almost total darkness. As he crossed the line he seemed to wink out of existence.

For a brief moment the falcon considered a desperate dash back toward the high zone. If she flew upward here in the blackness she might set enough distance between herself and her pursuer to elude him completely and disappear into the thick ferns and brushy growth of the high region.

She tried a few upward strokes of her wings. If she could rise far enough, her weight, too, would lessen. She could rise faster and more easily, the farther she rose.

But her injured wing, the one that the eagle had struck in his first attack, was growing weak and numb. She found herself circling involuntarily as she rose, then circling instead of rising. She had not the strength to climb to the high region!

She knew that she could not fly long, even in her horizontal path. Her only hope was to reach the ground and find some place of refuge there, before the eagle could reach her again.

He was here in the darkness, she knew, and almost certainly flying at a lower level than she. She would have to get past him to reach the dubious sanctuary of the ground.

With a quick shake of her head, she dipped her neck, spread her wings, and pumped against the air, pulling herself downward as rapidly as she could.

She couldn't see the eagle here in the shadowed zone. That made a distinct disadvantage, but the eagle might be equally unable to see her, which would balance the effect. Far below she could see a few glittering lights. These, she knew, marked the area where the humans stayed. She did not know the meaning of the lights, but she preferred to stay away from those strange creatures.

The air was cooler here in the darkness. Her injured wing throbbed dully when she held it against her body; it caused her acute pain only when she tried to use it, but she was forced to endure that pain. She could not afford to sacrifice the use of the wing.

She pumped downward, downward. She felt steadily heavier; she knew this would help her to fall more quickly, but it would do the same for her heavier opponent. As the disadvantage of darkness was shared, so was the advantage of increasing weight and speed.

The loudest sound in the falcon's ears was the rasping of her own breath. The throbbing in her injured wing seemed also to echo in her head, a steady, unpleasant, rhythmic thudding.

There was a heavy impact against her body, that sent her tumbling end-for-end. She flapped her wings and spread her tail feathers, desperately struggling to regain control of her attitude and trajectory. A line down her back felt strangely cold and hot at the same time. She spun once more and saw her foe rising above her, silhouetted against the remote twilight of the high region.

She had time for another brief dive, drawing still farther toward the ground and away from her enemy before he could find her and dive at her again. She strained to keep her attention from the sounds of her damaged body, to listen for the beat of the eagle's heavy wings as it dived at her once again.

As she picked up the sound of those wings, she flipped her body, holding her injured wing against herself and using her tail feathers and her uninjured wing to maneuver. The eagle's claws raked at her but she drove her own razor-sharp talons upward against the heavier bird.

With a solid, satisfying sensation she felt her claws rip at the belly of the eagle. She had raked them across his chest, ripping the pinion muscles across his rib cage, then plunged them into the soft part of his body behind the bottom rib. Her claws were caught in the eagle's belly, ankle deep.

The falcon gave a cry of triumphant joy. Her entire being was filled with a hot glory at the victory she had achieved against a heavier, stronger foe, against all but impossible odds. She had killed the eagle! She had killed the eagle!

Her cry ended when the eagle plunged his powerful hooked beak into her throat, tearing out jugular and carotid in a single powerful swipe. The eagle was still alive. He was mortally wounded and hopelessly tangled with the enemy who had been both his victim and his murderer.

He kicked and twisted but the dead falcon's claws were caught in his belly and could not come loose. He was filled with a hot agony and a dizziness that he could not long tolerate.

He beat his wings with all his strength, struggling to rise toward the high region. He had been hatched there and had lived there throughout his life. This was the closest to the ground he had ever flown, and beyond the agony and weakness of his wounds and the maddening burden of the dead falcon he felt a terrible weight that increased constantly.

He managed to achieve an approximation of level flight. He found his vision growing dim and blurred. He scanned the ground below him. Directly beneath him all was blackness, but he could see that he had not penetrated far into the dark zone. There was light on the ground, there were trees not very far away. If he could reach that area he might be able to land in a tree. If he could do that he might still work free from the burden of the dead falcon, dine on her carcass, regain his strength and, after a rest, make another attempt to fly back to the high region.

The heavy, warm, soft feeling in his belly was mixed with an agonizing pain. His head and wings were growing cold and numb. The darkness beneath him seemed to be spreading and thickening and reaching for him. He pumped steadily onward, struggling now and then to work his claws free of their burden.

The lighted region was drawing close. He could see now that he was over a wooded area. The tops of the trees reminded him of the ferns and shrubs of the high region. He crossed from blackness into a lighted area.

The sudden light dazzled him. He blinked, pumped his wings, strained against his burden. He struck the top of a tree, fell, tumbled through leafy branches, struck another, tumbled again, heard the sound of leaves brushing and twigs snapping as he passed through them, felt a terrible thump as his body struck the grassy earth beneath the trees.

He could see nothing, hear nothing, feel little. Beyond the agonizing weight and wounds of his body, there was still the feel and even more the scent of vegetation around him. It was like the nest in which he had been hatched. The sense of helplessness was not entirely unpleasant. It was like being a chick again. Helpless, yet safe. Cared for. Fed.

Surely his mother would come to feed him. Some delicious morsel that she held in her craw. Some wonderful blood-dripping gobbet that she could deposit into his own wildly hungry beak. He opened his beak, panting, yearning. He strained to see with his weak, dazzled chick's eyes. He was so helpless, so new that he didn't know even what his mother would look like. He knew only that she would care for him, protect him, love him.

She would feed him.

She appeared, a huge, strange figure, towering over him. She bent toward him. He blinked, stretched his mouth even wider. She would feed him. She would love him.

She looked down at the strange sight, feeling a cold shudder pass through her body. What an oddity. Two birds—big ones, birds of prey, not the little chirpers that made the park so pleasant near the hospital. One had a wingspread as wide as her own arms. The other was even larger. It might have been able to spread its wings the equivalent of her height!

The smaller of the two birds had not moved since they had fallen from the tree; the larger had been alive, although barely so, when they struck the ground. It had looked at her, opened its beak in a strange way, not as if it had been trying to attack her. What had it been doing, or trying to do?

She remembered a vidipic she had seen, of mother birds feeding their young. The chicks were apparently helpless, but they managed to hold their beaks open wide while the mother deposited pre-chewed and half-digested food into their craws.

Was that what the huge bird had been doing? Had it thought it was a chick again? Had it thought that she was its mother? The idea was grotesquely funny, and yet at the same time it was touching, almost pathetic.

Terminal regression in eagles. Huge birds at the moment of death reverting to the psychology of their own infancy. Was death itself a return to the egg, for these creatures, as it was, by some theories, a return to the womb in humans?

She knelt beside the tangled bodies of the two birds. They were not local wildlife. Royce knew the creatures of the parkland near the medical center, and no such large birds of prey as these were among them. They might have wandered in from another region of the Island, or perhaps even been residents of the null-sector in the center of the Island.

If creatures that had spent their entire lives in a state of little or no gravity had wandered closer to the ground here in the Island, had encountered earth-normal gravity for the first time, they might be trapped, unable to fly home. But these two had fallen victim to more than gravity. They had fallen victim to each other's formidable natural weapons, to the scalpel-sharp slicing talons and the brutal ripping beaks that nature had given them both.

"Doctor Royce!" There was a hand on her shoulder and an urgency to the voice. Still kneeling beside the birds' cadavers, she turned and saw a lab technician standing over her, almost out of breath.

"What is it?"

"You'd better get back right away, Doctor. Half a dozen people out looking for you. They need you, quick!"

She stood up and asked again what was the matter.

"It's Mister Kitajima. They were testing that new gadget of his, that one Mimir Monroe cooked up with Mister Kitajima's people. Something went wrong."

"You don't know what?"

"He just sort of passed out. Nothing really happened. It was like he was there, they were testing this new gadget, and he was looking out the window, somebody said, and he just wasn't there any more. I don't mean he walked away or disappeared or anything. He's still there, his body, but he's not responding."

Royce headed back for the building at a run, the lab tech trailing her, panting.

She raced through the lobby, into the high-tech intensive section where they'd worked on Kitajima. He wasn't there; he was in the adjoining conference room. She ran into the conference room. Kitajima had his back to her. People were milling around him.

Royce ran around the table so she could face Kitajima without disturbing him. No one had moved him; apparently, no one had touched him since he'd passed out. Good and bad. At least they'd done no further harm. But they'd done nothing for him either.

There were two semicircular chunks taken out of the edge of the table, where Kitajima had closed his hands on the wood and crushed it between those prosthetic fingers of his. Royce blew out a breath involuntarily at that sight.

Mimir Monroe was standing over Kitajima, agitatedly tugging at the tips of his moustache with both his hands. His Viking drag was missing at the moment. The constant tugs at his moustache turned his face into a continuously changing grotesque distortion of itself.

"We didn't touch anything," Monroe said. "We put out a call for you and Doctor Kimura. He isn't here yet. We—"

"Tell me exactly what happened," Royce snapped.

Monroe slumped into a chair. "We were just trying out a new feature on the converter for Mister Kitajima. Reverse perspective. Nothing very important, just a little feature he thought he'd like."

Monroe leaned close to the table, peered across it into Daniel Kitajima's slack face. He shook his head and continued.

"Everything seemed fine, we powered up, and Mister Kitajima just keeled over."

"You left the new feature running?" Royce asked."

"Yes'm. We didn't touch anything. Well, we touched Mister Kitajima, but he didn't respond and we didn't want to take any risks. So we just called you and Doctor Kimura."

"All right." She nodded, waved one hand in a vague gesture that seemed to make Monroe feel slightly better. He was tugging at his moustache with only one hand now. Kitajima's two associates, Decertes and Haddad, were flipping through projected schematics on a screen, talking through technical features in low voices.

"Can you offer any suggestions?" Royce asked them.

DECERTES raised her pale, close-cropped head from the screen. It cast an eerily colored pattern on one side of her face. She shook her head. "Nothing yet. Everything looks all right, but—" She nodded toward the unmoving Kitajima.

Royce leaned across the table and opened one of Kitajima's eyes with her fingers. As she did so she realized what a pointless act that was. There would be no organic clues in those optical sensors that she had personally installed in his prosthetic skull.

Kitajima saw Doctor Royce looking at him with an expression of concern, of puzzlement, of fear. He managed a feeble smile and was rewarded with a look of immense relief.

He started to straighten, pushing himself upright against the edge of the table. He noticed the two fistfuls of crushed wood in his lap. It wasn't sawdust: it was crushed and splintered hardwood. He saw the two jagged semicircles in the edge of the table.

"I was just—" For a moment he started to feel disoriented. He saw Doctor Royce gesturing to Mimir Monroe, saw Monroe's hands move over the equipment. Daniel's dizziness faded and he returned to normal

"I want to get you into the reader," Royce said. "I think you're all right now, Mister Kitajima, but I don't want to take any chances. Do you agree to that?"

Daniel nodded. "But not now. I'm really all right. I want to work on this. I think it might be useful."

Monroe clapped Daniel on the shoulder. "You're a cool one, you are! Pass out and scare the bellies out of all of us, and then just sit up and look around and want to get back to work. Well, I'll tip a horn of mead to that any time! What happened? For a minute I thought you were going berserker on us!"

"No. It was the new feature. That reverse-angle view. It worked—too well! I was looking out the window when you first cut in with it, right?"

Monroe nodded.

"I was looking at a squirrel. Suddenly I *was* the squirrel."

"Yes, looking back at the building."

"No! No, that was the design spec. But it worked better than that. I *was* the squirrel. I had all of its sensations. I could see what the squirrel saw, feel what it felt, smell what it smelled. You see? It was as if I *became* the squirrel."

Doctor Royce asked, "You mean—you took over the squirrel? You controlled it?"

"No. I had no control of it. Not even a will. I was strictly an observer. Well, but not a detached observer. I *was* the squirrel, at least I felt that I was. But I had no—human thoughts. No human will. I just became the squirrel."

"How did you get back to yourself?"

"The squirrel died." Daniel smiled sadly. "Poor creature. He was in rut. Caught the pheromones of a female in the next tree and got so excited he forgot to look before he leaped. Got snatched up in midair by a hunting falcon. She killed him. Killed him with one impact and started for home to give him to her babies for dinner!"

"And that's how you got back here? You were freed when the squirrel died?"

Daniel shook his head. "Then I became the falcon. I had all of her sensations and—thoughts. If you can call them thoughts. Everything was images, impulses. Recollections. Intentions. Fears. She didn't—conceptualize. But I *was* the falcon, the same way I'd been the squirrel. And that didn't last either. She set out for home with the dead squirrel in her beak, and an eagle attacked."

He grunted. "Little fleas have littler fleas."

Monroe said, "What?"

"Nothing. Just an old line. I guess it works both ways."

"I found an eagle and a falcon, together." Royce leaned across the table toward Daniel. "Or—I don't really know all the birds, but they were obviously birds of prey. One was medium size." She held her hands apart. "Must have weighed fifteen kilos. And the other—twenty-five at least. It was *big*. That would be a falcon and an eagle, wouldn't it?"

Daniel nodded.

"But how did you get back to yourself? Do you have any idea how you did it?" Royce was seated again. "When the eagle died also—that's what happened. I saw the bodies. The eagle must have attacked the falcon. I didn't see any sign of the squirrel, that must have been lost. But the falcon got her feet into the eagle's belly. She killed it, it killed her. Ugh!"

"Ugh indeed."

"And then you just became yourself again?"

"You saw the eagle die, Doctor. I *was* the eagle at that moment. I saw you bend over the two birds. I felt everything the eagle felt."

Royce's hand went to her mouth. "Did you—did the eagle regress? Did it think it was a new chick again, in its last moment? I had the strangest feeling, that it thought I was its mother, bringing it food."

"That was it exactly."

Royce began to cry. "I—I know this is silly," she managed. "But it was so sad. It was touching. That magnificent bird, so powerful. So fierce. And it was dying. And it thought I was— its mother." She managed half a laugh, then cried more.

Daniel stood and walked around the table. He put his arm around Royce's shoulders. She came out of her chair and he held her, feeling ineffably strange. His mind was filled with a jumble of notions. He was back to the artificial-man problem, the idea that he was a robot committing some insulting parody of a fleshly act. And the idea that he was Royce's patient; she, his physician. Doctors and patients didn't act that way. It violated their relationship. He was humiliating her before Mimir Monroe. He tried to hold her a hand's width away from himself, was startled at her momentary resistance before she let herself be moved back the few centimeters involved. She turned her face upward toward his own and for an instant it was crossed by an expression that pierced him to the heart and set his hands trembling.

Pierced him to the wankel rotary pump, he corrected himself. He turned angrily and stalked around the conference table.

"I'm really all right," he said. "There will be no need to take readings on my—machinery. Lydia." He addressed Haddad, deliberately selecting her from among the others. "I want to get this work completed and installed in my circuitry as quickly as possible. We can't hang around this Island indefinitely. We have a task ahead of us."

He turned back to Royce. "For your medical records, or whatever you're planning, when the eagle died my perspective was transferred to the nearest sentient organism." He saw her blink as if she had received a light slap. "When you returned here and pulled up the cover on this optical sensor," he popped one of his eyes wide with thumb and forefinger, "I got back into my own, ah, hardware.

"Monroe—" He turned brusquely to the engineer. "I want to keep that feature. You will get with Haddad and Decertes and modify it to include a programmable clock for automatic cancellation if I don't return before the clock runs. Put in a default feature on the clock, too. I'll give you the timer setting for that later."

He turned back to Doctor Royce. Her face was as pale as Tovah's. "Please call Doctor Kimura," Dan said. "I want this hardware toughened up a bit for operation in pressurized or caustic environments."

11

IT WAS A fledgling redwood grove, and its very presence said something about the intentions and expectations of those who had planted the giant trees' seeds. Carried from the surviving Pacific Northwest forests, they had been nourished and nursed as if the Island's future would be built upon them.

In a literal sense they meant little; any of a score of hardwood species would have done as well. But the fantastic size to which the redwoods grew and the immense longevity they were known to attain came to be a metaphor for the hopes of humankind in space.

The picnic setting beneath the young redwoods—and for a redwood anything under five hundred years was childhood; anything under one hundred was infancy—could have been a scene in any carefully tended grove from Monterey to Vancouver a century and half earlier. But the nearest building was the cyborging laboratory where Daniel Kitajima, over the span of the past eighty years, had been rebuilt from a shred of hard-frozen neural tissue into something outwardly resembling a man.

The picnickers included Daniel, Tovah, Lydia—and the doctors, Royce and Kimura.

They had packed and brought a picnic basket of real wicker, something that had been priced out of the market by plastic replicas on earth for three-quarters of a century. A cold ham, boiled eggs, long loaves of hardcrusted sourdough, wine. All the products of the space economy: nothing had been ferried up from earth.

The mood was strange and uneven.

Daniel was fighting melancholia: he was torn between a wish to recapture his humanity, his links with the past and with the world in which he had lived his first thirty-four years—and the emotional pain that recollections of that lost world inevitably carried.

His return to the replicated home that he had shared with his wife and children had been bittersweet. If he could do it over, he was not sure but that he would opt for some calculatedly sterile ultramodern cubicle that would meet his physical needs while offering no stimuli to the uncounted memories that reminded him constantly of his loss.

"Are you all right, Daniel?"

He turned toward Lydia Haddad.

"I'm okay." He managed a weak grin, convinced that it would fool no one. He looked around the table. "Is this all? I thought Mimir was going to join us."

Dr. Royce had been holding a glass of golden wine to her lips. Daniel saw it quiver slightly at his question. She lowered the glass.

"He said he was going to come. He wanted to wish you *bon voyage*."

There was a pause.

There were other picnickers in the grove. From somewhere among the trees Daniel heard a dog barking.

"But—?" he prompted.

"Oh, but he was called away. There was somebody in from earth, a client. You know Mimir's very good at his work."

"I know."

"Uh—well, he'd done some design work for this patient, some good prosthetic work. Some of the same technology that went into your own prosthetics, in fact."

"And?"

"Uh—I think he's coming back. He did want to see you once more before you leave."

"Yes, right."

The dog that had barked came charging across the clearing, spotted Daniel and others and detoured around them, pursued by a party of children. The dog was big and yellow, a retriever probably. He had a stolen joint of beef in his mouth.

The retriever disappeared around the bole of a young tree. The pursuing children, ignoring the picnickers, followed.

"When will you be back?" Kimura took Royce off the hook with the question.

"I don't know." Daniel shook his head. "It depends on a lot of things. Among them, whether Lydia and Tovah are ready to put in with me. To stay with me for a while longer."

Lydia put down a sandwich. "I think we are. What is there for us on earth?"

"You have jobs, They'll be safe. It's my company."

"No future in that. I think we'll stick. Tovah?" Her partner agreed.

Kimura nodded. "But what do you *want?* What are you after, Mr. Kitajima?"

Daniel managed a natural gesture. "I have to do something. What it is—I don't know. But something. Look, I'm—I guess, disconnected. I'm not working for a living. I don't have a family. I don't have a career. Everybody I grew up with has been dead for decades."

"You have family at Hokkaido Island, do you not?"

"Yes." Daniel stood and walked around the table. The grass beneath his feet was not a perfect replica of real grass: it *was* real grass. It grew from real earth, ventilated and fertilized by real earthworms.

He stopped. "Yes. I could go there. Maybe I will, eventually, I don't know. Certainly not now, though."

Voices came from a distance. Daniel could hear them before the others, could make out what they were saying before the others were even aware of them.

It was Mimir Monroe.

A second man was with him.

"Whatever I do, Dr. Kimura, I just have to—" Daniel made a motion with both hands, as if he were taking something out of his chest and throwing it into the redwoods.

"You see? Most people's lives are more or less controlled by the struggle for life. Do you see? They have to get jobs, work for a salary, take care of their homes. If they don't have work the struggle is even harder.

"Huh! We used to have an expression, the idle rich. People with so much money and time on their hands they didn't know what to do with themselves. We used to laugh at the poor things, having to run off to Aspen or Maui or St. Tropez."

Out of a corner of his eye he saw Dr. Royce headed toward the two approaching voices. Well, so she'd heard them at last.

"But they must have been desperate. Well—" He halted. Watched Royce reemerge into the clearing, trailed by S.S. Monroe. The third member of the party, as Daniel had known he would be, was Osvaldo Mgouabe.

Monroe hopped nervously, tugging at the ends of his moustache. "You, um, you know each other," he managed, swinging his head to include Daniel and Mgouabe alternately.

"We have had the pleasure," Mgouabe said. "Daniel visited me at Lilongwe, in fact. As I recall, it was a delightful little visit. The bureaucratic routine becomes oppressive after a while, you know. They say that bureaucrats are oppressors, and I don't doubt it. We aren't cruel but we have our rules and our procedures and so on.

"But the ordinary citizen has to deal with bureaucrats only on occasion. Think of dealing with them all day, every day. Such monsters! Think of *being* one! *Tch!*" He made a sound of eloquent self-pity.

Daniel glared. "Yes, I know Mgouabe. But I didn't know you all did. I know he's an important man on earth, but I didn't think that the Islands were under IGO authority."

"They're not." Royce was trying to conciliate. "We're— uh—certainly not countries, I suppose. But independent entities. Yes."

"Then suppose I just order you off the Island, Mgouabe?"

"How inhospitable."

"Never mind that."

Mgouabe flashed a look at Royce, then a longer one at Monroe. "I'd go, of course. It's your Island, Daniel. I can't deny that I would be distressed, but how could I quarrel with your wishes, right here on your own property?"

He reached for a wine bottle. "May I? These regional vintages can be intriguing. But Daniel, I wasn't planning to stay here on the Island very long. I just dropped in to chat with our Viking friend. Mimir is—you might say, a protégé of mine.

We've known each other ever since I had my accident. I've tried to keep in touch with him ever since, keeping tabs on the state of the art as it were."

He smiled.

"Mimir has even come to me for bits of advice on occasion."

"I didn't know you were an engineer, too."

"Oh, no. Just a bureaucrat. I had ambitions, once upon a time, of taking a more active role in things, but my injury, you know. Mimir did a wonderful job on my hands, but I lost several years. By the time I had recovered I'm afraid my career path had been shunted aside. Such are the workings of these large, impersonal institutions."

Daniel turned his back on Mgouabe, exasperated. The man's flow of ironies and calculated digressions defeated every attempt to challenge him.

"Dr. Royce," Daniel said. "Dr. Kimura. Monroe. Thank you for everything you've done for me." He shook hands with each of them ceremoniously, a quaint twentieth-century gesture that he insisted on retaining.

"Tovah, Lydia—if you're really with me, let's get out of here. The skitter's fuelled and stocked. Mgouabe, I want you off this Island now. You may be a high muck-a-muck on earth but this isn't earth."

"As you wish." Mgouabe inclined his head. "I wonder if you might include me in your own little excursion. Did I hear correctly that you had a jaunt of exploration in mind?"

Daniel felt himself trying to flush with anger. "Include you? Get back where you're a somebody, Mgouabe. I wouldn't—"

He felt Dr. Royce's hand on his elbow. "If you really want to get off the Island, Mr. Kitajima, you'll have to work out an accommodation with Mr. Mgouabe. Free space is open to anyone but free space means translunar space. We're in place between the earth and the lunar orbit. Cislunar space is under authority of the IGO. If Mr. Mgouabe says you can't travel, you can't."

"That's too much!" Dan sank onto a picnic bench.

There was a burst of noise and the big retriever came bursting through the clearing once more. The same gang of children came on in pursuit, screaming and tumbling. They disappeared among the redwoods once again.

"I don't see why you want to come with us, Mgouabe."

Mgouabe spread his hands. "Maybe for the same reason you want to go, Daniel. I'm comfortable enough in my job. Bored. Free of everyday obligations and seeking diversion. I suppose you wouldn't put it quite that way, but my search for diversion is my own way of—well, would you call it looking for purpose? The meaning of life, eh? Too bad we've all lost our hope of heaven—in the next life or in this one. It used to make the daily drudgeries bearable, I should think.

"But where is heaven now, eh? Where has it gone?" He spread his perfect black hands and looked down at them as if he expected to find heaven there.

Daniel said, "We're not going to heaven."

"I should have been astonished if you told me you were."

"And if you don't want us to leave—what then?" Dan addressed Dr. Royce. "What can he do?"

"Impound your skitter, I imagine. It's not a question that's raised very often. But IGO has the legal power to control travel in cislunar space. I don't know if they have the force to back it up."

"Come along then, damn you. Come along."

TOVAH piloted the skitter from the Island. Daniel and Lydia watched unspeaking. Osvaldo Mgouabe offered comments, showing a high degree of expertise.

"I didn't know you were a skitter pilot," Tovah said, over her shoulder.

"Oh yes. I have been many things."

Tovah's movements, at first tentative, rapidly increased in competence. After a while Daniel said, "You really know what you're doing. You're a fast learner!"

"Only insert-tab-A-in-slot-B fashion. The way bottom-level workers learn their jobs back in the zone. They don't know what they're building, they just know they'd damn well better do it right or they're out on their arses and somebody else has the job."

"Even so."

Daniel saw Mgouabe turn and lay his perfect hand on Daniel's arm. Mgouabe inclined his head and they retreated across the bridge. Lydia had slid into the copilot's seat beside Tovah.

"I trust we aren't out for a pleasure jaunt, Daniel." Mgouabe's voice was low, pitched to reach Daniel's ears but not the women's. "What is our objective?"

"You bullied your way onto this trip. I thought you knew."

Mgouabe's smile showed shining teeth.

"We're going to Zimarzla," Kitajima supplied.

Mgouabe nodded. "I'm all in favor of that, Daniel. But we'll need to make a small detour."

"We don't need to make anything. You're a passenger."

"Please, please." Mgouabe clucked his tongue. "Why must we quarrel, Daniel? I only wish to be helpful. There is so much you don't know about this modern world, my dear."

Dan bristled. "I sat in front of that screen till my eyes were ready to fall out. I know more about the past century than most people who lived through it."

"Indeed, indeed. I'm sure you followed every lead. But there are some topics not available through the screen. You understand that, surely."

"All right. What are you driving at?"

Mgouabe drew Daniel to a panel that showed the star-dotted blackness of space.

"You've never visited the planet Mercury, have you?"

"I've never visited any planet but earth."

"Daniel, I want you to trust me."

Kitajima's eyes popped at Mgouabe's words.

"Oh, I know you think I'm some sort of tricky fellow. Well, I suppose I am. It's the way of the bureaucrat, you know. The effective bureaucrat never violates regulation. Never defies a directive. But he always finds a way to get what he wants. One becomes—well, I shouldn't say corrupted, should I? But I suppose a certain deviousness creeps in."

Daniel waited.

"There are things on Mercury that you should see. We have a most interesting little station on Mercury. IGO has, that is. But before we go into that, Daniel, may we just go into orbit around your Island? I pledge my word to you, once we have talked this over, you shall have your way regarding our destination."

"You're too generous, Mgouabe!"

When Daniel didn't pursue the matter, Mgouabe walked back to the pilots' positions. He said, "Please."

Tovah and Lydia looked back toward Daniel.

He nodded.

Mgouabe reached between the women. Without hesitating, he slapped toggles, turned rotaries. The skitter rumbled and banked then settled smoothly into a new course.

"Look," Daniel said, "I want to know why you're riding with us. You're a powerful man."

Mgouabe inclined his head. "Indeed."

"You could have outfitted a ship of your own. Picked a crew of your own—or gone off yourself, for that matter, from the skill you show as a pilot."

Mgouabe repeated his move.

"Then—why on *this* ship? Why with us?"

"You are going to Zimarzla, Daniel. I am going there. It makes sense, doesn't it? Why send two expeditions when we can share?"

"You're not just saving equipment." Dan shook his head. "No."

"Just for our company, Mgouabe?"

"I will admit that your two lady friends are merely incidental. But you, Daniel—oh, you are another story. I will show you things. I will take you places."

Again he laid his hand on Daniel's arm. Daniel shook it off.

"Never mind that. This is no honeymoon. What's in it for you?"

"Daniel, you are the strongest man alive. I understand what you can do. Remember, I have some of you in me." He reached for Dan's hand, clasped it with his own in a semblance of a convential handshake. Dan felt Mgouabe's grasp. An ordinary man's bones would have been crushed.

"And there is some of me in you, as well." Mgouabe smiled icily. "Besides, you don't need to breathe. You don't need to eat. You have powers of perception that no ordinary man possesses."

"Yes. Me and Clark Kent. So what? Why don't you just have them build a robot for you?"

"That would have been ingenious. Just consider me impatient, then. Daniel, I want to show you something now." He reached inside his clothing and extracted a vidipic bead. "Come. We can all see this."

He slipped open the skitter's vidipic panel, dropped in the bead. An object glowed into being before the panel. "Come." Mgouabe gestured to Daniel, to Tovah and Lydia. "Look."

He held the object—seemed to hold it—between his hands, moving his hands around it like a gypsy's around a crystal ball.

It wasn't large—perhaps the size of an ordinary grapefruit. The skitter's cabin was in semi-darkness, illuminated by the faint, remote radiance of the stars and by the dim glow its instruments provided. The object was self-illuminated, a glowing blue that varied from a nearly green ultramarine to a near purple. Lines wove from the surface, drawing the eye into puzzling perspectives in the depths of the object.

The blue of the lines reflected off Osvaldo Mgouabe's black, graceful hands. They flew over its surface, never penetrating, as if the object were a real and solid thing and not merely the visual analog of the pattern stored in the vidipic bead.

The weaving lines formed pocketlike compartments, some of them vacant, others seemingly occupied by tiny shapes. Some of them were visibly organisms, vaguely humanoid or totally inhuman.

The interior of the skitter was eerily silent. Daniel could hear the sounds of the others' flesh: the slow alternation of inhalation and exhalation of three sets of lungs, the thudding of Osvaldo's and Lydia's and Tovah's hearts, the subdued gurgle of bodily fluids, the rush of their bloodstreams. He could hear the soft whir of the wankel rotary pump that served him in place of a heart.

Lydia Haddad reached past Mgouabe's arm and tried to touch the object. Her hand passed through it. She gasped.

"Please," Mgouabe hissed.

"I—I'm—"

The spell was broken. Mgouabe reached for the vidipic panel, clicked out the bead and dropped it back into his clothing. He spun a dial and the illumination in the skitter brightened.

Lydia said, "What was that?"

Mgouabe grinned, showing his teeth. "Should I really tell? I do so love melodrama and mystification."

Daniel said, "Cut it out."

"Eh? Oh, I suppose that's one of your archaisms, then. But you do not share my inclinations, do you? Very well. That bead was made on Mercury. The object is much larger than that, of course. It's one of the reasons we need to go there. It cries out for investigation."

"Yes, but what *is* it? And what were the things in those niches?"

"I do not know what it is, my dear. A piece of abstract sculpture, perhaps? And the things in the niches? How do I know? Biological specimens, perhaps? Who knows, maybe it's a storage rack for some giant's kitchen. Did you notice one of those things that looked like a cross between a spider and a squid? Some sort of crustacean? Maybe it's a sample kit for the special effects of an old space adventure film producer."

"That's on Mercury?" Dan asked.

Mgouabe said it was.

"All right. We'll go there."

Mgouabe grunted happily. "Very well then! And that is only one reason for going there before we try for Zimarzla. Also, there is a bit of refitting to do. I was very pleased, Daniel, that you saw to your personal refitting at the Island. I will confess that the staff there were under IGO interdiction from other contact, and that I used my influence to arrange your own, ah, modification.

"Ruggedized, that is the term I think you use in your own profession. Is that so, Miss Haddad? You ruggedize components that have to function under severe conditions, do you not? At one time, I think they called that beefing up. *Hah!* Beefing up. A marvelous expression.

"Well, and you are thoroughly ruggedized, Daniel. You will be very useful." He nodded in agreement with himself.

"But this ship will also have to be ruggedized. Beefed up. *Hah!* That, too, will be accomplished on Mercury. Did you know that Mercury is our largest source of heavy metals? The asteroids are valuable also, but Mercury is mostly metallic, under its rocky mantle. Imagine that! A whole planet of metals.

Like a BB. Do you know what BB's are? Mister Kitajima does, the ladies do not. Well, I suppose it is a function of the generational difference. I don't suppose Mister Kitajima knows what goes on in an urban dive, so there is a certain crude balance of ignorance, is there not?"

He swiveled so he sat staring through the transparent screen. The sun lay directly ahead of the ship; if Mgouabe had planned this journey to bring them to Mercury, then the planet must obviously lie between the ship and the blazing star, but in the glare of even the polarized sun, Mercury was not to be seen.

"Our forebears of a few generations ago used to play with toy weapons that propelled little round metal pellets at paper targets. They were called BBs. I have never been able to learn why, is that not odd? Well, and if you took a giant BB and rubbed it around in the dirt for a while so it accumulated a mantle of soil . . . you would have the planet Mercury.

"I think that is very picturesque. I think our forebears would have enjoyed that."

Mgouabe unlocked the control panel and flicked on an indicator screen similar to the one Ieyasu Hasegawa had shown Daniel as they traveled to Hokkaido Island. The brilliant dot glowed off-center. *"Ah-ha,"* Mgouabe exclaimed. "There is the beacon. And I certainly offer my congratulations to the pilot who brought us in so well."

He swiveled and bowed toward Tovah Decertes, then swung back to the controls and tapped in the corrections to bring them to the Mercury station.

"We'll see just where the station is today," he said over his shoulder.

Daniel exchanged glances with Tovah and Lydia.

"Oh, you had better settle in for our landing," Mgouabe said. "No landing disc here like the Islands, nor an Elevator as on the earth. We shall make an old-fashioned planetary landing here. Grand fun, splendid drama. We can just imagine ourselves a crew of those daring astronauts of the last century. They laid their lives on the line. None of our latter-day decadence for them! Oh, no. They learned what it was to be intoxicated on their own adrenaline.

"We shall learn that in a few minutes. Oh, I'm sorry. Miss Decertes and Miss Haddad and I will. Mister Kitajima, you'll just have to try and imagine what it's like."

THE planet appeared dead ahead of the skitter. Mgouabe had kept the controls while Daniel waited with Lydia and Tovah for their landing. This is what I wanted, Dan tried to tell himself. Not some drab job like my old one, and not an idle life. He'd been too busy lately, too wrapped up in matters of the moment, to slip into the sort of melancholic fugue that had plagued him in San Francisco.

The skitter's trajectory as it approached Mercury might have been selected for simple efficiency, but Daniel suspected that Mgouabe had specified their course for other reasons. His love of the melodramatic, even if it had not been proclaimed by word, had been obvious from Daniel's first encounter with him. The furnishings of his Lilongwe offices, the theatrical employment of the rose motif—and especially Mgouabe's use of a thorn to draw a drop of his own blood, and his blotting that drop with the petal of a dark red rose—all fit consistently with Mgouabe's theatrical behavior in the ship.

The skitter had been programmed to follow an orbit that would eventually have spiraled it into the sun, had the planet not intervened. As things moved, the skitter spiraled toward the sun and the planet appeared as a black point centered in the ship's transparent screen.

It was not centered against the sun.

Oh no, that would have been too simple an effect for Mgouabe. Instead, the skitter's trajectory was plotted to cause the point that was Mercury to spiral also. It started near the edge of the sun's disc, a scarcely discernible speck behind which the star's coronal flares danced like flame-gold silken curtains.

As the ship spiraled toward the planet, the speck grew to a tiny disc that enlarged steadily as it, itself, spiraled inward from the corona toward the center of the sun's own huge and growing disc.

There was silence on the skitter's bridge. Osvaldo Mgouabe and Tovah Decertes sat side-by-side before the control panel.

Daniel Kitajima and Lydia Haddad remained in other seats, farther from the controls.

Each remained silent for his or her own reasons. Mgouabe, Daniel thought, had the most to say, but chose to say no more. This, too, was part of his theatricality, and had the others been on an equal psychological footing with him, they should have carried on a conversation of their own.

But Mgouabe was able to dominate the psychic atmosphere of the bridge. The cards were all his. He possessed knowledge which the others lacked. He was the one accustomed to command; through his innocuous-seeming position as administrator of the International Geophysical Organization he had become, in effect, the most powerful individual on earth.

Yet he had chosen to leave the planet.

His rambling garrulity seemed ingenuous, but was actually the opposite. Kitajima perceived in Osvaldo a man who planned his every statement, who knew in advance every seemingly impulsive digression in his monologue, who said everything he said with a calculated anticipation of its effect.

And now he chose to say nothing.

And Daniel acquiesced, as did the two women. They had tacitly agreed to leave their destinies in the hands of Osvaldo Mgouabe. The prosthetic hands of Osvaldo Mgouabe.

THE Mercury beacon was bright and perfectly centered on the skitter's homing indicator.

The planet itself had become a huge disc. Features on its surface would have become gradually discernible by now, save for the angle of the ship's approach. But that angle was such that the planet appeared solely as a black two-dimensional figure.

Briefly it appeared as a great bull's-eye centered on the larger disc of the sun. Both discs grew, but the closer one of the planet expanded to cover more of the sun's glare. For a few minutes the sun's corona flared around the rim of the planet forming a breathtaking, almost geometric vision of the perfect black planet surrounded by dancing glories of fire.

Then Mercury's disc blotted out the flaring corona; the ship fell wholly within the long shadow of the planet.

Messages from the planetary station flashed onto the readout screens of the skitter's control panel. Osvaldo Mgouabe tapped back his replies, still declining to speak.

Daniel looked at the others. He could see Lydia's face as she sat beside him, her attention still fixed on the transparent screen above the control panel. Her eyes were wide, the pupils dilated and shining as if she had dissolved a tab beneath her tongue, but Daniel knew that the dilation was in response to the darkening of the bridge and the obliteration of the sun's disc by that of Mercury. He knew that the rapt expression of her face was a reaction not to some inner epiphany of mind or soul, but to the vision of the heavens they jointly experienced.

He felt, in a strange and disquieting manner, a sexual arousal. If he had been with Lydia alone, he knew that he would have reached for her. His hand quivered toward her but he drew it back. The presence of Tovah complicated the relational equation, though she might have been incorporated into the relationship, had only three of them shared this experience. Daniel felt a pang of disappointment that Mgouabe's presence made such closeness impossible.

Tovah and Lydia had been together a long time. They could lay aside all of their defenses, each of them confident that in the moment of voluntary, total vulnerability, she was wholly safe in the presence of the other. The admission of Daniel to that emotional nexus must have involved an act of great courage, a risk fearfully yet willingly undertaken. And his entry had involved the dropping of his own emotional armor, the baring of his scarred and severely injured psyche along with the baring of his perfectly reconstructed body.

None of them—not Lydia, not Tovah, not Daniel himself— was able to drop those defenses before Osvaldo Mgouabe, was able to say to him, in effect, My flesh and my soul are bare to you; I will not defend myself from you; you can do me harm; I will place my trust in you not to.

"Watch this now—you'd best hang on!"

Mgouabe's enthusiastic delivery ended Daniel's rumination. Wondering wistfully what Tovah and Lydia had had in their minds during those minutes, Daniel brought himself fully back into the present.

"We have to head for the station," Mgouabe said. He began

handling the controls of the skitter in classic space-jockey fashion. Daniel felt the G-forces induced by the ship's maneuvers and wondered if Tovah or Lydia would suffer a bout of nausea.

The ship's panel had depolarized as the ship fell deep into Mercury's shadow. The planet before them—or beneath them—grew from a huge disc that obliterated most of the sky into a great blackness that blotted out their entire view. Then features began to appear, ghostly suggestions of craters and occasional rilles barely visible in the faint light of distant stars.

Mgouabe wheeled the skitter into a swooping curve, leveled off a few kilometers above the cratered surface of the planet and sped eastward toward the distant terminator. The instrument panel showed the planetary station's beacon dead ahead.

"We'll have to leave the ship at the station," Mgouabe said. "They know we're coming. They know what we need. They'll work on the ship while we carry out our tasks elsewhere."

"Listen here," Daniel said, "you've found out all about us three, and we don't know a damned thing about you, Osvaldo. Why don't you use the time till we reach the station and give us an honest story."

Mgouabe laughed loudly. Daniel tried not to hear a note of contempt in the man's laughter.

"What would you like to know?" Mgouabe asked.

Daniel squeezed his eyes shut. "For starters, you seem to be a damned hot space pilot for a man who rides a swivel-chair for his living. What about that?"

Mgouabe kept his eyes on the screen and on the panel under his hands, but he nodded his head in concession of Daniel's point. "I did my share of piloting out here, before they gave me my desk. In fact, I'd never have got that desk, in all likelihood, if it hadn't been for these."

He held up his two hands, palms toward himself, so Daniel could see them over his shoulders.

"Yes, except for these, I'd probably be a hot-tailed skitter pilot to this day. Or a chief pilot, I suppose." He sighed dramatically. "I suppose the cosmos had a desk ready for me all along, and my getting to ride it was an exercise in inevitability."

He swung toward the others for a moment, before swinging back to his board. During the seconds that he faced them he said, "But here I am, off the planet, up in space, sitting at the controls again! So I triumphed after all!"

"What happened to your hands?" Tovah asked. She was close to Mgouabe and spoke in a low voice, but the bridge was otherwise silent and the others heard her speak.

"I lost them," Mgouabe said. "In fact, they're down there somewhere." He pointed toward the floor of the skitter, but it was now skimming across the surface of Mercury. *Down there* was the planet, not the ship.

"They're down there. I don't suppose anyone will ever find them. I don't suppose they're recognizable. But they're somewhere on Mercury. We'll see some interesting sights on Mercury! Look: the horizon! The terminator! You see that oblong with the sunlight reflecting off it? That's the planetary station! It moves with the terminator. Largest track-laying machine ever built. We'll skim in on the roof. You'll enjoy the commander. I've known her all my life. All my life."

He grinned roundly. "She's my big sister!"

12

THE GROUND-CAR'S tracks clanked into silence a few kilometers short of their objective. The car commander swiveled and addressed his passengers.

"I can't take you any farther. The ground structure here is unreliable. We could break a hole and get wedged, and we'd be in bad trouble. We could walk part way out if that happened, but they'd still have to send another car for us, and we can't afford it. Too expensive."

"Plus ça change," Daniel commented.

"Pardon?"

"Nothing. That has a familiar ring to it, that's all."

"That's all right," Mgouabe put in. "We'll walk the rest of the way in. More interesting that way. Not many folks get to stroll on a planetary surface any more. Not since the Islands started taking all the play."

The car commander made a disgusted sound. "Tin canners. Make all that fuss about being the new humanity, living independent of the planets. First time they spring a leak or need a few kilograms of anything, they come crying for help. 'Can we borrow a cupful of silica please?' And putting on airs all the time about being better than planet-lubbers. Planet-lubbers! The damned tin canners!"

"Yes, well, we all appreciate your feelings about that," Osvaldo said. He turned and started to rummage among the equipment he'd ordered packed aboard the ground-car.

"It isn't natural," the car commander added. "If the cosmos

had meant us to live in tin cans, it would have evolved us in tin cans. Life belongs on planets, it's a law of nature, that's what it is."

"Well, and here we are, aren't we?" Mgouabe said. He turned to the others. "These suits are just as good for the surface as they would be for space work. We don't need very much equipment. We can carry that along with us."

He handed a heavy carton to Tovah and another to Lydia. They opened the cartons and began carefully climbing into spacesuits. The flexible skins of the suits clung close to the body before they were sealed and inflated, so they required little extra space to work in. Mgouabe opened a third carton and sat down. He started tugging an insulated boot onto his foot.

"You sure you don't want a suit, sir?" the car commander asked Daniel.

"I really don't need it," Dan thanked him.

"It's your skin," the commander shrugged. "But I think you're committing suicide. It's over three hundred degrees out there, sir. And no atmosphere. You can't even exit the car without going through a lock, sir. I've never lost a passenger before. You'll be the first."

Dan smiled. "No, I won't. And don't worry. You want me to vidipic a release for your protection?"

The commander shook his head. "I've got it all, already, sir. In lieu of a log."

Osvaldo insisted on cycling through the ground-car's lock first. Daniel watched as the door slid open. The lock itself was a simple pressure booth the size and shape of a coffin tipped on end. Mgouabe smiled, locked his helmet and faceplate in place, and stepped into the lock.

The door slid shut.

Through the door's transparent panel Daniel could see Osvaldo's suit slowly ballooning out as the lock's mechanism sucked air from around him, reducing the pressure toward the external vacuum. Mgouabe smiled reassuringly, turned to look through the panel in the lock's outer door, turned back toward the car and waved.

The car commander said, "Here we go." He spoke into a small microphone. Daniel could see Osvaldo's face move as he answered the car commander through his suit mike.

The car commander hit a control and the outer door slid into the skin of the car. Osvaldo stepped out of the car, onto the surface of the planet. He walked away from the lock. Momentarily he was lost to sight, then he reappeared near the front panel of the car, waving cheerily toward the others.

Lydia Haddad exited next. Daniel and Tovah stood close together, watching Lydia through the panel. When she stood inside the lock her suit at first clung tightly to her. Daniel heard a tiny gasp from Tovah.

Daniel's eyes traced the same course that Tovah's had. He understood her reaction. The collapsed suit clung to Lydia's figure.

Daniel cast a sidelong glance at Tovah. She had not pulled her helmet over her head as yet. He raised his hand and held it a few millimeters from her cheek. She turned and looked at his hand, then raised her own, already in its thick-textured glove, and pressed Daniel's palm against her cheek.

She turned away and picked up her helmet.

Daniel watched Lydia's suit balloon as the pressure dropped in the lock. Shortly she was outside the ground car, standing near Osvaldo Mgouabe, moving slightly, taking a few steps in one direction, then in another, accustoming herself to the surface of the planet.

Tovah followed.

The car commander said to Daniel, "Your turn, sir. Will you take..."

"Let me have a radio."

The device comprised two beads, one that attached with a bit of adhesive material to Daniel's tooth; the other, to the outer channel of his ear. He tried the device and found that he had no difficulty in speaking with the three puffy figures outside the car.

He stepped into the lock. In his ear he heard the car commander's voice, making a final appeal to him to wear a suit. Daniel declined. The air began to hiss out of the lock as the car's pumps pulled at it.

The outer door slid back.

Briefly his skin felt puffy; he knew that this was caused by the pressure-differential between the interior of his body and the vacuum outside. His prosthetic skin was more than a decorative facade; it was a tough, chemically inert membrane that sealed his working systems from the exterior environment.

Autosystems sensed the pressure drop and vented his inert interior pressure valves through pore-like openers in his skin.

The sunlight, pouring in from a mere fifty-seven million kilometers, bounced off Mercury's rocky, cratered landscape. The sky was dead black; the rocks, a grayish off-white. Although Daniel's optical sensors adjusted rapidly to the brilliant light and the black contrast of the sky, he was mentally dazzled nonetheless.

He staggered back and threw his hand up, covering his eyes with his forearm.

He wore an ordinary set of clothes, form-fitting shirt and trousers, insulated boots, all fabricated of the material used for spacesuit covering, capable of withstanding the intense heat and radiation without vaporizing.

He slid his hand over his eyes and peered between his fingers like a child cheating at a game of hide-and-seek, then slowly drew his hand away from his face.

He walked toward Lydia, Tovah, and Osvaldo. They all stood facing him, their expressions hidden behind the polarized faceplates of their helmets.

A voice in Daniel's ear said, "Are you all right, sir? You seemed unsteady."

"I'm just fine," Daniel said. "Everything is working perfectly. I was just . . . it's quite an experience. That's all."

"I understand, sir. If you need anything . . ."

"Yes, yes. I don't think so. But thank you."

"I'll remain here, sir."

"We won't be too long, commander." That was Osvaldo's voice. "Keep this line open. If there's an emergency, you'll know it at once. We will not expect you to come for us, but you can talk with the main station. We should be back within a pair of hours."

Daniel saw Osvaldo turn away from the ground-car. There had been no need to face the car while he talked with the commander, but he had done so. The three spacesuits were coded with color patches. That hadn't changed in eighty years, Daniel thought. But he could have told them apart anyway by their size and shape: Mgouabe's large, athletic frame; Tovah's broad, heavy-set body; Lydia's slim litheness, all somehow influencing the shape of their balloonlike spacesuits.

And no one would mistake Daniel himself for anybody else.

Mgouabe raised one arm, pumped it slowly up and down, then pointed ahead and started to walk. It was the old infantry sign for a deliberate advance.

"How come we didn't bring any equipment?" Dan heard Lydia ask.

Mgouabe answered, "We're just going to look at some things. Some things that I want you to see. Especially you, Daniel."

They were walking in a loose cluster, perhaps a meter from one another. The ground under their boots was a gray-white mass with a consistency between that of coarse sand and pebbled snow. Daniel reached down and scraped up a small handful of it. He rubbed it on the palm of his hand, poking at the particles with his forefinger. He used the magnifying capability of his sensors to see the granular structure of the stuff. It was very ordinary rock, not unlike samples that could be picked up on the surface of earth's moon, or for that matter in the center of Arizona.

"I think you are duplicating previous research," Mgouabe remarked sardonically.

Dan grunted and tossed away the powder. The lighter gravity of Mercury was offset by the weight of the others' spacesuits, he knew. They had all been buoyed—if mildly discomforted— by the null-conditions in the skitter. On the surface of Mercury, in the great track-laying planetary station and in the ground-car, they had quickly adjusted to the resumption of weight at a fraction of earth-normal.

Now the extra weight of their spacesuits canceled that advantage for all but Daniel, whose tireless body felt no better or worse for its new lightness.

"I think we've all seen rocky plains and craters before," Daniel said. "I hope this is going to be more than a guided tour of a bleak landscape."

"Don't worry about that." Mgouabe pointed ahead. Against Mercury's short horizon it was hard to judge distance. "You see that small crater with the gap in its lip?"

They all halted and peered ahead. Daniel could see himself

reflected in Mgouabe's polarized faceplate. He looked to himself like a nineteenth-century desert rat.

"We can be there in another half-hour," Mgouabe said. "I would have liked to ride to the rim, but the ground gets weak here. That gap in the crater was apparently the result of a secondary impact from there—" He pointed to another crater, one with higher, more sharply defined edges. "Either that, or a later primary hit. Anyway, it saves us having to climb the rim. That's where we're headed. We can stroll right in."

"Yes. To see what?" Tovah demanded.

Daniel could almost hear Mgouabe's smile. "You wouldn't want me to spoil the surprise, Miss Decertes. Really!" He pumped his arm again and strolled ahead.

The ground-car commander called them once more. "You're just about out of visual contact, Mister Mgouabe. Can you still see the car?"

Daniel turned to look. The ground car was a white speck the size of a pebble on the horizon. He had to enlarge the image to see its communication dish at all.

"We're going on," Mgouabe told the car commander. "Everything proceeding as planned. Just wait there for us."

They turned away and walked forward. The sun seemed stationary in the black sky.

They reached the rim of their objective and halted at the opening Mgouabe had indicated. The ground still rose a few meters here, but they climbed easily and stood, peering down into the crater.

"Looks ordinary enough to me," Tovah commented.

"Look carefully," Mgouabe said.

"Is it safe? Should we go ahead?"

Mgouabe didn't answer, but moved over the lip of the crater, down the short distance into its bowl. The color of rock inside the crater was little different from that of the landscape they had crossed: a grayish off-white with perhaps the faintest suggestion of a blue tint. It seemed to be more finely powdered than the soil of the surrounding plain.

"You see?" Mgouabe lifted his arm. "Indeed, it looks quite ordinary. It is quite ordinary. No different from a thousand others on this planet, on Mars, on earth's moon, on most other moons for that matter. You see the mound there, the central mound?"

Daniel's mind flashed momentarily to other mounds, then back to the central rising of the crater.

"Those were a puzzle once," Mgouable lectured. "Then we devised a satisfactory model. The impact that created the crater heated the ground to a magma-like state. It flowed out from the point of impact, like a giant ripple in a pond. But slowly, and solidifying and cooling all the while. And then it slowly poured back toward the lowest point in the crater, the point where the original impact took place. And piled up there, a little, and solidified some more, and flowed back out again.

"But we have this mound left, a kind of fossil ripple a hundred million years old. Isn't that interesting? A hundred million years old. And underneath the mound—there may even be a chunk of the meteorite that landed here. If it wasn't destroyed by its own force. Think of that. A chunk of—whatever—a hundred million years old. My gracious!"

He turned and headed for the far side of the crater, toward a jumble of rocks tumbled there by some ancient impact or planet-quake and set now in bold relief by shadows of the sun.

"Daniel, I know you have marvelous powers. You can see by almost any spectrum you choose, is that not so?"

Dan grunted.

"Ah, but for the rest of us, there will be a few portable lamps. I left them here the last time I visited this spot. It's a very special little spot for me, you see." Mgouabe stepped between two boulders. The others were able to follow him in single file. He halted and bent. Daniel could see a heavy chest between the boulders.

Mgouabe, anticipating questions, said, "Standard IGO supply. We wouldn't normally leave things like this lying around, but rank still has its privileges." He opened the chest, withdrew three portable lamps and handed two of them to Lydia and Tovah.

"Now, I ask you to take a look straight ahead."

"I can't see past the rocks," Lydia said.

"Precisely. Well, let us advance."

They threaded their way through the passage. The rocks in places offered sharp edges to their spacesuits but the tough suiting material showed no tendency to rip. Mgouabe led the way. The others followed. Their order was unplanned but Daniel found himself bringing up the rear of the column.

At points among the boulders there were sharp turns, short climbs or drops. They passed from sunlight into black shadow. "Best turn on these lamps," Mgouabe said. "It will not get any lighter now."

Tovah said, "We've been tromping around here a long time. Why aren't we out through the crater edge?"

"Very good!" Mgouabe made a congratulatory wave. "I hoped that someone would notice. Yes, this is almost a maze. You'd be surprised at the sterling mind it takes to decipher every turn. I was almost lost here myself, the first time I came in. No one off the planet Mercury knows of this place, and very few of them on Mercury! Our car commander is one, of course, hey?"

The answering voice had a mild crackle to it. "Yes, Mister Mgouabe."

The rocks closed over their heads. The trail they followed dropped downward at a slight but definite pitch.

"You don't mean . . ." Tovah asked half a question.

"But I do mean," Mgouabe said.

"A cave? A cave big enough to walk into? On Mercury? I never heard of such a thing."

"Well that you didn't. This is one of the bits of information that IGO determined had best be kept under wraps."

"By IGO you mean Osvaldo Mgouabe, is that right?"

"I knew you were a bright person." Mgouabe halted. "But not just a cave, not just some fossilized bubble where the planet belched a billion years ago and didn't quite get rid of its distress. There is quite a system of caves here, the weakened structure above should have been a clue for you. Oh, it's strong enough to hold its weight up. There's no need to fear that the roof is going to collapse on us." He chuckled.

"But we don't want the weight of the ground-car added to the structural weight of the ground. Probably an excess of caution, but still . . ."

He continued down the passage. Daniel could have seen by infrared, but he chose to remain in the visual spectrum and see the passageway by the lamps that the other three carried. The passage seemed to have been formed by some sort of natural erosive process. It was roughly oval in shape, and varied in diameter so they were able to walk comfortably in some places, forced to crawl painfully in others.

Rocky Kitajima in the caves of Mercury, Daniel thought. When last we saw our vidipic hero, Kit was squirming through the dangerous passageway in pursuit of the beautiful but fiendish Madame Sverdlovsk and her mysterious Q-ray generator.

The tunnel opened into a low-domed chamber.

Daniel entered it behind Lydia Haddad. Three lamps threw their beams in patterns that wove across the walls of the chamber, its roof and its floor.

The chamber was roughly globular. Its inner surfaces were apparently rock, a darker gray than the rocks and soil of the planet's surface, but very likely, Daniel thought, of the same material.

"What do you think of it?" Mgouabe asked. His tone was almost proprietary, that of a man showing off his new home to old friends, hometown friends, small-town folks visiting their onetime neighborhood chum who had gone to the big city and made good. "What do you think of it?"

"I never knew," a woman's voice said.

"It's a surprise, but so what?" the other woman asked.

The first must have been Lydia; the second, Tovah. Those were the answers they would give. It didn't matter if you could tell their voices apart, they would react differently to Mgouabe's proud question.

"I suppose this was suppressed information, too," Daniel said.

Mgouabe grunted affirmation.

"But, yes," Daniel pursued. "So what? You didn't bring us ninety million kilometers to show us a little cave. It's a nice little cave, Osvaldo, but... *why?*"

"Always to the heart of things, Daniel. All I ask of you is a little patience. This isn't all. Come along."

He led the way around the chamber. The walls and floor fared into each other and their surfaces were fairly smooth, but they offered sufficient purchase to the four figures.

The far side of the chamber opened into a similar, larger cavern. Mgouabe halted in the opening that connected the two chambers. "We'll have to lower ourselves here. It's safe enough. We can climb back out. Just be careful."

He sat on the rim of the circular opening. He lowered himself slowly, turning as he did so, bracing himself with both hands on the lip of the opening, balancing his lamp momentarily on the surface beside his hands. His grunt came through the radios of the others as he released his grip on the upper rim, then reached back and took his lamp down with him.

The others followed, none of them with great difficulty or delay, Daniel with the least of all.

The second cavern was similar to the first, but easily three times the size, its far wall showing only faintly in the light of the three lamps. The walls were of darker rock, mottled with what looked like damp patches.

Daniel walked slowly across the chamber. He halted before a dark spot and touched it gingerly with the tip of one finger. He gazed at his finger, then turned back toward Mgouabe.

"Water?"

Mgouabe grunted.

"But I thought—"

"Were you a planetary scientist?" Osvaldo asked.

Daniel shook his head. The others were trapped within their helmets but he was free to smile, frown, shake his head and be seen.

"Even if you had been . . ." Mgouabe crossed the chamber, his color-swatched white suit making him look like a rubber-tire advertising figure. "Even if you had been," he repeated, "would you have known about this place? Had there been any landings on Mercury in your day?"

"No." Dan shook his head again. "No. But so close to the sun . . . it's so hot . . ."

"No it isn't. Come on, you are the one not insulated from this world by a spacesuit. How hot is it?"

Daniel shivered. It was the kind of emotionally generated tropism that could have come in any physical environment, but he realized that it was appropriate to the setting as well. It wasn't hot in the cavern. The surface of Mercury, where they had left it, had had a temperature on the order of 350 degrees. But here in this cavern there was liquid water, or at least dampness.

Daniel pressed his palm against the wall. It felt no warmer than an ordinary rock on a warm day on earth.

"Good insulation, eh?" Mgouabe laughed.

Tovah's voice asked, "How did this place get here?"

"Who knows?" Mgouabe responded. "God's design, eh? Or the blind workings of statistical happenstance?"

"Probably bubbles," Dan interrupted him.

"Are you serious?"

"Entirely."

"I didn't know you had a degree in extraterrestrial geology, Mister Kitajima."

"There was a place—out in Nevada. I went there on a school trip. There were fossil bubbles. Huge old globes, three, four meters across. Some of them piled up three or four high, above the ground. Some of them still below. They were old gas bubbles, old subsurface emissions, coming up through thick mud. Coming up so slowly, the mud was so thick, the sun was baking it into new rock, like a vidipic sequence slowing down, think of it, the bubbles moving slower, the mud hardening, the bubbles moving still slower, the mud getting thicker and drier, and finally the whole process stops, it ends, a freeze-frame. You know what a freeze frame looks like? The process didn't really reach its end, it just froze up at one point and stayed there. I don't know how many thousands of years, millions of years those old mud bubbles stood there. It never rained out there, there was nothing to soften them, to let the process start up again. So they just . . . they just stood."

He rubbed his palm against the wall and brought it away; it felt warm and damp but there was no visible sign of moisture on it.

"Does it get cooler farther down here?" he asked. "Are there any more of these caverns?"

"There's more to see." Mgouabe said. "Come along, my pilgrims. I rather like your theory, Daniel." He laid a gloved hand on Dan's elbow. It felt warm and dry through Dan's garment. "Yes, I like your theory. A nice image. The planet sending up huge bubbles of gas, the bubbles pressing and pressing against that layer of muck, that burden of muck, trying to reach the surface and win their freedom, and moving slower and slower, straining, striving, not quite able to break through, never able to break through. Oh, a pretty image.

"Now look!"

He knelt in the opening to another larger, deeper, darker

chamber. He didn't point his lamp through the opening. Daniel knelt behind him, let his optical sensors shift into an infrared mode, showing him the inside of the chamber by heat that radiated from the rocks.

Daniel braced himself against the sides of the opening, too stunned and astonished to speak, too dazed and startled to trust himself to move. He closed his eyes and opened them again. He said, "Let me take your lamp, will you, Osvaldo? Unless you want to go first. I want to see this by normal light."

"No need." Mgouabe took Daniel's elbow again, this time holding it between thumb and fingers of his gloved hand. "If you can climb down there—can you climb down there? Good. You just go ahead. You'll not need my lamp, I guarantee."

Daniel tried to look at Mgouabe's face. The faceplate of his helmet had cleared here in the darkened caverns, but the helmet itself shadowed and concealed Mgouabe's features. Daniel could have seen Mgouabe by infrared also, but he was reluctant, almost squeamish, to use what he still regarded as his "powers," especially as regarded other people.

He looked behind himself and saw Tovah and Lydia there, standing over him and Mgouabe. "I'm going down there," He pointed.

"Yes," he heard one of the women say. For a fleeting instant he worried for them, worried for the effect on them, should something disastrous happen to him. If he were injured, killed, lost in the caverns of Mercury . . .

. . . Rocky Kitajima, lost in the caverns of Mercury. The fiendish Madame Sverdlovsk has lured our hero into a deathtrap far beneath the sun-baked surface of remote, mysterious Mercury. As Rocky climbs through the ancient passageways in pursuit of his elusive prey, the sinister . . .

. . . what would become of Tovah, of Lydia?

But they didn't really need him, he knew. They were each other's lovers, each other's partners. Their destiny was plotted, had been plotted for years. He was the extra factor in their equation; his removal would not destroy them.

He nodded at them, ducked away, slipped into the lower chamber.

He had to drop a meter and a half to the curving floor of the chamber. He started cautiously across its semi-smoothness.

He was uncertain as to the size of this chamber, although obviously it was the largest he had entered. If there were any danger here, Mgouabe would have warned him of it.

He crossed fifteen, twenty meters of gently sloping rock.

Without warning he was dazzled by a blue-white glare.

His optical sensors compensated automatically, rapidly, for the unexpected outpouring of brilliant light, but he still staggered back a step before he regained control.

In his ear he heard Osvaldo Mgouabe's voice, confidential, insinuating. "What do you think of that, friend Daniel? Didn't I promise you more surprises? Don't you think I'm a man of my word? What do you think of that?"

Towering above Daniel, filling the cavern nearly to its roof, stood a huge replica of the object Mgouabe had shown them in the skitter. It glowed with a light of its own, like a sculpture cast in luminous material. But it was clearly not simple luminosity; it was not a sculpture in radium, for it had not glowed until he approached.

He gazed upward, able to see its top, able to see the roof of the cavern palely illuminated by the object.

It seemed so perfect a replica of the vidipic image Mgouabe had shown them in the skitter that the vidipic might have been imaged from this actuality. He turned toward the entrance of the chamber. Mgouabe had dropped through the opening and stood with his extinguished lamp in his hand, watching Daniel. He read the unspoken question in Daniel's eyes. "Yes. The vidipic was imaged from this. It was made here. I made it— that is, I summoned in the crew that made it. All veteran Mercurians, of course. We have no emigration from Mercury. It would provoke too many embarrassing questions. But, yes, this is the original."

He started across the chamber toward Daniel. Tovah Decertes and Lydia Haddad followed him, dropping carefully through the circular opening.

Daniel turned his back on the others and began slowly to walk around the glowing object. Perhaps it was a sculpture. He couldn't be sure. If it was a functional object—some sort of machine—what was its purpose? How had it got here? Who had built it, and when, and why? He had a crazy thought of an ancient two-dee cartoon he'd once seen, of a maddened

Noah building an ark in the cellar of a twentieth century dwelling.

How would he get it out the window when the deluge came?

How had the sculptor got his work into this bubble? Or if he had created the work here, how did he ever intend to get it out?

The thing towered four, five meters into the vacuum near the roof of the cave. Bits of something sparkled in the roof above it, and Daniel realized that there was crystalline matter in the cave roof. Mica, silicon, maybe even water ice.

"Osvaldo, up there." Daniel pointed. "Is that water ice?"

"It is."

"What is this thing?"

"Friend Daniel, you have the advantage. This spacesuit precludes the eloquence of the shrug. A mystery. I had hoped you would have a theory."

Daniel stepped closer to the object. He was bathed in its cold glow. He looked behind himself, toward the wall, to see his shadow lying black and elongated against the blue-white illumination of the object. "It looks like some old *avant-garde* sculpture. All neon tubes. I had a college roommate once studying art history. She showed me a book she had on something they called dekko. Dekko. Something like that.

"All straight lines and sweeping curves and burnished metal surfaces. Brushed aluminum, cobalt-blue mirrors, glowing tubes in brilliant red and blue and gold. Streamlined shapes on everything, even the people. Fabulous stuff. Fantastic. A whole world that looked like a stage set for a space fantasy."

He stopped.

Mgouabe said, "You think this is dekko? You think some secret space traveler from—when did you say?"

"I didn't. It wasn't my field. I don't know, a hundred years ago? Two hundred?"

"Anyway. Some secret voyagers from earth built this? Is that what you're telling me?"

Daniel shook his head. "Just a resemblance. What are those? Are those cracks in the wall?" He walked away from the structure. Its illumination blinked out. He cursed and stepped back toward it. It winked back to life.

Two figures moved. He saw Tovah and Lydia advance,

hand in hand, to stand beneath the glowing structure, heads and helmets tilted back as they gazed at it.

"Will you stay near it for a while?"

Tovah nodded clumsily.

"But don't—don't touch it, all right?" He saw them turn toward him. "I don't know what would happen. Probably nothing. But—just don't right now, all right? Osvaldo, did you ever—has anyone ever done more than look at that thing, more than make a vidipic image of it?"

"What were you asking about?" Mgouabe came close by Daniel. His face was visible through the faceplate. There was perspiration on his skin. In the glaring blue-white illumination the black skin took on a strange coloration, an almost metallic gray. The drops of perspiration made it appear that Mgouabe was slowly melting, that if Daniel stood and waited long enough Mgouabe's dull metallic flesh would soften and run down the inside of his suit, puddling up inside his boots, filling the suit perhaps as far as his sternum, leaving his naked skull exposed inside the helmet, staring with vacant eyes through the plate.

Daniel shook the image away.

"Those cracks." He laid one hand on Mgouabe's ballooned shoulder, pointed with the other. "I guess there could have been cracks in here from the freezing and melting of water long ago. Or just from the heat when the mud dried."

"You're sure your gas bubble and mud theory is valid, then?"

"No." Daniel shook his head. "It just—seems to fit."

"Well. Then I suppose they are cracks in the walls. I don't imagine this place is going to collapse on us." He turned his gaze full on Daniel, his eyes gleaming through the faceplate "What do you envision, friend? The temple of the Philistines collapsing upon Samson? I think not. Who is our Samson? Surely not I. You, perhaps? And who is Delilah? Which of your friends?" He paused before he spoke the last word and moved one shoulder in the direction of the women. The degree of movement inside the suit, Daniel could not gauge. Its appearance through the protective fabric was eloquent.

Daniel walked away from Osvaldo. Thirty centimeters from the wall he halted and reached out his hand, making a three-point balance of his feet and his one hand.

The cracks were definite, a webwork of them in the rock. Daniel was uncertain as to how hard the rock might be. If it was really just dried mud it might be easily chipped away or cracked. He was not in a mood to try it. For the time being, he would simply let it be.

He tried to see into the crack. It was not wide, just a matter of millimeters, but it might be deep nonetheless. The light from the glowing object behind him passed over his shoulder and illuminated the wall, but did not penetrate far into the crack. Daniel tried adjusting his vision up and down the spectrum. At last he found a wavelength at which he could see into the crack.

The superhero applies X-ray vision to uncover the lair of the mad scientist. Rocky Kitajima exposes Madame Sverdlovsk.

The crack was not wide, but it led to a network extending far into the wall. There were scratches on the insides of the cracks. Daniel blinked. It was absurd; more: it was insane. He thought they were drawings: impossible.

He tracked deeper and more carefully through the cracks. It was a test of his abilities, and he knew he was getting high grades—for whatever that might be worth.

The cracks might be natural phenomena, formed by the geological forces that had produced these odd bubble-caves. Odd, yes, but not altogether extraordinary. They might well be the products of natural processes, and he was not inclined to posit any more exotic factors in their presence than he needed to.

The object behind him, the glowing neon sculpture or whatever it was, that was another matter. That was clearly not the work of nature. Mgouabe's notion that the object had been placed here by ancient visitors from some forgotten civilization on earth was not entirely plausible. Nothing was plausible about the sculpture. But ancient visitors from earth did provide a workable theory.

But so did other theories. Native intelligence here on Mercury. There might be no survivors of that ancient race, nor any other evidence than the sculpture, but its presence alone was strong argument. Or—if not native intelligences, visitors from elsewhere.

Elsewhere.

That opened endless vistas. The whole notion of alien life, especially alien intelligence, had captured imaginations since people first had come to the notion that there were worlds other than earth. That idea was over three thousand years old. If tales of intelligent beasts, monsters, supernatural beings, gods with the bodies of humans and heads of animals—if these could be considered speculations on the existence of aliens, then the idea was far older.

The failure to find evidence of life other than that which had evolved on the earth had been one of the great disappointments of the era of space travel. Even the discovery of Zimarzla and its enigmatic transmissions had offered at best ambiguous data on the subject.

But the neon sculpture...

Here was an object that could be explained by only two means, each of them highly romantic. It was the product of an ancient and highly developed human civilization, a civilization totally erased and forgotten save for this one artifact. Or it was the product of some alien intelligence.

It was a must-win dichotomy.

Unless the object was a forgery, something created and emplaced by Mgouabe's IGO for some bizarre and unsuspected motive of their own.

That possibility Daniel refused even to entertain.

Sculptures in the caves, carvings in the cracks. Something caught Daniel's eye, a flickering shadow deeper in the wall. He tried to follow it with his vision and his consciousness. He knew that his body was still standing in the bubble-cave, balanced against the wall on one hand. His locus of awareness had not left his body in the almost astral sense that it had at the medical Island, but his concentration was so intense that his world had become the interior of this network of narrow openings in the cave wall.

Something flickered, wriggled.

He tried to follow it.

He was fascinated by the—by the carving, writing, drawing that he had seen on the wall of the crack. Probably it was nothing, probably it was merely some random feature of the sedimentation of the rock, something that nature had accidentally made in a shape vaguely suggestive of purpose, that his own mind had then interpreted from an abstract inkblot into a fantastic creature, a leering face, the body of a woman, the silhouette of a tree.

Something moved.

It couldn't see him, whatever it was. He wasn't here in the crack, he was outside in the bubble-cave looking into the crack. He hadn't moved in minutes.

But *something* had moved.

Daniel closed his eyes, issued a mental command that closed a neural switch in his half-organic, half-artificial mind. He called up the macro for reverse-angle vision, set the automatic timer that Mimir Monroe had installed for him, opened his eyes and sent an *execute* message to the macro.

He saw something flicker deep in the crack in the cave wall.

We saw the Light and a great excitement ran through us. We stopped in the midst of our myriad tasks. Awe and joy. Joy and fear. Our priests rose on pseudopods, waving cilia above their nuclei, roaring in triumph and vindication.

We stopped our mating. We stopped our feeding. We stopped our warring. Red ones, green ones, yellow ones flowed together, intermingled, merged, flowed, rose, bubbled, flowed. A great concentration generated a million pseudopods and rose on them, dancing, stamping our triumphant message to the Light.

We flowed through our cities, gathering ourselves by uncounted numbers, surging and pouring with excitement. How long had it been since the Light had come? How long had we waited, worried, believed, not believed, wondered, pondered, mated, died, grown, feasted, argued, danced, shouted, warred, divided, sorted, organized, merged, flowed, preached, quarreled, believed, worried, waited?

The Light had come.

We came to the Writings.

We pressed our body, our flesh, our stuff, against the Writings. We tasted the words of the Writings. We entered the Writings; and they, us.

We knew the Writings; and they, us.

We devoured the words of the Writings.

We knew that the Light would come. Our ancestors had

known and we knew. We pounded on the rocks with cilia. We danced on the rocks with pseudopods. We howled. We roared.

The Ones who bring the Light shall come.

The Light shall come.

If we wait, the Light shall come.

If we believe, the Light shall come.

We lived and died, warred and built, carved, waited, believed, waited, and the Light has come.

The Light has come.

We will go to the Light, and the Light will take us from this place to Heaven.

Heaven is a greater city in the rock.

Heaven is a finer city in a bluer rock.

In Heaven everything is blue.

In Heaven everyone is blue.

In Heaven the pseudopods of everyone are lithe, their cilia graceful, there is nourishment for all, the enemies in war are weak and we triumph always.

Those who believe shall be taken by the Light.

Those who believe shall know when the Light comes.

We knew the Writing. We flowed from the city. We flowed on the face of the created way. We held to the city and lowered first the priests, then the yellows, then the greens, then the reds. We flowed in joy. We stamped pseudopods and shouted.

The Light!

The bringers of the Light were here.

The bringers of the Light. The bringers of the Light will take us with them, with them, with them, with them to Heaven. They will take us to Heaven. To Heaven where our enemies are weak.

The bringers are strong.

Our priests show dismay. Our priests show surprise. Our priests show fear.

The bringers are not the bringers.

The bringers are not the bringers.

How can this be?

We stamp on pseudopods. A hundred pseudopods. A million pseudopods. We shake the world. We shake the world and the Light itself quivers.

How can this be?

The bringers flee?
Why do the bringers flee?
We flow to the Light itself. We touch the Light. Never have
we touched the Light. We touch the Light.
We are blue.
We are blue!

13

"BLUE!"

"What?"

Daniel saw concern reflected in Tovah's eyes as she bent over him. He tried to smile reassurance to her. The tension in her pale features lessened.

"Are you all right, Dan?"

He nodded and started to sit up but she pressed him back. He yielded. His prosthetic systems could have overcome her effort to hold him down, but it seemed more—human—to drop his head against a pillow. He was in a low-g environment, he realized. He turned his head, looked around.

He was in the ship that had brought them to Mercury, and the ship was off-planet, in space.

"What the hell—?"

"We got out of there. I'm just glad that you're all right, Dan. Lydia's taking a nap. Osvaldo is playing jockey."

This time Dan did sit up. He was lying on a folding bunk in a back compartment of the skitter. He looked around and saw that Lydia Haddad lay on a similar bunk, sleeping. A small screen, done up porthole-fashion, offered a view of space over each bunk.

Dan swung his feet off the bunk and placed them on the deck. Tovah sat on the bunk beside him. They put their arms around each other and held tight for a long time, not speaking. Dan felt Tovah's cheek against his own.

"I want to tell Lyd," Tovah said at last.

"Let her sleep. Tell her what?"

"I want to tell her you're all right. She kept saying that you would be. I guess she had more faith in Mimir Monroe than I had. I was afraid you were going to be a vegetable."

Dan shook his head. "More like a machine with its gears locked in neutral, if that happened. But—"

"What was that *blue* business, Dan?"

"I—oh. That's going to be hard to explain. I'll tell you, but it's going to be hard. But what are we doing here? I . . . look, the last I knew I was in that bubble-cave. We all were. Next thing, I look up and here I am in the skitter, and we're cruising somewhere, somewhere in space. How did we get back here, and where the hell are we headed, and why?"

He shook his head, stood up feeling disoriented and laid one hand against the bulkhead of the ship to steady himself. Rocky Kitajima of the space lanes!

"You were leaning against the wall in there." Tovah put her hand on his belly as if she wanted to make certain he was really there, as if she were afraid he was just a vidipic image and might vanish at any moment.

"Osvaldo got a radio message from the ground-car. The car commander relayed it from the big station. Osvaldo said we had to get out of there at once, it was an emergency." She shook her head.

"You were—it was as if you were catatonic. Like the time at the medical Island. We had to carry you, drag you." For the first time since the conversation had begun, Tovah smiled. "You are one *heavy* fucker, mister! It's a good thing this happened on Mercury and not on Jupiter!"

He grinned back. "If it happened on Jupiter you'd have had to swim for it!"

He was feeling steadier now. He held his hand out to Tovah and she took it and stood with him. They embraced again. He looked into her eyes and tightened his embrace. They shared a long kiss that left her breathless. "Maybe we should wake up Lydia," she said finally. "Low-g sex is supposed to be something!"

"I don't know, Tovah. I don't know if I could keep my mind on it. At this point. And Osvaldo—"

A security bar sealed the bridge from the rear compartment. Tovah tapped a series of instructions into it. That took one hand. The other was inside Dan's garment by then. "You seem to have your mind on it very well."

They moved to the other bunk. Tovah knelt, holding Daniel with one hand, laying the other gently on Lydia's dark hair. Dan saw the pale, heavyset woman bring her lips to Lydia's face. Lydia stirred. Tovah tightened her grip on Daniel's hand and drew him down onto the bunk. He embraced Lydia and Tovah, placing one arm around each of them as they came to each other.

LATER they tapped a release code into the hatch bar. The separator slid away and Lydia, Tovah and Daniel stepped into the bridge of the ship.

Osvaldo Mgouabe sat at the control board of the ship but the controls were preprogrammed and locked on program control; Mgouabe was gazing into space as the others entered the bridge. The vidipic projector was on the control board; a bead was in place and the glowing image of the Mercurian artifact filled the bridge with its blue-white illumination.

Although Mgouabe's eyes were fixed on the remote points of light outside the ship, his right hand—his prosthetic right hand—played over the intangible surface of the vidipic image, caressing its every contour with the sureness of long familiarity.

The sun still lay ahead. Its disc was huge but its brightness was cut to a pale luminosity by the ship's polarizing shield.

Mgouabe turned and looked up at Daniel and Tovah and Lydia. He smiled. "I'm pleased to see you all looking so well and so pleased. You must have had a very good rest. Daniel, I am most relieved to see that you are unharmed. My congratulations to you and to your employees. I had an explanation of your"—he laughed—"your astral projection device. Amazing. Truly amazing. First astral travel, next I suppose we shall witness a recurrence of table rappings and spirit trumpet serenades. Were such things a feature of your time? No? They must have been part of an earlier era, one even less enlightened. Hahah! Or perhaps *more* enlightened, who is to say?"

He turned and gazed at the vidipic image of the neon sculpture, then he spoke to them again, even though his back was turned.

"I suppose you'd like to know why we left Mercury so, ah, precipitously, eh?"

"I would," Dan said. "Tovah told me you'd got an urgent message, and off you went. Dragging me along like a sack of oranges."

"Oh, wonderful, wonderful! You old-timers use such marvelously colorful imagery. A sack of oranges indeed. Well, and that isn't really such a bad description."

He swung around.

"I'll tell you what. You want to know why we exited so rapidly from charming Mercury. I would like to know what you experienced during your mystical trance. You muttered about something blue after we'd got you back to the ship. What was blue?"

"You want to go first, Osvaldo? Or shall I?" Dan found a seat. He could stand indefinitely with as much—or as little—comfort as he could sit. But he felt better face to face with Mgouabe, rather than standing over him like a schoolboy called to task by the principal.

"You first," Mgouabe said.

Daniel shook his head. "No. You've played the mystery man too long. I want to hear your story."

Mgouabe gazed into Daniel's eyes. There was a silence. Then Mgouabe nodded. "Very well."

He stroked the intangible neon sculpture with one hand, the black prosthetic skin bleached to a metallic gray by its glow.

"As you've doubtlessly deduced by now," he purred, "the International Geophysical Organization is more than a scientific body."

"Doubtlessly," Daniel agreed.

"And our stations—the planetary station on Mercury, for one—are more than scientific research installations."

"Yes." Daniel looked at Tovah, at Lydia, then waited for Mgouabe to resume.

"Is that all?"

Osvaldo waited.

Daniel said, "Don't be dense. And don't assume that everyone else is dense. Even if I could have mistaken you for a run-of-the-mill bureaucrat—which I assure you I did not—Lydia and Tovah filled me in on who wields power on earth these days.

"In fact"—he jabbed a finger at Mgouabe's chest—"what

I'm puzzled over is, why are you here with us? Generals don't dig foxholes and bank presidents don't make change. What are you doing playing rocket-jockey?"

Mgouabe laughed. "I thought we'd been over all this. Back at that delightful picnic, and then before we started for Mercury. Why don't I just stay on earth and pull strings, live comfortably, let some little graycoat play space ranger, eh?

"Daniel, listen to me." He leaned forward confidentially and ran his fingertip in a circle around Dan's kneecap. "Machine to machine, eh? He grinned sardonically. "Do you know what's going to happen to earth in a few decades?"

Dan nodded. "I know. So do Lydia and Tovah. Things aren't going to get better. That's just the story you're using to keep the lid on. If word got out—"

"The end is nigh!" Mgouabe waved his hands in the air, rolling his eyes like a cartoon prophet.

"That's right. If the billions of people on earth found out that life is going to end on the planet in less than a century, there would be chaos."

Mgouabe pursued his lips. "Indeed there would. Twenty-six billion souls trying to skitter up to the few Islands that could take them. It would be disastrous."

"But you're keeping the lid on it. Pretty successfully so. As long as word doesn't get out you're safe. You can live in comfort—in luxury—for the rest of your life."

"Not the point. No, not the point at all." Mgouabe leaned back and ran his hand over the neon sculpture.

"Then what is?"

"Daniel, I do not think you really like me." Mgouabe's voice dripped mock pain.

Dan shook his head. "I don't."

Mgouabe clucked. "That is sad. I'm really quite fond of you, you know, Daniel. Why, I named a rose after you. I don't suppose you really understand what that means."

"I can imagine."

"And you do not respond. Well, I've given it my all." Mgouabe sighed conspicuously. "Whether you care for me or not, it makes little difference. Here we are, eh? How would you put it in one of your old space fantasies? I sampled the beads of a few. Really awful things. But we are plunging

sunward at a hundred microns per parsec, our fragile eggshell
of a space ship straining to survive against the fierce onslaught
of cosmic et cetera, eh?"

"Harmless trash," Daniel said. "I don't defend it, I never
cared for that stuff, but it was no worse than the Viking revival."

" *Touché!* Well, but to get this back on course, you wanted
to know why I don't just stay on earth and live on in comfort
for the next thirty or forty years, eh? And then die quietly and
let another generation cope with the problems we all know are
coming."

He steepled his fingers. "I suppose you asked the same
questions of your two, ah . . ." He cocked his head to indicate
Lydia and Tovah.

"Yes, he asked us," Tovah supplied. "but it wasn't the same
situation. The most we had to look forward to was a lifetime
of tough work and plain rations in the zone. That was our *best*
prospect. And if we botched, or if things just took a turn for
the worse, we'd have been out there in the dole lines with the
rest of the overpops.

"We're better off out here. A lot better off. Are you?"

Mgouabe smiled. "Very aptly put, Miss Decertes. Well,
and I must admit that I am not better off in terms of comfort.
The galley of this skitter can hardly compare with our facilities
at Lilongwe. By the way, would any of you care for a snack?
Here, let me punch in a few commands, eh? Rations for four,
with a bit of wine? Perhaps even a dash of cannabis?

"Oh, I'm so sorry, friend Daniel, I didn't mean to embarrass
you. Rations for three, wine, cannabis." He punched a series
of codes. "Ah."

The machinery responded.

"Of course, you have the advantage of us in some ways,"
Mgouabe continued. "You don't have to worry about any of
those messy and embarrassing little latrine duties, do you?
Well, every dark cloud, it's an ill wind and all of that. English
is so rich in metaphor, I think that is why I enjoy using it so
much."

He picked up a fried chicken wing and nibbled at its golden
crust, then washed it down with a sip of white wine. He made
a face. "I'm so sorry, ladies." He nodded slightly to Tovah
and to Lydia. "This Semillon Sec is normally quite adequate

for informal usage, but I'm afraid it just does not travel. A pity. Well..."

He swept the three of them with his eyes, obviously in command, obviously relishing the moment. "I have to say that there is more to me than a comfort-loving office-holder. I would really prefer to have someone else say that for me. I'm not modest you know. I just enjoy admiration more than self-praise, however well earned.

"But, you see, there's no *future* on earth. I don't want to be in on the end of history, I want to be part of its beginning. What ignominy, to preside over the antepenultimate generation of a planet facing extinction! Pooh! It makes my skin crawl."

"Then what do you want?" Lydia Haddad, quiet until now, leaned forward. "Where are we headed, and why? You've acted like the master of a game!"

"Tell me about blue." Mgouabe, suddenly serious, disposed of his meal. He fixed Daniel with a dark stare. "Tell me about blue, and I'll tell you a good deal else that you'll want to know!"

Dan returned his look. "All right. You know about the device that Monroe hooked up for me. It was a minor supplementary feature to the converter Lydia and Tovah developed— we thought. Turns out, it creates some form of... personality transfer."

"I know that," Mgouabe said. "I want to know what happened in that bubble-cave. What happened, what you learned, why you had so much to say, later, about blue."

"The caves are inhabited."

"By whom? By the people who built *this?*" Mgouabe swung the vidipic projector around so the miniature neon sculpture glowed in the center of the cabin, in the center of their four seats.

"I don't know," Daniel replied. "I don't think so. And I don't know if you'd call the inhabitants of that bubble people. They're more like..." He paused, trying to find the right way to characterize the creatures.

"Are they invisible?" Mgouabe interjected. "I didn't see anything. Decertes, Haddad didn't see anything. We compared notes in the ground-car. Maybe a faint shadow on the wall in front of you. We might have seen that for a few seconds as we hauled you away. A shadow. What did *you* see?"

"A shadow? A shadow flowing down the wall as if it was headed toward the sculpture?" Dan asked.

"You saw it, too?"

Dan smiled. "That shadow was an organism. Or maybe it was a million organisms, or a hundred million. Can you think of something as small as—Christ, I don't know! A spider mite? Something so small you couldn't even see it with the naked eye?"

"You could."

Daniel rocked back for an instant. "Yes, I could. But think of something that small, that highly organized. A living creature with organs, senses, even the ability to think. I think." He suppressed a giggle.

"And yet they aren't insects. In a way they're almost like— amoebae, I suppose. They can link up. I think their skins, they have some kind of exo-something on them . . . they can open up and flow together, they get like a giant single creature, they can share their experiences, they can act as one creature. And then they can separate again. I don't know if the—if the individuals that flowed into the amoebae retain their identities, if they regain their separate, separate, ah, lives. Or if the bigger creature just breaks down into new individuals. But . . ."

He stopped.

"They were blue?" Mgouabe asked. His tone, his whole manner had changed. He seemed to be oddly gentle, sympathetic to Daniel. "Is that what blue means?"

Dan shook his head. "No. They come in different colors." He smiled. "But *blue*—I think that was about the glow of the—" He held his hand toward the vidipic neon sculpture. He was not as practiced as Mgouabe. He missed the sculpture's contours and his hand disappeared into the image, up to the wrist.

He pulled his hand back.

"I think that's a kind of religious artifact for them. They may be the degenerate descendants of the race that built it. Or—they seem to have some kind of belief, a belief in something or someone or many someones—I didn't understand it all, you see, I just *experienced* it as *they* experienced it."

"Try."

"Someone returning."

"A savior? A messiah? A dead god?"

Daniel shrugged.

"That's a very common motif, friend Daniel. The Egyptians had it, the Christians—are you a Christian, by the way? I am not, but I find it a very interesting cult. Perhaps because of the Christian use of the rose as a symbol."

"Huh. I suppose I'm nominally a Christian." Daniel answered hesitantly. "In my time and culture, Christianity was a kind of default option for people with no real convictions."

Mgouabe smiled, "I like that! I like that a lot!" His face grew more serious. "But, you see, if those little blue spiders of yours have a religion, it's remarkable how it fits in with more familiar ones. The Incas, for instance. They expected their god to come back, and when the Spanish showed up, the poor Incas thought it was the millennium! Ho! They were more correct than they thought! And of course the Papuans—you're familiar with the Papuan cargo-cult?"

Daniel was not.

"Fascinating incident. Somebody was fighting a war, I don't remember who or why, don't suppose it really matters. But they used those primitive old wood-and-fabric airplanes for supplying their troops."

A frown creased his brow.

"Or had they gone on to jets by then? So many wars, can't keep the things straight. We could call it up, of course, but it doesn't matter."

Lydia interrupted. "Mister Mgouabe, what's your point? Who cares about savages throwing spears at each other in some ancient war?"

"Only this," Mgouabe said. "The Pacific Ocean is full of islands and the armies and navies kept pushing each other back and forth from island to island. The aborigines—well, it was not their war, they didn't care which group of outsiders conquered which other group of outsiders. But the warring nations needed the islands for bases. So . . ."

He paused and ran his hands over the sculpture.

"So the warring nations used to bring along gifts in their supply aircraft, and distribute them to the aborigines to stay on their better side."

He stood up and walked to the rear of the bridge.

"When the war ended the supply aircraft stopped coming. Years later anthropologists revisited the islands, and found the old landing fields perfectly maintained, and what looked like aircraft standing about, ready to take flight.

"They checked more closely and discovered that they were just bamboo mock-ups. But full-size, and lovingly crafted. Beautiful things. They asked the natives what they were, and the islanders explained that they were decoys. They were designed to lure the gods back so they would resume bringing gifts."

Lydia shrugged. "So what?"

Mgouabe smiled sadly. "You don't find it strangely—touching, Miss Haddad? All those years. The faith, the fidelity to their absent deities? All a misunderstanding?"

"Sounds stupid."

"Well, you are probably right. But don't you see—?" He let the question hang.

She frowned in concentration. "Sure. The, ah, spider people of Mercury—I'm sorry, Mister Mgouabe, I have a hard time taking this very seriously."

"Try, " Mgouabe said. "Just try."

"All right. The spider people of Mercury were visited long ago by a more advanced culture. Their—visitors—arrived in something like *that*. She pointed. "Something like that thing Dan calls a neon sculpture. The Mercurians thought they were gods.

"Then one day they stopped coming, and the Mercurians wanted them to come back. Maybe they brought them presents. Who knows, food or toys. So they built that—thing. That glowing sculpture. And they're waiting for their gods to come back."

"Yes, yes." Mgouabe nodded. "And now, one more bit."

Lydia said, "When we arrived and—turned on the lights—they thought their gods had returned. That was the experience Daniel shared with them. Is that what you're suggesting?"

"It is indeed. Although I cannot conceive of those tiny bugs building the sculpture. How? Out of what? That part doesn't fit. Still—we should not push the analogy too far. Maybe the sculpture was left behind by the—visitors. Rather than built by the aborigines. Who knows?"

Tovah shifted in her seat. "Look here, there's something the matter with that pretty theory."

Mgouabe raised his eyebrows.

"Those—bugs." Tovah spoke slowly, choosing her words with care. "Spider mites." She put a hand on top of Daniel's. "Amoeba creatures. Whatever they were."

Mgouabe nodded to encourage her question.

"Look, Mgouabe, how many ecosystems have we ever examined?"

"On earth?" Mgouabe responded. "I suppose it's a matter of interpretation. Just one, I suppose. We know that all life on the planet is related. It all interlocks. 'Who sees with equal eye, as God of all, a hero perish, or a sparrow fall.' 'Tis all one, young lady." He chuckled with his usual mixture of friendship and malice and irony.

"Well, yes," Tovah conceded. "but at least locally, we can separate ecosystems. A tundra system, a deep-sea system."

"Well, granted. And...?"

"And as far as we know, there's no such thing as a single-species system. How could it evolve? What would it eat? How would the population be held down? A thousand problems. It just wouldn't work."

"You suggest that the Mercurian spiders are all Daniel's fantasy?"

Tovah shook her head. "Hardly that. But—there has to be a lot more to that—that bubble-cave ecosystem than one species of little blue spiders. It just doesn't work, otherwise. What do they eat?"

Mgouabe shrugged. "Each other? Maybe they consume their own dead. Maybe they can draw minerals directly from the rocks and mud. Energy from the sun. Who knows?"

"I don't believe it. I don't think you do, either."

"Perhaps you are right. But then, whence came the tiny critters?"

Tovah shrugged.

Lydia Haddad said, "Maybe they were the visitors themselves. You—Daniel—you said they might be degenerate descendants of some higher creatures."

Dan nodded.

"Well, maybe they came in that—that—thing." She waved at Mgouabe's vidipic. "How do we know? Maybe they ran out of fuel, or the machine is broken. It needs parts, repairs. They were waiting for help to come, only it never came. How long were they there? A hundred years? A thousand? A million?"

Daniel shrugged. "They didn't remember. Or, at least, they didn't think about it while I was among them. It's a very strange state of being. I didn't have access to their memories and I didn't have any way of controlling them. I was just there, observing."

"How long could they preserve their traditions, then? Did they have any kind of records? Computer storage systems? Vidipics? Old-style books even?"

"They had a kind of writing, I think. The walls of their home—those cracks, you know, they're so small, to them they're as big as cities—they have some kind of carvings there. Writing or pictographs. The way they read them . . . they all flow together to become one social entity, and then they flow over the carving and it's physically pressed into them. They take on the shape of it. That could last a long time. You see, it wouldn't become distorted like an oral tradition. It's always carved there in the wall, and as long as the carving is preserved, the memory is renewed every time they flow over it. And it stays accurate."

Tovah broke in. "What happens to them now?"

They looked at one another.

"I mean"—she gestured— "we came into their world. They were programmed to react to the light of the sculpture. Don't you agree?" She waited for their nods. Daniel's came quickly, emphatically. Osvaldo's, perfunctorily. Lydia's was last, and came only after a thoughtful pause.

"All right." Tovah gestured again. "They were all primed for the light, for God knows how many generations, just waiting and waiting. Like Christians. Or Papuans.

"And the light came. Jesus walked the earth once more. The airplanes came back and landed beside the decoys. By the way," she grinned, "I really love that yarn, Osvaldo. Were you making that up? About the bamboo airplanes set out to lure back the supply flights?"

"Oh, no!" Mgouabe said. He looked down at Tovah's hand. She had laid it on his forearm. "I assure you, it really happened."

"Well, what did the Papuans do when the supply planes didn't come back?"

"They didn't give up, Miss Decertes, if that's what you are looking for. We had to move them, of course. Their home islands are too hot for habitation now. They're in the Falkland Islands, now, still building mock-up aircraft, still waiting for their old benefactors to return and hand out canned spam as they did in the good old days."

"Huh!" Tovah ran her hand through her brush-cut hair. Mgouabe leaned away, relieved to have her take her hand from his arm.

"Well, we changed the situation for those blue spiders," Tovah continued. "When Lyd and I stood by the sculpture and made it light up—I suppose it had sensors that we set off, that would be easy enough to build—the spiders thought their gods had returned. Or the rescue party had finally arrived. Whatever.

"Just think! They may have been very different creatures when they were first stranded. That close to the sun, I'd think the radiation rate, the mutation rate, would be pretty damned high. Good old genetic drift got'em. But they kept their traditions going. I guess that carved history, Dan, that flow-reading . . . that must have kept them going.

"And the promised day arrived, the lights went on, they came pouring out of their cracks to meet their long-lost brethren. Only we left! The lights went back off! How their priests gonna square that with the common folk? I think they're in for big trouble, friends. I think maybe there's going to be a revolution in the cracks of Mercury!"

"We shall never know about it," Mgouabe intoned.

"Hold on." Lydia pointed toward the vidipic image of the neon sculpture. "This thing seems to be some kind of display-case for biological specimens."

Mgouabe shoved out his lower lip. "Perhaps."

"Is there anything in it that resembles those creatures? Dan, can you tell?"

He leaned toward the sculpture. He gestured and Mgouabe manipulated the projector. The image rotated. Dan shook his head, gestured again; Mgouabe stopped the rotation.

"I can't tell," Dan said. "Look at that. Is that thing a sort of giant blue spider? That could be one of the mites, blown up. Or—I don't know. There's a certain—feel. It could be a related species, at least. I'm not sure. I don't know."

"Enough!" Mgouabe said suddenly. He snapped off the vidipic projector, then unlocked the skitter's control panel. He cut back on the screen polarization so the sun's brilliance filled the bridge almost—but not quite—to a blinding level.

The sun was huge now, filling the screen. No other objects were visible. "You wanted to know why we pulled out of Mercury so suddenly." He shot the words at Daniel Kitajima.

Dan nodded in reply.

"All right. You're going to learn. And also—I told you this ship was being refitted while we were at the bubble-caves. It's time for you to find out how it was refitted."

Mgouabe swung around in his seat, then stood. He was backlighted by the sun, a black man blackened further by the silhouetting effect. The others faced him, bleached by the same brilliance that silhouetted Mgouabe. Dust motes dancing in the atmosphere of the bridge formed a nimbus around Mgouabe. His shadow stood like a geometrical solid.

"First, we'd never have got this near to the sun if we hadn't refitted at Mercury. The skin of the ship is thickened and coated to get us by the sun. It looked normal on Mercury, didn't it, eh? But as we get closer the reflectivity increases. We should look like a perfect mirror soon, not that there's anybody around here to see us.

"We will skim within a million kilometers of the sun's corona."

"Why?"

"What?" Mgouabe was startled.

"Why?" Lydia Haddad asked again.

He shook his head. "If we didn't have the refit, we'd never get anywhere near this close. We'd have burned up by now."

"I didn't mean that," she persisted. "Why do we have to go so near the sun? Where the hell are we going anyway?"

Mgouabe burst into gales of black laughter. "I do beg your pardon, lady! You see, I was so involved with getting us safely to our destination, I didn't realize that only I know what it is. We're *en route* to Titan."

"Titan!"

He bowed mockingly, his long, solid shadow mimicking

the gesture. He stood straight once again. "The Russkies are headed there, and we need to get there before they do."

Dan spoke up. "Russians? What do they have to do with it?"

"We Marxists don't trust the Russkies. Did I mention to you my personal political convictions, friend Daniel? I don't make a big thing of them. The IGO is not a political body. No, don't snigger at me, please. We try to do our job. But my personal beliefs—well, you may be merely a nominal Christian, my friend, but you might find yourself drawn back to your church if it were attacked violently and viciously by apostates."

He shook his head. "And that is what happened to a great many Marxists. Merely nominal Marxists, not practicing. Like myself. When the counterrevolution swept Russia back into reaction, we found ourselves reasserting our Marxism. Oh, this was while you were in the deep freezer, Daniel. And before you were born, I think." The latter he directed to Tovah and Lydia with a mocking bow.

A frown drew deep lines in Dan's forehead. "I don't see what this history has to do with—what we're doing now. We're headed for Titan because a Russian expedition is headed there? From earth? And why? Why are they headed for Titan? And why is it so damned important for us to get there ahead of them?"

"Not from earth," Mgouabe shook his head. His jowls wobbled. "We would have no difficulty in reaching Titan ahead of them, if they left from earth. Saturn is far from us—far from earth just now. We have to cross the locus of the sun to get there. We have to hurry up because the Russkies are headed there by skitter from one of their Islands.

"Most of the Islands are independent but some were built and populated as colonies, and Tchaikowsky Island is still a Russkie outpost."

Daniel felt an impulse to spit. "I thought at least that we'd left *that* kind of bullshit behind. Well, what if they do get there first? And—what's the big excitement to get to Titan anyway? It was explored a hundred years ago and there's nothing there of any use I can think of. Unless somebody wants a big frozen-food locker."

Mgouabe bit his lip. "All right. To answer your second question first, the big excitement of getting to Titan, as you put it, my friend, is this. All sorts of wild transmissions are coming from that body. I can call them up on a screen and a speaker if you wish, but I'll tell you right now they don't make any sense.

"But there's never been more than background radiation from Titan until now. And these broadcasts seem to have started at the very moment that we set off the neon sculpture in that cave on Mercury!"

"Hold on." Lydia Haddad shook her head. "That doesn't make sense."

"Why not?"

"Because you were there before, weren't you, Mister Mgouabe? You visited those caves, you brought in a vidipic crew, you set off the—the neon sculpture before. And nothing happened elsewhere. Not on Titan and not anywhere else, isn't that right?"

"It is."

"Nor did the spider-mites react," Tovah added.

"Damn. That is correct." Mgouabe nodded grudgingly.

"Then why now?"

"I don't know. But I'm convinced there is some connection and I want *us* to get to Titan before the Russkies do."

"All right," Daniel said calmly. "That answers the second question, I suppose. At least it does as well as we can expect. But what difference does it make who gets there first?"

"It makes this difference, my friend. The Russkies do not know about the caves on Mercury. They do not know about the sculpture or the spider-mites."

"No," Daniel agreed, "but they know all about Zimarzla."

"Indeed. And while we do not know what connection there is in all these things, there has to be one."

"All right. So?"

"So—if we get to Titan first, we will have all the pieces of the puzzle in our hands."

"You think so."

"I do."

"But if *they* get to Titan first?"

"Then they have that piece, we have the sculpture, neither

of us have the whole puzzle. And we get back into political squabbling the likes of which humanity has not seen in decades. We may even get back into war."

Oh, Christ, Daniel thought, that's all we need. He said, "I'm not happy with this. But—all right. Where do we stand?"

"Look at this." Mgouabe extracted the vidipic bead from the projector and slipped another into its place. He repolarized the exterior screen to darken the bridge and snapped the vidipic into life. A new image glowed at them.

"Ever see one of these things? It's an orary. Very old device. I think Master Tycho Brahe invented it. A model of the solar system. The bodies are in scale to one another but they're exaggerated against the distances involved."

"I know about oraries, thank you."

"Don't be hostile," Mgouabe warned. "Now look. We're here, headed from Mercury toward the sun."

A tiny point glittered.

"Here is Saturn. Titan. Earth is back here—no problem if they left from earth. But look."

A miniature cylinder glowed at the edge of the asteroid belt, ninety degrees from Saturn in the plane of the elliptic.

Mgouabe traced a course from the miniature Island to the region of Saturn. With a finger of his other hand, he traced a course from the gleaming point that represented their skitter. "Look, if we maneuver away from the sun in the plane of the ecliptic we add so many kilometers to our course that we lose the race. Or we could climb above the plane, or drop below it. Really the same thing, just a matter of orientation." He traced alternate routes across the orary.

"No good." He shook his head. "But look here." He ran a line with his fingertip, from the present position of the ship, close by the edge of the sun and on to the far side, past the orbits of the intervening planets and the asteroid belt, to Saturn.

He turned toward the others, his face glowing. "We win!"

Daniel and Lydia and Tovah exchanged appalled looks.

"We win! What do we win? We get cooked, you mean! We'd never make it through the sun. We'd be disintegrated, but we'd be dead long before that."

"You did not listen carefully," Mgouabe said. "The very shortest course would be through the sun, but that is obviously out of the question. The longer courses I plotted would be safest and most comfortable. But with our ship's new shielding, we should be able to skirt the sun's corona with reasonable safety. And that will bring us to the target first."

"And what do you want us to do now?" Tovah asked.

"I want Daniel to help me with a little safety check before we get any closer to the sun. I told you about the new shielding this skitter got at Mercury. I didn't tell you about the auxiliary sled that's mounted to the ship.

"It runs directly off a nuclear power source. Yours, friend Daniel. You climb in, plug into the sled's network. It draws power and guidance from you."

"Are you serious?"

"Entirely."

"And what do you want me to do?"

Mgouabe grinned. "Just take a little flight. A little tour of the outside of the skitter. I'm sure our shielding is good. But I'm an old safety bug. I'd like to be doubly sure. If you spot any problem, fix it if you can. You can perform EVA, of course. Another advantage of yours. With no suit. Just hold your breath!"

He grinned. The others stared at him.

"I said, 'Just hold your breath!' Don't you think that's funny? That's a joke, son, a joke!"

Mgouabe roared with laughter.

14

ROCKY THE SPACESHIP.

Rocky the spaceship, Dan thought, a picture book for boys and girls age four and older. Not much older. Except they don't seem to have picture books for boys and girls any more, or any kind of books for any kind of readers. It all comes out of beads.

He could feel the little triangular planes of the sled, the skids that it would land on (if it ever had occasion to land anywhere), the control surfaces for atmospheric steering and the tiny vernier nozzles that could be used to move the sled in vacuum or atmosphere.

He could even feel the grapples that held the sled in its bay. He muttered a few words to himself.

"What's that? I couldn't quite . . ." The voice was Mgouabe's, speaking through the bead receiver in Dan's ear.

Dan answered. " I guess I'm ready to go. Want to hit that lever or however the hell you do it? Bomb-bay doors open, as they used to say."

He could almost see Osvaldo nod in agreement. The panel beneath Dan's sled rolled smoothly to one side. "Okay, lower now," Dan said.

He felt his sled, himself, shoved from its, his, closely nested niche. He could feel the solar wind, the blast of hydrogen and helium nuclei pouring off the sun's photosphere, streaming away in all directions. He felt the wind on his wings.

No, no.

How could he feel a wind in a vacuum? How could he feel anything on his wings? What wings?

Yet he did. The streaming nuclei of the solar wind, the deltoid fins of the sled. Those were the wind, those were his wings. He yelled at Mgouabe, "Here I go, now! Wish me luck!" He let go of the clamps that held him by the back of the neck and the base of the spine. He gave himself a gentle shove away from the belly of the skitter.

He was facing directly toward the sun. The sled was fitted with a polarizing screen like that of the skitter. The screen was deeply polarized. The sun appeared a coldly glowing green disc against a dead-black backdrop. The flames of the sun's corona danced and wove like petals of an evilly animated blossom.

Dan squeezed his eyelids partway shut, concentrated on shutting down his optical sensors while he compensated by clearing the polarized screen. Soon the screen was clear and his sensors were dealing with the direct sunlight. The disc now had its normal coloration, a brilliant white with suggestions of yellow-orange at its rim. Those were the corona.

The sky surrounding the sun was still the dead-black it had appeared through the polarized screen. There were millions of stars there, too, Daniel knew, but his sensors were stopped down to the point where they failed to register.

He powered the sled forward, moving still beneath the belly of the skitter. He leaned over the edge of the sled and looked beneath himself.

In a sudden panic he pressed his face against the body of the sled, clutched it with his hands. His instincts had told him that he was high, high, far higher than the top of a building or the top of a mountain, higher than the Elevator at Rejkjaviko or that at El Triunfo, higher than the moon, higher than an Island.

He was above the universe, and if he fell he would tumble endlessly through infinite space, through infinite blackness and emptiness, would freeze to absolute zero and tumble forever, forever, till he fetched up dead against the rime ice of some remote Thule. Gingerly he released his grip on the sled with one hand while clutching tighter than ever with the other. He pressed his hand against his eyes, then peered carefully between his fingers.

The sight was still there. He could still *feel* the distances, the unmeasurable millions of kilometers and the irresistible tug of gravity of the remote stars and galaxies as they pulled at him, drew him, tugged and stroked and caressed him to draw him like a lover.

He shuddered so hard that his cheek pounded the body of the sled. He held the sled with both hands once more, blinked, and was at least able to hold his eyes open. He regained some control of himself. He fixed his vision on one remote gleaming dot and carefully extended the focus of his optical sensors.

At last the dot resolved itself into a vaguely ovoid form, a glowing milky-white oblong. He struggled and saw it still more clearly: a spiral galaxy. He saw it three-quarters on, neither as the pinwheel it would have appeared seen broadside nor as the bulging lens it would have seemed end-on.

The nuclear-powered rotary pump that ran his body whirred at its normal rate but Daniel had the strangely familiar sensations of rapid breathing and elevated heart action that for thirty-odd years had signaled excitement.

He smiled to himself and spurted farther forward, emerging from beneath the skitter. He didn't know how long his panic-fugue had lasted, but there was no radio transmission coming from Mgouabe as there would surely have been, if Daniel's behavior had lasted very long. He took direct readings of the sled's condition and its performance. He felt good.

He had started with momentum identical to that of the skitter. His own forward acceleration, the acceleration of the sled, however modest in its own right, was added to that velocity. He calculated rapidly, determined that he was close to a hundred meters ahead of the skitter.

He used his verniers to rotate the sled on its long axis. As he came upright with his back to the sun he felt the warmth of its radiance and the gentle solar breeze. It was like sun-bathing on a balmy day. It was a pity that his new epidermis would not pick up a tan.

He tipped farther so that he was, effectively, lying prone, his feet toward the sun, sliding feet-first in that direction. The star-salted heavens swung before him and the skitter came into view.

The sun glinted off its thickened skin and heavy shielding.

The shielding had a mirrorlike finish. Every variation in the angle of approach and angle of reflection of sunlight had a scattering effect, an almost prismlike fragmenting effect on the sunlight. The shielding itself was nearly colorless. The sun's radiance, shattered and scattered by the shield, spread like a dazzling flower, like a million-petaled rose whose each petal vibrated at a different frequency. Like a shining giantess, a dazzling goddess opening herself to her chosen lover, her over-whelmed, obsessed, helpless, ecstatic lover.

He opened his mouth and called. He opened his arms and reached.

Osvaldo Mgouabe spoke loudly: "What, Dan!"

He covered his eyes with his hands. He felt his body trying to pant for breath. He said, "It's nothing. It's all right. It's—a kind of space-ecstasy. I have to calm down. Don't worry. Give me a minute."

"Is the ship all right?" Mgouabe gave him no time.

" It looks—uh—it looks okay. It's fine."

"That won't do."

"Uh?"

"Listen, maybe you'd better come back in, friend."

He wouldn't! They mustn't make him! Osvaldo mustn't command him to return, to abandon his flower, to abandon the goddess he worshipped with his flesh to return to the skitter.

Another voice, a woman's voice. It was the goddess, he knew, speaking to him. It was Lydia Haddad. "Please, Dan. Tovah and I need you here in the skitter. Please come back in. Dan, will you?"

He shook his head.

He looked around, looked at the blackness of space, the deepness of space, the brilliant unwinking points of distant stars. He kept his eyes away from the flower-ship.

"Dan?"

He made a fist and struck himself on the thigh. He felt his awareness coming back toward its normal condition.

"Dan? This is Tovah, Dan. Lyd and I—"

"I'm okay." He shook his head. A lot of good that would do. "I'm really okay, " he said. "I—can you all hear me? Osvaldo, too. Lydia. Tovah. Listen, it's a kind of ecstasy. Ocean divers used to get it. There was even a song about it, I remember it. A diver saw Jesus at the bottom of the sea. He met Jesus. And the spacewalkers. The first EVA experiments. You wouldn't know, it was even before I was born. You wouldn't know. This is another ecstasy. It was so beautiful. The solar wind. I can feel it. And the colors. The flower. The ship is a rose."

"All right, Dan. Will you come in?"

"I can do my job. What am I supposed to do?"

"Can you check the shielding?" It was Mgouabe's voice. "What does it look like to you?"

Daniel told him again, as calmly as he could.

"All right, then. You remain where you are. No, I think you'd better get closer. About twenty meters from the ship."

Daniel complied.

"Now I'm going to rotate the skitter. If I'm right, any flaw in the shielding should show up as a dull spot. Maybe just a point. But it will look dead-black against all that mirror-flare."

"Yes. And if I find a point like that, what then?"

"Then comes the fun. You look there within the body of the sled. You see a little panel—it should be right under your shoulder, Dan."

It was. Dan slid it open.

"This should be nicely nostalgic, for you," Mgouabe said. "Didn't you live in the hot-rod era?"

Daniel said, "Not quite. But there were tapes."

"Good enough. You spot one of those dead points in the shielding, all you need to do is apply some of the shielding material. You have a container of it there, in liquid form. Just use the applicator to cover the dead spot. What did they do a hundred years ago? Didn't they used to have something called lemonflake finish for hot rods?"

"I wouldn't know." But he opened the panel. It was precisely where Mgouabe said it would be. He found the shielding material and the applicator. He dabbed a speck of it on the body of the sled. It made a point of dazzling prismatic light.

He stared at it.

He thought: I could put this on myself. I could coat myself with it, cover myself with it. I could turn into a living flower of flame. I could swim in the sun.

He saw himself in his mind's eye, a double image perceived

from within and without. He could feel the flames of the sun's corona licking coldly at his body as he dived through them, rose again, casting darts of crimson, gold, chrome yellow, champagne yellow, rose.

"Are you all right, Dan?" Tovah's voice.

He shook himself. He set to work. The skitter, rotating slowly on her axes, showed him every bit of her shielding. He spoke with Mgouabe, warning him to halt the rotation when a point of black appeared against the coruscation.

He worked until no imperfections remained in the skitter's mirror-shielding.

He cast a final look at the sun, a lover's look at parting, and guided the sled back to its bay. He felt the hooks lock him into position at neck and spine, watched the panel slide into place, sealing him within the ship.

The bay sealed. Dan unhooked from the sled, waited for the inner panel of the bay to open, and returned to the bridge.

"Where are Tovah and Lydia?" he asked Mgouabe.

"Working on some new routine. They said it might be good for you some time."

Dan nodded.

"I was worried," Mgouabe said. "I thought we might lose you." He looked at Dan. "And the sled."

Dan sat. He looked through the screen at the polarized sun. It was dark green. The corona writhed.

"Was it that beautiful?" Mgouabe sat facing Daniel. He laid his hand on Daniel's knee. "Was it that beautiful? I envied you, out there, I thought, nobody has ever done what he's doing. No one has ever experienced what he's experiencing."

Daniel did not answer.

"What was it like?" Mgouabe tightened his fingers on Dan's knee. Prosthetic to prosthetic, Dan thought. Robot to robot. Where do baby robots come from, Mama?

"Rapture," Dan said.

Mgouabe turned from him and tapped out a series of inquiries on the skitter's control panel. Readout lights glowed back.

"You did a good job, Daniel. Look at these. If there were any flaws in the shielding, we'd know about it by now. We'd be heating up something fierce. I wonder what we look like."

"Nobody's watching."

Mgouabe smiled. "Of course. But if someone were?"

"A spark. A dart of flame. A glittering, mirrored flower."

Mgouabe grunted.

"All right. Here we go." Osvaldo punched at the control panel. "If this works the way it ought to, we will reach Titan safely. And well ahead of our friends from Tchaikowsky Island. If the program fails, we will not come in second." He grinned at Daniel. "Your friends wrote the program."

The ship veered. The sun, which had filled the screen, rose and swung to starboard. The ship dipped.

In orbit around Titan they were positioned, momentarily, to observe sunrise. It was a still moment. The sun, at a distance of nearly eight hundred million kilometers, was little more than a bright, yellow-white star. Its heat was negligible; its light, little more than negligible.

Still, looking down at the cloud banks that covered Titan, Daniel perceived a terminator. Solar day and night were not altogether meaningless even at this distance.

Their ship moved a hundred kilometers above the methane and nitrogen clouds. The ship's movement was less noticeable than the apparent advance of the terminator. Titan moved through a full series of phases, from sliver to disc to sliver. Then the sun fell below the horizon and the ship moved into night.

Daniel heard a gasp and saw Tovah reach for Lydia's hand. The rings of Saturn had begun to appear, their guiding moonlets policing each division. Then the planet itself, a gargantuan clouded globe, rose above Titan.

Where the sun had appeared tiny and weak, Saturn dominated the sky, a breathtaking vision of beauty.

"Good God," Osvaldo Mgouabe whispered.

"I thought you were a Marxist," Daniel said.

Mgouabe did not reply.

"All right. Here we are." Daniel stood up and paced. "We seem to have won the race, or whatever it was. What do we do now, wait for the Russkies and then shoot it out in the town square?"

Mgouabe dragged his eyes away from the magnificence of the planet. He tapped a series of commands into the control panel. The ship swung on its own axis until the planet was beneath it and Titan was directly overhead.

"I can't get over this constant reorientation," Lydia said. "Any time you want to turn up into down and down into up . . ." She spread her hands.

Mgouabe nodded. "I think this will be less distracting." He faced the others. "Our IGO monitoring stations have been keeping track of the transmissions from Titan. They still have not been able to read any pattern in them."

"Maybe that's because there's no pattern." Lydia said.

Mgouabe frowned.

"Maybe it's just some kind of alarm buzzer. Or a beacon."

Mgouabe made a face. "You may be right. In any event, we do have word on our rivals. They're still about—well, two to four hours from here. Two if they head straight in. Four if they do any reconnoitering *en route.*"

"And what do we do? Wait for them to arrive?"

" The rules," Mgouabe said, "would have us wait for them. Guide them in if they wish, offer assistance. Courtesies of the high seas."

"Somehow I detect a note in your voice," Tovah said.

"A note?"

" I suspect that you have other intentions than courtesy."

Mgouabe's laugh was a parody. "I want us to get down there and find whatever we can. And then get the hell out of here. Before the Russkies even arrive, if we can do it. If we can't, I still want us down there first, staking a claim."

"What do you expect to find?"

Mgouabe shrugged. "Something like the neon sculpture. Something related to it, anyway. That was no coincidence that all the sirens went off when we lit up the sculpture on Mercury."

"And then, what?" Daniel said. "This isn't a search for knowledge."

"But it is, my friend."

Dan shook his head. "Not in the scholarly sense. Not knowledge for its own sake."

"That I will concede. Things are building. History is moving toward a climax, a grand transformation." Mgouabe's eyes glowed. "The last days are upon us. There are signs and portents."

"You're turning into a mystic," Tovah said. "A fanatic! We're doing the bidding of a religious lunatic!"

Mgouabe shook his head. "No, no, no. I have no mystical vision, I assure you. I merely observe events. I make no claim of divine intervention, of cosmic pattern. How could I? I'm a Marxist. Atheism is my religion. I believe only in the inevitable working out of natural forces. Daniel here is the only certifiable mystic among us."

Daniel's eyes popped. "Me?"

"You are a Christian. Doesn't your faith speak of the last days, the second coming . . ."

"Yes, yes. And wars and rumors of wars. The skies will open and so on. Let's talk about something real. What's this business about landing and staking claims? Are you going to take this ship down and land it on Titan?"

"A metaphor. No, I doubt that a skitter could land safely and I doubt even more that it could get off Titan again. But the sled has a good chance to get down and back up. And of course there is the great advantage that you won't need a suit, Daniel. Or supplies. You can just go down there and do what needs to be done, and come on back up.

"We'll wait for you here in orbit." He spread his hands and smiled. "I think that's the way the original space explorers did their work. The first moon landings and such. A mother ship in orbit, and a lander to visit the surface. We'll be your mother, and you'll be our lander."

He turned away and worked over the controls of the skitter. Titan rolled beneath the ship, the tops of the moon's yellow clouds sliding past like an unending fogbank. Saturn itself rose and set again, a dizzying, magnificent sight as it moved across the sky, filling the view with its breathtaking beauty. The planet's rings, its major moons and numerous moonlets made a dazzling display but Osvaldo Mgouabe ignored them. He concentrated on the ship's controls and the moon beneath.

He turned in his seat. "I can't get us into the orbit I wanted."

Tovah asked why not.

"I wanted to put us into synchronous orbit over *this*." He jabbed a black finger at a screen on the control panel. "This is the chief locus of the transmissions. But there are too many forces at play. Saturn, Rhea, Tethys, Iapetus—we're being pulled in a dozen directions at once. And all the forces keep changing all the time.

"So we'll drop you, Daniel, on the sled. And keep in touch

by radio, of course. And we'll stay in an orbit that will bring us over your location as often as we can."

"But he'll freeze!" Lydia exclaimed.

"No, he'll be perfectly safe. Daniel, you have a nuclear furnace in your belly. And I think—if you're willing—you should coat yourself with the shielding material you used on the outside of the skitter."

"I didn't have any problems before."

"But you were in sunlight."

Dan grunted. "Okay. God damn it, I'm going to look like the Silver Surfer."

"The what?"

Kitajima smiled. "Nothing important. A cartoon hero. Long ago. Used to see screen adventures when I was this big." He held his hand at the height of a six-year-old.

THE sled fell away from the belly of the skitter and dropped toward the yellow fuzz of Titan's atmosphere. From this angle the ringed globe of Saturn hung low in the sky, a vision stretching from the moon's horizon halfway to the zenith. Daniel watched the planet briefly, filing the image with experiences to be relived when he had the time to enjoy them.

He ducked his head and glanced over the edge of sled. The sled's pointed prow dipped into the yellow clouds. Mgouabe's voice sounded in Daniel's ear, asking if he was all right. Dan said that he was. He was blinded, in the visual spectrum, by the murky clouds. The moon was so chilled that its radiation in the infrared was barely sufficient to identify shapes. Dan ran his sensors up and down the spectrum until he was able to see fairly well. A small scanner on the sled homed in on the major radio source. The transmission was meaningless as a message, but it offered a strong point-source beacon.

Something whizzed past Dan's face.

He whirled to see what it was—possibly a chunk of airborne ice or sleet—but it was gone.

He located the transmission beacon and set the sled into a spiral, gliding down toward it.

Another object whizzed past, too rapidly to identify.

Dan felt an impact as the sled was jolted from beneath. It bucked under his hands, then settled back into its course. "Some kind of atmospheric objects," he spoke into his radio. Mgouabe asked for details. "Don't know what they are," Dan said. "Couple of 'em missed me. One just struck the bottom of the sled. I don't think it did any damage. Probably a methane snowball."

Mgouabe said to be careful. Daniel thanked him for the useful advice.

An orange object thudded against Daniel's shoulder. It disappeared back into the murk. "Huh!" Dan spoke into his transmitter. "One of 'em whacked me!"

Mgouabe asked if Dan could identify the object. He could not. "Wait a minute! I think I see one!"

It was moving parallel to his sled, matching speed and course. "I don't think that's any snowball!"

Mgouabe asked what it was.

"I don't know," Dan answered. "Can't tell if it's—some kind of flying machine? A bird?"

"Impossible!" the voice sounded in his ear. "Titan is uninhabited."

"So is Mercury!"

Mgouabe said, "How's the seeing? Are you sure of . . . ?" He let the rest of the question suggest itself.

Daniel turned his attention from the conversation back to his surroundings. "I'll keep you posted, Osvaldo." The sled continued through the yellow murk. The flying objects continued to whiz in all directions.

The one that had paralleled Daniel's trajectory whipped past his face, then continued laterally and disappeared into the murk. Dan tongued his tooth-mike into quiescence. "You're some rare bird, buster," he muttered to the departed flying thing.

The chief sound he heard was the atmosphere whipping past his face. He peered down and saw a viscid, choppy sea. Yellowish icebergs poked up from the surface. A steady breeze— it must be a stiff one!—kept the liquid alive with whitecaps.

Again something matched the sled's trajectory. Daniel turned his face to get a good look at it. The thing looked back at him. "God damn it!" Dan tongued his mike back into life. "There's one of 'em not a meter from me, Osvaldo! I hope he doesn't take me for a meal!"

He didn't wait for Mgouabe to reply. He cut his mike and yelled at the creature. He didn't know if it had a sense of hearing, no less what it would make of his voice.

The creature swept forward with its wings. It reached start-ling speed and shot upward, leaving Daniel on his sled as if he'd been standing still.

Liquid nitrogen splashed from the sea, forming a fine spray across Daniel and his sled. He reached around the edge of the windscreen and scraped at the nitrogen ice that formed on it. He would have a harder time with the ice that formed on the sled's wings. Rather than scrape at it, he'd have to cut over more power from his own internal supply and use the wings themselves to melt the ice.

But that could wait for later.

He was nearly to the surface of the sea. He spotted a fairly even area on an ice floe. He checked the homing indicator on the sled's control panel. He was within the region where the radiation of Titan was centered. He looked overhead, hoping for a last glimpse at the skitter. It was impossible to see more than eight or ten meters into the methane murk. There was a single huge glow that filled a tenth of the sky. For an instant Daniel thought it might be the sun, then decided that it was Saturn. From Titan, Saturn *was* the sun for all practical pur-poses. The position of the huge glow suggested that it was late afternoon—but he didn't know how long the day was on Titan. He radioed the query to Osvaldo in the skitter, but failed to get through. The ship must have dropped below the moon's horizon, and the little tooth-mounted microphone-transmitter wasn't powerful enough to reach it. He should have checked the length of Titan's day before he dropped from the skitter, but he hadn't thought of it.

The ice floe was looming beneath the sled. Daniel circled over the sea, brought his sled in alongside a jagged ice peak that dominated one end of the floe, then banked in and cut power over the flat area. One of the flying creatures popped out of a murk-bank, flew straight at Daniel's face, then ducked at the last moment and disappeared beneath the sled's runners.

The sled touched down on a level stretch of nitrogen-meth-ane ice. Daniel unhooked from the sled and climbed off. He stood on the level ice beside it.

It was a pleasant afternoon on Titan.

"Hey, Osvaldo," Dan called.

Mgouabe was still apparently out of range of the tooth-radio Daniel used.

"Okay, never mind," Dan muttered. He stood surveying the scene. The sky glowed a dull orange-yellow near the horizon. Directly overhead it shaded off into a darker shade, and farther down it was black. The jagged nitrogen icebergs poked sharply into the air. Toward the setting sun—Saturn—they glowed, too, even more dully than did the sky. The ice underfoot had the look of dark urban slush, melted and refrozen.

The sea surrounding the ice floe looked completely black save for the low caps of foam where wind whipped up wavelets. The yellow clouds over Daniel's head scudded by in a brisk, icy wind. Large soft flakes of yellowish methane-nitrogen sleet fell on Dan's upturned face.

A pleasant afternoon on Titan.

Dan made another attempt to radio the skitter, then turned to explore his surroundings. The homing device on his sled had indicated that he was at the moon's radiation source, but there was no immediate evidence of any transmitter. Certainly no giant neon sculpture glowed blue here, as it had on Mercury.

Daniel heard a high, reedy cry. It must be one of the flying creatures he had encountered on his sled. The creature passed overhead, half-obscured by the murky atmosphere. It had wings, of that Daniel was certain. It seemed, also, to have a row of glittering, multifaceted eyes. Dan was unsure whether it was a bird or insect—or whether those categories could even apply to so alien a creature.

The blue spider-mites of Mercury were not really spider-mites, he knew. That was merely a convenient way of thinking of them. As for the flying creatures here on Titan...

There was another screeing, and one of the creatures landed halfway up an ice crest. It perched there, its face turned toward Daniel. Well, at least it had a face.

Daniel stood watching it, hoping not to frighten it away.

The creatures hunched its wings.

Daniel tried to imitate its cry, giving his voice a soft, re-assuring sound.

The creature leaped from its perch and disappeared into the murk. Well, that was a flop!

Dan examined the largest ice crest on the floe. Perhaps there was a neon sculpture—or something else—frozen inside the ice. The alien builders might have used the ice itself as a protective covering for their machine. But the ice seemed solid.

Another of the flying creatures appeared, circling over the sea a few meters from the ice floe. Daniel squatted on the ice, balancing on both feet and a fist like a football player at the line of scrimmage. He mentally set his internal clock, fixed his attention on the flying creature and made the mental leap to its mind.

The warm air buoyed his wings but the falling sleet gathering on his eyelashes was distracting. He partially closed his face-eye, squinting against the soft sleet-flakes, maintaining his circling course over the warm sea.

He kept his belly-eye wide open, scanning the wave tops and the water itself as deeply as he could penetrate with his vision. His neural sense had picked up the distinct presence of food in these waters. He had been preparing to dive and feast when a new source of neural activity had appeared. It was something strange, something he did not recognize as any species he had ever before encountered.

It was dangerous.

He had perched on a rock to study it, when the creature had spoken to him in his own language. Or so it had seemed. The creature's speech was so slurred that he had failed to comprehend its statements. It was a large creature, far larger than he himself, but it had shown him no weapons, had made no hostile move.

In fact, he had even made the breeding-challenge sign with his wings. The creature had not responded.

So he ignored it and resumed hunting for food.

An armored wriggler swam beneath him. He could pick up its neural activity, his belly-eye caught a slight glimpse of its movement beneath the water. He issued a piercing scream, commanding the wriggler to halt. He dived toward it, hit the water with his body drawn in to its most streamlined configuration.

With a . . .

Daniel blinked, rubbed his face with one hand. Sleet had accumulated on his cheeks and lips and he wiped it away. He shook his head, like a dog shaking away bath water. Methane-sleet flew in all directions.

He stood up.

"Daniel!"

"That you, Osvaldo?"

"I think we've picked up the Russkies. They're the bunch from Tchaikowsky Island, all right. And they're headed here."

Daniel grunted.

"How are you doing? What's it like down there?"

Dan smiled. "It's lovely. I wish you'd come down and join me. You'd love it."

"I doubt that. What have you found?"

"I'm afraid that your model of a solar system with nobody in it but us is all shot."

"The creatures on Mercury took care of that already, Daniel. You've found life on Titan?"

"We won't have to puzzle over a single-species ecology this time. There's one species here, a large flying creature. Seems to have eyes and a kind of neural sensor. I don't know how it works. Maybe it's electrical—some kind of built-in ability to detect the electrical fields of neural activity. I tried that personality transfer with one of them, and I found that it was out hunting."

"Are you in danger?"

"Don't think so. It gave me the once-over and flew away. Located its more usual prey. I caught only the fuzziest image. My flying friend thought of the food creature as an armored wriggler. Maybe some sort of eel with tough scales, I don't know."

"It's aquatic?"

"Yup."

Daniel heard Mgouabe grunt, then some off-mike conversation. "Look, this kind of exobiological research is fine but what about the radio source? These creatures don't show any sign of intelligence, do they? I mean, of being civilized. Could they have sent the radio message after our Mercurian contact? These creatures with their radio senses?"

"I don't know. I doubt it. Look, this place is pretty hopeless. Maybe I ought to come on back up to the ship."

"No."

"No? You want me to study the local birds and fishes?"

"I want you—listen here, Kitajima. The Russkies are on their way, and I don't want them picking up the piece of this puzzle that's on Titan."

"You're being awfully optimistic, Osvaldo. What piece of the puzzle? There's nothing here but icebergs and cold water.

Except it isn't even water. It's liquid nitrogen."

"What about those, what did you call 'em, armored wrigglers? Could they be the local intelligent species? Listen, if aliens landed on the earth and they first encountered parrots or jaguars or boa constrictors out in the jungle, they'd assume that there was no intelligent life on the planet. They'd have to find people."

"Right. And you think these birds and fish are just... well, the local birds and fish. Is that it?"

"I don't know. It seems like it."

Daniel rubbed his chin, looked at the sun. It had not grown perceptibly lower in the sky. "How long is the day here?" Dan asked Mgouabe.

"Hold on a second." Dan could imagine Mgouabe punching an inquiry into the ship's control panel. "Here it is. Just under sixteen days, earth normal."

"At least I don't have to worry about nightfall catching me unawares. Okay, I'll stay a bit longer. What do you want me to do?"

"Maybe you ought to try the sled again. I mean, what if there's an island a hundred kilometers away with a pyramid and a sphinx on it? Wouldn't you be embarrassed to give up and come home and then have the Russkies find the pot of gold?"

"Osvaldo, you're forgetting—the radio transmissions came from here."

Daniel tried to find the ship while he waited for his answer. His optical sensors were able to penetrate the murk better than a pair of human eyes would have, but he didn't succeed. He could hear Mgouabe conversing, off-mike, with Lydia and Tovah. Finally Osvaldo spoke again.

"Are you *sure* there's no transmitter there? Nowhere on that floe where you landed?"

Daniel assured him of that.

"Cojones!"

"Didn't know you were a linguist, Osvaldo."

Mgouabe laughed. "Without benefit of a built-in computer, either. Well, the discovery of life on Titan is still an important contribution. I don't suppose there'd be any point in trying to bring back samples. Anything that can live in a sea of nitrogen or fly in that atmosphere would never last here. We'll have to send an IGO party with the right equipment. Don't want to sign on as a sanctioned explorer, do you, Kitajima? You'd earn almost as much as a soccer player."

This time Daniel laughed. Then he said, "I'm plugging back into the sled."

He lifted off the ice, circled the jagged peak that dominated the floe, rose into the murk until the sea was barely visible beneath him.

"You're going to pass out of radio commo in a minute," he said to Mgouabe. "Talk to you next time around. Listen, before you drop away, what's the latest on the Russkies?"

"We've been talking to them. All very polite but *very* frigid. Pardon my use of that expression, Daniel. Considering what it's like where you are."

"On with it, you're fading."

"Yes. They'll be here in about an hour now. They'll want to take up orbit and send down a lander, more or less as we did."

"Agent on a sled?"

"Probably a bigger lander. Crew of—oh, four, six tops."

"I hope they're not hostile, that's all. Okay. Bye, Osvaldo."

"Wait! What are you doing?"

Dan said, "I'm going to check what's under that floe. It's drifting away anyhow." He pointed the nose of his sled straight down and dived into the nitrogen sea.

It took a few seconds for his sensors to adjust, but surprisingly the level of illumination beneath the surface of the sea was greater than that in the atmosphere. He couldn't tell how deep the liquid nitrogen was. He set the sled to spiral downward while he tried to locate more life.

The armored wriggler that the flying creature wanted for its dinner represented only one species, of course. There were more of the wrigglers, swimming singly. They ignored Daniel. He looked for other creatures—there had to be a food chain, and if the flying creatures that ate wrigglers were at or near its peak, there should be plenty of smaller creatures to build up to the wrigglers.

He found more fishes, some swimming singly, others moving in schools. Life in a liquid seemed to dictate pretty much the same kind of evolution in Titan's nitrogen ocean that it did in earth's water ocean. Daniel felt a sudden pang, so unexpected and so poignant that it seemed to cut to his heart and wring it. He was the wrong one to survive, to be the first to explore this alien ocean with its alien fishes. It was Marie-Elaine who should have lived to see this. With her passion for fishes she would have been enchanted here, classifying and naming the new species as fast as they were discovered.

Instead she was dead and gone, long since dead and gone, and her husband was slowly riding his sled through the nitrogen sea, looking for . . . looking for God knows what, he thought. For some exotic civilization. For some ancient, alien Atlantis. For some crumbled, fish-inhabited Grecian temple containing a glowing blue neon sculpture and some ancient transmitting device activated only recently by the incursion of himself into the bubble-caves of Mercury.

When he found what he was looking for, the absurd melodrama of it all sent him into gales of strange, silent laughter.

15 ◁══════

Not a Grecian temple nor a pyramid nor a sphinx. It was something incredibly graceful, even in ruins, and something that no comparison of Daniel's could fit.

It was clearly visible in the diffuse glow of the nitrogen sea. Daniel wondered if the glow was radioactive in origin. If it was, what effect might it have on him? He need not worry about losing his hair and teeth, he didn't worry about genetic monstrosities springing from his loins.

But he could develop cancer. If he did, how would he know? Loss of function? And if that occurred, and he returned to the Med Island, could his old friends Royce and Kimura simply replace his diseased cells with more electronic components? He wondered—not for the first time—how to define himself. At present, even though the bulk of his body was made of prosthetics, there did remain an organic core, at least a partially organic central nervous system that he could regard as his essential self. The rest of his body could be regarded as servomechanisms, super-waldoes built to serve the remaining fragment of Daniel Kitajima.

If the final bits of organic matter inside him were removed, replaced with silicons and plastics and inert metals, the last bits of flesh pickled for the specimen room—what then? He envisioned his body rising from an operating table and lurching like Frankenstein's monster while a fragile white dove, his departing soul, fluttered its way into the heavens, there to find eternal bliss nestled in the sacred heart of Jesus.

He put the absurdity from his mind and anchored his sled to the sea bottom. There was a solid bed of rocks and sand. Tall seaweeds rose through the liquid nitrogen, waving with every passing current. What bizarre chemistry functioned in their cells? One more puzzle for the inevitable IGO pioneers to work on, should they ever bother to visit Titan.

He entered the building. Its chambers were shaped like the insides of eggs; its corridors made obviously for swimming creatures who could move vertically or horizontally at will. Its scale was hard to determine: probably the builders were smaller than humans, but he couldn't be sure. If their habitual posture was horizontal that might account for the low ceilings.

In one room he found an astonishing picture. In an instant he knew the shape of the intelligent inhabitants of Titan. They resembled seals, but seals equipped with gill slits and with organs like clusters of tentacles that served in lieu of hands.

They were building a neon sculpture.

The picture was sealed into the wall. There was not a stick of furniture or any other sign of occupancy in the building. Surely there were none of the creatures.

Daniel swam from the building, then walked through the liquid nitrogen to his sled. He lay on it, plugged in, and rose toward the surface of the sea.

His head broke water—nitrogen—and he saw that the late afternoon glow of Saturn, Titan's sun, had barely moved toward the horizon.

What had he learned? In the normal course of events his observations would have made him an immortal of science. He had discovered an entire ecology. He had found the remnants of a previously unknown civilization.

But he had learned little that would contribute to the puzzle confronting himself and his companions. The ancient race who had built the neon sculpture on Mercury had apparently—no, he corrected himself, had *obviously*—visited Titan as well.

But who were they? What were their objectives? Had the seal-like creatures from Titan visited Mercury and built the sculpture there? It seemed wildly unlikely. The difference in environment was too great. How could a race that had evolved in an environment of liquid nitrogen at temperatures near absolute zero possibly achieve space travel? And if they did, would they visit Mercury, a world nearly as hot as their own was cold, and totally without atmosphere?

Assuming that the Titan race had once achieved space travel, they would use it to explore worlds that could support life of their own sort. Or where they could, at least, set up sealed—environment bases. Some of the other moons of the outer gas giants, of Jupiter and Uranus.

What would their spaceships have been like? Flying aquariums built to carry a liquid-nitrogen environment? Or possibly the seal creatures would simply have built spacesuits for themselves, personal life-support systems filled with nitrogen sea. There would then be no need for a sealed spaceship.

He shook his head.

There was no point in puzzling over the situation now. If there was anything left him to do on Titan, he had better get on with the work. Otherwise he would radio Mgouabe, plan a rendezvous with the orbiting skitter, and get back to the ship.

He tongued on his microphone but before he could call, the sky exploded.

A blood-red gout appeared in the midst of the yellow murk, billowing and spreading like the rush of blood from a swimmer caught in shark attack. Seconds after the discoloration's first appearance there was a deep, sustained thump resembling the sound of an old-fashioned howitzer.

Daniel leaned back, trying to locate the source of the phenomena.

Lightning crackled down from the deep red discoloration that dominated the roiling yellow sky. The ragged streaks danced between the ruddy patch and the wave-tossed nitrogen sea. The redness dropped toward the sea even as the lightning shivered toward Titan's horizon.

A blackened metallic cone appeared, descending slowly atop the discoloration. Lightning drove between the descending cone and the surface of the sea.

Daniel heard cracklings in his ear speaker. He caught a few fragments of Osvaldo Mgouabe's voice, but was unable to read the message. Little matter—it must be a warning that the Russkie expedition had arrived at Titan and was headed in for a landing. That much Daniel could see for himself.

The metallic cone descended tail first, like a military rocketship in some outlandish century-old space fantasy. Briefly it appeared to be aiming for the small ice island where Daniel had first landed. Then he realized simultaneously that the ship was far too massive for the ice island, and that it was headed for a different, a far larger, ice floe some kilometers away.

Daniel tried again to establish radio contact with his own ship, but the interference of the other craft's systems and the terrific electrical disturbances that they caused, totally overrode the link between Daniel and Osvaldo. Dan cursed silently. The interference would likely end once the Russkie craft had landed, but by that time the skitter would be over the horizon and out of range until its next orbit brought it back over the edge of Titan.

At Daniel's urging the sled rose higher in the nitrogen sea. His own weight and that of the sled itself would sink it in the nitrogen if he didn't exert an effort to keep afloat, but his own nuclear-power system, plugged into the sled's machinery, had more than enough wallop to keep the sled on top of the sea.

The Russkie craft's red flower had settled onto the selected ice island. The dancing lightnings now crackled and bounded within the cloud. The craft itself disappeared into the cloud. With its brightness reduced, even the red cloud faded into the thick yellow murk.

Daniel cranked up his sled so that it hydroplaned across the nitrogen sea on its runners. He made a final, futile attempt to contact the orbiting skitter, and returned his attention to the situation at hand. The rumblings and cracklings of the Russkie craft faded out. Daniel adjusted his optical sensors so he was able to see the craft, solidly down on the ice island, its rounded prow pointed at the sky.

The sled skimmed across the nitrogen ocean, thin walls of whitish spray rising on either side. When the sled approached the edge of the island where the Russkie craft stood, Dan slowed it. The sled dipped toward the surface of the nitrogen.

The runners slid onto a shelf of nitrogen ice, then rode up onto the island and slithered to a halt.

The red cloud had disappeared from around the Russkie craft. Daniel watched as a hatch opened in its hull a couple of meters above its base. A ladder was lowered and a monstrously bloated figure appeared, lowered itself slowly, then stepped away from the ladder.

Another figure appeared in the hatchway. Then another and another.

Four Russkies, unless there were more, remaining in the ship.

Daniel watched as the first spacesuited figure reached clumsily into a carrying pouch that hung from its shoulder. Behind him, the ladder was drawn back into the craft and the hatch slammed shut. There was at least one more Russkie aboard the ship, then.

The first figure had drawn a series of rods from the carrying pack. They fitted together, end to end, until a rod some three meters long was formed. The Russkies fitted a compact sliding mechanism to the rod, then one of them pulled a gadget from another carrying case and knelt clumsily. There was a brief glow as the mechanism hit the nitrogen ice. Daniel could see the infrared light that it gave off. The thicker end of the assembled rod was plunged into the melted ice. Perhaps they were taking cores, Daniel thought. Not that they'd learn much from nitrogen ice, but it was some kind of start. They were better equipped for a scientific investigation than he was.

One of them reached into a pack and pulled out a piece of furled material. Did they have maps of Titan? If so, they must not be the first Russkie expedition to the moon.

Daniel watched, fascinated.

The Russkie hooked the furled material to a mechanical slide on the rod. They all stood back and saluted. When the slide reached the top of the rod, the methane-wind snapped the furled material flat. It was the old Russian double-headed eagle.

They were claiming Titan as Russian territory! Daniel started to react, then stopped as they went on to the second part of their ceremony. From carrying packs they assembled the segments of a tall Russion Orthodox crucifix. They melted a second hole in the nitrogen ice and planted the crucifix.

They knelt.

One of them rose to his or her feet while the others remained on their knees. The standing figure walked from one to another of those kneeling, laying a hand atop each space helmet in blessing.

A priest!

It must be the ship's chaplain. Daniel didn't know whether to laugh or weep at the strangeness of the Russkie crew setting up their Imperial standard and double-armed crucifix, claiming this frozen worldlet in the names of their Tsar and their God.

He unhooked from the sled and stood up. He walked toward the Russkies. The priest was the only one of them facing Dan. Simultaneously the kneeling Russkies rose and turned. The priest must have told them he was approaching. If they were transmitting on a radio band he should be able to pick up the transmissions and use his universal conversion circuits to communicate with them.

Daniel started across the ice. Osvaldo Mgouabe had warned him that the Russkies were hostile to the IGO, that the Marxist society of Daniel's former lifetime had been overthrown and a reactionary counterrevolutionary regime established in its place.

But Osvaldo was himself a Marxist. He would have the lowest regard for these latter-day Russians. Daniel didn't know them, had nothing against them. He strode carefully toward their ship.

There was a voice in Daniel's mind. "Get out of there!"

Daniel froze. Was it one of the newcomers? Had he tapped into their radio band?

"Daniel! You're in danger!"

It wasn't exactly a voice, yet it carried the same overtones of personality that a voice would have carried with every accent and intonation.

"Osvaldo?"

"They haven't seen you yet. Get back to the sled and get off that floe."

"How are you talking to me?"

"Never mind. A kind of radio. I told you Monroe did some work for me. But you have to get out of there before they see you."

"God damn it! How dare you tamper with my circuitry—my mind! You have no right to—"

"There isn't time! They've spotted you!"

The spacesuited figure nearest Daniel had turned toward him. It was pointing and gesturing.

Daniel raised both his hands, showing that he had no weapon.

"That won't do any good," the voice whispered. "Get—"

"Can you see down here? Where's the skitter? Damn you, Mgouabe, are you using my eyes?"

One of the Russkies had drawn something that looked like an electronic gun from a compartment on his suit. Another followed course.

"There isn't time," the voice whispered in Daniel's mind.

A crackle of sound: Daniel knew the Russkies were communicating by radio. He picked up their signal, kicked in his translator macro, caught stray words. He had no radio transmitter, couldn't speak to them.

He waved both his hands, emphasizing that he had no weapon.

A Russkie pointed a gun at Daniel. Something shot from it, sped past him and skimmed to a halt on the ice.

Daniel threw himself sideways and began to scuttle away from the spacemen.

Another projectile struck near Daniel and skipped past him. It left a gouge in the methane ice where it bounded.

"Get out of there!"

"You bet!"

He could settle his score with Mgouabe later. Right now he had to get to his sled. But the spacesuited figures were trotting forward, trying to reach him. They didn't know about his sled but they were nonetheless cutting him off from it.

He could pick up their conversation in bits. One of them was a military commander. He could pick up the voice as well as the words. It was a husky voice, the intonation blunt. He couldn't tell whether it was a man or a woman.

"Kick in your circuit-booster," Mgouabe commanded.

Even as Daniel asked what Mgouabe was talking about he could feel himself shifting into a faster electronic pace. The spacesuited figures were moving at a fraction of their former pace. "Another Mimir Monroe special?" he whispered bitterly to Mgouabe.

He could almost feel the other nod agreement.

With his new advantage he could sprint past the spacemen and get onto his sled before they could stop him. He moved at top speed, his feet pounding the methane ice like a sprinter on a cinder track.

He could see his sled.

Even the colors of the weird Titan twilight had shifted down toward the red end of the spectrum as Daniel's circuitry read incoming signals at its accelerated pace.

"Cut back! Cut back," Mgouabe warned. "If you hit the sled at this speed you'll smash it!"

About to launch himself in a dive, like a bobsledder jumping to a start, Daniel realized that Mgouabe was right. He shifted back to normal speed. He had no idea how he did it; Monroe's wizardry had given him the ability and he just did it.

He gave a final shove, his three hundred kilos of mass crashed onto the sled and shoved it toward the edge of the ice even as Daniel fumbled frantically to plug his own circuitry and power systems into the sled's.

A clot of white-hot ball lightning smashed into him, sank claws like a viper's fangs into his shoulder.

The sled skipped forward, tilted, hung for a moment at the edge of the ice. Daniel could still hear a confused jumble of voices, feel the thud of heavy boots crossing the ice.

A film of fire was passing over his skin. The spot on his back where it had first struck felt like a growing lump of hot lava, slowly spreading through his flesh—his silicon-and-metal body. The film of flames spreading over him was like a sheath of lightning. As it spread his artificial nerves sent screaming messages of pain to his brain. His muscles clenched and thrashed in meaningless, violent convulsions.

His sled tipped farther, then the violence of Daniel's own movements pushed it over the edge. It tumbled through a meter or so of Titan's atmosphere, then splashed into the methane sea.

As the sled revolved Daniel was turned so he could see upward. A cluster of space-helmeted figures knelt at the edge of ice, pointing after him.

One pointed its gun and fired again. A heavy projectile the size of an old-style flashlight battery plunged into the sea and flashed past Daniel, disappearing into murk.

Daniel and his sled sank.

Agony gripped him.

A million years later, still hooked into the sled, he reached sea bottom. The sled had landed prow-first and had struck sea bottom with sufficient force to bury its front fifty or sixty centimeters in the frozen stuff like a dart in a corkboard.

Daniel managed to unhook from the sled, tumbled backward, thrashed until he stumbled backward into a jagged projection of ice or rock.

As if a fist had ripped a huge gobbet of flesh from his back the fire was gone. The lava was gone. The lightning was gone.

He staggered, steadied himself against the jagged ice. He stood panting, as if he had lungs and could breathe.

"What?"

Mgouabe's whisper returned. "Daniel, I think you'll be all right now. We've got to get you out of there, but it should be all right."

"What happened? What did they get me with?"

"It was a tazer, Daniel. There was nothing else it could have been. It would have knocked out any organic man. I'd have had no guess at what it would do to a cyborg like yourself, but apparently it overloaded your circuits."

"I felt like I was burning."

"You were short-circuited. You're lucky it didn't burn out your circuits completely."

Daniel rubbed a hand across his face. "I owe you one, Mgouabe. They were pretty unfriendly types."

Mgouabe did not reply.

"What's the position of the skitter?"

"We've crossed the terminator and are on the daylight side of Titan. We'll be passing your position in less than an hour."

"All right. Stand by while I check the sled."

He was feeling steadier now, able to walk across the Titan seabed on steady legs.

He knelt beside the upended sled and plugged into its circuits. They checked out undamaged. He was able to get his arms around the prow of the sled where it protruded from the seabed. He strained back but couldn't budge the sled.

He stood and planted his feet firmly, put his shoulder against the sled and shoved, leaned his full three hundred kilograms into it. He felt a little movement, a little give, but not enough to help.

He circled the sled and tried it from the other side. It was shaped like an elongated delta, a stretched and narrowed version of the hang-gliders of Daniel's boyhood or of the folded paper airplanes he had made in school when lessons were too dull to bear.

He knelt again and used his hands to loosen some of the material around the sled's embedded tip, then plugged into its circuits again. The little craft strained, raised itself a fraction of a meter, then tumbled over sideways taking Daniel with it.

He managed to extricate himself, climb back onto the sled and plug in properly. "Osvaldo?"

"Here, Daniel."

"I'm coming up. I don't want to tangle with my visitors again. I don't know how they landed so close to me anyhow—on a world this size, how could that be?"

"I wouldn't fret over that. They homed in on the same signal that we did. They must have."

"Huh. Anyhow, listen here. I don't want to cruise around this area. Once I rise, I'm going to head straight up and I want you to be ready to rendezvous. If that won't work, I'm just going to zip out of this place and settle into an orbit of my own till we can meet. What do you think?"

"I think we can rendezvous. We're about—hold on. Very good. We're in Titan-polar orbit, headed south-to-north. We're roughly seventy degrees from horizon headed toward zenith."

Daniel nodded. "All right. What kind of beacon can you set? I don't imagine you want our visitors to see you. Not that they could do a hell of a lot."

"I would rather not have anything to do with them. We'll put out a beacon in the X-ray spectrum. I doubt greatly that they would be scanning upward, but even if they do, it's most unlikely that they'd look for anything in that range. But I know you can home in on that, you can detect it."

"You know too damned much, Osvaldo. But I think you're right. Here I come!"

The sled moved across the seabed, tilted upward, accelerated until Daniel felt the extra g-forces pushing him back.

The sled's prow broke the surface of Titan's methane sea, then slid into the atmosphere like an upended hydroplane. The liquid methane streamed back off the sled and off Daniel itself. He peered back, over the edge of the sled.

The visitors' spaceship was an incredible thing. It looked like an old-fashioned magazine illustration, massive plates of blackened metal studded with bulging rivets and heavy metallic protrusions for power systems, guidance systems, observation and communication gear. It was something out of a wild Tsiolkovskian dream.

The Russkie spacers were scattered around the ice island,

gesturing angrily, searching out any evidence of Daniel's stay or of any presence other than their own.

They would find nothing there, Daniel knew. They might encounter the same species of Titan marine life that he had observed. They would surely home in on the signals that emanated from the submarine structures, and would find the same evidence of former habitation that he had found.

But by the time they had completed their work on Titan, the skitter would long since have come overhead, Daniel's sled would have made its rendezvous, he and Osvaldo and Tovah and Lydia would be well on their way to Zimarzla, the true goal of their expedition.

The sled emerged from Titan's atmosphere.

Saturn hung above him, filling most of the sky with its glorious pattern of colored bands.

Even in this moment Daniel paused, his eyes hot with nonexistent tears at the beauty and splendor of it.

Then a weird glow edged into his field of vision. It flared in its nameless color unlike any color ever seen in the normal optical spectrum.

It was the skitter's X-ray beacon.

Daniel plotted a converging orbit, accelerated toward the spot where his own course would intercept that of the skitter. The rings and their magnetic spokes wheeled behind the X-ray glow of the skitter. Saturn's glow lighted them.

"I can see you fine, Osvaldo. Hold your course."

Mgouabe assented.

Daniel could feel the absolute cold of space, the radiation coming to him from the planet above, the particles impinging on his skin and on the skin of the sled, particles that had traveled hundreds of millions of kilometers from Sol or uncounted light-years from remote stars and galaxies.

The journey from earth to Titan was barely a hop from one grain to the next on the cosmic beach. Zimarzla would be a similar hop.

Even the Islands that had opted to leave Sol's realm and head for nearby stars were traveling little farther on that same scale. If Daniel could live indefinitely, his cyborged parts carefully fuelled and maintained, his organic remnant regenerated or replaced by microcircuits, he might see a truly distant shore!

But Zimarzla was his present goal. What might be found there, what might be learned there, could represent the sole hope of survival on earth for the teeming billions or for their descendants less than a century hence.

The skitter's X-ray glow filled Daniel's vision, overwhelming the beauty of Saturn's rings. Visions filled Daniel's mind, visions of Marie-Elaine, of Lydia and Tovah, of Royce and Kimura and Mimir Monroe, of Daniel's daughter Elizabeth, his grandson Ieyasu and the geisha Kodai-no-kimi.

They blended, blended into the black stalking figure of Osvaldo Mgouabe, naked and tumescent and holding a miniature rose for Daniel.

He shook his head violently.

The X-ray beacon shone less than a decimeter from him.

INSIDE the skitter Daniel embraced Tovah and Lydia. Osvaldo extended congratulations on Daniel's escape.

"Never mind that. Let's get moving for Zimarzla, Mgouabe."

"You don't really appreciate me, Daniel. We're on course already. As soon as we completed the rendezvous, our little ship broke orbit." Mgouabe patted the skitter's panel as a horseman would pat an animal's neck. "We're on our way now."

"We should have been long ago," Daniel countered.

"You don't think Titan was important? You don't think it's important that we know now that the aliens visited both Titan and Mercury?"

Daniel stared at the screen. Outside the sky was calm, a blackness whose infinite depths baffled the eye, a midnight beach of obsidian crystals whose facets yet reflected the light of countless remote beacon-flames.

"I suppose it means something. Whatever the aliens were. You really think the neon sculptures on Mercury and Titan were both—cargo-cult totems?"

Mgouabe nodded. "That and more. There was function, too. The old technology was preserved in them, as well as the form of the old constructs."

"Bamboo propellor blades that turn in the wind." Lydia spoke for the first time.

Tovah said, "You think the whole thing originates on Zimarzla, Osvaldo?"

He turned slowly. He brought his perfect prosthetic hands together, made a rising, opening motion with his fingertips as if they were the petals of a fresh bud opening to drink in morning dew and sunlight.

"I think it does, and I think it is important. But I'm not certain." He moved until he stood beside Daniel, gazing out at the flame-studded obsidian. Mgouabe was the taller of the two men. He felt Daniel's shoulder against his biceps, Daniel's hip against his outer leg.

"There are many small mysteries in the solar system, endless treasure chests of knowledge waiting for us to smash their locks and tip back their lids. But there is only one great mystery left, and that is Zimarzla, the greatest mystery of them all.

"The only shimmering goal beyond Zimarzla would be to join the Islanders who have left the solar system entirely.

"But life is too short for that," he breathed. He waved his black hand at the outer blackness, as if he could send dust motes with the movement of his hand across the light-years to alien stars. "Life is far too short. Who would set foot on Procyon's emerald shores? Who would embrace the flowing denizens of Al-ghoul? Who would explore the labyrinths that wind through the tertiary Magellanic Cloud?

"Not we!" He shook his head ruefully. "Our boy Daniel might do it. He might! But we mere organic creatures, we bits of animated clay—why, it would be for our descendants' descendants. I fear that I lack the sense of continuity with my seed required to undertake that expedition."

16

LIKE THE SUN.

How like the sun it was.

Daniel had the advantage on Tovah, on Lydia, on Osvaldo. He could turn his eyes into telescopes.

"I'm amazed." He managed to drag his focus away from the marvelous view of Zimarzla and its family of satellites, turn his attention at least for the moment to his three companions. "How could that..." He gestured toward the transparent screen, was nearly caught up in the vision again before returning his attention to the bridge.

"How could that be there all the while...all the millions of years that people scanned the skies...and never be detected?"

"I wondered at that myself," Osvaldo Mgouabe said. Mgouable had turned over the controls of the skitter to Lydia Haddad. He sat at his ease, feet stretched before him, fingers laced in his lap. He held a tiny bud vase in his lap. A single minuscule Daniel's Passion rose stood in the vase.

"Did you ever find out?" Tovah Decertes asked.

Osvaldo smiled and turned his face toward her. "I found out, yes. But it isn't much of an answer, I'm afraid. No mysteries here, no plots. Just happenstance. Zimarzla isn't quite massive enough, or hot enough, or bright enough, to make much difference on earth. And it's so far away—twice as far as anything else in our system—none of the old naked-eye astronomers would ever have had an inkling it was there."

He gently stroked the still-closed calyx of the Daniel's Passion.

"But its peculiar orbit—that was the main reason. That's what kept it from discovery once telescopes came into use. It only crosses the plane of the ecliptic every three hundred years. Think of the odds. Somebody would have to be looking at just the right point in the heavens, all the other factors would have to be just right, the position of the earth in its own orbit, I mean. And it could only happen at three hundred year intervals anyway. For practical purposes, there's only been one such opportunity since the telescope was developed. And now is the second, of course, and we don't need to use telescopes, we can *go* there."

Lydia Haddad shook her head. She had been punching figures into the control panel of the ship, not altering its course, but running computations on astronomical data.

She looked up from her screen. "What about orbital perturbations? That much *mass . . .*"

Mgouabe nodded. "Of course. Of course. And your data will tell you"—he pointed vaguely at Lydia's work—"orbital mechies have been sweating over perturbations for a couple of hundred years. That was how Neptune and Pluto were both discovered, eh? Wouldn't our man from the past know about that? And every time the mechies accounted for one perturbation by discovering a new body, they'd notice that there were *still* perturbations to be accounted for. They were fighting the hydra!" He laughed merrily. "That was what got Annabel Smirkova interested. That was how she finally found Zimarzla. Bright woman. Bright."

"And now we're headed there." Daniel stood watching the distant objects, still using his optical sensors as telescopes. He lifted his shoulders, flexed backwards like a bird making a mating gesture. It was the closest he could come to heaving a sigh. He had felt the impulse so often, felt his inability to make that human sign of complex emotions, that he had finally devised a substitute.

Suddenly Daniel sat down. He said. "I'm afraid."

The statement provoked surprise. Tovah asked, "Why now?"

"I don't know." He shook his head. He looked at his hands. They were trembling. He realized that he was shivering.

"Look at me," he said. He raised his hands. The tremor was not great but it was clearly discernible. "This body—it doesn't have any need to shiver. I don't have the physiology for it. But I'm shivering."

Tovah leaned from behind him. She put her hands over his shoulders, crossed them against his face and held him. He felt her upper arms pressed against his face, her breasts against the back of his head. He closed his eyes and tried to breathe deeply, knowing that he could not.

He took great comfort from his contact with Tovah.

He said her name.

She laid her cheek on the top of his head.

"They shot me," he said.

"They're back at Titan. They can't do anything."

"They shot me with a tazer. It did things to me. It was like a—like having pain and madness poured into me, until I couldn't do anything, couldn't think of anything. They—it was my whole being."

"It's gone."

"But it happened."

"They won't come."

"It will be with me."

"It will go away."

He turned, burying his face in her. She pressed him gently to her. After a while he turned back and gazed out of the skitter. She still stood behind him, holding him. He could feel her warmth, hear the coursing of her blood. He reached and disengaged her hands, carefully. As she straightened from behind him he held one hand a moment longer, held it to his face and put a kiss on her palm. He said, "Thanks," softly.

"Do you want to go to bed?" she asked him.

He nodded. "Yes."

They lay together in the bunk for a long time. He managed to fall asleep. When he awoke, Tovah was still there, holding him. He touched her face and thanked her. "Do you know how far we've gone?" he asked. "How long to Zimarzla?"

She shook her head.

They rose from the bunk. She straightened her clothing. He still wore none. The mirror-shielding that covered his body served some purpose; it was not equivalent to wearing clothes, it made the wearing of clothes superfluous. By now, for Daniel

Kitajima to put on clothing would have been like a robot or a statue putting on clothing. It didn't make sense.

They returned to the bridge. Lydia was concentrating on the controls of the ship. Osvaldo was seated near her, looking through the screen into space. He turned as Tovah and Daniel reentered the room.

"All right, now?"

Daniel nodded. Zimarzla loomed huge before the ship. It appeared the size, now, at normal vision, that it had appeared to Daniel earlier using telescopic vision. The main object, Zimarzla itself, was utterly gigantic, larger by far than Jupiter. The only object in the solar system larger than Zimarzla was the sun itself. Zimarzla was large enough to be a small sun, and in fact it glowed, giving off a good deal of both light and heat.

"Those Russkies," Lydia said. She turned from her position at the ship's controls. "Do you think they'll come after us? Picking a fight, I mean? Or they might try and beat us to Zimarzla."

Mgouabe shook his head. "I doubt it very much. The Russkies are incredibly centralized authoritarians. An old tradition of theirs. Whatever happens, they'll almost certainly buck it all the way to the Palace in Tchaikowsky Island. Somebody high up in the Imperial government will have to make a decision. Maybe the Tsar personally. I wouldn't worry about them."

The instrument panel sounded a warning.

"Look at that." Lydia pointed. The skitter's homing screen was glowing.

Mgouabe tapped an inquiry into the panel. When the answer appeared he nodded. "We're homing in on a transmitter near Zimarzla."

"Not *on* it?"

He shrugged. "Can't tell yet, for a certainty. But I doubt it. Zimarzla isn't exactly a planet. Well, or even if it were, do you think you'd put a beacon right on Jupiter or Saturn, if you were trying to set up some sort of base? And get other species to visit you?"

Tovah grunted. "Huh! Depends on what kind of creature I was, and where my home was."

Mgouabe laughed softly. "Point well taken. I suppose some

kind of animated blobs might have evolved in a gas-giant environment."

"Or in the sun?"

Mgouabe rubbed his nose.

Daniel Kitajima, watching, thought of Santa Claus preparing to rise up the chimney.

"I don't see how anything could evolve inside a star. The heat and pressure would disrupt complex molecules long before they reached the potential for life."

Tovah shook her head. "I wouldn't be so sure of that. You think of just how different the environments are where we've found life. From the Mindanao Trench to the Amazon jungle to the mountaintops of Tibet. Not to mention Daniel's little friends on Mercury. And his seal-people or whatever they were on Titan."

"They aren't there any more," Daniel said. "They don't seem to be, anyway."

"Beside the point. They evolved in that environment. They lived and built a civilization at the bottom of a nitrogen sea. I wouldn't write off the chances of finding life anywhere. Not anywhere!"

Mgouabe spread his hands. "I think you win, Tovah." He peered at the homing screen. "Wherever they have their beacon set up, it's doing its job."

Daniel said, "You don't think Zimarzla is a planet. Then what is it?"

"I'd call it a sun. Or a proto-sun. Look at that . . ." He pointed, not to the instrument panel but to the transparent screen above it. Zirmarzla was now visible in the normal optical range, unamplified. It glowed with its own light.

"It's bigger than Jupiter," Mgouabe said. "I think it's big enough to ignite. I think it's already warm enough to support life on its own planets . . ."

"What planets?" Lydia demanded.

"That, we shall have to see. Soon. But I expect that it has some. I don't see why our own sun should be special. And if there are planets, there might well be life."

"Then you think the neon sculptures that we found on Mercury and Titan—"

"I think they're either cargo-cult artifacts, just like those bamboo airplanes on earth. Designed to lure back the, yes, the

Zimarzlans who had visited Mercury and Titan. Or maybe they were built there and left there by the Zimarzlans themselves. For whatever reasons they had."

"Why Mercury and Titan?"

"Eh?"

"Why Mercury and Titan?" Tovah demanded. "Why not, oh, Venus or Uranus or Ganymede or Ceres?"

"I have no idea." Mgouabe shook his head. "Maybe they deliberately chose two extreme environments. You can hardly get much different from those bubble-caves on Mercury and the bottom of a nitrogen sea on Titan."

Daniel said, "Wait a minute. How do we know they picked out Mercury and Titan?"

"Because, dearie, that's where we *found* their artifacts. Or cargo-cult copies of them."

"Nope. Not nearly good enough." Daniel shook his head. "We don't know they were on, uh, let's say, Venus. We don't know they were on Venus because we never found any sign they were there."

"We never explored Venus," Mgouabe countered. "Some quick preliminary surveys and we quit. Even the IGO didn't think that hell was worth landing on."

"Yes, Yes," Daniel grinned. "You're making my point. We never found any artifacts on Venus but we never really looked on Venus. The Zimarzlans might have been there and left— good God, a library, a museum, a whole university. It might be there just waiting to be discovered. Or it might have been there at one time and been covered up by sand or eroded into dust or . . ."

"I get the point," Mgouabe said. "All right. For all we know, these mysterious aliens have been all over the place. The fact that we found evidence of them only twice doesn't prove that they didn't leave it in a lot of other places that we haven't been to."

He pointed at the homing screen on the control panel. "We'll find out soon enough."

THEY approached Zimarzla and its satellites. The proto-sun in fact had a family of satellites orbiting it that rivaled those of Sol. Planets ranging from meagre rocks that resembled Mercury and Pluto, through earth-type worlds, to gas-giants. The largest of Zimarzla's satellites was a ringed and moon-rich world nearly as large as Uranus.

"Can you see it yet?" Daniel asked.

"Not yet," Lydia said. "But I can detect it with the ship's instruments."

"You'll see it. Too bad I'm the only one with telescopes in my eyeballs!" He laughed. "It's beautiful."

"I don't think the beacon is on a planet," Lydia told him. "The screen shows it right at the main object. At Zimarzla." She ran her hand over her hair and down the back of her neck, working her fingers as if her period at the controls had left her with tense muscles.

Dan stood behind her, rubbing her shoulders and neck. "One other possibility," he said. "If the beacon is located on an object in a straight line with us and Zimarzla itself—between us and it, or directly beyond it—we'd get the same image here. Wouldn't we, Osvaldo?"

Mgouabe grunted affirmation.

They drew nearer to the beacon, nearer to the Zimarzlan system.

The outermost object of the system became visible in the transparent screen of the skitter. Tovah Decertes was the first to spot it.

"Look at that! It looks like an explosion going on!"

Mgouabe leaned past Lydia Haddad, tapped commands. An image of the object appeared.

"Can you get that up?" Tovah peered at it. "Can't you call it out, like a vidipic image?"

Mgouabe turned momentarily toward her. "Sounds like something worth working on. But I can't do it with this hardware."

"Huh! Lyd and I could work that out, I think."

"Now?"

She shook her head. "Would take a while. Writing up the software, building a breadboard. Forget it."

Mgouable nodded thoughtfully. "I will—for now. But after this is over—if we come through it—I want you to build that device for me. IGO will fund it, of course. Daniel, my friend, I think you will agree to give up your employees to an IGO project. Especially since we can draft them if you refuse."

Daniel Kitajima was standing behind Lydia, his hands resting lightly on her shoulders. He was watching the approaching planet. To his normal vision it was now a barely visible speck against the darkness. He called in his telescopic vision, ran through spectral ranges examining the object by ultraviolet, infrared, X-ray, radio spectra.

"Looks like Io!"

Tovah asked what he meant.

"Volcanoes going like crazy. Not just an eruption now and then, like we have on earth. It's some kind of homeostatic system for the planet."

"But that isn't what we want," Osvaldo said. "We're not doing a general survey of this system. Maybe we will some day. I'm sure my planetary station kids would love it. A whole new system of worlds to explore! But look—"

He pointed to the homing indicator.

"We have to bypass this world."

At the next orbit Daniel used his telescopic vision to examine a suspicious area. He gripped Lydia's shoulder more tightly, turning toward Mgouabe as he did so. "I think we'd better check out that planet." He moved his head to indicate the direction.

"Are you in command of this ship?" Mgouabe asked.

"What does that have to do with it?"

"I said, we are seeking the radio source at Zimarzla. Not exploring its planets. That comes later—if at all."

Tovah stepped close to Mgouabe. Broad-shouldered and heavily fleshed, she was nearly his equal in mass. "I'm with Daniel. So is Lydia."

Mgouabe stepped back, an expression of incredulity—or perhaps of mock-incredulity—on his face. "Is this a mutiny?"

"Mutiny? Who said anything about mutiny? Who said you were captain of this ship, Mister Mgouabe? If anything, I think you might claim the status of stowaway."

"What!" The mocking quality was absent, now. "I am the director of the IGO. Who do you think you are?"

Daniel whirled. He grabbed Mgouabe by the front of his garment and lifted him off the floor. "This is *my* ship, Osvaldo. It came from my Island, don't you remember? But never mind that. Think of this."

He dropped one hand to his side. With the other he still

held Mgouabe off the floor. He raised him slowly toward the ceiling.

"I am not a normal man. I have a rotary pump for a heart. I have a nuclear reactor in my belly. I could take you in my hands and tear you in half if I wanted to!"

Mgouabe nodded slowly. Perspiration had broken out on his face.

"I don't want to." Daniel lowered Mgouabe slowly, then released him. "And I don't want to set up as a two-bit dictator, either. We'll discuss this thing and we'll decide what to do. But forget about playing boss. You aren't boss. Do you understand?"

Mgouabe nodded again.

"All right. Lydia, can you see the world we're headed for?" She said she could.

"It looks earthlike to me. I want to take at least a fly-by. What do you think?"

She flashed him a small smile. "I think that's a good idea."

"Tovah?" Daniel said.

"Yes."

"All right."

Lydia ran up some figures from the ship's data bank and its computer. She punched instructions into the panel. The skitter quivered gently as it made a course adjustment to meet its new instructions.

Daniel sat down beside Lydia.

From behind him, Osvaldo said, "So, the *uebermensch* takes command, is that it?"

Daniel tried to heave a sigh. "No, Osvaldo, that is not it."

Mgouabe grunted.

Daniel turned to Lydia. "I'll be damned, that looks like the earth. Not the land masses, but the coloration. Blue and White. Swirls of cloud. You'd almost think . . ." He let it trail away.

The skitter took up a polar orbit. The ship's instruments measured the planet. Its mass was close to earth's. Its spectrum was almost identical. There was no sign of life. No radiation above the normal background emissions of an earthlike planet.

"Can we drop down closer? If there's anything alive . . ."

Lydia dropped the ship into closer orbit.

Forestation became visible.

"What do you think now?" Daniel turned toward Osvaldo Mgouabe. Mgouabe had taken a seat and was watching the scene through the bridge's screen.

"I didn't say there was no life here." Mgouabe frowned. "I said *we* were here to check out that radio source. Listen to me, Kitajima. Those neon sculptures—that evidence of a cargo cult, of technologically advanced aliens—that's the only hope we have to calm down the solar activity. You know the figures. You know the reality. The human race isn't doomed, Kitajima. The Islands will survive. Most of them will stay near Sol. A few will take off for other suns. A couple already have."

"I know that," Daniel said.

"But if we don't find some way to damp the solar increase, *earth* will die and everybody on it. Twenty-six billion poeple. Twenty-six billion!"

"Somehow I am not too convinced by all this." Daniel looked into Mgouabe's face, trying to read what lay behind the bland eyes, the calm, cynical mouth. "Pardon me, Osvaldo, but you never have struck me as a great humanitarian. You take too good care of Number One to pass for Albert Schweitzer."

Lydia Haddad's slim hand reached out and grabbed Daniel's wrist. "Look at this!" she hissed. She pointed at the planet beneath them. They had crossed the heavily forested area. It stretched for a thousand kilometers or more, from the lower slopes of a great mountain range to a rocky seacoast. There was a bight where two rivers converged and emptied into a dark ocean.

Apparently a city had once grown up around the bight. It was natural. It was obvious. The rivers would have made natural highways for loggers and farmers bringing their products to sell. The bright offered protection for ocean-going vessels.

A semicircle thirty kilometers in diameter had been flattened. It stretched from the edge of the sea inland. Beyond it, smashed and ruined buildings poked raggedly into the air.

Osvaldo Mgouabe turned a bitter face toward Daniel. "What is the commander's decision? Shall we land and arrange a treaty with the natives, sir? I suspect they'll be quite docile."

Daniel made an ugly face. "Something went wrong here."

"Obviously."

"Do you think they were attacked?"

"By the blokes from around the next bend in the river? Or by your blue friends from outer space?"

Tovah said, "It doesn't really matter, does it?"

Osvaldo's eyes widened. "It matters greatly, my dear. Very greatly. If the blokes from around the bend did it, that means that the local folks couldn't keep their civilization civil. And they went smash. Rather the way some of the pessimists of Mister Kitajima's time expected us to go smash. Isn't that so, Daniel?"

Kitajima nodded absently.

"But if our blue friends did it—ho-*ho!* We've been assuming that these hypothetical aliens are benevolent creatures, just as eager as eager can be to lend a helping hand. If only we could reach out and grasp it. You see? But what have we to base that upon? A piece of dekko sculpture in a gas-bubble-cave on Mercury? A picture of some trained seals on Titan—pardon *me*, Daniel—still, a picture of some of those supposed denizens of the nitrogen sea, found in a ruined building?

"How do we know they're such benevolent beings? When we find them, they might just cook us for dinner. It's been known to happen, you know." His grin was wolfish.

"Okay," Daniel stopped him. "Here are our options. First, we can return to earth and live out our lives in relative comfort. You with your job with the IGO and your base of operations at Lilongwe, Osvaldo. And I have plenty of money of my own. Lydia and Tovah, I have promised jobs as long as they want them."

He took two strides, peered from the skitter to the landscape below and tried to heave a sigh. "Let's get out of here, Lyd. This is too depressing. Let's just home in on the beacon, eh?"

He strode the other way. "Second, I could go back to my medical Island and play guinea pig for Royce and Kimura. I'd still like you with me, working with Mimir Monroe. Third, I could head out for Hokkaido Island. Back to the new land of my ancestors and descendants. I won't even have to worry about studying Japanese, now that I have those new circuits you folks cooked up for me. I could pretend that it's a few hundred years ago and I'm some sort of small-town *daimyo-san* and live it up."

He shook his head. "I don't think you two would fit into that scenario very well. But you could get work at almost any

Island you wanted. Or sign on with somebody who's getting ready to go to the stars. I almost think that's more appealing than anything we can do around here. Just write it all off and head for Procyon or Spica.

"But I can't write off twenty-six billion people."

He sat down and put his head in his hands. "Besides, you'll all be dead in a hundred and ten years. Will I be?" He held his hand up for them all to see. "I don't think I'll wear out. If I do, I can always pick up some spare parts down at the nearest factory and hire a grease monkey to put 'em in for me. This body isn't going to grow old and shrivel up. I have enough fuel . . ."

He jabbed a thumb at his belly and it struck, making a metallic sound. The mirror-like shielding flashed as if a piezoelectric spark had been struck.

"I have enough fuel to last me for, God, I don't know. But if I ever run down, I can tank up again at the nearest nuclear depot." He managed a brief, bitter laugh.

"But, no. I can't believe that the aliens who built those glowing sculptures, who set off beacons for us—I can't believe they just want to cook us for their lunch. There must be some better purpose than that. Or—at least I'm willing to give it a try, on the chance that there is."

They were still in the atmosphere of the earthlike planet. The air outside their skitter hissed against the shielded surfaces of the ship. Inside the bridge the sound resembled the humming and shrieking that Daniel remembered from old vidipics of ancient fabric-and-wire aircraft as they wove their way above the battlefields of centuries-old wars.

"All right." Mgouabe broke the silent tension. "All right. I'll concede that you're the altruist, Daniel. Not I. You want to head for the beacon. Still. So do I. And you, Lydia? Tovah? Then let's get on with it before somebody suggests that we sell all that we own and give to the poor."

THE beacon came from one of a pair of twinned planets in orbit less than a million kilometers from the surface of Zimarzla.

"Who did you say discovered this system?" Tovah asked Mgouabe.

"She didn't know it was a system, you understand." Mgouabe

had dropped a vidipic bead in the projector and sat with a huge bowl of yellow and deep-red roses in his lap. He caressed their petals and avoided their thorns as if they were real. He looked from the nonexistent flowers to Tovah. "She only knew of Zimarzla itself. A pity she did not live to see what she had found! But her name was Annabel Smirkova."

He emphasized the second syllable of both the astronomer's names.

"Huh! And she never knew about the sculptures, or the beacons?"

"No." Mgouabe had returned his attention to the vidipic roses. By manipulating projector controls with one hand and slowly moving his other hand in his lap, he created the illusion that he was turning a real bowl of flowers.

"A pity," Tovah said.

Daniel was seated beside Lydia. He leaned toward her. "I can see the worlds. They look like—uh, miniature gas-giants. I don't see how that can be. They'd dissipate. They must be composed of heavier gases. Or maybe there's some small, dense core in each that holds the light molecules. Damn it, why don't we have a real astromomer on board this ship!"

Lydia concentrated on her piloting.

Daniel stood up, stepped away from her. She didn't seem to notice him. He looked at Tovah, at Lydia, at Osvaldo. All were intent on other matters than himself. Lydia divided her attention between the control panel of the skitter and the sight of the twinned planets, yellowish with rose-pink markings. Tovah was watching Lydia. Daniel could almost feel Tovah caressing Lydia with her eyes. He felt a pang of jealousy. The two women had given him what he most desperately needed in his time of crisis in San Francisco. They still shared their bodies with him, and to some extent their emotions, but it was manifest that they were chiefly for each other, not for Daniel. And Osvaldo? Osvaldo appeared to be immersed in contemplation of his roses. But where his real commitment lay was no more penetrable here, a million kilometers from Zimarzla, than it had been on the beach of Lake Njasa.

Daniel bent and whispered briefly to Lydia.

She turned toward him, surprised.

He reiterated his instructions, adding assurances that the

skitter and those in it would be safe.

The skitter plunged toward the twin planets. The homing screen on its control panel pulsed and glowed. The target image remained in dead center.

Daniel retreated to the rear of the bridge. He watched the others: Lydia and Tovah, Osvaldo. He looked at himself, at his naked body covered in the mirror-like shielding.

He opened the hatch at the rear of the bridge and made his way to the sled.

The skitter had plunged into the gas-envelope of the nearer twin. Swirls of rose and of chrome-yellow whipped past the ship. A voice from the bridge came to Daniel, asking what he was doing.

"Never mind, just keep this ship on course," he said.

"You are in full command, then?"

"No." Daniel thought about it. Those three humans up in the bridge. Those three creatures with their clumsy metabolisms. Those groaning, pain-filled organisms. Those crude energy mills converting the corpses of slaughtered animals and plants into piles of stinking shit to draw enough by-product energy to keep them going. All the while they were dying. Dying day by day. Hair falling out. Skin drying and wrinkling. Arteries slowly clogging, slowly filling up. Teeth rotting. Skin spotting. Brain cells dying, dying, dying by the millions and not being replaced. Turning to stinking hulks that would drool and quiver their last years away locked in corners, hidden from the horror-stricken eyes of younger ones lest they cringe and shudder and puke with disgust and terror at the sight of their own future selves.

"No," Daniel called again.

He climbed into the body-niche of the sled and plugged into it. Once more he had wings.

"I'm not in command," he said.

He operated the inner seal of the airlock. He was in communication with the others now by radio.

"I'm not in command. You three can do what you want. I thank you all for everything. For everything."

The air pump sucked precious molecules out of the lock.

All that remained of the old, protoplasmic Daniel Kitajima was the bit of brain tissue and spinal cord encased in his new, mirrored body. That protoplasm would die eventually. Cell by cell his brain would die. He would find some way to replace the slimy, fleshy circuits with clean and sterile prosthetics. He would find a way. He would rid himself of the slime.

He opened the outer seal. The atmosphere of the gas-planet swept in.

He disengaged from the ship.

He dropped away, feeling his wings like the wings of an eagle as it leaps from its aerie.

The gases of the planet were like champagne and roses, like liquid gold and red wine. He opened his mouth. He tried to inhale but the neurons to control his diaphragm dead-ended. His only real regrets were that he could not smell or taste the atmosphere of this splendid rose and gold world.

He looked above him. The ship was a dark deltoid shadow that hovered above him. It was a shark and he a pilot fish.

Voices sounded in his ear. The rich baritone of Osvaldo Mgouabe, the husky contralto of Tovah Decertes, the light, sweet mezzo of Lydia Haddad.

What were they talking about?

What were they talking about?

Bothersome gibberish about a star ten billion kilometers away. Something about pathetic grubs that squirmed on a planet somewhere. Something about slimy protoplasmic things that would be wiped away, that would be removed by antisepsis.

Daniel cut out his receiver. The nonsense was bothering him.

He dived toward the heart of this planet. His wings were strong. The sensation of atmosphere passing over them was a thrill. He felt stimulated by it, joyously aroused. He felt that he had an erection. He raised his head from the body niche so the atmosphere could whip his cheeks. He could feel droplets of moisture carom off his face, each impact a minute sting of pleasure and pain.

He drove his consciousness farther into the sled and felt every droplet, every molecule that bounded from its wings and its streamlined fuselage.

The thick atmosphere around him was lighted by the reddish glow of Zimarzla. Too bad that Annabel Smirkova could not be here, could not share this moment with him, could not know the joy of immersion in the worlds that she had found decades ago.

He could not see Zimarzla as an object; it was not even as distinct as Saturn had been from the surface of Titan. It furnished this world with a widely dispersed, vague illumination.

"A noble thought, Daniel."

He was startled.

"Yes, there is that streak in you. Western idealism. How one admires it!"

He clicked off his radio link with the skitter—or tried to. The link was already cut.

"Is that you, Mgouabe?"

"I am here, Daniel."

"You son of a bitch! You had Monroe sneak that circuit into me! Get the hell out! I don't want you here!"

"Oh, but here I am."

"No, you're not. You're on the skitter with Lydia and Tovah. You'd better get to work, figure out what to do if they follow on out from Titan."

A chuckle, "That isn't my problem. Let Osvaldo Mgouabe and the two ladies worry about that. Surely they're smart enough to—"

"What was that?"

"I said—"

"Never mind what you said. You're Osvaldo Mgouabe. I don't want you whispering in my ear. Get out!"

"Ah, but I am not whispering in your ear. I am here, Daniel. Tiny passion, Daniel. That is the fleshly Osvaldo on the ship, he with his fleshly appetites and his artificial hands. But I am not he—any longer. I am here with you. I told you that there was something of me in you. Something that Mimir Monroe constructed and installed at my direction. I'm right here within you now, and very pleasant it is, Daniel."

"Get out, Mgouabe! You don't understand! I'm not going back there! I—"

"I understand fully well, Daniel. Of course you are not going back. You are not so enigmatic as you might believe. I never thought you would go back. I told you that you were important to me for your special talents. What more could one ask—to live forever, to visit alien worlds, to plumb the mysteries of

the universe not for a few puny decades but for millennia, for
eons!

"Together, Daniel. Always together!"

"I won't let you! I'll plunge into a star, Mgouabe! I won't
be your hag-ridden flunky!"

He bucked, arching his back, arching and turning the sled
with him like a bronco.

Again Mgouabe's icy chuckle. "It's no use, Daniel. And
why so eager to be rid of me? Think of it—a companion down
the ages."

"Shut up! Shut up!"

"As you will." Mgouabe left a silence like a blank audio
tape running over capstans.

"I'll offer you a bargain." Daniel told Mgouabe. "We'll find
a way to separate from each other. You'll mind your own
affairs. You'll stay out of my thoughts and out of my feelings."

"But Daniel—"

"There's no *but!* I swear, Mgouabe, I can find a way to
destroy myself and I will do it, I will do it and you'll go with
me unless you agree."

"You would take my word?"

A pause.

"Yes."

"Done."

Another source of illumination came into play. It was the
planet's twin, rising above the horizon. In his mind Daniel
named them, Annabel and Smirkova, in honor of the Czech
astronomer who had discovered their primary, Zimarzla.

And yet a third object appeared, a greater dawn subsuming
the lesser, Zimarzla herself rising behind Annabel, its colors
blending and mixing with the colors of the twins.

A new color flared brilliantly from the heart of Zimarzla a
glaring, brilliant turquoise.

The gases of Smirkova changed coloration. The rose deep-
ened to maroon, then to purple. The yellow became chartreuse,
then a dazzling green.

The glow from Zimarzla had become a brilliant ultramarine.

Daniel boosted the full power of his sled, burst away from
Smirkova. It had been his intention to land on that planet, but
he was held now in a force greater than his rational will.

The sled headed for the center of radiance.

Direction lost its meaning. Up was down, fast was slow. Time sped or halted or wove, he could not tell.

He plunged into the glittering ultramarine.

He felt himself grow, as if the wings of the sled, the wings of himself, were unfurling, extending.

The source of the radiance became visible.

It was a neon structure, huge, it was huge, at least the size of earth's moon. It was incredibly complex. The copies he had seen on Mercury and on Titan and in Osvaldo Mgouabe's vidipic projection were nothing compared to this reality. They were the simplest of children's sketches compared to the truth of this great. complex, subtle structure.

He rushed to it, accelerating with every instant, and yet time did not compress but rather seemed to slow to his perception, to unfurl itself, to ooen like the petals of a moss-rose revealing new reality and new beauty with its new revelation.

The surface of the construct was as smooth as velvet from afar, and from closer in its revealed all the complexity of a living cell revealed in a photomicrograph. It was covered with uncountable millions of niches and chambers, compartments and projections, extrusions of wholly unguessable purpose.

What would a Papuan make of an external radio antenna mounted on the fuselage of a Martin B-26?

What could Daniel Kitajima make of the millions of small and large, round and ovoid and trapezoidal and tesseractal projections on the skin of this alien globe?

Would Osvaldo—no! Mgouabe was keeping his bargain; leave him out, keep him out, keep him shut away!

Daniel adjusted the spectra and the focus and the scale of vision of his optical sensors. He was able to see through the surface of the object. There were layers and sectors and realms within it. Reqions of glowing green and glittering silver. Kingdoms of heat and palaces of absolute cold. Seas of sand and deserts of ice. Volumes packed with matter in incredible density and volumes of vacuum that would make intergalactic space seem as thick as porridge by contrast.

Lydia or Tovah might have some idea—

He shut that away.

He was alone. He was himself, only himself, purely himself.

He was Man, Not-Man, Not-Not-Man.

He was energy.

He was movement.

He plummented toward it.

He grew.

For a moment his mind raced backward. He wanted to share but only with one.

His velocity overwhelmed him. His purpose, his excitement filled all of his being.

In a picosecond flash as long as a lifetime a face glowed in recollection.

Ma —